The Baron's Daughter

The Baron's Daughter

Laura Beers

Phase Publishing, LLC
Seattle

Cover art by Tugboat Design
http://www.tugboatdesign.net

Phase Publishing, LLC first paperback edition
April 2019

ISBN 978-1-943048-78-6
Library of Congress Control Number 2019937295

Cataloging-in-Publication Data on file.

More Romance from Phase Publishing

Chapter One
England, 1814

The coach slowed to a creaking stop outside an unobtrusive, two-level, white building, near the outskirts of the fashionable part of London. Reaching out of the small, opened window, Lord Morgan Easton turned the latch and exited the carriage, not bothering to wait for his footman to come around.

A group of rough-looking men in tattered clothing loitered near the shabby building, surreptitiously watching as he stepped onto the pavement. A dark-haired man holding a donkey's lead grunted a command, and the group of men straightened, their eyes never wavering from him.

He tilted his top hat towards the group of ruffians as he approached them. Their gruff exterior didn't intimidate him. These men guarded the building with their lives. Behind the plain walls, which were in dire need of a lime wash, were the offices of Lord Charles Beckett, England's Chief Spymaster.

"Want any potatoes, gov?" the dark-haired man boldly inquired, tugging the donkey forward. Two wicker baskets filled with potatoes were strapped across the donkey's back.

Lord Morgan chuckled before lowering his voice to ensure their conversation stayed private. "When did you add the donkey bit, Joshua?"

Grabbing a potato from the basket, Joshua tossed it high and deftly caught it. "It adds authenticity, does it not?"

Morgan ran his hand down the donkey's neck. "Poor donkey," he murmured. "I am not sure which one of you is the biggest arse."

"You offend me, sir," Joshua sniffed, returning the potato to the basket.

Reaching into the pocket of his waistcoat, Morgan pulled out a sixpence and tossed it to the man. "Distribute my potatoes to any street urchins that you see. And for pity's sake, man, move these men about. They look as though they're waiting for something or someone."

"As you wish, my liege," Joshua replied flamboyantly, dropping into a low bow.

As Lord Morgan started towards the entrance of the building, Joshua shouted gruffly, "Me wife thanks ye for yer donation, milord."

Morgan shook his head, amused. It was a shame that his friend worked for the agency. Joshua could have had a career in the theatre. He walked into the entry hall, which was barren except for a single desk in the center of the room. No pictures hung on the walls, and no tables or other furniture graced the chamber.

A lanky, young man sat at the lone desk, his left hand hidden from view. He offered no welcome salutation. This man's job was not to entertain the guests that walked through the door, but to evaluate whether they were a potential threat.

Stopping short, Morgan introduced himself. "Lord Morgan Easton to see Lord Charles Beckett, if you please."

The guard nodded and visibly relaxed. "He is expecting you, Lord Morgan," he said, rising from his chair and holstering the pistol in his left hand. "Please follow me."

Morgan followed the man up towards Beckett's office on the second floor. As they approached the familiar red door, he could hear muffled shouting and a loud bang coming from within.

The young man stopped at the door, seemingly unfazed by the disturbance coming from within. "Would you like me to announce you, my lord?"

"That won't be necessary," Morgan assured him as he knocked on the door. In response, the shouting subsided, and a long pause ensued before the door was wrenched open, revealing Benedict, the Marquess of Lansdowne.

"Easton," Benedict greeted with a welcoming smile. "Do come in." He looked over his shoulder and lowered his voice, his eyes full of merriment. "You should know that Beckett is in a foul mood, and I would run while you still can."

"Do shut up, Benedict," Lord Charles intoned from his seat. "I'm glad that Easton has decided to finally grace us with his presence."

Benedict stepped aside, smirking. "You should have run when you had the chance."

As Morgan entered the room, he saw Eliza, the Marchioness of Lansdowne, sitting gracefully in an armchair, glaring at her uncle. Turning in her chair, Eliza's face softened as her eyes landed on him. "Morgan. It is good to see you looking so well."

"Likewise, Lady Lansdowne," he replied with a tilt of his head.

Eliza humphed. "I believe we are past formalities, *Lord Morgan*."

He grinned. "I could not agree more, Eliza."

Morgan had suspected that Eliza was the legendary spy, *Shadow*, when they'd served together to rescue her friend, Lady Martha, or Mrs. Emmett Maddix, as she preferred to be called now, from Martha's father's evil clutches over a month ago. However, he was not brazen enough to ask that question directly. He had no doubt there was a reason he was not privy to that information.

The tension in the room was palpable, and he turned his questioning gaze towards Benedict. "What did I interrupt?"

Beckett slammed his fist on the desk. "My stubborn niece is the most infuriating woman I have ever encountered." Despite his harsh words, his eyes were filled with pride. "She is asking permission to go undercover."

Morgan raised his brow. "Undercover?"

"Yes. She seems to think she is the only capable spy in all of England."

"Do not exaggerate, Uncle," Eliza chastised. "This assignment will require a female agent."

Beckett shook his head firmly. "True, but it will not be you." He frowned before he gestured towards the chairs, inviting Benedict and Morgan to sit. "Allow me to explain to Lord Morgan what we are facing."

With a solemn expression, Lord Charles explained, "The French spy, known as *Genet*, will be attending a house party on the English

Channel in Devon near the seaside town of Torquay."

Morgan sat straight up in his seat, suddenly very sharp and alert. "How did you discover this?"

He had been tracking *Genet*'s movements for years, but the spy had always managed to elude him.

Reaching for a piece of paper on his desk, Beckett handed it to Morgan. "An agent smuggled a note out of France, detailing that *Genet* would arrive on England's shores and attend Lord Paxton's house party."

"But for what purpose?" Morgan asked, reading the brief missive, detailing what Beckett had just revealed. "Why would a French spy wish to attend a simple English house party?" He extended the paper back to Beckett.

Eliza shifted towards him. "The agency has been tracking a growing number of anti-monarchists in Torquay, and we have reason to believe that *Genet* may be colluding with them."

"What is known of Lord Paxton?" Morgan asked.

Glancing down at a paper, Beckett's eyes perused the document for a moment before answering. "Hugh Moore, the Viscount of Paxton, is a highly respected architect and has been responsible for many notable renovations throughout London. He owns two estates, not including his London townhouse, but prefers to spend his time at his estate on the cliffs overlooking Oddicombe Beach. Furthermore, he owns a majority stake in a coal mine located in Champagney, France." He glanced up. "Lord Paxton appears to be a staunch Tory. We see no outward indication that he is not loyal to the king."

Benedict leaned forward in his seat, appearing concerned. "Perhaps it's a trap?"

Beckett nodded. "I'd considered that, but we have no choice. We must act on this information, despite the inherent risks."

"Which is why Benedict and I must go," Eliza insisted. "We must infiltrate that party."

"I agree that we must act, but I forbid *you* to go," Beckett declared.

Eliza curled her fingers around the armrest of her chair and repeated, "You *forbid* me?"

Beckett gave his niece an exasperated look. "Do you intend to go as yourself? Pray tell, why would a couple with the social standing of the Marquess and Marchioness of Lansdowne request an invitation to Lord Paxton's house party in a small seaside town?"

Removing her hand from the chair, Eliza waved it dismissively in front of her. "You question my abilities, Uncle. I have no doubt that Benedict and I could create an impressive alias."

Beckett shook his head, turning his gaze towards Benedict. "I hope that your daughter, Caroline, will not be nearly as stubborn as my niece."

Stifling a smile, Benedict glanced lovingly at his wife. "I disagree, my lord. I hope that Caroline grows up to be exactly like her mother."

"Bah," Beckett huffed. "You are still blinded by love, son." His words may have been hard, but his tone was anything but. "Regardless, I have come up with a different plan." He turned his resolute gaze towards Morgan. "Lord Morgan will attend the house party. He has been tracking *Genet* for years."

Morgan nodded approvingly. "I accept the assignment, my lord. I will not let you down."

Leaning forward, Beckett placed both his forearms on the table and interlocked his fingers. "You may want to save your kind words until I have explained my plan."

Morgan glanced curiously at Benedict, and his friend simply shrugged.

"Eliza is correct about one thing. This assignment will require a married couple, but the Crown does not officially employ female agents," Beckett said, his tone growing determined. "Fortunately, Eliza has kept me apprised of Miss Josette's training. I was briefed on the bravery she displayed in Gravesend. Which is why I propose we bring her in… as your wife."

"My wife!" Morgan exploded, leaping from his chair. "You want me to… *marry* the girl? Impossible!"

Beckett shook his head. "No, but I do want you to *pose* as a married couple. Originally, I had considered having you pretend to be betrothed, but then we would have had to deal with chaperones." He untwined his fingers and tapped the file on the desk, more impassioned than Morgan had ever seen. "However, you are not truly married, and if I discover that you have become too familiar with Miss Josette, there will not be a place you can hide on this earth that I will not find you." His eyes narrowed menacingly. "Do I make myself clear, *agent?*"

Morgan swallowed slowly as he nodded, acknowledging Beckett's harsh warning.

"Good." The aging spymaster nodded approvingly. "Your first assignment will be to obtain an invitation to Lord Paxton's house party without arousing suspicion."

"When is the house party?" Morgan asked.

"Six days." Extending him a file, Beckett added, "An informant has confirmed it will be a four-day house party."

"Six days?" Morgan repeated, accepting the file. "It will take at least three days to travel to Torquay by carriage."

"Then you'd better hurry and go woo your bride," Benedict teased. His smile evaporated when Morgan shot him a baleful look.

"Those three days in the carriage will give you time to review the documents and grow accustomed to each other," Beckett stated, before giving him a stern glare, "but not *too* accustomed."

Morgan gripped the file in his hand. "Even if I wanted to go find Miss Josette, I have no idea where she would be."

Eliza faced him. "Are you aware that Miss Josette became the headmistress at The Beckett School for Girls a little over a month ago?"

"I was vaguely aware of that, yes," Morgan replied, attempting to keep his expression neutral.

"Interesting," Eliza murmured. "Then I must assume that you have not told Josette that you have taken it upon yourself to hire guest lecturers for the school."

"How did you…" he began.

"I am a spy," she reminded him with a twinkle in her eye. "I also happened to notice your coach driving past the school last week."

He cleared his throat, and his eyes darted away from Eliza's knowing smile. "I must have had another appointment in the area," he lied. He had no desire to reveal that he'd made it a point to covertly check in on Josette regularly. In addition, he had hired street urchins to monitor the school and to inform him if anything was amiss.

"I see," Eliza murmured. "What appointment *did* you have on the East Side?"

Benedict laughed loudly. "Please do not attempt to invent another lie. We all know that you were smitten with Miss Josette on your last mission."

"I beg your pardon! I most certainly was *not* smitten," Morgan declared. "My assignment was to guard Lady Martha and that included guarding her companion, Miss Josette. There was nothing more to it than that."

Why did he feel the need to venture to the East Side to check on her? He had no doubt that Miss Josette could take care of herself, if the need arose.

Turning back towards Beckett, Morgan said, "Miss Josette and I did not leave on the best of terms. What if she does not agree to partner with me in this mad ruse?"

Beckett leveled a firm gaze at him, his eyebrows lowered. "It is of paramount importance that we discover the identity of *Genet*, learn the reason for his attendance at the house party, and put all this anti-monarchist resistance to rest."

Rubbing a hand along the back of his neck, Morgan asked, "Even if I could convince Miss Josette to act the part of my wife, how do we finagle an invitation to a party that is only six days away?"

Beckett huffed loudly. "You are the spy. Invent something!"

A soft chuckle came from Eliza. "My uncle did fail to mention that a neighboring estate, Harrold House, was available to let, and the lodgings have already been secured by our solicitor, Mr. Briggs. All done anonymously, of course." She fingered the reticule around her wrist. "It's only a short ride from Lord Paxton's estate."

"Additionally, it is fully staffed," Benedict shared. "But bear in mind that these servants have no affiliation with the Crown, so you must maintain the ruse of a married couple at all times."

Morgan took a moment to compose himself. "How do I propose the idea of a sham marriage to a woman who would rather see me dead?"

"It surely can't be that bad," Beckett admonished. "From what I have witnessed, Miss Josette is personable, engaging, and a beautiful young lady." He pointed towards the file in his hand. "Normally, I like to do a thorough investigation on any potential agent, but in this case, we have no time to launch one."

"Miss Josette has kept her past private," Benedict confirmed. "Although, it is clear she was born into privilege."

"And we know that her mother was French," Eliza added.

Morgan continued to object. "We also know she is fiercely independent, contrary, opinionated, and takes unnecessary risks." He frowned as he rose from his seat. "I fear that she may be more of a liability than an asset."

Eliza lifted her brow at his last words. "I have personally trained Josette, and I have full confidence in her ability to act as an agent."

"Be that as it may..." Morgan started.

Rising, Eliza cast him a look filled with cold censure. "You will not discount Josette. Not only did she protect Martha with valor, but she was the reason we learned of Lord Waterford's deceit."

Benedict walked over to his wife and placed an arm around her shoulder. "Don't cause a ruckus, dearest. Morgan is just nervous about approaching Miss Josette again."

Morgan held up his hands in a show of surrender. "I apologize for my insensitive remarks, but truthfully..." He hesitated, attempting to formulate the right words. "I find that I would rather stand at the battle front than ask Miss Josette to partner with me and pose as my *wife*."

Beckett rose from his chair and adjusted his coat. "Do not take no for an answer, young man. Your king and country are depending on you."

Morgan shuddered a bit and nodded gravely. Before exiting Lord Charles's office, he tucked the file in his coat. How was he going to convince Josette to partner with him? Not only had she taken almost an immediate dislike to him after their first encounter, but he truly believed that she would rather see him dead!

Headmistress Josette wore a rich, green gown with a high neckline and held a stack of books in her hand as she walked down the hall of The Beckett School for Girls. As she came around the corner, she saw a group of chattering students, all wearing donated dresses. She stopped next to them and waited until their chatter died down.

"Girls, where are you supposed to be?" she asked firmly.

The girls ducked their heads. A freckle-faced girl named Sophie said, "In astronomy class, headmistress."

"I will inform Mrs. Dawson that all of you will be doing one extra chore tonight before dinner." Josette attempted to maintain her stern look, but her lips twitched at the sight of their downcast eyes. If only these girls knew what a mischievous child she had been. "Now, off to class with you."

The girls scurried off in the opposite direction as she smiled at their retreating forms. She had been the headmistress of the school for the past month, and never had she been so happy. The Beckett family had supplied the funds to allow for almost twenty girls to attend the school, all of whom came from similarly dreary backgrounds.

Resuming her walk down the hall, she could hear Miss Cosette's voice drifting out from one of the classrooms. "No, Bertha, that stitch will never do," she corrected, her voice calm. "Try it again."

Josette stopped and leaned up against the door as she watched her dear friend teach a group of six girls how to sew. Both she and Cosette had chosen not to reveal their surnames to anyone, for fear of someone discovering their true identities.

Picking up the handkerchief from her seat, Cosette gracefully sat down and held out the needle in her hand. "Whitework embroidery is used on muslin dresses, tablecloths and christening gowns. By the end of this course, I hope you will have learned various techniques and how to follow the patterns that are featured in ladies' periodicals."

Before Cosette pushed her needle into the handkerchief, she glanced up and smiled at her employer. "Good morning, headmistress."

"Good morning, Miss Cosette," she answered, wondering how her friend always appeared so fresh-faced and beautiful with her creamy white skin and black hair.

In unison, the class stated, "Good morning, headmistress."

"Good morning, class," she replied, smiling.

Cosette rose from her seat and placed her handkerchief on the chair. "Girls, I must speak to Miss Josette for a moment. Please continue to practice your embroidery silently."

Once Cosette stopped in front of her, she asked, "How is your day going?"

"Very well," Cosette responded. "This morning, I met Mrs. Somerville, the new guest mathematics and astronomy teacher."

"Isn't she impressive?"

"Heavens, yes," Cosette confirmed. "I have often considered attending her astronomy lectures just for the fun of it."

"It is amazing the caliber of guest teachers that Lady Lansdowne and her family have acquired for this school."

Looking down at the books in her hand, Cosette gave her a knowing look. "Please, don't tell me that you are planning on another late night."

Josette smiled as she brought the books up to her chest. "Actually, I am returning these books to the library."

"Good," Cosette declared. "You have been working much too hard this past month." In a hushed voice, she added, "Between you sneaking off in the early morning for your training sessions at Lady Lansdowne's townhouse and burning the midnight oil, I don't know when you rest. I'm worried about you."

Stepping back into the hall, Josette gave her a mischievous smile. "Where is the fun in being idle?"

Cosette let out an exasperated huff as she started walking backwards in the hall. "We will finish this conversation later," her friend said.

Josette shifted the books in her hand, so she could give Cosette a salute. "Yes, Miss Cosette."

Rolling her eyes, Cosette just laughed. "I'll see you at supper."

Josette turned and headed towards the library on the first floor. As she descended the stairs, her housekeeper approached, holding a calling card in her hand. "Headmistress, a Lord Morgan Easton is here to see you."

Lord Morgan? She stared at the card in Mrs. Dawson's hand and wondered why *he* would call on her? Did that man have no sense at all? The sign by the front door specifically stated that no men were welcome at this school. She would make no exceptions, especially for a man as infuriating as Lord Morgan.

After a long moment, she reached out and accepted the card, tucking it into her pocket without sparing it a glance. "Inform Lord Morgan that it is inappropriate for him to call here and that I will not receive him."

Mrs. Dawson stared at her in disbelief. "To confirm, you wish me to turn a handsome lord away?"

Feeling no need to defend her position, she replied, "Trust me, Lord Morgan is a pest that needs to be dealt with."

"As you wish, headmistress."

Squaring her shoulders, Josette headed straight for her office. As she walked into the room, she dropped the books onto a chair, reminding herself that she'd need to return them to the library later. Why did she lose rational thought whenever her mind turned to that infuriatingly annoying man? She hadn't even seen him yet, and her thoughts had become jumbled!

It had been over a month since their last encounter, and he had made no attempt to contact her since then. Why now? Banishing her wayward thoughts, she sat at her desk, reached for the newspaper, and flipped it over to scan the society page. Sure enough, an article about Lord Morgan and his antics at Viscount Phillipson's ball were highlighted. A list of women who danced with him was also carefully outlined. Why is the ton so enamored with this man, she wondered.

Eliza had always taught Josette to learn as much as she could about her opponent, and she considered Morgan exactly that. It was perfectly natural for her to want to learn more about him. He may be a proficient agent of the Crown, but his words were too smooth, too rehearsed. Why did that bother her?

Rather than dwell on it, she placed the newspaper under the large stack of papers laying on the edge of her desk. Later, if she had the time, she would revisit the puzzle that was Lord Morgan.

The squealing of several girls' laughter from the cobblestone courtyard caused her to shift her gaze out the window, but she couldn't see what had the girls so riled up. She wasn't overly concerned because the courtyard had various hiding spots but was mostly open for the children to play. The tall, stone walls ensured their safety from the ruffians of the rookeries.

She heard a loud, masculine roar and quickly stood, stepping closer to the large bay window. The girls shrieked with laughter as they ran past with bright smiles on their faces, plaited hair streaming behind them. A dark-haired man, well-dressed in a blue jacket and buff trousers, chased the girls across the courtyard.

Feeling angry and protective of her girls, Josette pushed the window open and reached for the pistol in the pocket of her dress. She climbed out the window easily and looked around. The girls were huddled in a far corner, their eyes wide with excitement, as the man moved slowly towards them, his hands outstretched like a bear's claws.

Josette kept her steps silent as she approached him from behind. The man roared again, making the girls laugh and scream simultaneously. Taking advantage of the noise, Josette lifted her hand and pressed the barrel of the pistol against the man's spine.

He stopped in his tracks and stood with his hands still in the air.

"This is your only warning," Josette declared. "Do not move."

She turned to look at the girls, her pistol not wavering. "Girls, go inside at once and fetch Miss Cosette."

The girls ran past her obediently, although several gave her confused looks. When the last one was safely indoors, Josette lessened the pressure of the pistol against the man's back but did not remove it.

"You are trespassing, sir."

"You left me no choice, Miss Josette."

Josette sighed as she recognized the deep, baritone voice, and lowered the pistol to her side. "What in the blazes are you doing here, Lord Morgan?"

Chapter Two

Slowly and deliberately, Morgan turned around to face Josette, not wanting to give her any cause to shoot him.

Keeping his eyes trained low, he saw the pistol by Josette's side, but he could see her fingers twitching. He donned his most dashing smile, the one that he knew worked on the ladies, then he brought his gaze up to hers. However, he was not prepared for his reaction to her incomparable beauty. His breath hitched, and his heart began to pound. How was it possible that she was even more beautiful than he last remembered?

Josette wore a simple gown, and her hair was pinned back into a low chignon with small tendrils framing her delicate face. To say that Josette was a beautiful woman would be inadequate. She was far more than just a pretty face. She was radiant with green eyes that shone bright with cleverness and a bearing that projected determination. From the moment he'd met her in that dimly lit alleyway, Morgan knew he had met his match.

The memory of Josette striding towards him in the alley with a dagger in her hand, made him smile. She'd had no fear when she approached him, demanding to know why he was watching Lady Martha.

Josette's voice broke through his musings. "Will you stop grinning like a bloody fool, Lord Morgan?"

"Language, my dear Josette," he teased as he adjusted the sleeves of his blue riding coat, "and just Morgan will do."

"No," she said with a shake of her head. "I would prefer if we kept formalities between us. We are barely acquaintances."

Morgan chuckled. "I daresay we are far more than just acquaintances after fighting side-by-side to save Martha from her father and that despicable fiancé." He grinned, hoping to disarm her. "Plus, we spent many hours in a coach driving back and forth between Gravesend and the hospital in St. George's parish. If you'll recall, you allowed me to call you Josette then."

"I recall it differently, my lord," she contested. "You began using my given name without my permission."

Josette tucked the pistol into the pocket of her dress, but her stony demeanor did not indicate she had softened towards him at all. This was not going well, he thought, before deciding to try a different approach.

"How have you been?"

Her eyes narrowed slightly as they scanned his face. "Why are you here?"

"To visit a friend," he answered smoothly. He was becoming more and more frustrated with his inability to woo her. Why did she not respond to his flattery like other women?

She again shook her head. "We are not friends, Lord Morgan."

"We are," he declared, taking a step closer to her.

In response, she took two steps back, clasping her hands in front of her. "We each had a job to do, and we successfully completed the task. If anything, we were more colleagues than friends."

"Would you care to sit for a spell?" he asked, gesturing towards an iron bench.

She moved to the far side of the bench. Taking her cue, he sat on the other end, maintaining more than enough distance to be proper.

Shifting, he angled his body towards her. "I will tell you, but first, I was hoping to hear how the school is operating."

"What specifically would you like to know?" she asked with cool politeness.

He rested his arm on the back of the bench. "Are you happy here?"

Obviously, that was the right thing to ask because her eyes lit up, and she actually smiled a little. "I am, very much so," she admitted softly. "Thank you for asking."

14

"Why is that?"

A wistful expression crossed her face. "We are teaching skills to these girls that will help them find employment when the time comes for them to leave our school." She shifted her eyes towards the building. "The staff demonstrates kindness, love, and tolerance, and we hope the girls leave the school knowing that they are enough."

Seeing a vulnerable side to her that he had not seen before, he pressed, "Is that what happened to you, Josette? Did someone think you were not enough?"

Her expression grew guarded. "No, something far worse happened to me, Lord Morgan." She rose quickly. "If you will excuse me, I have work that needs doing."

He rose, reluctantly. "I need to speak to you privately."

Josette gave him a questioning glance. "Are we not alone?"

Glancing over his shoulder, he took in all the faces of the girls watching them from the windows of the second level. He turned back with an uplifted brow. "It is a matter of the utmost importance." When her expression didn't change, he added, "I come on behalf of Lord Charles Beckett."

Tipping her head, she acknowledged, "Follow me. You may speak freely in my study."

Feeling as though he had secured his first victory, Morgan clasped his hands behind his back as they walked towards the door. "Lord and Lady Lansdowne send their regards," he remarked, attempting to engage her in casual conversation.

Josette smiled with genuine affection. "I hold Lord and Lady Lansdowne in the highest esteem, and I am most grateful for their friendship."

Leaning in, he nudged her gently with his shoulder. "From what I understand, Eliza has been training you as well."

Her lips drew into a tight, white line. "You are remarkably well-informed, Lord Morgan," she stated in a tone that was anything but complementary.

Morgan opened the door and stood aside as Josette entered the hall. She walked swiftly, not looking to see if he was following her. She stopped near the base of the stairs and tapped her slipper as he approached her. "You appear to be dawdling, Lord Morgan."

He grinned. "Not in the least, headmistress."

She rolled her eyes at his use of her title. "Follow me. My study is just around the corner."

As she started to brush by him, Morgan placed his hand on the small of her back.

She stiffened, and she stopped in front of him. "Kindly refrain from touching me."

Dropping his hand, Morgan opened his mouth to apologize but stopped when he heard a pistol cocking. "Step away from Miss Josette," a woman ordered from the top of the stairs.

His first instinct was to reach for the pistol tucked into his trousers, but he thought better of it. Instead, he slowly raised his hands, turning his head towards the voice. A woman with black hair, beautiful, creamy-white skin, and red, pouty lips descended the stairs with a pistol aimed at his chest. With each step, she kept her gaze riveted on him, and her aim never faltered.

Morgan glanced at Josette, and she had the nerve to smirk at him. "I would do as you are told, because Miss Cosette is an expert marksman," she advised.

His eyes grew wide. "*She* is Miss Cosette?" he asked in disbelief. He had been briefed that the former condemned spy had received permission to work at the school teaching embroidery, but he had not been prepared for the striking beauty in front of him.

"She is," Josette responded with pride.

Miss Cosette's eyes regarded him with contempt. "The girls informed me that a *nice* gentleman had climbed over the walls and was playing with them. Fortunately for you, Miss Josette only placed a pistol to your back in the courtyard. However, I may not be as lenient since I just witnessed you becoming too familiar with our headmistress."

Morgan offered her a dashing smile, but Miss Cosette just lifted a brow. Why were these ladies immune to his charms? "This is simply a huge misunderstanding," he tried to assure her. Then, glancing at Josette, he implored, "Tell her."

Josette gave him a one shoulder shrug. "I think her perception is quite accurate." She smiled at Cosette. "I say shoot him. After all, he has trespassed onto our property."

"Wait!" he shouted. "I tried to come to call, but I was turned away at the door."

"And yet, you didn't take the hint, Lord Morgan," Josette said dryly.

"*He* is Lord Morgan?" Cosette asked in surprise. She lowered her pistol, and her eyes perused the length of his body. "Based on Josette's description, I imagined you to be quite hideous and much hairier."

Relieved that the pistol was no longer being pointed at him, he adjusted his paisley waistcoat. "How did Josette describe me?"

Cosette chuckled softly. "Akin to the offspring of a one-eyed monster and an ogre."

Aghast, he turned to Josette. "Is that how you perceive me?" He found himself wounded by her harsh description of him. Why did he care what she thought of him?

"Of course not," Josette declared in a rush. Her blush was barely discernible, but he caught it nevertheless. "Cosette has the most vivid imagination, because I never once described your appearance."

Feeling elated that Josette wasn't completely oblivious to his charms, he decided to take advantage of this moment and tease her. "Just how often do you speak to Miss Cosette about me?"

Expecting a witty retort, he was surprised when she simply huffed, "You are a jackanapes, my lord."

An unexpected burst of laughter escaped Cosette's lips, but she covered her mouth with her fingers. "I believe I'm not needed here, but I'll stay close for propriety's sake." She tucked her pistol back into the folds of her dress.

"Thank you," Josette replied. "We shall be in my study." Without waiting for him, she turned and walked across the hall.

Morgan tipped his head graciously to Miss Cosette. "It was a pleasure to meet you, Miss Cosette."

"You as well," she said, giving him a slight curtsy.

He glanced towards the door and watched Josette enter her study. Taking a step closer to Cosette, he asked in a hushed voice, "What am I doing wrong?"

Cosette watched him with careful deliberation for a long moment before he saw compassion creep into her eyes. "Be patient with Josette. She guards her secrets fiercely and hides her emotions behind a mask."

However, before he could respond, any sign of warmth in Cosette's eyes disappeared, and she closed the distance between them. "I will give you one warning," she said, her words becoming thick with a French accent. "Josette is like a sister to me." Her finger reached out and stroked along the length of his right cheek. "And if you hurt her in any way," she paused, leaning closer, "then I will have no qualms about killing you in the most excruciatingly painful way possible, *comprenez-vous?*" Her gaze was unrelenting, leaving little doubt that she would follow through on her threat.

"Understood." He swallowed nervously.

Cosette stepped back. Her cheerful smile belied the fact that she just threatened to kill him. "Off you go, Lord Morgan. Josette is expecting you," she said in her usual, more subtle, French accent.

Morgan nodded before moving towards the study. Wondering if Cosette might attack him from behind, he glanced over his shoulder. To his surprise, she offered him another bright smile and a wave of her fingers.

As Morgan walked into the office, he wasn't sure which lady he feared more.

Josette took a deep, calming breath and forced herself to think. Why did Morgan's presence cause her to act like a simpering girl? Yes, he was handsome. But he was also rude, conceited, cocky… Her thoughts trailed off as she sighed in frustration. Her life would be much simpler if Morgan was not involved.

Before she could dwell on her wayward thoughts any longer, Morgan entered the study and closed the door behind him. She moved around the desk and sat on her chair, waiting for him to explain why he was here. Instead of following her lead, Morgan stepped to the shelves which lined one side of her office.

He clasped his hands behind his back as his eyes perused her array of books. Finally, he spoke, "You have quite the impressive collection."

"Most of those books were gifted by the Beckett family."

His hand came from behind his back as he selected a book. "Have you read any of them?"

"Most of them, in fact."

Turning to face her, he held up a small, worn book. "You've read *New System of Chemical Philosophy*, by John Dalton?" The disbelief evident in his voice irked her.

"I have," she replied smugly. Truth be told, she barely understood it, but she refused to share that bit of information with Morgan. "The book contains a scientific description of the atomic theory and accurately describes the law of multiple proportions."

"You are a woman of many talents." His words almost sounded like a compliment. Tucking the book back into place, he turned to face her. "I've just left a meeting with Eliza, Benedict, and Lord Charles."

"Is that so?"

"A French spy, known as *Genet*, plans to attend a house party near a seaside village of Torquay, and possibly conspire with a group of anti-monarchists." He walked to the window and looked out. "I have tracked this spy over the years, and he is ruthless."

Noticing the pain etched on Morgan's face, she asked, "How so?"

For a long moment, he said nothing. "While the British army fought in the peninsula, somehow *Genet* managed to learn the location of our troops." Breaking his gaze from the window, he turned and leaned against the window sill. "Because of him, thousands of our soldiers were killed," he paused, his voice hitching with emotion, "including my brother."

"My condolences for your loss." His gaze remained on the ground, so she shared, "I have experienced the loss of loved ones as well, and I understand the feeling of an all-encompassing grief. It consumes your entire being."

His gaze rose to meet hers, and she was surprised by the compassion in his eyes. "Who have you lost, Josette?" His voice was barely a hoarse whisper.

She hesitated, knowing she was about to admit something she had not previously shared with any of her friends. But the way he looked at her, with such tenderness and care, caused her resolve to shrink. "I lost my parents."

"At the same time?"

She ducked her head, careful to give nothing away. "No, my mother died first."

Josette brought her gaze up when she was met with silence and saw Morgan watching her closely. Fortunately, he was wise enough not to pester her with more questions. If he had, she would have refused to answer.

"An agent intercepted a note stating *Genet* will be at Lord Paxton's house party in six days." Morgan pushed away from the sill. "Beckett has tasked me with obtaining an invitation to the house party, discovering *Genet*'s purpose, and arresting him as a traitor to the Crown."

Josette scrunched her nose. "Why would *Genet* attend a house party in Torquay?"

"That's all we know right now, but we must act on this information. Which is why…" he began, but stopped, shifting his gaze to a point behind her. If Josette didn't know any better, she would think that he was too nervous to say his next words. He cleared his throat and met her gaze. "Which leads me to the reason I'm here."

Leaning forward, Josette closed the ledger in front of her and gave him a faint smile. "I must admit that I am quite curious about that."

Morgan stepped closer to the desk, keeping his gaze aimed at the stack of papers in the corner. He began lightly tapping the edge of her desk, which suspiciously looked like a stalling tactic. However, his finger stilled, and a line appeared between his brows. Not understanding what captured his attention, she moved her ledger to the side of the desk and saw the newspaper sticking out from under the papers.

As she reached out to grab it, Morgan slid the newspaper from the pile and a wide, infuriating smile came to his lips. "Are you keeping tabs on me, Josette?" The way her name slid off his tongue made her want to stab him with her dagger.

"No," she declared, rising and reaching for the paper.

"Interesting," he said, still maintaining the same annoying smile on his lips. "Were you by chance reading about Countess Whitenhall or of her dandy of a son, Viscount Brown?" He made a showing of reading the paper before he continued. "After all, we are the only three featured on this society page."

Josette fought a blush, but she could still feel her cheeks growing warm. Attempting to save some dignity, she placed her hands on the desk and leaned forward. "If you must know, I was doing some research."

Morgan gave her a look that lay somewhere between smugness and pity. "Is that the best you could come up with?"

"It's true," she admitted, shrugging. "For some reason the ton seems to be smitten with you, but I can't for the life of me figure out why."

"Because I'm charming."

"No, that's not it."

"Handsome." He gave her an impish grin.

She huffed, lowering herself back on the chair. "You are far too conceited for your own good, my lord."

"And you are a bad liar," he challenged as he placed the newspaper back on her desk. "However, as much as I would like to tease you about your newfound obsession with me…"

Josette spoke over him. "How dare you insinuate…"

Morgan put his hand up to interrupt her. "Be that as it may, I am not here to fight with you." He paused, and she saw a vulnerable expression half-hidden deep within his eyes. "I am here to convince you to be my wife."

Chapter Three

Morgan held his breath, waiting for her answer, hoping it would be yes. He had expected her to rail at him and had even considered the possibility that she might try to shoot him. But he was not prepared for the deafening silence that filled the room.

Watching Josette carefully, he saw emotions flickering across her face as she simply stared back at him. Finally, she rose slowly from her chair, her movements precise, keeping her back stiff. "I apologize if I gave you any indication that I was interested in receiving an offer from you, but I must decline." Her words were deliberate, devoid of nearly all emotion.

Taken aback by her rejection, which seemed to sting deeply for some reason he could not fathom, he asked, "Why am I not a suitable candidate?" He felt his anger rising. "Am I not wealthy enough for you?"

Josette shook her head. "That's not what this is about…"

"Is it because I am only a second son?" he barked, then frowned at his own irrational behavior.

"I'm sorry if I…"

"Do you take issue with the fact that I'm an agent?"

"Stop!" Josette came around the desk and stood in front of him. "I have no problem with you personally, Morgan. The truth is that I have no desire to marry."

He gave her an odd look, despite being secretly pleased that she had just called him by his given name. Did she even realize the slip of her tongue? "All women wish to be married."

"You mean controlled," she countered.

Looking down at her, he softened his tone. "No, I mean loved, protected, and cherished."

"You've read too many fairy tales," she replied, lowering her gaze to his lapels.

Morgan reached out to offer her comfort, but when he saw her body tense, he immediately lowered his hand. Josette took a step back. "Thank you for your kind offer, but I must decline." She started to move behind her desk. "I assume you can see yourself out."

Her quick, dismissive tone bothered him, and he reached out to grasp her arm. "Wait, I still need to speak to you."

Lifting a brow, she glanced down at his hand on her arm. "Unhand me, Lord Morgan." Confounded woman, he thought. She's back to using my title.

Dropping his hand, he offered an apologetic smile. "I am going about this all wrong." He pointed at the settee against the back wall. "I would like to discuss something with you."

Seeing the indecision on her face, he placed his fingers to the bridge of his nose and sighed loudly. He was butchering this proposal, despite the speech he'd practiced during the carriage ride.

Morgan stepped to the settee and waited as Josette cautiously approached him. Once she was situated, he sat down next to her, and offered a dashing smile before he tried again. "I have no intention of actually marrying you, but I need you to act in the role of my wife."

As soon as the words left his mouth, he was thrown against the back of the settee, and Josette had a dagger pressed against his throat. "How dare you!" Her eyes burned with anger, but he could see the hurt buried deep within. "I will never be your mistress."

To his surprise, her eyes filled with tears as she removed her dagger from his throat and jumped up. "I was wrong about you," she declared, pointing her dagger towards the door. "Get out!"

"No!" he shouted. "You completely misread my intentions."

"Your intentions? Are you not looking for a woman to play the role of your wife?"

"Yes... but no..." His voice trailed off as he rose and stood in front of her. "You misunderstood me. I need you to pose as my wife, so we can infiltrate Lord Paxton's house party as a married couple."

Josette didn't speak as she scrutinized him warily, her fingers twiddling the dagger in her hand. "Why ask me?"

Frustrated, he raked his fingers through his hair. "Because, apparently, you are the only woman Lord Charles feels is capable of this assignment. The Crown does not officially hire female agents."

Her lips pressed together. "To clarify, *you* did not select me to be your partner?"

"Aren't you pleased that Beckett thinks so highly of you that he is allowing you to work as an agent for this assignment?"

"I see. I should feel flattered, then?" Her words were dry, which irritated him greatly.

"Obviously, you don't understand," he proclaimed. "Why are you being so infuriating?"

With a tip of her head, she replied, "Again, I must decline your offer." Josette started to turn away.

"Wait! You can't decline!" Morgan exclaimed.

She sighed heavily. "Even if I agreed, we would never suit. We can barely be in the same room without arguing. I thank you for the great honor you've bestowed upon me, but…"

"I will give you £15,000 if you agree to partner with me!"

Her eyes grew wide, her lips parting in shock. "That is a fortune."

Not to him, but he didn't feel the need to clarify that. "Please, Josette," he pleaded softly. His shoulders slumped, his burden too heavy to bear. "My brother is dead because of *Genet*. I must stop him." His voice choked with emotion. "But I am unable to stop him without your help."

Josette stared deeply into his eyes, and he could see depths of compassion in them, but he also saw vulnerability. He knew that she was not one to trust easily, and frankly, neither was he. But he trusted Josette. He'd seen her bravery when she'd helped save their lives at The Cloven Hoof in Gravesend. He knew what she was capable of.

Her eyes drifted reluctantly towards the door. "I'm not sure if I should leave the school."

To their surprise, the door was wrenched opened, and Miss Cosette entered the room. "You should go, Josette." They stared at her in amazement as she tsked. "Did you assume that I wouldn't listen at the door?"

Miss Cosette turned to address him. "As an agent, you may have been informed that I was a former French spy." He nodded, so she continued. "I had no direct contact with *Genet*, mind you, but even among French spies, he was considered ruthless. You must be careful around him."

"Is there anything else you remember about *Genet*?" he asked eagerly.

Miss Cosette brought her fingers up to her lips and tapped them as she thought. Then, her fingers stilled, and she dropped them. "I do recall that my father told me that *Genet* was fond of sweets."

"Sweets?" he huffed. "That is my only lead? A French spy who enjoys sweet delicacies."

Cosette's eyes twinkled with amusement. "I have succeeded with less, Lord Morgan."

Turning his gaze back to Josette, Morgan said, "Please say that you will partner with me."

Her dagger had disappeared back into the folds of her dress, but she still eyed him with trepidation. "Just to clarify a few things," she began, her voice taking on an edge, "we are not truly married, and you will not expect any of *those* benefits."

He tipped his head. "That goes without saying."

Josette nibbled on her lower lip, drawing his attention to their fullness. "Will I be expected to continue working as an agent once this assignment is complete?"

"I suppose that is between you and Lord Charles," he replied.

She walked to the window and looked out. "What if your information is wrong, and *Genet* is not at the house party?"

Morgan took a few steps closer to her. "Then you will still be entitled to the £15,000."

"And you will manage the school without me?" she asked Cosette.

"Yes, headmistress," Cosette confirmed. "The school will be here when you get back."

Meeting his gaze, Josette's eyes grew determined. "I won't play the role of a submissive wife."

"Nor would I expect you to," he responded, his words filled with sincerity. He had no desire to silence this beautiful creature. He had enjoyed their previous conversations and knew she was a woman with a sound intellect.

"And I want to play a role in *Genet*'s capture."

He smiled, his eyes reflecting respect. "I have no doubt."

Returning his smile, Josette's eyes held a mischievous twinkle. "Then, I agree."

With those words, Morgan felt buoyed by the hope that he would finally catch the French spy that had plagued their continent for years. Now, he just had to remind himself not to get too close to Josette. He must keep a professional distance between them. After all, he was, first and foremost, a spy.

After depositing her last gown in the trunk, Josette latched it and sighed. Was she doing the right thing? Could she pretend to be married to Lord Morgan?

"I heard that sigh," Cosette said after she closed the lid of another trunk. "Will you stop doubting yourself?"

Josette's eyes roamed over the three traveling trunks in her room, which were stuffed full of everything that she would need to attend a house party. "I still believe three trunks is simply too many for four days."

Cosette waved a hand dismissively. "Nonsense. You will need matching gloves, gowns, ballgowns, a riding habit, a traveling habit, bonnets…"

As she continued listing articles of clothing, Josette's mind wandered. Would she be able to prove her worth as an agent? If so, perhaps she could go on other assignments and travel the world.

Cosette broke into her musings. "Have you stopped listening to me?"

Josette gave her an apologetic look. "I am sorry. I was woolgathering about the possibility of going on other missions after this assignment is complete."

A haunted look appeared in Cosette's eyes before she blinked it away. Walking over to the camelback settee, she sat down and patted the cushion. "Come sit for a moment."

"I know that tone," Josette teased, as she stepped to the settee, "you plan to provide me with some much-needed, but unsolicited, guidance."

Cosette smiled. "It's true." The smile dropped from her face as she shared, "Being a spy will require your full attention. You must never get distracted or lull yourself into a false sense of security." She grew quiet, and she seemed to disappear into her own thoughts. "There are dangerous men afoot, and they will kill you without regard for your gender, age, or status."

Reaching for her friend's hand, Josette ventured, "I understand. When I was working as Martha's companion, I dealt with her father and Lord Allister, and I daresay that they were ruthless."

"It's not the same. You were working with a team of agents to keep Martha safe," Cosette insisted. "When you are on an assignment, partners can be killed, and you have to prepare yourself for the worst-case scenarios." She clasped her hand tightly. "Promise me that you will always have an exit strategy in place. You must never rely solely on Lord Morgan to save you."

Josette watched her friend closely. The sadness in her features was visible, but it was the pain in her voice that alarmed her the most.

"You sound as if you are speaking from experience."

Cosette pulled her hand away as her face grew expressionless. "Being a spy may sound exciting, but it is a life full of misery, torment, and loneliness." Her eyes searched Josette's before she shared, "Believe me, if I could do it all over again, I would never have become a spy."

"Then, why did you?" Josette pressed gently, knowing that Cosette had never shared this much about her past before.

"It was either work as a spy or be killed by my own father," she admitted.

The headmistress reached over and embraced her friend. "I am so glad that Lord Camden was able to obtain permission for you to come work at the school with me."

"As am I," Cosette expressed. "My dream was always to open a dress shop, but teaching girls embroidery is a close second."

Sitting back, Josette asked, "Do you think I am mad to partner with Lord Morgan on this assignment and pose as his wife?"

Cosette shook her head. "I do not, because £15,000 is a fortune."

"It is," Josette admitted. "With the £5,000 that Lady Lansdowne gave me to act as Martha's companion and £15,000 from Lord Morgan, I would be financially secure for the rest of my days."

A playful smile came to Cosette's lips. "Besides, I think you might enjoy playing the role of Lord Morgan's wife."

Josette's lips grew tight. "I hope I can hold my sharp tongue around him." She huffed. "He just makes me so… angry."

"Angry?"

"He can be so mulish at times."

Cosette raised her brow. "Mulish?"

"Yes," she said. "Haven't you noticed it?"

Cosette laughed. "No, I have not."

"And when he smiles that infuriatingly cocky smile, a dimple appears on his left cheek," Josette revealed. "It's as if he knows how dashingly handsome he is and is using it to his advantage."

Her smile faded, and Cosette asked, "You think Lord Morgan is dashingly handsome?"

Josette's mouth snapped shut as a blush crept up her cheeks. "I… uh…"

Cosette rose and stepped to the trunks. Opening a lid, she started removing the gowns that Josette had just packed. "What are you doing?"

Taking the gowns over to her bed, Cosette laid them down before she headed back to the trunk. "You were right. This was a bad idea."

Josette jumped up. "Why?"

Cosette stopped and frowned, her left hand holding a gown. "I fear that your attraction to Lord Morgan could jeopardize your mission. It could get you killed."

"No, it won't," Josette rushed to reassure her. "Lord Morgan may be handsome, but he is a known rake. We both are aware of his reputation from the society page, and I have experienced it firsthand." She walked closer to her friend and reached for the gown in her hand. "I have no intention of letting down my guard and falling prey to his flattery."

Cosette's eyes grew sad. "Men are a tricky sort; they offer promises with no intention of keeping them."

Placing the gown back into the trunk, Josette asserted, "You don't need to worry about me. I am proficient in multiple weapons, and I am excited to prove myself in the field. If Lord Morgan becomes too familiar, then I will shoot him."

Cosette pulled her into a tight embrace. "Promise me that you will come back to the school unharmed."

"I promise you," she replied, returning the embrace.

Leaning back, Cosette looked sad. "I wish I could help you, but I am not allowed to leave this school; it's punishable by death." She gave her a weak smile. "But if you need me, I will come to you and assume the risk."

"I assure you, my friend. I will be fine."

Cosette's eyes filled with unshed tears. "Either way, I don't think you'll be coming back."

"What do you mean?"

"You'll see," she replied vaguely as she left the room.

Watching Cosette's retreating figure, Josette couldn't help but repeat those words back in her mind. *I don't think you'll be coming back.* What did she mean? Of course she was coming back! This was her home now. This school, these girls… this is where she belonged.

But that thought barely had time to surface before a feeling of uncertainty crept into her mind.

Chapter Four

Morgan yawned as he rested the back of his head on the plush bench of his post-chaise. He'd had a restless night. Every time he closed his eyes, he'd thought about Josette. She was an anomaly to him. For some inexplicable reason, she did not respond to his charms or good looks. It was as if she was immune.

He reached over and closed the window of the carriage as the smell of excrement floated in from the bustling street. Returning to his thoughts, he realized that it might be a good thing that Josette showed him no favor. After all, this partnership was for business purposes only... not pleasure.

The carriage jerked to a stop in front of a large three-story brick building with a painted sign proudly announcing The Beckett School for Girls. Despite being surrounded by blackened buildings, waste of all kinds, and a hideous, foul-smelling odor that was synonymous with the rookeries, the school was in excellent condition, and the pavement in front of the school had been recently swept.

The footman opened the door, and Morgan started to exit when Benedict and Adrien, the Earl of Camden, hopped into the carriage unexpectedly.

Morgan watched as they sat across from him before asking, "Did I miss a meeting?"

Removing his top hat, Benedict placed it on the bench next to him. "No. However, Adrien and I wanted to speak to you privately for a moment."

His eyes flickered between the two men's uncharacteristically stern and reprimanding faces, and he was trying to think what he could have done to earn their anger. He cleared his throat. "May I ask what this is about?"

Lord Camden crossed his arms over his chest. "We wanted to explain the repercussions if you become too familiar with Miss Josette."

"Or even attempt to become familiar," Benedict added.

Morgan shifted uncomfortably in his seat. "Gentlemen, I have no..." His words stopped when he saw both Benedict and Adrien lean down and pull pistols out of their Hessian boots. "Threats are not necessary. I do not intend to mix business with pleasure where Miss Josette is concerned."

Adrien's eyes grew hard. "Your reputation precedes you, Easton."

"What reputation is that?" he asked.

"A rake of the worst kind," Benedict said, answering for his friend.

Morgan smiled tentatively, hoping to ward off their disdain. "It is just an act, a cover," he insisted. "I can assure you that I am not a rake."

Jaw clenched, Adrien did not seem convinced. "Then perhaps you can explain why the society pages seem to feature you on a regular basis." He lifted his brow. "And every time you are seen with a different lady."

Leaning his head back, Morgan looked at the top of the carriage and sighed. "It's all strategic. I may play the part of a jovial, charismatic..." he paused, smirking, "...devastatingly handsome rake, but I do not go home with any of those women." His smile dropped. "It's just an act to obtain certain invitations, so I can be kept abreast of what the ton are gossiping and whispering about."

Benedict eyed him suspiciously. "Regardless, Josette is a dear friend to my wife and Lady Camden, and we think of her as family."

"And we protect our family," Adrien stated, his voice taking on a dangerous tone. "Do I make myself clear?"

Morgan nodded his understanding. "Perfectly. But you have nothing to fear. Josette and I are just partners, nothing more."

After dropping the pistol back into his boot, Benedict pulled out a piece of paper from his waistcoat. He held it up as he explained, "Larson wanted me to read this to you." He opened the slip of paper and read, "If you touch Miss Josette then I will cut slits in your belly, place hungry cats..." he paused, and squinted his eyes, "what does that say?"

Adrien leaned over, pointed at the note and stated, "Rats. It says rats."

Benedict nodded and continued, "...I will cut slits in your belly, place hungry rats in those slits and watch while they devour you from the inside." After he finished, he folded the note and placed it back into his waistcoat.

Morgan chuckled nervously. "That was very specific."

"I would not discount Larson's threat," Adrien instructed with a firm gaze. "Or ours."

"I understand your concerns, but I give you my word as a gentleman that I will not compromise Miss Josette," he vowed.

"Thank you. Now, on to happier things," Adrien said, returning his pistol to his boot. "If you need any assistance during your mission, please let us know."

Morgan gave him a pointed look. "Didn't your wife just have a baby?"

A smile came to Adrien's lips as he replied, "She did. A little girl." He reached for the door. "Since we are finished threatening Easton, let's go home to our families."

Morgan waited until Benedict stepped out of the carriage before he exited and walked to the front door. The marquess's crested carriage rolled down the street as he lifted his fist to knock. Unexpectedly, it was partially opened, and Miss Cosette slipped out, closing it behind her.

"Lord Morgan, I want to speak to you for a moment," she announced.

Another threat perhaps, he thought to himself. He gave her a charming smile, curious about her intentions. "I'm listening."

Leaning closer, she revealed, "Tomorrow is Josette's nineteenth birthday."

He hadn't expected that. "Tomorrow," he confirmed.

Cosette's eyes held compassion. "Josette would be furious if she knew I told you, but she hid it from us last year. We had planned a celebration tomorrow evening, but now I am hoping you might do something special for her on the way to Torquay."

Morgan smiled reassuringly. "I can arrange for something."

Happiness filled Cosette's eyes. "Thank you, Lord Morgan. We don't know much about Josette's past, but we did manage to discover her birthday… after it passed, of course." Turning back towards the door, she pushed it opened and walked into the entry hall. She pointed towards three trunks by the door. "Those are Josette's."

Snapping his fingers to alert the footmen, Morgan pointed towards the trunks to be loaded. While the footmen hauled them to the carriage to be strapped down, Josette came to stand at the top of the stairs, wearing a dark blue traveling habit. She offered a tentative smile as she placed her hand on the railing and descended the stairs. A young woman dressed in a servant's uniform trailed not far behind Josette, carrying a valise in her hand.

Morgan admired the way the dress fit Josette's curves perfectly, rendering it nearly impossible to look away. Her dark brown hair was piled high on her head and small curls framed her face. Why did his partner have to be the most beautiful woman he had ever known?

Cosette cast him a concerned look before whispering, "You're staring."

Reluctantly, he shifted his gaze towards Cosette. "Just anxious to depart, I suppose."

She frowned as her eyes assessed him. "I assume that Lord Camden and Lord Lansdowne threatened you with bodily harm if you touched Josette."

"How did you know that?"

Cosette looked disappointed. "Please do not ask ignorant questions, Lord Morgan. It is beneath you." As Josette stepped down from the last step, she rushed to continue, "If you hurt my friend, in any way," she stopped, her thick French accent returning, "I will make their threats look like child's play. Do we understand each other?"

He cleared his throat. "We do."

"What exactly do you understand, Lord Morgan?" Josette asked as she stopped in front of him.

"Miss Cosette just informed me that I need to return you back to the school in one piece," he replied smoothly.

Reaching for her hand, he was surprised when Josette placed it out of his reach. "There is no need for prevarication between us. Complete honesty will save us considerable time."

He lifted his brow at Cosette in question, but she just smirked back. Turning his gaze back towards Josette, he asked, "Are you ready to depart?"

"I suppose so," she murmured, her eyes roaming the entry hall. "I have already said my goodbyes to the girls, and I assured them I will be back within two weeks."

"Hopefully sooner," he stated.

She gave him the smallest of smiles. "One can only hope."

Morgan offered his arm to Josette and was pleased when she accepted it, allowing him to escort her out to his carriage. Once she was situated, he sat across from her and braced himself as the coach lurched forward. He attempted to catch Josette's eye, but she kept her gaze firmly out the window.

He sighed. This was going to be a long three days unless he could convince her that he really was a likeable fellow.

Josette kept her attention firmly on the passing countryside. Still, she could feel Lord Morgan's eyes on her. "Will you please refrain from staring at me?" she asked, without shifting her gaze.

"Did you just acknowledge me?"

She turned her head and gave him a baffled look. "Didn't your parents ever inform you that staring is rude, Lord Morgan?"

"No ruder than ignoring your companion in a carriage." He softened his words with a smile.

Pressing her lips together, Josette chose her next words carefully. "We are not friends. We are partners. Thus, we do not need to engage in polite conversation."

"I consider you a friend," he stated, maintaining his gaze.

She gave him a knowing look. "We barely know each other."

He gave her a one-sided grin that made him look devilishly handsome. "I learned everything about you on our last mission, without you even saying a word."

"Is that so?" Josette challenged.

"It is," he replied smoothly. "I discovered that you are a brave, capable woman who is not afraid to risk her life to save a friend, which means you have a compassionate side that you keep tucked away."

"That is—"

He spoke over her. "You prefer to wear men's clothing, but you are comfortable in expensive gowns, informing me that you were raised in privilege."

She lifted her brow. "Are you finished?"

He clucked before adding, "You are a strong, determined woman. I can see the fight in your eyes, leading me to believe that you sculpted yourself to be your own hero."

"Interesting," she murmured. "You presume that flattery will soften my stance towards you, do you not?"

He shrugged. "I just spoke the truth."

Straightening her spine, she challenged, "You prefer truth then?"

"I do."

"I observed you as well."

His lips twitched in amusement. "Well, go on."

"You are an entitled lord who has relied on good looks and charms to achieve your purposes, but behind your handsome exterior, you are insecure with your role in society," she stated matter-of-factly, placing her reticule on the bench next to her.

A flash of hurt filled his eyes before he blinked it away. Realizing that her sharp tongue had gone too far yet again, Josette opened her mouth to apologize, but Morgan spoke first.

"You think I am handsome?" he asked with an impish grin.

"Good gracious!" she exclaimed. "Do you ever take yourself seriously?"

"I do, entirely too much."

"I want to make something clear to you," she started with a firm gaze, "I will not be one of your conquests. I am here to do a job, and I have no intention of falling for your flowery words. Do I make myself clear?"

To her disbelief, Morgan looked back at her with a bemused expression. "May I ask a question of my own?"

"You may."

"What makes you think I am attracted to you?"

Taken aback, she felt her cheeks grow exceedingly warm. "I… uh…"

Morgan lifted his brow.

She lowered her gaze to the bench and saw a file labeled "*Genet*". "I believe it would be best if we focused on the mission," she managed to say without showing her discomfort. "Don't you agree?"

"That would be for the best," he agreed, picking up the file and extending it towards her. "I have already read through the documents."

"I assume that we will be using an alias."

He nodded. "I have settled on the surname Addington."

"I like it," she said, opening the file on her lap. "Should we assign ourselves new Christian names?"

"I don't think that's necessary," he stated. "Besides, I am particularly fond of your name, Josette. It just rolls off the tongue."

Ignoring him, she pulled out a piece of paper and started reading. "The Home Office has been monitoring a growing number of anti-monarchist groups in South East England. One of these groups is in Torquay. Their agenda is clear; they wish to replace the monarchy with a republican government," she paused, skimming the paper, "and a few skirmishes have already been put down by the constables." She looked up at Morgan. "Is Lord Paxton the head of this movement?"

Morgan gave her a hapless look. "According to Beckett, Lord Paxton is not affiliated with the rebels."

She read through the notes about the anti-monarchist groups, noting various members but not designating a leader. "Then how does he tie into this?"

"We don't know yet," he confessed. "An agent smuggled out a note from France, detailing that *Genet* would arrive on England's shores and attend Lord Paxton's house party. That is all we have to go on."

The carriage felt extremely stuffy as she started to read more of the documents. She reached over and opened the window, but it provided minimal relief. Unfortunately, most of the papers were agents' accounts of the skirmishes and did not mention the famed French spy. "Why do you suppose *Genet* is coming to Britain to attend a house party of all things?"

"I have been asking myself that same question."

Taking the paper in her hand, Josette started fanning her increasingly warming face. "The war is over. Napoleon abdicated in early April, restoring the Bourbons to power, and he is now exiled to the island of Elba. King Louis and England are allies. Why would they jeopardize their alliance by sending a spy to our shores?"

"Perhaps *Genet* is not welcome in France anymore now that Napoleon has been defeated?"

Feeling overheated, she was having a hard time concentrating on his words. Deciding the paper was not sufficient, she reached into her reticule, pulled out her fan, and started waving it in front of her face. "How do you suppose we secure an invite to a house party that most likely was planned months ago?"

"That's where you come in."

"I am not a miracle worker," she contended, her voice shaky. The carriage jerked to the side, causing her head to start spinning. She placed her hand against the side of the carriage as she closed her eyes.

"Are you all right?" Morgan asked in a concerned voice.

Her stomach began churning, and she could feel every rotation of the wheels on the uneven road. "I will be fine."

"You don't look fine. Would you like me to stop the coach?" He must have leaned closer because his words were spoken next to her ear.

Josette shook her head, and she instantly regretted her action. Feeling that she was about to do something extremely unladylike, she reached for the door handle and pushed it open. She heard a shout ordering the driver to stop. The moment the wheels skidded on the ground, Josette jumped out and ran towards the cover of the trees.

Chapter Five

Morgan stepped out of the coach, watching helplessly as Josette ran towards the trees that lined the road. It hardly took a moment for him to decide he needed to help her. Reaching back into the coach, he grabbed the canteen and started in the direction he'd seen Josette disappear.

"My lord," a young woman's voice called from behind him. He spun back around and saw Josette's lady's maid holding a cloth against her chest. "Perhaps *I* should go help Miss Josette?"

He shook his head. "No, I will go."

A frown appeared on her lips, but she did not question his choice. She raised the cloth towards him, keeping her gaze lowered.

"Thank you, Miss…" He let his voice trail off.

"Abagail," she replied, dipping into a low curtsy.

Morgan waited until she looked at him before he smiled. "Thank you, Miss Abagail."

He raced into the cover of the trees and saw dainty footprints leading deeper into the woods. As he followed Josette's path, he heard a trickling stream up ahead, but his view was hampered by moss covered branches. He dipped under a thick branch and saw his partner sitting on a boulder next to the stream, splashing water onto her face.

"Josette," he said quietly, not wanting to startle her.

She ducked her head away from him. "Go away." Her plea was soft.

"Is that what you wish?"

"Yes, it is."

He took a step closer towards her. "Unfortunately, I have to deny your request."

"Please leave," she urged. "I don't want you to see me like this."

Morgan was unsure why she was embarrassed. "As your husband, I feel it is my duty to help you," he teased lightly.

Cupping her hand, she placed it in the stream and brought it up, pouring the water onto the back of her neck. "We are not truly married."

He walked closer to her, but she still refused to look at him. Placing the cloth into the water, he squeezed the excess water out and gently placed it on the back of her neck. "Allow me to assist you."

"Thank you," she murmured, placing her hand on the cloth.

Sitting on the boulder next to her, he tried again to make her feel more at ease. "In all the times we traveled back and forth between Gravesend and London, you never once got sick."

She placed a hand on her stomach. "It must have been because I was reading in the coach."

"Ah," he replied, "and that is exactly why women should not be permitted to read."

A soft chuckle left her mouth, but she did not speak.

He decided to try again. "I must inform Lord Charles that my wife is broken. After all, it has only been three hours since we left London, and we already had to stop because of your delicate constitution."

She leaned back on the boulder but kept her eyes downcast. "Please stop referring to me as your wife. This is a ruse. We are not truly married."

He extended the canteen towards her and was pleased when she accepted it. "Thank you," she said before taking a sip. "Please give me a moment to collect myself, and I will join you shortly at the carriage."

"I will stay with you," he replied, relaxing back against the boulder.

Josette glared sternly. "I can take care of myself."

He nodded. "I know you can, but I want to help you."

"I don't need help."

He studied her flushed face for a moment before asking, "Do you refuse help from everyone, or just from me?"

The fight seemed to drain out of Josette as her shoulders slumped. "I have learned that asking for help is a sign of weakness."

"I disagree. I believe it is a sign of strength."

She sneaked a glance at him, and he could see emotions flickering across her face. It was clear that Josette did not like to show any sign of vulnerability. What had happened to her that had caused her to lock her trust away?

Rising quickly, she announced, "I am ready to depart."

She took a step but stumbled back. He jumped up and wrapped his arms around her waist. "I don't think that's a good idea," he remarked, tightening his hold on her.

Josette looked up at him, her cheeks still pink. "You, sir, are too familiar." She might have intended her words to be sharp, but they came out breathless.

"My apologies," he said, his eyes roaming her beautiful green eyes with unique flecks of yellow in them. He had never been this close to her before, and he found he quite enjoyed it. "I will release you, assuming we can sit for a spell."

She nodded, and he reluctantly lowered his hands. He assisted her as she sat down on the boulder, then he returned to his seat. For a long time, neither of them spoke. They simply sat together, listening to the birds sing. Occasionally, a bullfrog croaked loudly, yet still they sat.

Morgan finally broke the silence. "Are you feeling better?"

"I am. Thank you," she confirmed with a smile.

Not wanting this moment to end, he asked, "Will you tell me about yourself?"

Josette's smile dimmed. "That was not a part of our deal."

"True," he admitted, "but we are supposed to play husband and wife. It would be conceivable that we would know something about each other."

Morgan could see indecision rippling over her features. "There are some things I will not discuss," she stated adamantly.

"Fair enough. If a question is too personal, then you can say 'pass'."

"What would you like to know?" she asked hesitantly.

He had many things he wanted to discover about her, but he

decided to start small, slowly peeling away her defenses, layer by layer. "Did you have a happy childhood?"

"I did." A wistful smile graced her face. "I had loving, devoted parents that doted on me from the time I can remember. Whenever my father was home, we would have a picnic by the stream on our property." Her voice became so soft that he almost missed her next words. "It was perfect."

Morgan placed his hand back behind him and leaned back. "That seems like an ideal childhood."

"It was," she replied. "What was yours like?"

"Pass," he declared.

Josette turned towards him with her lips parted in disbelief. "You can't pass."

He smiled. "I was just teasing," he said. "Let's see. I am the second son of the Marquess of Bath. I am the spare heir and a complete, utter black mark on my family's perfect legacy."

Her expression became puzzled. "I find that hard to believe."

"Is it because I am so ruggedly handsome?"

"Humility is not one of your strengths, is it?" she replied, rolling her eyes.

He grew serious. "My father wanted me to go into the Royal Navy, but I was recruited by Beckett out of Cambridge. I am gone on assignments for months at a time, and I maintain a rake persona when I am amongst the ton. My family believes I court scandal, and my father has even referred to me as a 'rakehell' on more than one occasion."

"Rakehell?"

"It means that I am worse than a rake."

"Your family does not know that you are an agent of the Crown?"

"No. That is a well-guarded secret," he informed her.

Josette bit her lower lip. "You only pretend to be a ladies' man?"

He flashed her a flirtatious smile. "To some degree. After all, it is not my fault that women cannot resist my charms."

Josette bristled at his teasing remark. "Will you kindly refrain from flirting with me?"

"Does it work?"

She shook her head. "No. I find it rather annoying."

Impossible. Maybe he wasn't as charming as he thought he was? "All right," he conceded. "I will not flirt with you, but I will hold you to the same bargain."

Josette laughed loudly. "I assure you that will not be a problem."

Hearing her laugh, Morgan realized how badly he wanted her to be happy. He had seen glimpses of the woman that she was, but she hid behind a wall of secrecy. He wanted to help her, to free her. But how? He didn't know much about her, including her surname.

Without thinking, he asked, "What is your surname?"

All humor was stripped off her face and a betraying flush of anger stained her cheeks. "Pass."

"But…"

Her eyes grew guarded. "I said 'pass', Lord Morgan."

He stifled a groan. He had pushed her too far. "I thought we previously decided that you would call me Morgan."

"I will when you stop being a nincompoop," she countered.

Morgan pressed his hand to his chest, feigning shock. "Watch your language, Miss Josette."

He saw her lips twitch, but she resisted smiling. Glancing towards the direction of the road, she asked, "Should we return to the coach?"

He rose and extended his hand to help her rise. "I have a better idea."

She eyed him curiously. "Which is?" she asked, placing her hand in his.

"You shall see."

Riding tall in her saddle, Josette brought up her hand to cover her mouth as a burst of laughter escaped her lips. "I can't believe you put slugs in your governess's boots."

Morgan gave her an unrepentant smile. "It was only five slugs, but my father punished me nonetheless."

"You deserved to be punished."

"You wound me, fair maiden," he said, laughing.

After they'd arrived back at the coach, Morgan had ordered two footmen off their horses and ordered a side saddle to be placed on one of them. He'd told her that it would help with her sickness if she could feel fresh air blowing on her face.

The sun was starting to dip low in the sky, and Josette had enjoyed learning more about her sham of a husband. He had spent the day sharing the outlandish things that he and his brothers did growing up.

Furthermore, there were few things that Josette loved to do more than riding. It was exhilarating. When she was younger, she used to race her horse around her parents' property for hours every morning. Her father found her behavior amusing and even looked the other way when she started riding astride. She smiled fondly at that memory.

"What are you smiling about?" Morgan asked, bringing his horse up next to hers.

"I was remembering the first time my father caught me riding astride."

"What did he do?"

Adjusting the reins in her right hand, she smiled. "At first, he chastised me. He told me that it was inappropriate for a woman of my station to ride astride," she paused, before adding, "but then he told me I ride better than most men."

Morgan watched her, seeming to evaluate every word that came out of her mouth. "What station would that be exactly?"

She sighed. "It would be wise of you to remember that I am not a mystery to be solved. I am your partner on this case."

"At least tell me if you rank higher than me among the ton?"

Turning her gaze towards the road, Josette admitted, "The answer is no. I am not the daughter of a duke or a princess."

"Do you have a title?"

She gave him an exasperated look. "No. I do not. Happy?"

Morgan gazed at her, and it felt as if he could see into her very soul. It greatly unnerved her. "I won't be happy until I learn all of your secrets."

"That will not happen, I assure you," she huffed.

"Don't you trust me?" he asked as their two horses walked side by side up an easy road.

She nodded. "I do trust you... as my partner."

He pulled his horse to a stop and looked at her. "That's not what I am asking, Josette."

Wanting to avoid this futile conversation, Josette saw a billow of smoke over the horizon. "Is that the village where we will be staying tonight?"

Morgan shifted his gaze towards the smoke. "It should be. The groomsman suggested we stay at a coaching inn known as The Bear Tavern."

"I will race you to the inn!" she shouted over her shoulder as she kicked her horse into a run.

Riding low in her saddle, Josette urged her horse to run faster as the inn came into view. She turned her head and gave Morgan a radiant smile as they raced up to the stable yard of the inn.

"I won!" she announced, reining in her mount.

Morgan laughed, his rich baritone voice echoing off the walls. "I would consider that a draw."

"That's what losers say, Lord Morgan," she joked.

He dismounted and came around to assist her off her horse. Two stable hands came and collected their horses just as their coach pulled into the yard.

Miss Abagail exited the carriage and approached with a wide smile. "Thank you for letting me ride inside the carriage."

"How did you enjoy it?" Josette asked.

"It was nice not having to worry about swallowing a bug," Abagail said.

Morgan attempted to stifle a laugh, but it came out as a cough. He cleared his throat. "If you will excuse me, I will go secure our rooms."

Following behind Morgan, Josette asked Abagail, "Were you able to rest your eyes?"

She nodded. "I was. It was splendid."

Scanning the establishment, Josette saw a brawny man leaning up against a column in the main hall, holding a drink in his hand. He had dark eyes, and his piercing gaze had latched on to them the moment they'd arrived. Rather than ignore him, she returned his gaze, challenging him to look away.

He winked at her and blew her a kiss. In response, Josette rolled her eyes and turned away from him, grateful that she had a dagger strapped to her right thigh and a pistol strapped to her left.

Just then, Morgan walked up and informed her, "There are only two rooms available. Would you prefer residing with me or your lady's maid?"

She flashed him a look of annoyance. "I will share with Abagail."

"Pity," Morgan teased.

At that moment, her stomach growled, and she placed a hand over her dress in an attempt to cover the noise.

Morgan smiled knowingly at her. "I have requested that our supper be brought to a private room. Would you prefer to rest before we eat?"

"That's not necessary," Josette replied as she noticed her lady's maid was watching the brawny man with fear in her eyes. She stepped in front of Abagail to block her view and asked, "What's wrong?"

Abagail lowered her voice. "That man has been staring at us since we arrived."

"Just ignore him," Josette instructed. "Would you like me to walk you up to our room? I can order your dinner to be sent up."

"That would be preferable," Abagail replied with relief in her voice.

"Will you order supper for me?" she asked, turning back towards Morgan. "I will join you after I escort Abagail up to our room."

Morgan stepped closer. "I would be happy to escort you both up."

Josette shook her head. "That's not necessary. I will be down shortly," she assured him as he extended the key towards her.

Josette and Abagail walked up a narrow set of stairs towards their room. Once Josette had unlocked the door and pushed it open, she saw two thin mattresses on iron frames, a small table with a basin on top, and a window on the far side.

Abagail followed her into the room and dropped down on one of the beds. "I can't believe how comfortable this mattress is," her lady's maid said, running her hand along the sheets.

A loud knock came at their door. Before Josette even turned

around, the door was thrown open and the same brawny man from downstairs strode into the room, holding a pistol. He sneered as he closed the door and latched it. "It looks like I got two women to pleasure tonight."

Josette considered her opponent. He was tall, muscular, and his pistol had not wavered. He appeared confident that they would go along with his evil intention. A muffled sob came from her lady's maid as the man's lecherous gaze perused her body.

Snapping her fingers, Josette drew the man's attention. "Do you intend to kill us after you finish 'pleasuring' us?"

The man's right eye twitched as he glared at her. "Not if ye do what I say." He was lying, of course, which infuriated her even more.

Clasping her hands together, she tilted her chin defiantly. "We must refuse your offer. Please leave our room."

He chuckled menacingly. "Lady, ye make me laugh. Ye don't have a choice."

She smiled sweetly at him. "I am not a lady."

"Just get on the bed," he ordered, pointing his pistol towards the bed.

Glancing down at the lumpy mattress, she shook her head disapprovingly. "No."

"No?" the man repeated.

Her right hand slowly slid into the pocket of her gown, and she found the slit that allowed her to access her ivory-hilted dagger. "If you leave now, we will just pretend this never happened." She slid the dagger out of its sheath and past the layers of clothing.

The man took a commanding step towards her, his pistol pointed at her chest. "Ye will do as ye are told."

Abagail let out a low sob from behind her. "As you wish," Josette conceded. She walked to the head of the bed and stood next to it.

"Get *on* the bed," the man hissed.

Because her assailant was so close, she shifted the dagger until she pinched the blade, ensuring the weapon would rotate more quickly. "Please don't make this worse for yourself. Just turn around and leave."

The man turned the pistol towards Abagail. "If you do not get on that bed, I will kill her now."

"Do not threaten my friends," Josette warned.

The man's eyes narrowed as he watched her. "You are not in a position to order me around."

Shifting her weight to her right leg, she leveled her gaze at him. "This is your last warning. Put down your weapon and walk out of here."

In response, the man cocked his weapon. Josette transferred her weight to her left leg while simultaneously bending her wrist back towards her forearm. She released the dagger, and it plunged deep into the man's chest. He stared at her in shock as he dropped to his knees. The pistol slipped from his hand before he slumped to the floor. Unfortunately, when the pistol hit the wood floor, it discharged, the sound echoing loudly in the small room.

After ensuring that the man was dead, Josette rushed towards Abagail. "Are you all right?" she asked with concern.

Abagail looked up at her with wide, tear-filled eyes. "He was going to kill us."

"We are safe," she assured her lady's maid. "No one will hurt you."

She looked up as someone banged loudly on the door, rattling the locked latch.

"Josette, are you all right?" Morgan shouted. "Open up! It's me, Morgan."

Rising from her crouched position, she went and unlocked the door. Morgan stormed into the room and came to a stop when he saw the dead body on the ground. He turned his gaze towards her.

"What happened?" He stepped closer to her and placed his hands on her shoulders. "Did he hurt you?"

She shook her head. "No, but he had designs to. My dagger stopped him."

His eyes scanned her face, and he looked scared. "But I heard a gunshot."

Josette's gaze turned to the dead body. "I didn't want to kill him, but he left me with no choice. I tried to stop him before he cocked his pistol, but I wasn't fast enough."

Morgan's hand came up and cupped her cheek. "Look at me, Josette. Don't look at him." His eyes were filled with compassion.

"You did the right thing."

Abagail's sob filled the room again, and Josette reluctantly stepped away from Morgan's tender care. "Would you mind if we switched rooms?"

"Not at all," Morgan said, producing a key from his waistcoat. "I'll take care of this mess."

Josette's eyes strayed back towards the dead body sprawled out on the floor. She walked over and crouched down, pulling out the dagger. She wiped the blood off on the man's shirt, then stood. "This was my father's dagger," she explained, breathing shallowly.

She looked up to see Morgan watching her with such care that Josette almost broke out in tears... almost. She had never killed anyone with her dagger before, and it unnerved her more than she would have thought. This is what she had been training for. This is why she spent countless hours outside, aiming at targets. She'd never wanted to feel helpless again.

And it worked. Then why did she feel so horrible?

Chapter Six

Morgan stood next to Josette as they watched the stage coach pull away from the inn, taking Miss Abagail and a footman with it. "I'm sorry you couldn't convince her to stay."

Josette sighed. "She was quite frightened. It's best that she goes back to the school to recover."

"Were you close with Miss Abagail?"

She shook her head. "Not particularly. She is one of the older girls from the school and just recently became my lady's maid. Cosette thought it would be a good experience for her to join us."

Turning to face her, Morgan noticed the dark circles marring her pale face and the haunted look deep in her eyes. "Did you sleep at all last night?"

"No," she admitted softly. "Between Abagail's sobbing and the image of that man's body, I had difficulty closing my eyes."

Josette looked so young and vulnerable, causing a surge of fierce protectiveness to wash over him. Morgan started to place his hand on her arm to provide her comfort, but she stepped out of his reach.

He watched as their horses were led into the stable yard. "If you are not opposed, it might be best if we just rode hard to Torquay. If we make good time, then we could arrive as early as tomorrow morning," he informed her.

She nodded methodically. "I think that is a splendid idea."

After he helped Josette mount her horse, they rode hard for the next few hours, stopping only to let their horses rest. During one of these breaks, their horses walked side by side up the tree-lined road. His eyes strayed towards the birds jumping merrily in the trees.

Glancing over at his partner, he asked, "That man last night...

he wasn't your first kill?"

Josette shook her head. "No. I killed two men at The Cloven Hoof." She sat erect, her body rigid. "But he was the first man that I've killed with my dagger."

"Was the experience different?"

"Yes. It seemed more personal." She looked over at him and he could see sadness in her features. "I didn't want to kill him."

He rushed to assure her, "I know."

"I warned him, multiple times," she said, her eyes downcast.

"Look at me, Josette," he prodded softly, waiting for her gaze to come up. "You did nothing wrong. You protected yourself."

Josette let out a heartfelt sigh. "I didn't kill him for myself, but, when he threatened Abagail, I killed him." They rode in silence for several moments before she shared, "Eliza told me that every person I kill will stay imprinted on my soul, and it will slowly destroy me if I let it."

Morgan ran his left hand through his wind-tossed hair. "Eliza is wise."

"When I began training with Lord Camden, I wanted to feel empowered, to take control of my life," Josette stated. "I wanted to ensure that no one could hurt me ever again."

"You have succeeded."

"Have I?" Her eyebrows drew together, mirroring her anguished frown. "Or am I still that same scared little girl, only now with weapons training?" Her tone was filled with doubt.

"Whoa," he said, reining in his horse. He dismounted and walked over to Josette.

She gave him a baffled look. "Why are we stopping?"

Morgan reached up and placed his hands on her waist. She stiffened but didn't pull away.

"Trust me." His words had the intended effect. She placed her hands on his shoulders and allowed him to help her dismount.

Leading the horses to a small clearing, he found the ruins of a medieval chapel. He secured the horses and walked over to a stone fence that partially bordered the ruins. He sat down as Josette came closer, but she made no effort to sit next to him.

He looked out over the green countryside. "I remember my first kills, practically down to the minute detail." He brought his gaze up to Josette's. "As a new agent, I was given the task of trailing a lord that had suspected ties to the French. I followed him to a pub that was deep inside the rookeries. My job was to return and report, but I saw a known French informant walking through the doors of the pub."

Josette stepped closer. "What did you do?"

"I couldn't just let that French blackguard go free," he insisted. "Once he left the pub, I pulled out my pistol, intending to arrest him. Unfortunately, he was not alone, and I ended up killing three men that night."

"Were you able to arrest him?" she asked, sitting down next to him.

He shook his head. "No. After killing his guards, I chased him through the streets and caught up to him in an alley. I ordered him to put his dagger down, but it was obvious that one of us was not going to leave that alley alive." He winced. "Beckett was furious that I disobeyed his direct order and relegated me to desk duty for a whole month."

Josette reached down and plucked out a red flower from the ground. He felt prompted to ask, "Why did you feel the need to start weapons training?"

She stayed quiet for so long that he feared she wouldn't respond. Finally, she said, "I was thrown out of my home and…" Her voice hitched. "I was near death when Lord Camden found me. He brought me back to his estate, which he had converted to a refuge for women, on behalf of his wife, Lady Camden." Raw pain came into her eyes. "When Lord Camden offered to train us in the use of various weapons, I jumped at the chance to protect myself, to ensure that no one would ever have the power to hurt me again."

Morgan felt curious about one other thing. "How did you end up training with Lady Lansdowne?"

Josette's eyes softened at her friend's name. "Whenever Eliza came to Lady Camden's estate, she would spend time training me with the longbow or helping me perfect my aim with my dagger. After she hired me as Martha's companion, she increased our training regimen. I'm grateful for her friendship."

"Why were you thrown out of your home?" he asked in concern.

"Pass," she replied sternly.

He sighed in frustration and kicked at a rock near his boot. "Let me in, Josette. Let me help you."

Instead of a quick retort, he was met with silence. He turned to gaze at Josette, but she was looking out over the countryside. Finally, she brought her gaze back to him and pain was etched on her face. "The less you know about me the better."

"And why is that?" he asked with a skeptical look.

"I am not worth knowing," she whispered, torment lacing her words.

Nothing she said could have been further from the truth, and he opened his mouth to respond, but she raised her hand to stop him. "You are an honorable man, but there are some people that even you can't save."

He shifted his body closer to her. "I don't believe that. I *will* earn your trust."

She smiled sadly. "If you believe that, then you have overestimated the effect you have on me."

He rose and placed his hand out to assist her. When she stood up, he informed her, "I am going to embrace you now." He smiled gently. "That is how friends offer each other comfort."

Rather than step back or retrieve her dagger, she gave him a slight nod. Slowly, he brought his arms up and around her, being mindful not to pull her in too tightly. The delightful smell of rosewater reached his nose as he rested his chin on top of her head. Despite Josette remaining rigid, she did not try to flee from his arms. That was a promising sign.

Morgan lowered his arms and stepped back. "That wasn't so bad, now was it?"

"I have experienced worse," she murmured.

Surprised by her cheeky remark, he chuckled. "You sure know how to keep a man humble."

Josette took a hesitant step towards her horse. "We should get on the road again."

"Lead the way."

He followed her to the horses, still thinking about her story and puzzling over what she hadn't revealed. He would get Josette to trust him and reveal her past. Perhaps it was because he was a spy, or a man who found her intriguing; either way, he would solve the mystery of Miss Josette, even if it was the last thing he did.

Josette glanced at the shops lining both sides of the narrow cobblestone street of Barnsley Village. She anxiously reined in her horse in front of The Bawdy Boar Inn and immediately dismounted. Her whole body ached from being in the saddle.

Morgan gave her a disapproving look from atop his horse. "Dearest, you should have waited for me to assist you," he said in a chastising voice, tilting his head towards the groomsmen watching them.

Remembering her role to play, she waited for him to dismount before she gave him an apologetic smile. "It won't happen again."

He gave her a stern look. "See that it doesn't." He softened his words with a wink.

Accepting his arm, they strolled into the well-maintained inn and were met by a tall, bulky man with a receding hairline. "May I get you a room, Mr...?"

"Addington," Morgan replied. "Besides a room, my wife would also like a bath before supper."

"Of course, let me just get my wife," the innkeeper said, his eyes surveying the crowded hall. Long tables ran the length of the room and every seat was filled. His eyes landed on someone, and he gestured adamantly. A plump woman in a brown dress made her way towards them through the crowd.

As she neared them, the woman admonished, "Dear heavens, Frank. A simple wave would have sufficed." She turned her gaze towards Josette. "What a beautiful lady you are!"

"Mrs. Addington is interested in a bath," Frank informed his wife.

Josette smiled at the kind woman. "We decided to ride ahead of our coach. Do you have a spare nightgown?"

"We can find something for you," the woman said, returning her smile, "but you must call me Florence, Mrs. Addington."

"Only if you call me Josette."

Florence's smile grew. "I will, Josette. We have a room that is designated for baths, so we don't have to lug around the tub." Her gaze turned towards Morgan. "Would you like to share a bath with your wife?"

To her surprise, Josette saw a pink blush stain his cheeks. Morgan cleared his throat, which was husky, and stammered, "I... will wait for her in our room."

Florence nodded her acknowledgement before leading Josette towards a room off the main hall. The small, square chamber had one window, and it was surprisingly warm. Florence smiled at her. "If you will stay here for a moment, I'll see to the bath," she requested before disappearing.

In a moment, Florence re-entered the room and held the door open as two men started the arduous task of bringing buckets full of water and dumping them in the tub. Once the tub was full, Florence assisted Josette as she removed her clothing, but her hands stilled at the sight of the weapons strapped to her legs.

Josette opened her mouth to explain, but Florence spoke first. "The roads are a dangerous place. I'm glad that you and your husband are taking proper precautions."

"Thank you for understanding," Josette replied, grateful for the innkeeper's acceptance.

Florence folded her clothing and placed each item onto the table, tucking the dagger and pistol beneath them, and then excused herself from the room.

Stepping into the warm bath, Josette found herself relaxing back against the tub. She must have dozed off because the next thing she knew, Florence was gently tapping her arm.

"Dearie, the water is cold."

Opening her eyes, she saw Florence holding a towel for her. "I can't believe I fell asleep."

"You must have been very tired," Florence replied gently.

Josette rose from the tub and quickly wrapped the towel around her body. "I was. I didn't sleep well last night."

Florence smirked. "With a handsome husband like yours, I can't imagine you get much sleep."

Josette found herself speechless by the woman's suggestion.

"I was able to find you a nightgown," Florence said, extending it towards her.

"Thank you."

After she dressed for bed, Josette retrieved her clothes and weapons and followed Florence up a back staircase and down a narrow hall. The innkeeper's wife led her towards the last room on the left and knocked before disappearing back down the hall.

The door was opened, revealing Morgan in a state of undress. His jacket, waistcoat, and cravat had been removed, and his shirt hung open. She stood frozen in place, and her eyes couldn't seem to look away from his expansive chest.

"Josette," Morgan said, causing her to bring her eyes up to his. "Aren't you coming in?"

She took a step closer and admonished, "What do you think you are doing?"

Morgan's eyes scanned the hall before bringing his gaze back to hers. "I'm not sure what you're referring to, but perhaps we should have this conversation in private?"

Josette reluctantly stepped inside, and her eyes took in the single bed, a table, and a chair in the corner. Immediately, she headed to the furthest corner of the room. She placed her clothing on the bed and retrieved her dagger, pressing it against her leg.

Morgan frowned when he saw the dagger. "Why are you holding that?"

She gripped the ivory hilt tighter. "Why did you remove articles of your clothing?"

He glanced towards the chair where his jacket and waistcoat were draped. "Would you prefer that I put them back on?"

She nodded. "I would."

"All right." He complied silently. When he was once again dressed, he turned and asked, "Happy?"

Again, she nodded, despite his shirt remaining partially opened. She placed the dagger on the bed without saying a word.

Morgan watched her, a wry smile on his face and an amused twinkle in his eyes.

"Your virtue is safe with me, Josette. I already told you that."

She tilted her chin. "I just didn't want you to assume anything, since we are not truly married."

"I have not forgotten that fact," he assured her as there was a knock at the door.

In one swift motion, she had retrieved her dagger and hid it behind her back. Morgan reached behind him, pulled out a pistol and held it against his side. Carefully, he opened the door a smidgeon, then grinned and opened it wide.

Florence entered, carrying a tray. Placing it down on the small table, she said, "Here are two bowls of mutton stew and some freshly baked bread." Glancing curiously between them, she added, "When you are finished, just place the dishes in the hall."

Josette tipped her head graciously. "Thank you, Florence."

Florence smiled tenderly at her. "You're welcome, child. I hope you sleep well tonight."

After she departed, Josette placed the dagger back on the bed and sat down, leaning her back against the wall.

Morgan picked up the tray and stepped closer. "Would you like to eat your stew on the bed?"

She nodded. "That sounds wonderful."

He glanced down at the bed, and back up at her with a curious look. "May I join you?" He smirked. "I promise not to ravish you."

A laugh escaped her lips. "You may."

"Thank you," he said, sitting down and resting his back against the wall.

He extended a bowl and a spoon towards her. "This is most uncivilized," she commented, just before she took her first sip of stew.

"I won't tell if you won't," Morgan teased.

After they finished their supper, Morgan accepted the dishes and placed the tray in the hall. He latched the door and placed a chair under the door handle.

He took a few steps and sat back down on the bed, angling his body towards her. He reached his hand into his jacket pocket and pulled out a brown package tied with string. "This is for you."

Josette eyed the package suspiciously. "I cannot accept a gift from you. It's most inappropriate."

Morgan waved the package in front of her and asked, "Don't you want to see what I bought you for your birthday?"

Her eyes snapped up to his. "What did you say?"

"Happy birthday, Josette," he said, a slow smile forming on his lips.

She began fidgeting with the sleeves of her nightgown. "How did you know?"

"Cosette told me." He extended the package towards her. "Open your gift."

Tentatively, she reached out and accepted the package. A flood of memories overcame her as she held the brown-papered package in her hand. Tears filled her eyes.

"Have I done something to upset you?" Morgan asked, concerned.

She looked up at him through unshed tears. "No one has wished me a happy birthday since my parents died."

"Are you saying I did something right?" he jested.

She swallowed back the lump in her throat. "I suppose I am."

"Open your gift," he encouraged.

Removing the strings, the brown paper fell open and revealed a single-strand coral necklace. She ran her fingers over the small stones, reminding her of the one her mother wore. Regardless, she could not except a gift of this monetary value. She extended it towards Morgan.

"This is too expensive. I cannot accept it."

His face softened with understanding. "The correct response when receiving a birthday gift is 'thank you'."

"But, Morgan…"

"No buts," he chided her gently. "I want you to have something you will always remember me by." He reached for the necklace and fastened it around her neck.

"When did you have time to buy me a gift?"

Morgan wore a look of amusement. "You were in the bath for a long while. It allowed me ample time to visit the shops."

Josette ran her fingers over the necklace, unable to find words to express her appreciation. The necklace was exquisite, but it was the fact that he remembered her birthday that touched her deeply.

Bringing her eyes up, she hoped her gaze conveyed her overwhelming sense of gratitude for his thoughtfulness.

Morgan's eyes crinkled at the corners as he watched her. "You're welcome, Josie."

Josie. Tears welled in her eyes. "No one but my family has ever called me Josie," she admitted weakly.

"Would you permit me to call you Josie?" he asked, uncertainty showing in his eyes.

She nodded. "I would like that very much."

Their gazes locked, and she saw that his usual cocky self-assuredness was gone, replaced by vulnerability. He blinked away his emotions and leaned back.

"Good night, Josie."

Rising from the bed, he moved towards the opposite wall and tossed down a blanket. He blew out the candle before he laid down.

Josette watched him before she laid down in bed. As she placed her head on the lumpy pillow, her hand played with her necklace.

"Thank you, Morgan," she said, closing her eyes.

For the first time in years, she felt safe enough to drift easily into a deep sleep.

Chapter Seven

The sun was high in the sky when Morgan and Josette rode up the long road to arrive at Harrold House. A pillared portico ran along the façade to a large, grey, three-story estate, with mullioned windows and a timber roof.

Reining in his horse, Morgan dismounted before he helped Josette off her horse. Surprisingly, she waited for him. He placed his hands around her waist, and while lowering her to the ground, remarked, "Thank you for allowing me to assist you."

Her eyes shifted towards Harrold House. "I am now playing the role of a dutiful wife."

"This will be fun to watch."

Josette's eyes snapped back to his. "What exactly is that supposed to mean?"

He leaned closer and whispered in her ear, "You have to pretend that you are enamored by me."

"And what of your behavior?" She tilted her head, bringing their faces only inches apart.

"I am a spy. I can play any role."

A mischievous smile came to her lips. "Then I propose a challenge."

"I'm listening," he said, amused.

Josette brought her gloved hand up and traced her fingers along his jaw, slowly and deliberately, making it exceptionally difficult to focus on her words. "It's simple. Whoever best plays the role of a smitten spouse, desperately in love, wins the bet."

He cleared his throat. "And what does the winner get?"

"One favor," she responded coyly.

His eyes darted towards her lips. "Deal."

With a triumphant smile, Josette leaned back. Shifting her gaze over his shoulder, she said, "I believe I am in the lead."

Turning his head, Morgan saw the whole household staff had assembled themselves outside, waiting for them. The maids all had dreamy expressions on their faces as they watched their interaction. He turned back towards her. "You are a minx."

Josette's hand flew to her chest as she feigned shock. "I hope I did not offend you, my love."

He dropped his hands from her waist, turned, and offered his arm. "We have only just begun the competition," he stated softly.

Sliding her hand into the crook of his elbow, she leaned up against him. "What will my favor be?" she murmured under her breath. "Perhaps I will ask you to embroider a handkerchief for me."

He chuckled. "I don't embroider. Besides, aren't you getting a little ahead of yourself?"

They walked up the rounded cobblestone path towards the estate. About thirty servants were standing outside in a line watching them approach. A short, thin man with grey hair stood at the head of the line. He stepped forward and bowed.

"My name is Mr. Miles Croft. I am the butler of Harrold House."

"I'm Mr. Morgan Addington," Morgan said, stopping in front of him. "I hope you received the missive that I sent informing you of our arrival."

Mr. Croft nodded. "Yes, sir. It will be a pleasure to serve you."

Morgan patted his wife's hand. "This is my wife, Mrs. Addington. Her lady's maid was unable to complete the journey, and she will require a replacement."

"That won't be a problem," Mr. Croft assured them.

"Thank you, Mr. Croft," Josette acknowledged gratefully. "That is most kind of you."

"If you will follow me," Mr. Croft invited, leading them under the pillared portico towards the main door.

Following the butler into the estate, Morgan saw the entrance hall boasted a dominating chimneypiece and tapestries on the wall.

He asked Josette, "Was your estate similar to Harrold House?"

Her eyes scanned the hall as she responded. "Our country estate was much larger. We had the most beautiful bay windows..." Her voice trailed off as she turned to look at him. "What of your estate? Was it much grander than this house?"

He smirked. "Which one?"

She rolled her eyes as Mr. Croft stopped and turned to face them. "This is the dining room," he informed them, pointing towards a room with a long rectangular table. A fireplace sat at the far end of the room, linen-fold paneling hung on the walls and the ceiling had exposed, carved beams.

Josette walked into the room and ran her finger along the table. "This is a beautiful room," she murmured, her eyes focusing on the carved beams.

Mr. Croft nodded approvingly. "This room dates back to the sixteenth century. The Harrold family has taken care to keep it intact." He turned to continue his tour of the first floor.

Josette offered Morgan a sad smile as she joined him. They walked side by side, learning the layout of the lower level, but Morgan noticed that her countenance had dimmed. "Mr. Croft," he interrupted. "I need a moment alone to speak to my wife."

"Of course, sir," Mr. Croft acknowledged, walking away to grant them privacy.

Morgan gently placed his hand on her arm and led her into a room off the main hall.

"What has upset you?" he asked gently, removing his hand.

"My father's hunting lodge had a similar dining room to this one," she replied wistfully. Suddenly, a guarded look came into her eyes. "It's silly of me to fret over trivial matters from the past."

Morgan regarded her with concern. "Why do you assume your emotions are trivial?"

"No matter how much I mourn my parents' death, it won't change the fact that they are not coming home... to me," Josette shared, her tone holding an intensity he did not expect. "And it is all my fault." She reached up and ran her fingers along the coral necklace, which pleased him immensely.

"How did your parents die?" he asked delicately.

Her lips pressed tightly together as she shifted her gaze over his shoulder. "Pass."

"All right," he said, backing down. "Should we resume the tour?"

"Yes, I would prefer that."

He extended his arm to her , and she accepted it. They walked out into the hall as Mr. Croft appeared from another room.

"May I show you the second level now?"

"We would like that very much," Morgan answered.

After they discovered the library and guest chambers, Mr. Croft led them towards the far end of the hall. He stopped at an ornately carved door and pushed it open. "This is Mrs. Addington's room which connects with your room, sir," he informed them.

When Josette entered, her eyes lit up with pleasure. The room had bright, floral wallpaper, wood paneling around the windows, and elaborate coordinated curtains and bed hangings. The mahogany four poster bed sat against a wall and a chaise lounge rested next to two large windows.

"This will do quite nicely," she murmured as she stepped to the windows and unlatched them.

Mr. Croft acknowledged her comment before walking to a door near the bed. He opened it and announced, "This is Mr. Addington's bedchamber."

Morgan stepped into his room and immediately noticed the more masculine wallpaper and furnishings. It had not escaped his notice that Josette looked into his room but did not enter.

"Thank you, Mr. Croft. That will do for now."

The butler bowed. "As you wish, sir."

Morgan moved to the doorway that separated their rooms and watched as Mr. Croft exited. He leaned up against the frame and saw Josette sticking her head out the window she'd opened.

"May I ask what you're doing?" he inquired curiously.

Without looking back, Josette leaned out even further before saying, "I will easily be able to scale these walls, assuming there is a need." She ran her hand along the brick wall.

"Remember, my dear, we must use discretion around the staff here," Morgan reminded her. "They believe we are renting the house for a limited time and have made our money in trade. They won't be expecting you to be scaling the walls."

Josette turned back around and wiped off her gloved hands. "Do not worry about me. I just wanted to ensure that I located the quickest way to exit the room."

Pushing off from the doorway, he asked, "Would you like to take a nap before dinner, or perhaps you'd prefer a bath?"

She looked at the floor clock. "If we hurry, we can take a tour of the village before we dress for dinner." She looked thoughtful. "Actually, I won't be able to dress for dinner since my trunks haven't arrived yet."

"The coach should arrive tomorrow morning, barring any unforeseen delays."

"Should we leave through the main door, or shall we scale down the walls?" she asked, with an uplifted brow. "If you prefer, we can race."

She was goading him. He was sure of it. "It will be best if we walk out the main door like civilized people," he said with humor in his tone. "After all, we don't want to arouse any suspicion about our conduct."

Josette nodded in approval. "Good point. Although, it is much more fun to be uncivilized."

After leaving their horses at the livery, Josette kept her hand in the crook of Morgan's arm as they strolled through the seaside village of Torquay. The aged cobblestone streets were lined with cottages with thatched roofs and many had whitewashed walls. In between the homes, she could see glimpses of the harbor and boats anchored in the water.

Morgan tipped his hat at the couple walking past them on the footpath as Josette watched the children dart out between the cottages, thoroughly enjoying playing with each other. A smile came to her lips as she heard their lighthearted laughter. A child's laugh was like music to her ears.

They turned the corner and sauntered along a row of shops with large windows and spruced up shop fronts. She stopped to admire the brightly colored ribbons and floral bonnets displayed in one of the windows.

"Do you see something you like?" Morgan asked.

"There are many things that I like, but not anything that I need," she replied, fingering the coral necklace that still hung around her neck.

He glanced over at her. "You are my wife, for the time being," he paused, with a twinkle in his eye, "and I would be happy to buy you anything your heart desires."

She shifted towards him. "If you have extra money to spare, then I encourage you to donate it to The Beckett School for Girls."

"I could do both."

Josette resumed walking and pulled him away from the store front. "We are not on a holiday," she chided with a smile. "Torquay's economy has consisted of fishing and agriculture for centuries."

He chuckled, drawing her attention to him. "Thank you for that informative, yet rather dull, fact."

She swatted at his arm playfully. "I wasn't sure if you read the documents in the file that Lord Charles gave you."

"I read it, but I didn't memorize it like you apparently did," he teased.

The streets widened as they approached the main square of the town. A large group of men and women were standing in front of The Gutted Fish pub, listening to an orator standing on a barrel, his head visible above the crowd.

As they approached, Josette heard the man shouting, "Who is running our country, a mad king or his prince-of-pleasure son? The prince regent has built extravagant and exotic palaces. And who pays for those?" His hand gestured over the crowd. "*We* pay for those!"

The crowd started booing. "We have suffered because of heavy taxation, and we have barely enough food to scrape by, but our Queen is philandering through Europe. Who pays for that?"

"We do!" the group complained.

"Precisely!" the man exclaimed. "Our children are starving, and we are supporting a monarchy that does nothing to help us. They only help themselves."

"Hear, hear!" the group shouted.

The orator pounded his fist in the air. "Just last week, members of this town marched to Williams & Co. to protest the use of stocking frames, which are putting our hard-working stocking knitters out of work. It was a peaceful protest." He paused dramatically. "However, the constable shot into the crowd and called it an uprising. Two people were murdered by the constable's hand. But was he punished? Was he taken to the gallows?"

Men and women started shaking their heads, grumbling, "No."

A tall man from the crowd shouted, "Yeah, but we showed them. We smashed all those frames and beat *that* constable to a bloody pulp."

A cheer went up from the crowd, and the orator chuckled. "Yes, you did. But who is speaking for us?" He pointed towards a man. "Are you?" He pointed towards another man and asked, "Are you? No! No one is speaking for us. No one in Parliament is representing us. Only the wealthy are entitled to vote, and they refuse to help. It's time we help ourselves!" The man pumped his fist in the air again. "It's time we take back what is ours! This is *our* country, and we deserve to have a say in what happens!"

Loud cheering erupted from the group as the orator continued to pump his fist in the air. After the noise died down, he exclaimed, "If you want to hear more, join us tomorrow night for more debate." He jumped off the barrel and reached down to pick up a stack of pamphlets.

The orator began handing out the pamphlets as Morgan and Josette stepped into the line that quickly formed. When it was their turn, Morgan stuck out his hand and accepted one.

"What time is the meeting tomorrow night?"

"Nine p.m. It will be at this here pub," the orator answered as he continued to give pamphlets to others in the group.

"We'll be there," Morgan said, tucking the pamphlet into his jacket.

The orator stopped and introduced himself. "I am John Blount. I am speaking on behalf of a club of free thinkers."

"Free thinkers?" Morgan repeated. "That sounds quite radical."

John shook his head. "I am promoting the idea of a forum for political debate amongst the lower levels of society." He cocked his head and scanned Morgan's face. "You're new here, aren't you?"

"I am. My name is Morgan Addington, and this is my wife."

Mr. Blount tipped his hat towards Josette. "It's nice to meet you, ma'am. I hope this political talk is not hurting your delicate constitution."

Josette smiled politely. "I assure you it is not. Mr. Addington often speaks to me about social reform, but I'm afraid it doesn't make a lot of sense to me."

"That doesn't surprise me. Women often have a harder time comprehending social reform because it is such a complicated issue," Mr. Blount said. "Besides, political activism is not for the faint of heart."

"No, it's not," Morgan agreed, glancing behind him at the long line of people still waiting for pamphlets. "Good day."

As they headed back towards the livery, Morgan pulled out the pamphlet and handed it to her. "What do you think about that?"

Josette took a moment to review the pamphlet before replying, "This is a partial reprint of *Common Sense*, which was written by Thomas Paine."

"How exactly are you familiar with *Common Sense?*"

She lifted a brow at his curious tone. "Are you asking because it is American propaganda, or because I am a woman?"

"Both."

"I was raised in a home where politics were discussed, and free-thinking debates were encouraged," she paused, giving him a pointed look, "even amongst the women."

Rather than commenting on what she had just revealed, Morgan glanced down at the pamphlet. "That was written with the purpose of advocating independence from Great Britain to the people in the Thirteen Colonies."

"It worked," Josette commented. "He encouraged the people to fight for an egalitarian government."

"Equality for all," he murmured. "In 1789, under a similar notion, the French Revolution put forth The Declaration of the Rights of the Man and of the Citizen."

"*Liberté, égalité, fraternité*," she quoted. "Most of my mother's family was killed during the Reign of Terror, despite many of them belonging to the Jacobin Club."

Memories of the times she spent with her family in France

flooded her mind, and she sighed as a great wave of sadness washed over her. Morgan's voice broke through her thoughts. "How did your parents meet?"

"An arranged marriage," Josette revealed. "They were first cousins, once removed." The sadness lifted as she shared, "My grandfather was under house arrest in Paris, but he had made arrangements for my mother to flee in the night to England. She was eighteen and very beautiful." A wistful smile appeared on her lips. "My father said he was besotted from the moment he laid eyes on her. He secured a special license, and they were married the next day."

"Do you have any family left on your mother's side?"

She shook her head. "They were either killed or succumbed to illness while in hiding."

Two children ran past them on the pavement, and Josette leaned closer to Morgan, feeling the taut muscles through his coat. "On a positive note, we have located the anti-monarchist leader for this radical group."

Morgan's jaw tensed. "No. That was too easy. There is more to it. I can feel it."

"Considering we have been here for two hours, I think we are making good progress," she said lightly.

His jaw relaxed. "Come. We need to hurry if we want to arrive home before the dinner bell."

Chapter Eight

Early the next morning, Morgan dressed and prepared to break his fast. He stepped over to the door separating his room from Josette's and knocked softly. Hearing no movement on the other side, he smiled. Josette must still be sleeping. Good, he thought. She deserved to sleep late.

They had stayed up late last night playing games, and he assumed that ladies required more sleep than men. At least, his mother and sister did. But Josette was nothing like his mother, or any woman of the ton for that matter. She was brave, confident, and rivaled most men in weapons training. Yet she had a compassionate side, and he couldn't help but notice how she smiled whenever she saw a child.

After he'd given Josette the coral necklace, things had shifted between them. She was still fiercely private about her past, but she had become more open with her affection and wit. For her birthday, he had planned to give her a ribbon or a chain, but when he saw the coral necklace in the shop window, it just felt right. She had hesitated because it was so expensive, but to him, it was a symbol of their budding friendship. Because that's what they were... friends. Only friends. At least for now, he mused.

Morgan walked into the dining room and saw a bountiful buffet. He grabbed a plate, filled it with food, and then sat down. Mr. Croft handed him a newspaper and announced, "Your coach arrived moments ago, sir."

"Excellent," he replied, feeling relieved. "It will be nice to change out of these clothes."

After eating breakfast and reading the whole paper slowly, Morgan sighed as he placed the paper on the table. He had hoped that Josette would join him for breakfast, but at this late hour, she would probably request breakfast in bed.

He rose, pushing back his seat. "When will Mrs. Addington be served breakfast?"

"She has already eaten and left for a ride, sir," Mr. Croft informed him.

"When was this?"

"She left about an hour before you came downstairs." He lowered his voice. "Should I have prevented her from leaving the estate?"

As if you could have stopped her, Morgan thought. "No, my wife is free to come and go as she pleases."

"Good, good," Mr. Croft muttered.

Leaving the house, Morgan strode out towards the stable and was pleased to see his horse had already been saddled. A young, black-haired groomsman walked up to him with an apologetic look on his face. "Mrs. Addington told us you would be joining her, but we had assumed it would be much sooner. That's why we saddled yer horse already."

Morgan smiled reassuringly at the groomsman. "Good thinking. Thank you." He led his horse out of the stable. "Do you know which way my wife went?"

The man pointed to the south. "She headed towards Lord Paxton's estate over those hills, passing through the meadow."

"Thank you," he said, mounting his horse.

Morgan kicked the gelding into a run as he admired the green countryside on one side and the beautiful, expansive ocean on the other. He rode hard until he saw a lone rider near a white-washed lighthouse, her long, brown hair blowing in the wind. As he rode closer, he saw that Josette's eyes were closed as she lifted her face towards the warmth of the sun.

He slowed his horse's gait as he approached her. She opened her eyes and turned towards him. "I see that you finally decided to rise for the morning," she teased.

Morgan chuckled as he reined in his horse next to her. "I had incorrectly assumed that you were sleeping late."

"No. That's a luxury that I do not enjoy anymore," Josette

admitted.

"Why not?"

She turned her gaze back towards the ocean before sharing, "When I lived in Bermondsey, everyone rose before dawn. I suppose the habit just stuck with me."

"Bermondsey? You lived in one of the worst rookeries in all of London?" he asked in disbelief, hoping he'd simply misheard her.

Her lips pressed tightly together as she looked at the ground. "I thought you knew," she replied with a little catch in her voice.

"And when would I have learned that tidbit?" he questioned, hearing the mocking chide in his voice. Why did he find this so unbelievable? "After all, you haven't exactly been forthcoming about your past."

Her fiery eyes flew up to meet his gaze, and he could practically see her erecting barriers between them. Josette's horse pawed at the ground, as if sensing the tension of its rider. However, rather than reply with a witty retort or shout at him in anger, she deliberately turned her head back towards the ocean.

What had he done, he wondered. Why had he spoken to her in that tone? He knew she had secrets, but he'd never imagined that she'd once lived in the rookeries. A vile, filthy place saturated with putrescent matter. How did a woman of her station end up in the cesspit of London?

Without saying a word, Josette turned her horse and trotted away from the cliff.

"Wait!" he shouted after her retreating form.

Josette stopped and turned her horse back towards him. "I never asked you to be my friend," she said, sounding hurt. "I am not proud of my past, nor do I want to discuss it, but you keep dredging it up."

"I want to understand what happened to you," he replied, bringing his horse closer to hers.

"This is me now!" she exclaimed. "That is all you need to know."

"You're wrong," he stated with a shake of his head. "To truly know someone, you have to know their past."

She sat tall in the saddle, her back stiff. He witnessed a myriad of emotions flickering across her face. Adjusting the reins in his right hand, he asked, "Who hurt you, Josie?"

Her expression was solemn. "Pass."

He stifled a groan. Josette was the most private woman he'd ever known. She guarded herself with a ferocity he'd never seen before. He knew that, yet he had still pushed her too far. He was becoming far too invested in discovering the truth about her.

Morgan decided to change topics. "The coach arrived this morning."

Looking down at her gown, Josette replied, "That's good. I couldn't very well wear this traveling gown to call on Lady Paxton."

It dawned on him that she had worn these clothes for the past three days, but she never once complained. He had as well, but this wasn't the first time that he didn't have a spare change of clothes. Josette was a remarkable woman.

"If you come closer, you can see Lord Paxton's estate." She pointed past the lighthouse.

He rode his horse closer to Josette and saw a large estate on a cliff overlooking a cove. She gave him a side-long glance. "Any ideas on how to secure an invitation to a house party only two days away?"

"I plan to charm Lady Paxton," he revealed.

Josette gave him a look of disbelief. "Your entire plan is revolved around you being charming? What happened to '...That's where you come in'? I believe those were your exact words in the coach on the way here."

"Well," he hedged, "I need a wife in order to gain access to Lady Paxton. It would be inappropriate for me to call on her as a single man."

Josette just glared.

"What? It's a solid plan," Morgan defended.

"You are entirely too full of yourself, Lord Morgan."

Blast it! She used his title again. "Do you have a better idea?"

Her eyes grew alert as she scanned the estate. "Not at the moment."

"Then, we move forward with my plan." He grinned. "Just so you're aware, I can make almost every woman fall in love with me."

Morgan saw Josette stiffen at his words, and he instantly wished he could take them back. "I'm more than aware of your reputed sexual prowess amongst the ton." Her words were sharp.

He clenched his jaw. "I am not the rake that you think I am. I already explained that." It greatly bothered him that Josette could even think he was a rake. He was not that man.

"And I am not a woman that will simply fall in love with you because you charmed her," she countered.

Deciding to take hold of the conversation, he said, "I already promised that I wouldn't flirt with you, and I have no intention of making you fall in love with me."

"Good," she declared in a firm tone.

"I am glad that we agree on that... again." He smiled at her.

He could see the tension drain from her, and she offered him a tentative smile. "I'm sorry, but sometimes I find your cocky nature a bit irritating."

"Really?" he teased. "I wasn't aware."

Josette's smile widened. "All right. Prove to me that you can get Lady Paxton to swoon over you and extend us an invitation to her house party."

"Challenge accepted."

Josette sat at the dressing table as Annie, her lady's maid, created an elaborate chignon on top of her head. "Will you explain again why my hair has to be coiffed to perfection?" she asked, attempting to ignore the tugging on her hair.

Annie just smiled. "Lady Paxton is very particular, and she has been known to reject callers, telling them that she is not home."

"But a fancy hair style and clothing will make a difference?"

"Oh, yes," Annie confirmed. "She is very much about appearances, ma'am." She took a step back. "You look beautiful."

Rising, Josette smoothed out the wrinkles of her muslin primrose gown with a modest neckline and puffy sleeves. Annie had just handed her matching gloves when she heard a knock on the side door.

Annie opened the door and curtsied while Morgan walked into the center of the room. He eyed Josette with approval, making her feel desirable.

"You look beautiful, my dear."

Aware that Annie was watching them, Josette smiled coyly at her pretend husband. "You flatter me entirely too much." She walked over to him and took a moment to straighten his cravat. "You are looking especially dapper, as well."

Morgan continued to look down at her , and she took a moment to peruse his handsome face. Noticing a small scar on his chin, she reached up to run her fingers along it. "How did you get this scar?"

"I fell out of a tree," he answered, his eyes watching her intently.

With lingering fingers, she said, "It suits you." She dropped her hand and stepped back. "Perhaps we can find a tree to climb after we call on Lady Paxton."

Her words elicited a giggle from Annie and a smile from Morgan. "Shall we?" Morgan asked, offering his arm.

He led her down the stairs and assisted her into the coach. Morgan sat on the opposite bench as the coach lurched forward. "It's vital we secure an invitation to this house party," he reminded her.

Josette dreaded her next question, but she asked it anyway. "And if we don't?"

He sighed as he turned his head to look out the window. "Then, we will have failed."

Noting the seriousness of his tone, she hoped that it would not come to that. However, whenever her mother threw house parties, the guest list had been decided upon months in advance and invitations sent out shortly thereafter. Rooms had been assigned and menus had been carefully selected. The thought of inviting guests at the last-minute was inconceivable. How were they going to secure an invitation when the house party was only two days away?

She attempted to hide her growing concerns by turning towards the window and appearing to enjoy the meandering drive through the beautifully landscaped gardens. The coach pulled up in front of the large stately home of Lord Paxton, and a footman opened their door. As Morgan assisted her out of the coach, she looked up at the impressive outer stairway that led to the main door.

"We can do this," Morgan whispered. She wondered if those words were to encourage them both or just him.

The door was opened before they knocked, and Morgan handed

the butler a calling card.

"Wait here, sir," the sharply-dressed butler said, opening the door wider and allowing them to step into the entry hall. As he walked away from them, his steps echoed off the tiles and papered walls of the imposing great hall. An enormous gold chandelier hung from the ornately painted ceiling, and expensive art was on display in the alcoves.

Josette lifted an eyebrow. "Is one of your estates larger than this one?"

"Most of them are," he replied smugly.

The sound of shoes on the tile alerted them of the approaching butler. "Lady Paxton will see you now," he proclaimed with a stiff upper lip.

Following behind the butler, they walked through the expansive halls, and Josette's eyes were focused on the beautiful art work and furniture. The butler stopped at an open door and held his hand out, indicating that they should enter first.

Josette stepped into the room and saw a grand pianoforte, with exotic veneer and banding, and an elegant French frame. Reluctantly shifting her gaze towards Lady Paxton, she smiled cordially before curtsying. "Thank you for allowing us to interrupt your morning, Lady Paxton."

Lady Paxton was a tall, thin woman with faded red hair and sharp features. She was dressed in an expensive gown with long strands of pearls hanging low around her neck. She rose from her seat. "I understand from Mr. Clark that you moved into Harrold House."

Morgan bowed and answered, "Mr. Clark is well informed."

Lady Paxton gave him a haughty look. "I make it my business to know all my neighbors, Mr. Addington." With a softer look, she pointed at the settee near her. "Please sit down. I have a few moments to become acquainted."

Josette felt immediately at ease around Lady Paxton. Sitting on the settee, she asked, "Have you lived in Torquay long?"

"About thirty years," she replied. "We raised our children here."

"How many children do you have?" Josette asked.

Lady Paxton smiled proudly. "Four. Three boys and a girl."

Nodding towards Morgan, Josette revealed, "My husband came

from a large family as well. He has two brothers and a sister."

"Is that so?" Lady Paxton asked, shifting in her seat to face him.

Morgan nodded. "Yes, we had quite the adventures in our youth. We drove our mother to distraction."

Lady Paxton's laugh filled the room. "Yes, children can bring such joy in your life..." she paused, then continued with sadness in her tone, "and such disappointment." She turned her gaze back towards Josette. "And you, Mrs. Addington?"

"Pardon?" Josette asked.

With a lifted brow, Lady Paxton restated her question. "Do you have any siblings?"

She could feel Morgan's eyes on her as she forced a smile. She could lie, but she decided to tell the truth. "I have a brother. My sister is deceased."

Lady Paxton's eyes filled with compassion. "I am sorry. Was the loss recent?"

"It has been a few years now," she admitted, blinking away her emotions.

With a tender look, Morgan reached over and placed his hand over her fisted one.

Josette hadn't even realized she had clenched them. With a glance towards the window, she asked, "We are new to this area. Can you recommend sites to visit?"

For the next short while, Lady Paxton informed them of all the coves and ruins that were near Torquay. She shared stories of pirates and smuggling along the coves and described a nearby cave system that her boys used to explore for hours.

Josette had been enjoying conversing with Lady Paxton and was saddened when the matron stood up, indicating their visit was over. "Well, I am afraid I must be about other business. Perhaps I will call on you next week."

Morgan rose and offered her a dashing smile. "If you are so inclined, we would love to invite you and Lord Paxton over for dinner in the next few days."

Lady Paxton shook her head. "Unfortunately, we have a house party planned and won't be available to dine at Harrold House till at least next week."

Josette smiled as she rose. "A house party. What fun! My mother and father would bicker constantly before a house party. He was more interested in hunting, shooting, and drinking cherry brandy than he was planning outdoor couple games."

Lady Paxton laughed. "Husbands appear to be universally similar."

Josette reached out and touched Morgan's sleeve. "I was fortunate enough to be blessed with a good match." She smiled at him, hoping it conveyed love.

Morgan returned her smile before turning towards Lady Paxton. "If you find your numbers are odd, bear in mind that I am an excellent marksman."

Lady Paxton tipped her head graciously. "We will remember that, Mr. Addington."

With an invitation still not forthcoming, Josette attempted to think of something else she could do to change Lady Paxton's mind. Her eyes strayed towards the pianoforte. Her heart sank. She knew of a way. Could she though?

Josette moved towards the pianoforte and ran her fingers lingeringly over the keys. She sighed. This was the only way. Taking a moment, she attempted to calm her racing heart before turning to Lady Paxton.

"Would you mind if I played something?" she asked. "Harrold House does not have a pianoforte, and we have yet to order one."

Lady Paxton smiled graciously at her as she lowered herself back down onto the chair. "Of course. I always love to hear music in my home."

Josette sat down at the bench and closed her eyes. It had been so long since she had last played. She started playing a piece by Beethoven, tentatively at first. Her touch became more confident and heartfelt as she felt the rhythm of the music come over her. By the end of the piece, she played the pianoforte effortlessly as her fingers danced over the keys. The practiced movements were as familiar to her as breathing.

When she finished, Josette observed that Lady Paxton was entranced, but she still had not won her over. Her eyes sought out Morgan's, and he was watching her, admiring her. She knew what had to be done. But was she strong enough? For this was something she might not ever recover from.

Morgan's eyes grew warm, inviting, as if he knew she needed encouragement. She could do this… for him.

"If it is permissible, I would like to sing a song," she said, keeping her voice neutral.

Fingering the long strands of pearls around her neck, Lady Paxton nodded. "I would very much like that."

Her fingers rested on the keys, as she garnered the strength from within. She could do this. Without conscious thought, Josette's fingers began the opening phrases of *Fidelio Op. 72,* which was Beethoven's only opera. When she reached her mark, she closed her eyes, knowing they didn't need to be open to feel the music. She opened her mouth and began singing the words of *Komm Hoffnung.*

Chapter Nine

The moment Josette sang her first note, Morgan was entranced. When she began singing, her voice was almost a whisper, but a whisper of such strength it was palpable. Never had he heard such a beautiful soprano voice. It held heartbreak and passion, blending those emotions perfectly, allowing the listener to experience the journey with her.

From his position on the settee, he saw pain etched on Josette's face. As he continued to gaze at her, he felt that pain carving itself upon his own heart. He watched as her fingers glided effortlessly over the keys and listened to the power in her voice that erased every emptiness and every troubled thought, replacing them with beauty.

A tear slid down Josette's cheek, and that was his undoing. Morgan rose from his seat, surprising even himself. He sat down on the bench next to her, hoping his presence would offer her comfort. As she sang the last word, her hands hovered over the keys for a moment before she allowed them to fall into her lap.

Loud cheering erupted from the other side of the room. Morgan turned his head to see the room was filled with liveried men and women. Many of the female servants had tears streaming down their faces as they clapped with enthusiasm.

A finely-dressed older gentleman stood in front of the household staff. His eyes did not waver from Josette. He was of large stature, had silver hair, and a wide jaw.

Clearing his throat, he stepped over to Lady Paxton and asked, "Will you introduce me to our distinguished guests?"

As if by magic, the servants quietly disappeared as he spoke.

Lady Paxton's smile softened as she looked at him. "This is Mr.

and Mrs. Addington. They are our new neighbors." She looked over at them and completed the introduction. "And this is my husband, Lord Paxton."

Morgan rose and helped Josette to rise before he bowed. "It's a pleasure to meet you, Lord Paxton."

Lord Paxton acknowledged him with a brief nod but turned his piercing gaze back towards Josette, who curtsied. "You have a beautiful singing voice, my dear," he praised kindly.

Josette gave him a grateful smile. "Thank you," she murmured humbly.

Turning back towards his wife, he remarked, "We must have them join us at our house party this weekend."

Lady Paxton attempted to avoid frowning, but it was clear that she was not pleased. "The guest list is full. We don't have any additional rooms open."

A male voice came from the doorway. "They can use my bedchamber," he said, walking further into the room. "I can sleep in the hunting lodge."

Morgan looked over and saw a young gentleman with red hair and faded freckles on his face. Turning back towards Lady Paxton, he put his hands up and pretended to object. "We don't mean to impose. We will just…"

"Nonsense," Lord Paxton declared, cutting him off, "we would love to invite you to our house party. Wouldn't we, dear?"

Rising from her seat, Lady Paxton's smile was tense. "Of course. Please excuse me while I make the necessary arrangements."

Everyone's eyes were on Lady Paxton as she exited the room. The young man chuckled. "Poor Mother does not like surprises."

Lord Paxton grinned. "That's true." He looked at Josette, his eyes fixating on her. "I'm hoping you will grace us with more of your musical talent during the party."

Josette nodded, but her words were surprisingly hesitant. "I would be honored to."

"Excellent," Lord Paxton replied in a pleased tone. "Where are my manners?" He tore his gaze away from Josette and gestured towards the young man. "This is my youngest son, Geoffrey. He is on holiday from Oxford."

"Oxford is a decent school." Morgan smirked. "I assume you couldn't get into Cambridge."

Both Lord Paxton and his son roared with laughter at his joke. After a moment, Lord Paxton replied, "We are an Oxford family, but I take it that you went to Cambridge."

"Yes, sir," Morgan confirmed. "I studied to be a barrister."

"A barrister?" Lord Paxton repeated. "Is that your profession?"

"No. I decided there was more money in trade and cargo ships," Morgan replied.

Lord Paxton nodded approvingly. "That there is. Pray tell, have you considered investing in mines?"

Morgan rubbed his chin thoughtfully. "I own percentages of two mines up north, but I am always interested in expanding my investments."

"This is wonderful news," Lord Paxton said. "I own a majority stake in a coal mine in Champagney, France, and the house party is to entertain the French investors."

"French investors?" Morgan asked with an uplifted brow.

Lord Paxton dismissed his comment with a wave of his hand. "The war is over, Mr. Addington. Now that Napoleon has been exiled, it's time we move on from our differences with France."

Dropping down onto the settee, Geoffrey asserted, "We would do well to model our society after the French government."

"Hush," Lord Paxton stated harshly. "We do not wish to hear any of your radical nonsense today."

Geoffrey put his hands up in front of him in defeat and remained silent.

Morgan placed his hand on the small of Josette's back. "Well, if you will excuse us," he said as he started leading her towards the door.

"You will come to the house party, won't you?" Lord Paxton asked Josette, hopefully.

Josette responded with a sweet smile. "We would be honored to attend."

Lord Paxton's face broke into a wide, relieved smile. "This pleases me immensely. We will send a carriage around to pick you up in two days' time."

"That won't be necessary," Morgan assured him. "We will see to our own transportation."

Tipping his head graciously, Lord Paxton said, "Until the house party, then."

In response, Josette offered a shy smile before allowing Morgan to escort her out of the drawing room. As they walked down the steps and into the awaiting carriage, he felt exhilarated that they had secured an invitation.

Sitting opposite of Josette, he waited until the carriage jerked forward before he let out an excited whoop. "We did it," he paused, correcting himself, "*you* did it."

Josette kept her gaze out the window. "We did it together. We are a team," she replied in a low, calm voice.

"We are one step closer to discovering *Genet*," he said, attempting to engage her in the conversation.

"That we are."

Morgan studied her, noting her withdrawn demeanor. "Lord Paxton seemed quite infatuated with you."

"I'll be on my guard."

Blast it! Why was Josette being so dismissive? They had just secured a critical advantage on their mission. She should be elated. He decided to change tactics.

"You have a beautiful voice, Josie."

"Thank you." She barely glanced his way when responding.

Morgan sat forward in his seat and adjusted his riding coat. "What is it?"

"It's nothing," she said, bringing her gaze down to her lap and wringing her hands in obvious agitation.

"Clearly, it is not nothing," he replied encouragingly.

"This is the first time that I have sung since my mother died."

Sensing there was more to the story, Morgan reached out and placed his hand over her twisting hands, stilling them.

"I am here for you, whether you want to share or not."

Her vulnerable eyes latched onto his, and she didn't speak for a long moment. With a shaky breath, she confessed, "My mother died because of me."

He tightened his hold on her hands. "I doubt that."

"It's true," she whispered. "Due to the complexity of my singing voice, my mother insisted that I be trained by only the best sopranos, including Miss Cecilia Davis. We traveled up to York for an extended lesson with Miss Cecilia, and my mother became ill on the return trip." Her voice grew distant. "She died in the carriage before we even arrived home."

"I can't imagine how hard that must have been for you," he said, his voice hushed.

"Thank you," she acknowledged in a quiet voice. "To make matters worse, my younger sister contracted the illness and died shortly thereafter." Tears came to her eyes, but she did not attempt to wipe them away. "The cruel irony was that I was spared."

"Why is that ironic?"

Her face grew pale. "It was my fault they died. We traveled all over England, seeking out the best opera singers… for me. Not them. I should have been the one who died."

Morgan shook his head. "No. You did nothing wrong. Did you not say that your mother sought out the best tutors for you?"

"I could have said no."

"How old were you when they died?"

"Fifteen," she admitted, wincing.

"Dear Josie," he said gently, "their deaths were not your fault."

Her eyes sought his. "I thank you for that, but you are wrong."

In a swift motion, he moved to sit next to her on the bench, not removing his hand from hers. "You were but a young girl when they died. Your mother wanted what was best for you and sought out the best tutors to enhance your prospects. She wanted you to be happy."

A wistful smile came to her lips. "My mother said something similar to me before she died."

"Did she ask you to stop singing?"

Josette bit her bottom lip. "No, quite the opposite. She encouraged me to never give up my voice. She thought it was a gift from God."

"I agree," he expressed. "Your singing cleansed my soul, Josie."

"After my sister died, I vowed never to perform again," she shared. "I thought it was penance for my selfish behavior."

"Again, you did nothing wrong," he reminded her. "If that was the case, then why did you offer to sing for Lady Paxton?"

A slight blush came over her cheeks as she murmured, "It was the only way to secure an invitation."

Morgan shifted to face her. "You are more important to me than this mission." His eyes implored hers, hoping to convince her of his sincerity.

Bringing her head up, her eyes were wide, uncertain. "But I know how badly you want to capture *Genet*."

"I do," he assured her. "I want to find *Genet* and watch him die a slow, painful death," he hesitated, "but not at your expense."

Josette's eyes filled with tears , and she started blinking them away. He reached up and captured one of the stray tears. "You don't have to be brave all the time."

"But I do," she whimpered.

"Lean on me," he said. "We will be brave together."

"I have been alone for so long. I don't think I can."

Morgan reached out and pulled her gently against him, determined to offer her comfort. She provided no resistance as she rested her head against his chest.

"We will decline the invitation to the house party, and we will find another way to capture *Genet*." He had no idea how they would accomplish that feat, but they would find a way.

"You will do no such thing," she insisted, relaxing in his arms. "It would compromise the mission."

He rested his cheek against her head. "I will agree, assuming you won't push yourself more than you can bear."

"I promise," she answered.

Lifting his head slightly, Morgan kissed the top of her head, his lips lingering on her skin. His brave Josie had sacrificed a part of herself to help advance their cause. What bravery! How could he *not* care for this woman?

Josette narrowed her eyes and debated about reaching for her dagger. If she killed her partner, would Lord Charles be upset?

"Are you even listening to me, Josie?" Morgan asked, frustration filling his tone.

She crossed her arms over her chest. "Yes, but everything you are saying is senseless."

He threw his hands up in the air and spun around. She could hear him muttering under his breath, and it sounded like he was counting down from ten. He sighed loudly and turned back around. "I am the lead agent on this assignment, and I forbid you to go to The Gutted Fish tonight. It's not safe, even if you are wearing men's clothing."

"I know what I'm doing," she assured him, dropping her arms to her sides. "I can slip in and out, and no one will be the wiser."

Morgan gave her an exasperated look. "You can't walk into a pub and not expect people to notice that you're a woman." He took a commanding step forward. "It could put our whole mission in jeopardy. It could put *you* in jeopardy."

Walking over to her bed, she sat down. "Do you expect me to just stay behind while you put your life on the line?"

"Going to a pub is hardly a life or death experience," he replied dryly. "I need to see what this radical group is planning."

Josette lowered her gaze to the bed and debated about how to answer. They had been arguing about this off and on for hours. Now the conversation had moved upstairs to her bedchamber. Morgan was adamant that she would not go to the pub for fear that her gender would be discovered. However, that was preposterous. She had become proficient at slipping in and out of buildings.

Tugging down on his coat, Morgan informed her, "I need to depart if I want to arrive before the meeting starts."

"Then go," she said with a flick of her wrist. "I won't stand in your way."

Morgan eyed her suspiciously. "This has nothing to do with your abilities, but it has everything to do with the mission." He stepped closer to the bed. "If you were discovered, then how could we explain your presence?"

She lifted her brow. "Why do you assume I would be caught?"

"Just stay here," he ordered. "I will fill you in on what was discussed the moment I arrive back from the village."

"All right," she conceded.

He let out a relieved sigh. "Thank you."

Josette rose from her seated position on the bed and walked up to him. She reached up and adjusted his skewed cravat. "Be safe."

A smile crossed his lips. "I can take care of myself."

"I have no doubt," she replied, grabbing his top hat from the table. Holding it out to him, she waited as he approached her.

"Thank you for being reasonable, Josie." He offered her a dashing smile as he accepted the hat.

She tilted her chin. "Why would I not be? After all, you are paying me to be your partner."

Morgan's smile dimmed. "Josie…" he started off hesitantly, "please don't say that." His eyes reflected hurt.

"Just go," she encouraged him.

He turned towards the door and put his hand on the handle. Before he opened it, he said, "We will continue this conversation later."

She nodded but didn't say anything. After he departed the room, she ran to her trunk and opened the lid. She pulled out a white shirt, tan trousers, a small pair of Hessian boots, and a cloth cap. She quickly removed her nightgown and put on the men's clothing.

She locked the bedroom door before heading towards the window. She had anticipated that Morgan would refuse to allow her to go to the pub and had arranged an alternate plan. She may not be able to walk into the pub, but she could climb in through an open window.

Sticking her head out of the bedchamber window, she glanced down and saw that a horse was waiting for her below. She climbed out carefully and felt for hand holds on the brick before she began scaling down the wall.

Jumping the last remaining feet, she landed and turned towards the young groomsman who held the reins to a horse. She handed him a coin. "Thank you," she said, accepting the reins from him.

The groomsman placed his hand on the horse's neck and asked in a hushed voice, "Should I remain here until you return?"

"No, I will return the horse to the stable." She placed her right foot into the stirrup and mounted easily.

"Do you recall the directions I gave you?" he asked as he stepped back.

"I do. Thank you." Josette gave him a grateful nod before she kicked her horse into a run. The young groomsman had provided her with an alternate course towards town, ensuring she wouldn't run into Morgan along the way.

As she approached the street where the pub was situated, she saw an older woman standing in front of her cottage, looking out towards the horizon. She dismounted and cautiously approached the white-haired, frail-looking woman.

"Good evening," she said, announcing herself.

The woman turned towards her with a guarded expression. "Evening."

"May I pay you to watch my horse?"

"For how long?"

Josette rubbed a hand down her horse's neck. "About an hour."

Taking a few tentative steps closer, the woman asked, "How much will you pay me?"

"A pound."

The woman's wrinkled face lit up with a smile. "Your horse will be safe with me. I swear to you."

Extending the reins towards the woman, Josette returned her smile. "Thank you. I will return shortly."

She didn't look back as she ran the short distance towards the pub and circled around the back. The pub had a gated rear courtyard and two small structures sat in the corners. She had no trouble hopping over the fence. Moving silently from shadow to shadow, she peered into the windows on the lower level.

Looking into the first window, she saw a small hall with tables and chairs near an open fireplace. Men were sitting around, chatting and drinking merrily, but there was no sign of Morgan or Mr. Blount.

Josette crouched low and approached the window on the far side of the inn. She peered in and saw this larger hall was filled to capacity. Men were seated at rounded tables, but many of the patrons were leaning up against the walls. Their attention all seemed to be focused on Mr. Blount, who was standing in front.

Her eyes scanned the room , and she saw that Morgan was sitting down next to Geoffrey, Lord Paxton's youngest son. Bringing his glass up to his mouth, Morgan paused as he laughed at something

Geoffrey had said. Both men then directed their gazes back towards Mr. Blount.

Josette placed her hand in between the bricks and started scaling the wall, looking for a way to enter the second level. To her left, a darkened room had a window that was slightly ajar. Perfect. She quickly opened the window wide enough for her to slip through.

Her intention was to locate Mr. Blount's room and learn who his co-conspirators were. She glanced around the vacant room before she carefully made her way to the door and looked out. No one was in the hall , and she counted eight doors along both sides.

She moved over to the next room, knocked softly, and waited for a response. When no response came, she knelt down to pick the lock. Once she heard the click, confirming it was unlocked, she opened the door and peered into the room. She saw a satchel on the bed and walked over to it, hoping to find any sign of Mr. Blount. After pulling out a change of clothes, she saw nothing else that gave indication who this room had been rented to. She shoved the clothes back in the satchel and left the room.

After the fourth room she searched, Josette let out a frustrated sigh. Perhaps Mr. Blount wasn't staying at this public house. Still, she must not give up. She knocked on the next door and waited. When no one answered, she unlocked the door and slipped into the room. After closing the door, she locked it and headed over to the desk. The rooms all had the same layout. A small desk, a table with a basin of water and pitcher, and a lumpy, straw mattress on an iron frame.

A set of clothes was laid out on the bed and two sets of pamphlets were stacked up on the desk. The only light came from the moonlight shining through the window, but it was enough. Picking up a pamphlet from the first pile, she saw that it was the one that Mr. Blount had given Morgan. She returned it to the exact same position so as not to arouse attention to her search and reached for a pamphlet from the second pile.

Josette attempted to read the pages but there was not enough light, and she didn't dare light the candle sitting on the desk. Gripping the pamphlet, she walked closer to the window, but the writing was too small. There had to be something incriminating in this room. If not, this was a wasted trip, and she risked Morgan's ire for no reason.

The thud of heavy boots came from the hall, along with muffled men's voices. She returned the pamphlet to the correct pile and dove under the bed.

The door was unlocked and pushed open. She could see a set of worn, black boots and a set of shiny boots walk into the room. The door was closed behind them, and the man with worn boots walked over to the bed. He sat down on the mattress, and the iron frame squeaked in protest.

The man next to the desk asked, "How are the new recruits?" Yes, that was Mr. Blount's voice.

"Gullible as the other groups," a deep voice answered from the bed. She was sure she had never heard this voice before. "And this Mr. Addington?"

"He checks out." Mr. Blount pulled out a chair from the desk and sat down. "When does *Genet* arrive?"

"In two days," the voice above her said. "Lord Paxton provided passage for him to sail into English harbors."

Mr. Blount scoffed. "We should thank the fool for graciously bringing the French investors under his passport. I highly doubt the Royal Navy would suspect a British merchant ship of transporting a French spy."

A silence descended over the men before the man above her asked, "Have you met *Genet*?"

"No. Have you?"

"Me neither. When do you expect to hear from him?"

"Not sure. But it will be at some point during the house party."

The bed squeaked as the man rose. "I am leaving tonight to join the rebels in London. Everything is going according to plan."

"Good," Mr. Blount confirmed, standing from his seated position. "It's been planned down to the last detail." She heard a ruffling of papers. "It will serve England right for putting their support behind the traitorous Bourbons."

"Those blackguards. After everything Napoleon did for us." The man walked towards the door, but spun around, causing his boots to grind the dirt on the floor.

"Come," Mr. Blount urged, walking over to the door and opening it, "let's go distribute these pamphlets."

After the men left the room, the door was locked, and Josette came out from her hidden position. She headed back towards the desk and started quickly searching through the drawers. But there was nothing that indicated what these groups had planned.

Josette cautiously went over to the door, unlocked it, and opened it a crack. A man was walking down the hall towards her. She closed and locked the door before moving to the window. Opening it wide enough for her to escape through, she placed her legs out and found arm and foot holds on the bricks. She kept a firm hand on the wall as she used her other hand to close the window.

With quick precision, she scaled down the wall until she was able to land softly on her feet. Before she turned around, a hand gripped her upper arm, squeezing firmly.

"What do you think you are doing, lad?" the man asked in an infuriated tone. He shook her forcefully before yanking her back towards him. "Do you really think you can just steal from my boarders?"

In a fluid motion, Josette retrieved the dagger strapped to her right thigh and plunged it deep into the man's leg. When he released his hold on her, she removed the dagger and ran towards the fence. Behind her, the innkeeper screamed curse words, no doubt waking the whole village with his vile tongue.

As she scaled the fence, the back door of the public house was thrown open, and a group of men ran out. "Go after the lad!" the innkeeper shouted. "He went that way."

Keeping herself hidden in the shadows, Josette ran quickly towards town until she found a darkened cottage. She scaled up the white washed building and laid low on the thatched roof as the men ran past her, heading towards the main part of town.

She waited until the men had disappeared from her view before dropping down from the roof. Carefully, she made her way back towards the house where she'd left her horse. The woman was sitting on the porch of the cottage holding onto the lead. With quiet steps, she was within a few feet of the woman before she was noticed.

The woman jumped up, her eyes wide and fearful. Hoping to put the woman at ease, Josette murmured in a hushed voice, "It's only me. I am the person who paid you to watch my horse."

After accepting the lead from the woman, Josette reached into her pocket and removed two gold coins.

The woman's eyes widened, but she made no attempt to retrieve the coins. Looking up, she asked, "Are you injured?"

Looking down at her right hand, Josette realized that it was coated in blood. "No. This is not my blood."

The woman froze, and Josette rushed to assure her, "I didn't kill anyone." She extended the coins again. "Please. I need to depart, and I want to pay you for your services."

The woman brought her hand up , and Josette dropped the coins down to her. The woman stepped back as she quickly mounted her horse, kicking it into a run on the cobblestone street.

Racing towards her estate, Josette continuously glanced over her shoulder to see if she had been followed. When no riders appeared, she sighed in relief, but did not slow the horse's gait until she saw her estate looming ahead.

A smile came to her lips as she reined in her horse near the stables. That was a crazy adventure, she thought.

Chapter Ten

Morgan yawned loudly as he slid his cravat off and dropped it on the floor. After removing his waistcoat and jacket, he placed them on the settee near the fireplace. He would let the valet pick up his clothes tomorrow.

Sitting on the bed, he removed the pistol from his right boot and slid it under his pillow. He kicked off his boots and put them to the side. Except for a ruffian stabbing the innkeeper, the night had been mostly uneventful. He had sat next to Geoffrey at the pub, and they'd chatted about politics, sports, and gambling.

He sighed. It was clear that Geoffrey was a radical thinker, but his youthful naiveté was evident tonight. He didn't think that his new friend understood the ramifications of attending these types of meetings.

Mr. Blount spoke to them at length about social reform, but it was nothing that he hadn't already heard from members of the Whig party before. As he stood to leave, he was handed another pamphlet, and encouraged to spread the word.

Before he rode away from the inn, he took a moment to read the pamphlet. It was anti-Bourbons in nature, opposed the restoration, and praised Napoleon's achievements in educational, religious, and administrative reform.

Morgan stretched his neck as he looked over at the door that divided his room from Josette's. He didn't see a light under the door, so she must have gone to bed. Would she still be angry with him tomorrow for ordering her to stay home tonight? He had been correct in his thinking. Her presence certainly would have been detected.

Before they adjourned for the evening, Geoffrey had invited him to tour the ruins tomorrow during his morning ride. That would be a good opportunity to persuade Geoffrey of the error of his ways. Orators, such as Mr. Blount, did not care about the repercussions to the people that followed them. They only cared about pushing their reforms and getting paid.

He blew out the candle and laid back on the bed. Josette had been eyeing that bonnet in the village. Perhaps that would bring a smile to her face. He loved making her smile. He had no right to tease her, or crave her laugh, but he did both.

Morgan had never met a woman like Josette. The more he discovered about her, the more he wanted to learn, to unearth. He could never rest until he learned why Josette was the most remarkable, complicated person he'd ever known. She was a puzzle, but he was certain that puzzle had a solution.

A muffled noise came from Josette's room. He jumped up and grabbed his pistol all in one quick motion. Reaching the door in a few strides, he placed his hand on the door handle and waited to see if perhaps he imagined the noise. After a moment, he heard a moan coming from behind the door. He tossed it open and charged into the darkened room. However, instead of finding an intruder, he saw Josette tossing on the bed, sweat covering her brow.

Morgan stepped closer to the bed. The muttered words on her lips seemed incoherent, but he started to recognize a pattern.

"Please don't... I'm sorry..."

His heart could take no more of this. Tucking his pistol into the waistband of his trousers, he sat down on the bed next to her.

"Josette," he whispered softly.

When she didn't respond, Morgan gently brushed the hair off her sweaty brow and whispered again, "You're safe."

His words had the intended effect, and her tear-filled eyes opened. "Morgan," she whimpered. Then, she surprised him by throwing her arms around him.

Instantly, he reached out and pulled her close. "I have you, Josie. You're safe," he assured her in a hushed tone. Feeling her tremble in his arms, a surge of love and fierce devotion washed over him. He would do whatever it took to care for Josette, even if it meant that she would never be his.

She sobbed into his white shirt, and it soon was drenched with her tears. Gently, he kept her close, hoping he was providing her with some comfort. After a few moments, she dropped her arms from his neck and leaned back, wiping her eyes with the white sleeves of her nightgown.

"I'm sorry," she apologized through shaky breaths.

Feeling the loss of her contact, he reached for her hand, encompassing it in his own. "You have nothing to apologize for."

Josette lowered her gaze. "I haven't had that nightmare in weeks."

Standing, he moved to a side table where a basin and a pitcher of water sat. Pouring a glass, he brought it back to her.

"Thank you," she mumbled, then took a sip.

"Would you like to talk about it?" he asked, sitting back down on the bed.

She shook her head, keeping her eyes downcast.

"All right." Attempting to keep the disappointment out of his tone, he rose and added, "If you change your mind, you know where to find me."

Seeing the crestfallen look on her face, his heart lurched, but he couldn't force her to trust him. It must happen on her terms, when she's ready. Regretfully, he walked back to the open door between their rooms. As he placed his hand on the door, Josette's soft voice stopped him.

"A few months after my mother and sister were buried, my father and I took a holiday to our country estate near Dover."

Morgan removed his hand from the door and turned to face her, waiting for her to continue. Even in the dim light, he could see her bottom lip tremble.

"My father took me along while he went hunting with the gamekeeper." She hesitated. "He said I needed a distraction." She leaned over and placed her glass on a small side table. "He... um..." Her voice trailed off.

Taking a step closer to her, Morgan prodded gently, "He what?"

The sadness was evident on her brow as she replied, "He died when his shotgun exploded."

"Oh, Josie!" Morgan exclaimed as he moved swiftly back to the bed. He sat down and wrapped his arms around her again. "What a horrible thing for you to witness."

She buried her face in his chest. "I wanted to go get help, but I didn't know the way back home," she cried. "Mr. Ritter told me to stay with my father, and he raced back to the estate. But he was too late."

Morgan placed a hand on the back of her head and held her close. He couldn't imagine the depth of the trauma she'd had to endure. "How old were you?"

"I'd just turned sixteen."

"You have borne such terrible losses," he stated, unable to keep the emotion out of his voice. He knew his words were not adequate, but what does one say in such moments? "Is that what your nightmare is about?"

Josette surprised him again by snuggling closer. "One of them."

"You have more than one dream that plagues you?"

She nodded. "I do, but they come and go. They are less frequent now that I am the headmistress."

"Do you know why that is?"

"I now can protect myself." She sighed before continuing, "But more importantly, I feel safe there."

"Were you not safe before?" he asked, hoping she would reveal more of her past.

"The overwhelming grief of losing my parents and my sister became imprinted on my very soul, but I did not have the luxury of time to grieve properly until I arrived at Lady Camden's estate."

Gently, he leaned her back so he could look into her eyes. "Why was that?"

Morgan could see the vulnerability on her face and realized she was about to erect the barrier between them again. He slowly lowered his forehead until it rested against hers.

"Don't shut me out, Josie," he pleaded earnestly. "Let me help you."

Her voice started off weak as she shared, "After a brief stay with my Aunt Winnie, I returned back to our London townhouse. My older brother was enraged. He blamed me for all the deaths." Morgan felt her shudder as she tried to stifle a sob threatening to erupt from deep within. "He told me that he wished I was the one that had died."

"That's a cruel thing to say."

Josette brought her arms around his waist as she revealed, "He ordered me to leave and never come back."

In disbelief, Morgan asked, "Your brother kicked you out of your own home?"

Her grip tightened around his waist. "He was inebriated and kept raging at me for what seemed like hours. When he finally ordered me to leave, I just stood there. I couldn't believe he really meant it. Then, he tossed his glass at me. It shattered against the wall, and the glass cut my arms."

"He threw a glass at you?" Morgan felt the rage churning inside of him.

"I don't think he meant to hurt me," Josette clarified weakly. "I… um… ran upstairs and my lady's maid helped stitch me up. I had hoped that my brother was not in earnest, but he followed me upstairs. He told me not to bother going back to our aunt's estate, because she hated me, as well."

Josette hiccupped through her tears. "I started crying, and he told me that I had ruined his life."

"*You* ruined *his* life?" Morgan asked incredulously.

"He had been studying at Oxford, but he was forced to come home and take over for my father."

"That included taking care of you," Morgan pointed out.

"My brother was so angry, and I was scared," Josette admitted. "When my brother left my room, I collected all of my mother's jewelry, and I ran out the front door."

"What did your brother do?"

"I don't know. I just ran… and ran."

"Where did you end up?" he pressed gently.

She looked up at him. "My new life."

"Will you please tell me your brother's name, so I can find him and kill him in the most excruciatingly painful way possible?" His words were forced through clenched teeth.

"I will not, because I want no ill-will to befall him."

Morgan stared at her in surprise. "After everything he did to you?"

Tears pooled in her eyes as she replied, "If it wasn't for me, then my mother, father, and sister would all still be alive. It was my selfish actions that contributed to their death."

Taking his hand, he cupped her right cheek. "Why do you believe that?"

"If I hadn't acted so irrationally about my mother and sister's death, then my father wouldn't have felt obligated to take me away from London," she explained.

Morgan's brow furrowed. He thought her words seemed rehearsed. Suddenly, it dawned on him why.

"Did your brother tell you that?"

Her lips tightened as she tried to look away.

Ignoring the overwhelming anger that coursed through his body, he kept his hand firmly on her cheek. "Josie," he began gently, "your father saw his daughter hurting and wanted to help you. That's why he took you on his hunting trip. He loved you."

Tears streamed from her eyes. "I miss them so much," she whimpered. "Not a day goes by that I don't think about them and wish they were here."

"It's normal to feel that way," he said, trying to console her. "You were so young. None of this was your fault. You must believe me, you did nothing wrong. Your brother was the one who was in the wrong. Not you."

Her eyes searched his and a weak smile came to her face. "I haven't told anyone about that part of my life."

"Not even Eliza?"

She shook her head. "No. I was worried that Eliza would use the Crown's resources to identify my brother and kill him."

Morgan stifled a groan. Josette had just laid out his exact plan to enact revenge. "I daresay that she would have probable cause."

"Please," Josette said, "my brother is in my past, and I have moved on. I don't wish any harm to come to him."

"Fine," he agreed reluctantly, pulling her close.

No more words were exchanged as Josette clung to him. After a while, her breathing deepened, and he could tell that she was falling asleep. Kissing the top of her head, he started to slowly lay her down on her pillow. But her hand shot out and grabbed his.

"Don't leave me," she pleaded.

"Never," he replied as she scooted over in the bed.

He leaned his back up against the wall, and she placed her head on his chest. Within moments, her breathing became deeper, letting him know that she had fallen asleep at last.

Morgan was in trouble. He knew, without a doubt, that Josette had become his future.

Josette was having the most wonderful dream. She was in Morgan's strong arms, and she felt safe, protected. The sun streamed through the windows, and the birds chirped merrily outside. Fighting the idea of waking up, she snuggled her head against her pillow. Suddenly, her heart stopped. Her pillow was hard and was slowly rising and falling.

Opening her eyes, Josette realized that her pillow was really a man's chest, and his arm was draped familiarly over her waist. She tilted her head slightly and saw Morgan sleeping. What is he doing in my bedroom, she wondered. And why am I in his arms?

She felt her blood start to boil. How dare he come and take advantage of her! He had no right to sleep with her. They were not truly married and never *would* be.

Carefully, she moved out of his arms and reached for the pistol tucked under her real pillow. She would have grabbed her dagger, but it was under the pillow Morgan was currently sleeping on.

She moved to the opposite side of the bed before she pointed the pistol at Morgan. "Why are you in my bed?"

To her surprise, he opened his eyes and blinked lazily at her.

"Why are you holding a pistol?" he asked, seemingly unconcerned.

"Because you are sleeping in my bed," she answered.

In slow motion, Morgan sat up and leaned his back against the wall. He brought his hand up and rubbed the back of his neck.

"You invited me to stay, Josie."

Her jaw dropped. "Impossible! I would never share a bed with a man."

"I'm not just any man; I'm your husband." An impish grin formed on his lips. "As such, I am entitled to my husbandly rights."

Glancing down at her nightgown in alarm, she looked for any signs that it had been removed last night. Her eyes widened as she looked up at him. "You didn't... we didn't," she stammered.

He laughed heartily, much to her annoyance. "No, we didn't," he reassured her, amusement in his tone. "I promise you that it would have been a more memorable experience."

Josette had never wanted to shoot a man as badly as she did at this moment. "Then, pray tell, why are you in my bed?"

Running his hand through his disheveled hair, he sighed. "After I came back from the village, I heard you moaning and thrashing about, and I came in to check on you." His eyes held compassion as he asked, "Do you remember having a nightmare?"

She nodded, albeit reluctantly. The past evening's events washed over her, filling her with shame. What must Morgan think of her? She had been in such a vulnerable state last night and revealed far more than she intended to. Lowering the pistol, she placed it on the bed and looked away.

"I remember now," she mumbled.

"Josie," Morgan said, "please look at me."

She felt panic swelling up in her chest and had the sudden, familiar urge to flee from the room. Unfortunately, this was *her* bedchamber, and she wore only a nightgown.

"I need to change," she declared, hoping that Morgan would leave the room so she could collect herself.

"Why?"

She brought her gaze up at his ridiculous question. "Because I am dressed only in a nightgown."

Deliberately, his eyes ran down the length of her attire. "First of all, I have already seen you in your nightgown. Secondly, your sleeping gown offers more modesty than the gowns you wear during the day."

"Be that as it may, it's inappropriate for you to see me in such a state of undress," she replied haughtily.

Morgan shrugged. "I daresay that I'm exposing more than you are, and I'm not the least bit concerned."

Without thinking, her eyes dropped to his broad chest peeking through the opening in his white shirt.

"Nor am I complaining that you are ogling me."

Once his words registered in her mind, Josette's eyes shot back up to his. Her cheeks felt exceedingly warm as she realized she'd been caught staring. "I, sir, am not ogling you," she huffed.

"It's all right. I give you leave to do so." He smiled roguishly at her.

Her lips pressed into a white line at his flirtatious comment. "You are the most infuriating man that I have ever known."

Morgan laughed before he rubbed his eyes. "You're probably curious about last night."

"I am," she replied, grateful for the change of subject.

His face grew serious. "Mr. Blount handed out another pamphlet and spoke at length about social reform. It's evident that this momentum is leading to something, but nothing specific has been mentioned."

Josette nodded. "I concur. When I snuck into his room, I discovered…"

"You did what?" he roared, cutting her off. "I specifically forbade you to go!"

She waved her hand dismissively. "You didn't think I was going to stay back, did you?"

His mouth gaped as he stared at her. "Yes, I did. We agreed!" he shouted in a tone that clearly invited no argument.

"No, *we* did not agree. You ordered me to stay behind," she pointed out. "Besides, don't you want to learn what I discovered about *Genet?*"

Josette watched Morgan clench and unclench his jaw. "Proceed," he said tersely.

She smiled victoriously. "As I was saying, I saw the pamphlets on his desk. However, my search was interrupted by Mr. Blount, and I had to hide under the bed."

Morgan let out a loud, frustrated sigh. "Were you the thieving lad that stabbed the innkeeper in the leg?"

"Yes, that happened as I was leaving," she confessed, seeing no need to deny it. "While I was under the bed, I heard Mr. Blount confirm that *Genet* will be at the house party. Furthermore, I learned..." she began, filling him in on the whole conversation.

Morgan pressed his fingers to the bridge of his nose. "You were almost caught," he complained. He lowered his hand and balled it into a fist, dropping it to his side.

"I had it under control." Her voice was firm, insistent.

Anger darkened his features, and he stared at her wordlessly for several moments. "You went against my direct order."

She gave him an exasperated look. "Am I truly your partner, or do you see me as someone that you need to protect?"

"Partners protect each other," he remarked.

"True, but partners also trust each other," she responded. "While you were busy downstairs at The Gutted Fish, I snuck into Mr. Blount's room. We need to work *with* each other, not against each other."

Morgan watched her closely for a moment before he conceded. "You're right. Sneaking into Mr. Blount's room was a smart move."

Toying with the lace on the sleeves of her nightgown, she smirked. "I thought it was quite brilliant myself."

"I see humility is not one of your strengths, is it?" Morgan quipped with a grin.

Josette laughed, remembering that she'd used those exact words on him not so long ago. "I saw you sitting next to Geoffrey. Do you think he's a member of this radical group?"

Morgan wiped a hand over his face. "No. I think he is a naive young man that is siding with these radicals because they fall in line with the Whig's values."

"Is Lord Paxton a Whig?"

"No, he's a Tory. Whigs have repeatedly called for reducing Crown patronage and establishing a constitutional monarchy. They have a belief in liberty, advocate for drastic parliamentary reform, and idolize Napoleon."

"Whereas Tories support a stronger monarchy, are supporters of the Church of England, and push the agricultural interests of British farmers," Josette shared.

"You are well informed," Morgan praised. "The Whigs were heavily against the Bourbons coming back into power."

Josette looked curiously at him. "You seem to know a lot about the Whig party. Do you side with them?"

He looked forlorn. "That's a ticklish question. My personal views fall in line with the Tories, as do my father's, but my job as an agent forces me to publicly side with the Whigs."

Noticing the sadness in his voice, she asked, "Do you regret hiding who you are so you can be an agent?"

"At times," he revealed. "My family views me as an embarrassment, a black sheep."

"Everyone?"

He turned his gaze towards the window. "Not my mother. She writes dutifully to me every week." His jaw tightened as he admitted, "But not my father. He won't acknowledge me in polite society. He believes I court scandal."

"That's awful." She moved closer and placed her hand on his arm. Once he brought his gaze up, she spoke from her heart. "I know you to be a brave, honorable man."

Morgan's eyes softened. "Thank you, Josie. That means a lot."

She retrieved her pistol and held it up. "Would you like me to go speak to your father?"

He laughed as she hoped he would. "I have no doubt that my father would do your bidding."

"Because of my pistol?" she teased.

His eyes roamed her face slowly before saying, "No, because you are an extraordinary woman."

Uncomfortable with his praise, she slid her pistol back under her pillow. "I wish you would not say such kind things to me, Lord Morgan," she said, using his title intentionally.

"Why not?"

She met his gaze. "After our mission is over, we both will go back to who we truly are."

"Will we?"

"Yes," she confirmed, nodding. "I am the headmistress at a boarding school, and you are society's golden boy."

"Perhaps I could change my image," he suggested, watching her carefully.

"But why? After all, you play the rake so well," she jested.

"That is not who I am." His tone sounded hurt.

Josette gazed at his handsome face. "Who is it that you want to be?"

Before he could respond, there was a soft knock at the door. As it opened, Morgan reached over, placed his arm around her waist, and pulled her against his side.

Her lady's maid walked into the room with a tray. Annie stopped and gasped softly. "My apologies, Mr. Addington. I thought Mrs. Addington was alone."

Morgan leaned down and kissed Josette's cheek, much to her surprise. "No harm done." He rose from the bed and directed his next comments to Josette. "I'll go prepare for the day. Would you do me the honor of joining me when I call on Geoffrey after breakfast?"

"I think that is a fine idea, husband," she replied, finding herself smiling playfully. She refused to let him have the upper hand.

He winked at her. "I am full of them, wife."

With a side-glance at her lady's maid, she lowered her voice to give the appearance of shyness. "Thank you for a memorable evening."

In response, a deep blush stained his cheeks as he cleared his throat, his eyes refusing to meet her gaze. "Yes… um… as you were," he stammered out, walking swiftly through his opened door, closing it behind him.

"It is refreshing to see a couple in love," Annie sighed.

Josette's heart lurched. How she wished that this could be real, but it was only a ruse. Morgan was her partner, and she was just a lonely orphan.

Chapter Eleven

Josette's pale blue gown caught for a moment on the carriage door as she exited in front of Lord Paxton's estate. Morgan's hand squeezed tighter around hers, preventing her from tumbling to the ground.

"Thank you, Morgan," she murmured, removing her hand from his.

She took a moment to smooth her rounded neckline and fluff her puffy sleeves before accepting Morgan's arm as they walked towards the main door. The butler admitted them into the entry hall, took their calling cards, and instructed them to wait.

After a few moments, they were escorted into the drawing room, but before they sat down, Lord Paxton and Geoffrey entered.

"Mr. and Mrs. Addington," Lord Paxton welcomed them. "What a lovely surprise."

After pleasantries were exchanged, Geoffrey informed his father, "I invited Mr. Addington to come along on my ride to see the ruins."

Josette took a moment to admire Morgan's broad shoulders beneath his green riding jacket. Briefly, she allowed herself the indulgence of remembering how his arms felt around her, comforting her.

His voice cut through her thoughts. "Please, call me Morgan."

"Pardon?" she asked.

"You already have leave to call me by my given name, wife." Morgan gave her a boyish grin.

"That is so gracious of you, *husband*." She smiled. "I apologize. I was woolgathering for a moment."

Lord Paxton glanced curiously at her. "Do you not wish to join them for a ride, Mrs. Addington?"

Her eyes drifted longingly towards the beautiful instrument in the corner of the room. "If you would permit me, I would prefer to practice on the pianoforte."

"We would be honored," Lord Paxton replied kindly.

Smiling, she stepped over and ran her finger along the keys. "Where is Lady Paxton this morning?"

Geoffrey chuckled. "Mother is acting like a chicken with its head cut off."

Lord Paxton attempted to hide his smile. "Son, it's not nice to compare your mother to poultry. Besides, she is just overwhelmed with the upcoming house party."

"I told her to drink some chocolate and take a nap, but she wanted to go over the schedule again," Geoffrey stated lightly.

"It's good to be prepared," Morgan replied, his eyes lingering on her as she sat down on the bench.

"Come, Morgan," Geoffrey encouraged, walking towards the door. "It's best to travel to the ruins before the sun gets too high in the sky."

"Of course." Morgan approached her and asked in a hushed voice, "Will you be all right here?"

"I have a pistol and a dagger strapped to my person. I assure you I will be fine."

The corners of his mouth dipped downward. "I have no doubt that you can protect yourself, but I am more concerned about your emotional state after you practice."

Touched by his words, she gave him a grateful smile. "That's kind of you, but I will be all right."

For a brief moment, Josette thought Morgan might kiss her cheek before departing, and she found herself anticipating it. However, he gave her a curt nod, then spoke in a normal tone. "If you wish to retire to our estate when you are finished, I can always walk home."

"Nonsense," Lord Paxton said. "If Mrs. Addington chooses to leave before you return, I will gladly arrange a carriage to take you home."

"Thank you," Morgan acknowledged before he shot her a look

filled with meaning. He was worried about her.

Josette gave him an encouraging nod, confirming that she would be all right. Her eyes remained on the door long after he left the room. It warmed her heart to know that he cared for her. She frowned. She needed to be careful not to become attached to Morgan. After all, this was a mission. Nothing more.

Lord Paxton pulled her from her thoughts as he moved closer to the pianoforte. "Would it bother you terribly if I listened to you practice?"

"I would be honored," she replied. "After all, this is your estate, and I am just a guest."

Lord Paxton acknowledged her words before sitting on the settee.

As her fingers began to glide over the keys, the memory of her mother singing her a French lullaby came to her mind. She started playing the simple melody of *Au Clair de la Lune*, or the English translation, *By the Light of the Moon*. Her voice filled the room as she sang the French folk song with the same love and devotion that her mother used to.

The image of sitting on a rocking chair, cuddled in her mother's arms, listening to her mother's voice, caused her words to falter. Those memories were too painful, too raw. She removed her hands from the keys, hoping to swallow her building emotions.

Perhaps Beethoven would be best, she thought, as she returned her hands to the keys. It was safer. It would not be wise to act like a simpering female in front of Lord Paxton.

After she played a few pieces, Josette was preparing to start on another when Lord Paxton's voice interrupted her.

"Would you mind taking a break? I have something I would like to discuss with you."

"Of course," she replied, shifting her position so she faced him.

Rising, Lord Paxton stepped over and closed the door. He returned to his seat and regarded her closely. "May I be so bold as to ask what your given name is, Mrs. Addington?"

"It's Josette."

"Josette," he repeated slowly. "How are..." His voice stopped. Lord Paxton held his hand over his mouth as if to hold back his emotions, keeping his gaze firmly on her. "Where do you hail from?"

Remembering to play her role, she replied, "Leeds."

He allowed his hand to drop. "What was your surname prior to marrying?"

Surprised by his question, she recovered quickly and lied, "Denton."

Lord Paxton frowned as he watched her… no, studied her. "You don't remember me, do you?"

She shook her head, becoming uncomfortable with the intensity of his gaze. "No, but I have never been to Torquay before."

"I am not speaking of Torquay," he responded. "I'm referring to Christmases at Berkeley Hall with Lord and Lady Craven. Their little girl would serenade us for hours." He gave her a sad smile. "Yesterday, when I heard your voice drift out from the drawing room, I could scarcely believe it. Then, when I saw you …" tears welled in his eyes as he continued, "I knew it was you."

Admiration filled his voice. "You look just like your mother."

Josette caught her breath, and her eyes grew wide. She couldn't seem to formulate any response to his words, and her eyes darted towards the closed door.

"Josette," Lord Paxton said in a reassuring tone. "You have nothing to fear from me. Please believe me."

She brought her gaze back to him, surprised by the depth of compassion in his eyes.

"Where have you been these past two years?" He paused, waiting for her response. When she was not forthcoming, he pressed, "Why have you been lying about your past?"

"I'm afraid I can't answer that," she admitted solemnly.

He leaned forward in his seat, his brow furrowed as if he was sorting out a puzzle. "Did you run away to get married?"

Josette shook her head. "No, I did not." She didn't dare tell him where she had been and what she had suffered to get here.

"Is Mr. Addington a good husband to you?" His direct question was asked with an underlying meaning. He wanted to know if Morgan treated her fairly.

"He is," she answered honestly.

"Good." Lord Paxton looked confused. "May I ask why you

have not contacted your brother? He's been worried sick about you."

Startling her out of her shock, she huffed. "I think not."

"It's true," he said. "Hudson has been searching for you since the day you went missing."

Biting her tongue, she didn't want to unleash her rant about what she thought of her brother. "My brother and I had a falling out, and it was best that I left," she stated instead.

Lord Paxton gave her a baffled look. "I don't understand. If that's true, why has your brother hired Bow Street Runners to search for you," he hesitated, before adding, "discreetly, of course."

"I do not presume to know the complexities of my brother, but it's best that he does not discover that I'm here," she assured him.

"Why wouldn't you want to claim your inheritance?"

Now, it was her turn to be confused. "What inheritance?"

"You don't know?" He lifted his brow in surprise.

"Know what?"

"Your father's will stipulated that you and your living siblings have equal partnership in Craven Steelworks," Lord Paxton explained. "Were you not aware of this?"

"No, I was not." She rose and walked over to the window as she attempted to understand. "I had assumed that Hudson had inherited everything."

"He assumed that as well, but he was only entitled to the entailed properties and half of the company," he informed her. "Hudson has been running Craven Steelworks admirably, but you should be handling the business dealings together."

"If I had never claimed my inheritance, then what would have happened to it?"

"It would resort to your brother," Lord Paxton said, rising from his seat. "But that won't be the case. You are a wealthy woman."

Josette turned her back towards Lord Paxton as she fought a growing desire to seek out her brother and challenge him to a duel. It was no less than he deserved. Her own brother had sent her away to lay claim to her portion of the inheritance. She had defended him to Morgan, to *herself*, but he was a lying, conniving man.

At least, now she had a fighting chance. She may have struggled on the streets in the rookeries, but she'd risen above the squalor and torment to become stronger than she ever thought possible. He will not get away with this, she thought.

Lord Paxton came to stand next to her. "Your father and I were business partners, but we were also good mates at Oxford. I considered him a dear friend. Allow me to assist you when you go speak to Hudson."

Tears welled up in her eyes at the mention of her father. "I miss my father dearly," she whispered.

"I have no doubt, my child," he said, his words filled with love. "I can only imagine the pain you have gone through after losing your parents and Lizette so close together."

Hearing her sister's name on his lips was her undoing, and a deep sob escaped her. To her amazement, Lord Paxton stepped forward and wrapped his arms around her, holding her tight. She found herself relaxing into his arms, because she felt as if she was wrapped in her father's loving embrace.

A slamming of the door caused them to jump apart. A stone-faced Lady Paxton was watching them. "May I ask what is going on here?"

Lord Paxton looked at Josette, as if to seek permission. She nodded. He turned towards his wife and said, "Darling, this is Josette Northcott."

"The baron's daughter?" Lady Paxton asked, confused.

"Yes. This is Lord Craven's daughter," Lord Paxton confirmed.

Within moments, Josette was wrapped up in another tight embrace, but this time it was from Lady Paxton. "My dear, dear child," she murmured. She leaned back and brought her hands to cup her cheeks. "How did I miss this? You look just like your mother." Her eyes roamed her face. "Where have you been?"

Lord Paxton interjected, "She hasn't been very forthcoming about that, my dear."

Not bothering to acknowledge her husband's comment, Lady Paxton pressed on, "I haven't seen you in more than six years. You were such a gangly girl, but you have grown into an extraordinarily beautiful woman." A sad smile came to her lips. "I remember the day that you went missing. Your brother, Hudson, sent us a missive informing us that you had disappeared. In fact, he contacted all your father's friends."

Seeing the love in her eyes, Josette found herself revealing, "I didn't disappear. Hudson kicked me out."

Lady Paxton removed her hands from her face and straightened to her full height. "Nonsense! That was your home, too. Hudson had no right to do that," she declared forcefully.

"Why didn't you seek out your aunt?" Lord Paxton asked. "Or any of your friends."

Josette lowered her head in shame. "I didn't think Aunt Winnie would have wanted to see me, considering I caused Uncle Edwin's death. Furthermore, none of my friends would have received me either."

"Why would you think that?" Lady Paxton asked. "Edwin was on death's door before you even went to stay with your aunt and..." Her voice trailed off. Then, sadly she continued, "I think I understand. You must have seen the articles."

"Hudson pointed them out each morning," she shared softly.

Lord Paxton cursed under his breath. "Your brother needs to be called out for his cruel, unfeeling behavior towards you."

Reaching for her hand, Lady Paxton guided her over to the settee. "No one took those articles seriously. You are not unlucky. You just had a series of unfortunate incidents that occurred in a relatively short time."

"Hudson told me that gentlemen were placing bets at White's about who I would cause to drop dead next," Josette admitted, wincing.

Lord Paxton let out a low growl. "Your brother should have protected you..." He turned away from them, and Josette tried to hide her smile at the long list of expletives she heard him mutter under his breath.

"We will call for our solicitor immediately," Lady Paxton proclaimed. "We will get this all sorted out for you."

"No!" Josette shouted.

Lady Paxton gave her a curious look. "Why not, child? Do you not want this matter resolved quickly?"

Think, she thought. "Morgan doesn't know about my past," she confessed. "I would prefer to speak to him about this matter *after* the house party."

"Surely, Morgan will be thrilled to know that you are entitled to such a large fortune," Lord Paxton pressed.

Josette decided to be partially honest. "I informed Morgan of my parents' death, but I left out that my father was a baron." She was met with silence and shocked expressions. "I would like to tell him on my own terms, which means I would like to wait until after the house party."

Lady Paxton cast a concerned look over at her husband. "I'm afraid I don't understand your reasoning, but we will respect your choice."

"At least until after the house party," Lord Paxton said. "I am quite vexed at your brother's treatment of you."

Josette bit her lower lip. "I'm worried about Morgan's reaction when he discovers Hudson's identity."

Lord Paxton smiled at her. "Husbands can be fiercely loyal to their wives, but I can't believe that Morgan would go half-cocked on Hudson."

Stifling a laugh, she knew that is exactly what Morgan would do, because that is what she would have done if the situations were reversed.

Lady Paxton patted her hand. "Must we pretend that we don't know you?"

"I'll tell Morgan that you recognized me and are friends of my parents," she said. "But I will leave it at that."

"And he will let the matter drop?" Lord Paxton huffed disbelievingly.

No, she thought, but nodded instead. "I believe so."

"I wish things had been different." Lady Paxton smiled tenderly. "After all, you were supposed to be betrothed to our eldest son, Arthur."

Her eyes widened at this unexpected news. "Arthur?"

"We had a contract, but that matters not. You are now married, and Arthur won't ever know," Lord Paxton replied, sitting next to his wife.

Outraged, Josette asked, "Why would my parents do such a thing?"

"A parent will do just about anything to ensure that their child is well cared for," Lady Paxton said wistfully. "We thought it would be best to bind our two families together and wholeheartedly believed that you and Arthur would suit nicely."

Lord Paxton shook his head. "Water under the bridge, now."

Josette rose. "This has been a lot to take in. Would you mind if I retire to my estate?"

"Must you?" Lady Paxton asked, her voice holding a hint of a plea. "At least stay for the mid-day meal."

Lord Paxton stood up and placed his arm around her shoulder. "If you stay, I will share stories about your father at Oxford."

"How can I refuse that?" Josette smiled.

Chapter Twelve

"I will give you £20,000 if you tell me who your father was," Morgan offered as he watched Josette reach for the reticule on the table in her bedchamber. Her maroon gown fitted her body perfectly, and he found his eyes admiring her comely figure.

"We've been over this." She shook her head, causing the curls around her face to swish back and forth. "My parentage is not something I am willing to discuss."

"Let's review what I have discerned about you," Morgan mused, leaning his shoulder against the wall. "You were born into the peerage, but you don't have a title. You were raised in privilege, and your parents socialized with Lord Paxton, most likely making your father a staunch Tory as well."

"He was," she confirmed, walking closer to him. "Will you please let the matter drop? You have been talking incessantly about this since we left Lord Paxton's estate yesterday."

"I will," he smirked, "if you give me one more clue."

Josette looked frustrated as she stopped in front of him.

Morgan pushed away from the wall.

"You are a very infuriating lord." Her hands came up, unfolding his cravat and began the arduous process of retying it. "Why are your cravats always slightly askew?"

"Most likely because I tug on them." He watched as Josette focused her attention on the cravat, and he admitted to himself that he enjoyed her doing this intimate task for him. "I'm still waiting for the clue."

After she smoothed out the cravat, she brought her gaze up to meet his. "If I give you this clue, then you give me your word that you will let the matter drop?"

"I promise," he said, resisting the urge to reach out and take her into his arms.

She tilted her head and a mischievous smile came to her lips. "My father," she paused dramatically, "had a dog."

"A dog?" he repeated back. "That is the clue?"

She laughed and began backing up. "You didn't say it had to be a meaningful clue."

"That is not a clue. That is a fact," he argued in a teasing tone.

"You are a poor sport," Josette joked, mocking him with a pouting lip.

He walked purposefully towards her, maintaining her gaze. "I have been very tolerant of your errant behavior, *wife*, but you need to be taught a lesson."

"Oh, is that so?" she replied amused and continued to back away from him.

Morgan advanced towards Josette until her back was pressed up against the wall. He stopped in front of her, forcing her to tilt her head to look up at him. As he reached out and captured one of the silken brown curls that framed her face, he heard her breath hitch, causing his chest to puff out with pride.

It pleased him immensely that she was not impervious to his charms.

His eyes roamed over her olive skin and stopped to admire the sprinkling of freckles on the bridge of her nose. Josette seemed completely oblivious to her own beauty. How was that possible?

Once his gaze captured hers, there were no shadows in her expression, no fear, but her green eyes were warm and inviting. She trusted him, and it nearly brought him to his knees.

Without thinking, he leaned closer and murmured, "You are so beautiful."

Josette tensed before she stepped to the side, creating more distance between them. "We should leave for the house party," she said with a shaky breath.

Annoyed at his inability to break through all of Josette's defenses, Morgan jammed his hand through his hair. "I think that would be for the best."

She looked up at his hair and rolled her eyes. "What is the point of a valet if you mess up your hair at your first opportunity?"

He took his hand and smoothed down his hair. "Sufficient?"

Walking over to her dressing table, she picked up the brush and ordered, "Sit. I refuse to have an unkempt husband. What an embarrassment!"

He chuckled as he sat on the chair. "Noted. Disheveled hair is not permitted."

Josette brushed his hair forward before placing the brush back down on the table. "Much better."

Rising, Morgan was in a perpetual state of confusion. He could not seem to get an accurate read on Josette. One moment she seemed to flirt with him and welcome his attentions, but then she would become guarded and withdrawn. What was holding her back? It was clear that she trusted him because she allowed him to touch her. However, whenever he complimented her, she retreated as if protecting herself.

A knock came at the door. Josette walked over and opened it. He could hear a woman's voice say, "Your carriage is ready, Mrs. Addington."

"Thank you," she acknowledged as she closed the door.

She turned back towards him. "Are you ready to go to the house party and discover the identity of *Genet*?"

"I am," he confirmed as he extended his arm.

As they walked down the hall, Josette gave him a sidelong glance. "Just so you know, I am winning our wager."

"Wager?"

"We placed a wager on who could play the role of a doting spouse more convincingly. Do you not remember?"

"I do. Although, I clearly won that bet," he replied smugly.

Josette patted his arm. "It's adorable that you think so."

"No?" He smirked. "I believe the large bouquet of flowers I ordered for you definitely put me in the lead."

"Have you not noticed that custard is served every night?"

"I have. It's my favorite dessert."

"I know. That is why I asked Mrs. Hudgins to serve it," she grinned.

Morgan stopped at the top of the stairs and turned to face her. "How did you discover what my favorite dessert was?"

With a twinkle in her eye, she replied, "I am a remarkably astute woman."

He eyed her with interest. "You have piqued my curiosity."

"One always researches their opponent to gain the upper hand," she shared, smiling.

"Are we opponents?"

She shook her head. "Not anymore, but it was best to come prepared."

"How did you prepare?"

Placing her hand on the bannister, she replied over her shoulder, "I read the society page. Apparently, you are also quite fond of lavender cheesecake."

He laughed, offering his arm. "How long have you been keeping tabs on me, Josie?"

"About as long as you have, I suppose."

"Meaning?" he asked, glancing at her inquisitively.

Her eyes remained straight ahead as she replied, "On occasion, I have noticed your coach pass in front of my school."

His steps faltered, and embarrassment coursed through him. He turned to face her on the stair.

"You noticed that?"

Josette shrugged. "The school is in the rookeries. There are not many black carriages leisurely driving around on the East Side."

"Oh," he mumbled as he resumed his walk down the stairs.

He nodded at the butler as he held the door open for them. Morgan assisted her into the coach and sat on the opposite bench to face her.

"I will focus on the gentlemen at the house party, and you work on befriending the women. However, you must be on guard. *Genet* is not a man to be trifled with. He is dangerous."

She arched an eyebrow, challenging him. "Why do you assume that *Genet* is a man?"

Shifting his gaze towards the window, Morgan adjusted his jacket, attempting to avoid this awkward conversation. "Men tend to be more adept at espionage. It's a known fact."

"I disagree, Lord Morgan," Josette contended, who was now fingering a dagger in her gloved hands.

His mouth parted in surprise. "How did you retrieve your dagger so fast?" He had never seen someone who could access their weapons with such speed. It was unnerving.

Ignoring his question, she said, "We know that *Genet* would somehow discover the location of British troops and is a fan of sweets."

"Men like sweets as well," he pointed out, keeping his gaze on the dagger in her hands.

"We know that the French have used female spies before."

Leaning forward, he asked, "Why do you have your dagger out?"

Her hands quieted, but she still maintained her grip on the dagger. "I suppose it provides me comfort knowing that I can defend myself."

"Do you fear me, Josie?" he found himself asking.

She shook her head. "No, but holding my dagger provides me with comfort."

He felt his heart lurch at the sadness in her tone. Reaching out, he placed his hand over the dagger and slowly lowered it to her lap.

"I will keep you safe."

"No man fights my battles for me," she replied, her eyes flashing with determination.

Morgan lifted his hand and pointed at the dagger. "May I?"

She nodded and extended it towards him.

He ran his hand along the ivory hilt, admiring the craftsmanship. "Who gave you this dagger?"

"I took it from my father's desk," she revealed. "After my brother tossed his glass at me, I snatched it off the desk as I ran up to my room." She shifted her gaze towards the window. "I have had it near me ever since. It reminds me of what happens when one isn't strong enough to defend oneself."

"You were just sixteen years old. You should never have needed to defend yourself from your brother," he said with compassion.

Josette continued gazing out the window.

"Why haven't you confronted your brother for his behavior?"

Her eyes darted towards him in surprise.

"After all," he continued, "you are more than capable of defending yourself."

"At first, I was frightened by my brother and knew I needed to flee the house while I still could." She cast her eyes downward. "That night, I huddled in the deplorably filthy alleyway, shivering from the cold, and my brother's words kept playing in my head over and over. I suppose it's easy to believe horrible, vile things about yourself when no one is around to defend you."

He extended the dagger back towards her. "And now? Do you believe those words?"

She shook her head. "No, but I have been forced to grow up a lot since then."

"If you would like me to be there when you confront him, I would be honored to stand by your side and defend you," he expressed gently.

A small smile played on her lips. "You're just worried that I will kill him."

"I would be more than happy to do the honors," he pressed.

Taking her dagger, she slid it into the folds of her skirts. "I now know that my brother's actions were motivated by greed, and I have every intention of confronting him after this assignment."

"Does this mean you plan to rejoin Society?"

"No." She shook her head. "I will remain the headmistress of my school. I finally know where I belong."

Morgan wanted to contradict Josette and declare that she belonged with him. However, before he said something foolish, the carriage jerked to a stop in front of Lord Paxton's estate. He needed to brush aside his feelings for Josette.

It was time to catch a spy.

Morgan exited the carriage and reached his hand back to assist Josette. She placed her gloved hand in his and offered him a smile. How easy would it be to believe that this was her life? To be happily married to a ruggedly handsome lord that had a smile that made her go weak in the knees. But this was not her life. They were both acting a part. Besides, even though Morgan insisted he was not a rake, she still had some lingering reservations.

When he looked at her, Morgan made her feel like she was the most special person in his life and that her happiness mattered to him. But that was ridiculous! They hardly knew each other. This was just an assignment. He was *paying* her to pose as his wife.

As much as she tried to resist, Josette knew she was falling prey to his charms, his flattering words, and to the dimple in his left cheek that appeared when he gave her an impish grin. Those are things that she should definitely *not* notice about her partner.

Morgan leaned closer as they walked towards the main door.

"There are five exits to the exterior. Besides the front door, three in the rear and the servant's entrance." He pointed his hand towards the west side of the estate. "The stable is behind the estate and tucked into the corner of the property."

"Thank you," she murmured.

Two footmen opened the wide doors as Josette suppressed her nervousness. She could do this. The more time she spent with Morgan, the more she was afraid of letting him down. What if they didn't learn the identity of *Genet*? Would he blame her for the failure?

Stopping in the entry hall, Morgan cast her a questioning look before asking, "Why are you nervous?"

Her eyes grew wide as she glanced at him. "How did you know I was nervous?"

"I'm a spy, remember," he teased, smirking.

His words had a calming effect on her, and she found herself returning his smile.

Lady Paxton's voice came from the far side of the hall. "Welcome, Mr. and Mrs. Addington." She came closer and embraced her. "I am so glad that you are here, Josette." Stepping back, Lady Paxton regarded Morgan with the same kindness she had bestowed upon Josette. "I am so pleased that you are our neighbors." Her voice hitched and tears came to her eyes. "Thank you for choosing Torquay to live, Mr. Addington.

Morgan's lips twitched, but his face remained impassive. "We are grateful for your kindness and for the invitation to your house party."

Lady Paxton waved a hand in front of her, dismissing his

comment. "You are always welcome in our home. *Always.*" She turned to walked towards the drawing room. "Please follow me. You are the last guests to arrive."

"I apologize if we caused the festivities to be delayed," Josette said, keeping pace with her.

"You're right on time," Lady Paxton assured her. "The ship arrived earlier than expected. Apparently, the sailing conditions were excellent."

As Lady Paxton stepped into the drawing room, the noise died down and everyone turned their expectant faces towards their hostess. "Our dear neighbors, Mr. and Mrs. Addington have just arrived. Please allow me to provide the introductions."

Extending her hand towards a middle-aged couple, Lady Paxton shared, "This is Mr. and Mrs. Michael Perier."

Josette curtsied and murmured, "It is a pleasure to meet you." Mr. Perier was tall, had a receding hair line, and his eyes were sharp. Whereas his wife was short, had grey hair, and appeared bored.

Lady Paxton opened her mouth to introduce the next couple, but the gentleman stepped forward, speaking in a delightfully thick French accent.

"My name is Mr. Antoine Clemens," he paused and pointed his hand towards a woman with a large pair of spectacles on her nose, "and this is my sister, Miss Adalyn Clemens."

Miss Clemens gave her a cordial smile, but it didn't reach her eyes. "It's nice to meet you, Mr. and Mrs. Addington," she said, her French accent barely discernable.

Moving her gaze towards the men next to Miss Clemens, Josette saw two handsome gentlemen with dark brown hair, pointed noses, and strong jaws. The first man bowed in her direction, but not before she saw him brazenly perusing the length of her body.

"My name is Christophe Mancini, Madame," he stated in a smooth tone.

The other man stepped forward and bowed, his movements exaggerated. "And I am the much handsomer, younger brother, Gaspard Mancini," he shared, offering her a private wink.

Despite finding their blatant flirtation amusing, Josette heard a low growl come from the back of Morgan's throat. She shifted her gaze towards him and saw that his jaw was clenched so tight that a muscle pulsated below his ear. He couldn't possibly be jealous. Could he?

She hoped to diffuse the situation by tucking her hand into the crook of his arm. "My *husband* and I are pleased to meet you." After she said her words, she could feel the tension drain from Morgan's frame.

Lady Paxton spoke up as she pointed towards an older gentleman and a young woman who had stepped forward. "To round out the introductions, please allow me to introduce you to Mr. Lemaure, and his daughter, Miss Ernestine Lemaure."

A portly, white-haired Mr. Lemaure acknowledged them with a bob of his head. However, his beautiful, blonde-haired daughter, with expressive eyes and a pointed chin, was not as subtle. Keeping her piercing gaze on Morgan, she curtsied low, offering him a coy smile.

Resisting the feeling of jealousy that welled up inside of her, Josette tilted her head and replied, "It is a pleasure to meet you, Mr. Lemaure, and your lovely daughter." She was pleased that her voice sounded relatively calm.

Lady Paxton smiled at the group. "You have all traveled a great distance," she glanced their way, "except for our neighbors who live on the next hill. If you will adjourn to the entry hall, the maids will show you to your rooms. Feel free to lay down and rest before you dress for dinner."

Geoffrey's jovial voice came from the doorway. "For any of the gentlemen who don't require time to rest, please join my father and I in the billiard room."

Morgan turned towards her, giving her his full attention. "Do you mind if I join the men?"

She smiled up at him, skillfully acting like a dutiful wife. "Not at all. I will adjourn to our room and rest," she said, even though she had no intention of spending her time in her bedchamber.

He leaned closer, his lips brushing against her ear, causing her to shudder with delight. "Good luck, my dear." Due to his nearness, and his warm breath on her skin, Josette found she couldn't formulate a response. His hands came up to gently rest on her shoulders. "I'm enjoying this temperate side of you."

"Don't get used to it," she replied, immensely pleased that she found her voice again.

She offered him a parting smile as she hurried to catch up to the other women.

Chapter Thirteen

Josette opened her bedchamber door and peered out into the hall to ensure it was empty. When the young maid, Suzanne, showed her to her assigned guest bedchamber, she had been sure to inquire who was staying in each room. Armed with that information, she decided to search the men's rooms first.

Josette kept her feet light on the carpet as she walked down the hall to Mr. Lemaure's room. She looked both ways to ensure no one was watching. Placing her hand on the handle, she slipped inside the door.

The room layout was similar to hers with a large four poster bed against the wall opposite a fireplace. The window was open, and the curtains were blowing in the wind. Her eyes scanned the room, focusing on the small round table and writing desk, but nothing was stacked on them. Walking over to the bed, she placed her hand under the pillow and mattress but found nothing.

An unopened trunk sat against the wall, but an iron lock held it closed. Not deterred, she knelt in front of the trunk and pulled two pins out of her hair. She picked the lock with careful precision and opened the lid.

Being careful to return everything to its precise location, she started rummaging through his clothing and personal effects. Tucked between shirts were two pistols and a velvet bag filled with coins. She continued to search through the trunks but found nothing that would arouse suspicion.

Josette had just locked the trunk when she noticed the door handle slowly starting to turn. Quickly, she dove under the bed. A pair of men's black shiny Hessian boots came into view as the person started walking around the room. Stopping at the trunk, she heard the man reach for the lock, but within moments it dropped to the floor.

The trunk was opened, and the man started searching through the items. She had to find the identity of that man searching Mr. Lemaure's room! With slow, deliberate movements she moved until she could peek out and saw a man with dark brown hair, wearing a black jacket. From the back, it appeared to be one of the Mancini brothers. However, she couldn't discern whether it was Christophe or Gaspard, and she didn't dare risk becoming more exposed.

Mr. Mancini let out a deep sigh as he organized the items and locked the trunk. Standing up, he strode out of the room without any sign of hesitation.

Josette waited for a few moments before she came out from under the bed and approached the door. Why would one of the Mancini brothers want to search Mr. Lemaure's room? What was he hoping to find?

She exited the room and walked down the empty hall to Mr. Antoine Clemens's room. She lightly tapped the door before pushing it open and closing it behind her. Again, nothing was out in the open, and she walked over to the bed. She ran her hand under the pillow and found nothing. However, as she placed her hand between the mattress and iron frame, she felt a stack of papers. Pulling them out, she saw that they were letters, bound by string.

Untying the string, Josette placed the stack of letters on the bed and unfolded the first missive. It was written by Mr. Blount. He was requesting additional funds to produce more pamphlets. As she poured through all the letters written by Mr. Blount, it was clear that the rebels were building up to something, but no specifics were mentioned. Nor were there any return letters from *Genet*. She found herself wondering if this was enough evidence to prove Mr. Antoine Clemens was the French spy, *Genet*? Or, did he just help finance the rebel groups?

Returning the letters to their original location, she stepped to the unlocked trunk and opened it. In the bottom corner, there were small, worn books. She picked up the first one and read the title, *New System of Chemical Philosophy*, by John Dalton. She had read this one. At least Antoine had good taste when it came to reading material. Opening to the front page, she realized that she did not see any familiar words, but it was written in a language she was not familiar with. She opened the other books, but they appeared to be untampered with. *Interesting.*

Closing the trunk, Josette slipped out of Mr. Clemen's room and started walking down the hall. She didn't dare search Christophe or Gaspard's room since she didn't know which one she had seen previously. As she walked towards the drawing room to practice the pianoforte, she turned the corner and saw Miss Adalyn Clemens standing at Lord Paxton's study door.

Adalyn glanced over and relief washed over her face. "Do you know how to get into the library?" She placed her hand on the door handle, but it wouldn't budge. "It's locked."

Josette smiled. "The library is further down the hall. You are trying to break into Lord Paxton's study."

"Good heavens," Adalyn declared as she withdrew her hand quickly. "I do not wish Lord Paxton to think ill of me. I was tired of resting, and I was hoping to find a book to occupy me until dinner.

"Would you like me to show you to the library?"

Adalyn nodded as she pushed her spectacles further up on her nose. "Yes, please."

Josette started down the hall, and Adalyn walked next to her. "How are you enjoying your trip to England?"

Glancing over at her, Adalyn replied, "It feels like coming home to me. I worked as a governess for a family in London for almost six years."

"How old are you?" Realizing the bluntness of her question, Josette started to apologize, "Please forgive me. I have no right…"

Adalyn put her hand up and smiled. "It's all right. I am twenty-nine. As you would say in England, I'm a spinster."

"I did notice your French accent wasn't as thick as your brother's."

Adalyn let out an exasperated sigh. "Antoine intentionally thickens his accent when beautiful women are present. It's quite maddening."

"Why are you traveling with your brother, then?"

Adalyn kept her eyes on the large portraits as they walked down the hall, delaying her responses. "After my employment as a governess ended, I couldn't find another position that was lucrative. Sadly, many members of the gentry are interested in obtaining a governess for their children, but do not wish to pay more than a beggar's salary."

Adalyn stopped and looked up at the portrait of a young mother surrounded by her children. A wistful look crossed her face before she resumed her story. "After I returned to France, I leapt at the chance to accompany my brother to England. Even if it meant that I had to endure his presence for four whole days."

They had just stepped into the library when Josette asked, "I take it that you and your brother are not close?"

"Heavens, no," Adalyn replied. "As the heir, my brother inherited a fortune, two large estates, and a sister that he considers a burden." Her eyes lit up with excitement as she looked at the stacks of books neatly arranged on the shelves.

Josette took a moment to observe Adalyn, undetected. It was hard to miss the long strands of light brown hair that had come untucked from her messy chignon and hung down the length of her back. She had an oval face, a straight nose, and deep-set eyes, but the large, round spectacles distracted from her beauty.

Feeling a connection with her, Josette shared, "My brother and I aren't close, either."

Adalyn turned her gaze back towards her, and her eyes reflected sadness. "My brother and I were close growing up. Sadly, we have drifted apart. He is focused on work, chasing women, and radical reform. Whereas I..." she sighed, "am content to be alone with a good book."

Walking over to a shelf, Josette's eyes skimmed the titles of the books as she admitted, "Books are my escape as well. I love learning new things, pondering philosophies and questioning why things are a certain way."

Adalyn reached up and removed a book from the shelf that housed scientific books. "Unfortunately, we are just women. We don't have a right to enact change."

"I disagree," Josette expressed. "If we don't stand up for change, then who will?"

With a sad smile on her lips, Adalyn pressed the worn green book with gold writing against her chest. "I'm the opposite. I do not wish to cause a ruckus, and I prefer to be a wallflower."

Josette glanced at the floor clock and noticed the late hour. "It's time for me to dress for dinner. Would you like me to escort you back to your room?"

Adalyn shook her head. "No, I will find my way back. Thank you."

Nodding graciously, Josette turned and started walking back towards her bedchamber. She couldn't help but feel bad for Adalyn, who appeared timid and disheveled. Perhaps she could spend more time with her and help strengthen her. Maybe she could teach her to stand up to her brother?

She laughed at her musings. It would be good practice for her, as well.

Morgan shrugged on his dinner jacket and revealed, "Nothing of importance happened when we played billiards."

Josette sat on the settee, facing away from him as he dressed for dinner. "Nothing was discussed?"

He took a moment to adjust his sleeves, not wanting to reveal that all the men had fawned over how beautiful Josette was, declaring him the luckiest man alive.

"Just the usual topics of hunting and shooting," he replied.

"I was able to search Mr. Lemaure's room and found nothing that would implicate him as a French spy," she informed him. "However, in Mr. Antoine Clemens's room, I found letters from Mr. Blount."

Now she had his full attention. "What did they say?"

"Mostly, they asked for additional funds and provided updates about the rebels and their propaganda."

"You may turn around now," he stated, reaching up to tie his cravat.

Josette turned in her seat and faced him. "I also ran into Mr. Clemens's sister, Adalyn, in the hall. She seems a little absentminded."

"How so?" he asked, intentionally ruining his first attempt at tying his cravat.

With an amused smile, Josette rose and walked over to him, stopping in front of him. "Allow me," she said, bringing her hands up to his cravat. "As I was saying, Adalyn mistook the locked study for the library, she would become distracted when we were chatting, and I fear those spectacles are too heavy for her face."

He chuckled. "Do you think Adalyn is spying alongside her brother?"

She shook her head. "No, I don't believe Adalyn is interested in politics or social reform. Even the book she grabbed today was sorted amongst the scientific section of books."

"How did you know the layout of the..." He stopped. "Never mind. Do you think Mr. Clemens could be *Genet*?"

A crease appeared in her brow as she finished tying his cravat. "It's possible. Not only did he have letters from Mr. Blount in his possession, but I believe that book held codes." Instead of stepping back, she ran her hands along his shoulders. "There. Now you look handsome."

Meeting her gaze, he asked a question that had plagued his thoughts. "Do you find me handsome, Josie?"

In response, her eyes grew wide and a deep blush spread to her cheeks. "I... um ..." She turned her head towards the door. "It's time for us to go down to dinner."

Bringing his hand up, he captured her chin with his fingers, bringing her gaze back to his. "Not until you answer my question."

Her lips pressed tightly together before he heard her mutter, "I do. Satisfied?"

Oh, he was satisfied. Elated, even. He had been called handsome by many women over the years, but no one's opinion mattered as much as Josette's did. Morgan lowered his eyes to the coral necklace that hung around her neck and reached up to touch the cool stones. "You are still wearing the necklace I gave you."

"It's the only necklace I own."

He heard her voice tremble as she spoke. He snapped his gaze back up to hers. "I thought you took your mother's jewelry when you left your brother's house?"

A look of sadness came to her eyes. "I had to sell them for food," she responded reluctantly.

"All of them?"

"Yes," she confessed, a tear leaking out of her right eye.

He captured the tear on her cheek with his finger. "If you were my wife, I would shower you with jewels."

She tilted her chin before saying, "I wouldn't want jewels."

"What would you want?" His voice was hoarse.

"I would want a husband that would love me above all else. Someone that would be true, kind, and allow me to capture his heart. Not a part of it, but his full heart," she confessed.

He stepped closer, so no distance was between them. "Does this mean you might one day consider courting?" he asked nervously.

Her eyes sparked with vulnerability. "I have been betrayed so many times. I believe that's what is holding me back. If the man I truly loved betrayed me, I don't think I would have the strength to go on."

He gently cupped her right cheek. "Would you be willing to take a chance on me?"

Her face crumpled. "Please don't ask me that, Morgan."

"I have enjoyed spending time with you, and I think we would suit," he pressed.

Stepping back out of his arms, she shook her head. "This is a ruse. We are only pretending to be married," she said, her tone deflated. "You're confused."

He took a step closer to her, but she stepped back and put her hand up. "This is not the time to discuss these matters. We are here to catch a French spy, not to see if we suit," she expressed, her voice turning sarcastic near the end.

Watching her closely, Morgan knew he had pushed her too far. Josette did not like to be caught off-guard or put in a vulnerable position. "All right," he conceded. "But when the mission is over, I hope to revisit this conversation."

A minute smile touched her lips. "By the end of the mission you might discover you find me intolerable, my lord."

Never, he wanted to say. Instead, he returned her smile, hiding behind the mask he wore so well. "Or you may find yourself deeply in love with me."

He could see her spine straighten. "I believe I told you that I would not be foolish enough to fall in love with you."

"We'll see," he remarked smugly, walking past her towards the door.

Josette met him at the door and replied, "I am surprised your head hasn't fallen to the ground with such a large ego to bear."

He placed his hand on the handle. "Are you finished?" he asked, giving her a knowing look. "Once I open this door, we have to pretend to be a *loving* married couple."

She tapped her finger against her lips. Her mouth parted as a twinkle came to her eye. "Your ego is so large that your head can't fit into certain rooms."

He gave her a disapproving head shake. "That was awful."

"I know," she admitted. "It wasn't one of my finer insults, but I will think of better ones over dinner."

"See that you do." Morgan opened the door and waited for Josette to walk through before saying, "Frankly, I am embarrassed for you."

She laughed as her alert eyes scanned the length of the hall. "We still need to search the remainder of the rooms tonight, if possible."

Morgan nodded. "I agree. Perhaps you could serenade the group longer tonight?"

"That could work," she replied. "I know just the opera."

Offering his arm, they walked towards the large staircase. He looked over and admired her green gown with embroidered flowers and rounded neckline. Even though she dressed in the finest gowns, he was quite confident that she would look breathtaking even in a shapeless frock.

"You look beautiful tonight, Josie," he said as they took their first step onto the stairs.

Rather than stiffen, she looked at him and replied, "Thank you."

He stopped and shifted his body towards her. "Did you just accept a compliment?" he asked, feigning shock.

She swatted playfully at his chest. "You are being overdramatic."

Continuing down the stairs, he kept teasing her, knowing he always wanted to make her smile.

As they entered the drawing room, Adalyn waved at Josette and broke off from Miss Lemaure and Mrs. Perier. She headed straight for them, stopping next to Josette. "Thank goodness you are here. If I am forced to comment one more time on the nice weather we are having, I fear that I might literally go mad."

Josette smiled. "Polite conversation can be rather dull."

"Mr. Addington, it is good to see you here," Mr. Blount said, drawing his attention.

What's he doing here, Morgan wondered. "Mr. Blount, what a pleasant surprise. I didn't realize you'd been invited." He smiled politely.

Geoffrey came to stand next to Mr. Blount. "I invited him. I am hoping to convince my father that his views are archaic. Regardless, Mr. Blount will help round out the lively debate."

Adalyn leaned closer to Josette and whispered, "I hope not around the women. I fear that my delicate constitution could not take such political banter. It's so unsavory."

Josette laughed with a most unladylike snort and covered it with her gloved hand.

Mr. Blount's eyes lewdly perused Josette's frame, focusing a considerable amount of time on her neckline, and Morgan had the urge to beat the man for even daring to look at her. His whole body tensed, and Josette cast him a worried look.

Turning her gaze towards Geoffrey, Josette's voice was low as she asked, "Where did your mother find a place for Mr. Blount? I have to assume that she became a bit flustered by yet another unplanned guest."

In response, Geoffrey nodded. "It's true. I had to convince my mother to open the east wing to accommodate Mr. Blount."

With a coy grin, Josette looked at Mr. Blount. "Won't you be frightened sleeping all by yourself?"

Mr. Blount returned her smile, causing Morgan's blood to boil. "I am the first room in the east wing, facing the courtyard. Perhaps I won't have to sleep alone tonight," he suggested boldly.

Morgan's hands balled into fists. Then he felt Josette's gloved right hand encompass his. With no resistance on his part, she intertwined their fingers. He immediately felt the tension drain from his body. He was elated by her intimate gesture. How was it possible that her touch affected him to such a degree?

At that moment, Lady Paxton stepped into the room and announced dinner.

As everyone lined up, Morgan continued to hold Josette's hand. He had no desire to relinquish his hold on her... now or ever. They followed the group in silence across the expansive hall. Just before they entered the dining room, he brought their hands up and pressed a quick kiss to her knuckles. "Thank you," he mouthed to her.

After assisting Josette into her seat, Morgan sat down, and waited as the first course was served. Most of the conversation centered around hunting, fishing and other polite discussions. When Mrs. Perier brought up the nice weather, he saw Adalyn turn towards Josette and roll her eyes.

Addressing Lord Paxton, Mr. Gaspard Mancini asked, "Will you be in attendance when King Louis addresses both houses of Parliament in the House of Lords?"

Lord Paxton brought his linen napkin up and wiped the sides of his mouth. "Sadly, my wife had already sent out the invitations for this house party before I received the missive about the special assembly." He smiled regretfully. "It's truly a shame, since it is a rare privilege for a foreign leader to address both houses."

"Will the building be ready for the French king?" Geoffrey asked.

Lord Paxton huffed, amused. "It depends on your definition of 'ready'."

"Is the House of Lords under construction?" Morgan asked as he reached for his glass.

"It is perpetually under construction it seems, as are the rest of the buildings that make up the Palace of Westminster," Lord Paxton shared.

Lady Paxton smiled approvingly at her husband. "The prince regent has great confidence in my husband's ability to restore the Palace of Westminster to its former glory."

Mr. Christophe Mancini chuckled dryly. "I have heard that it's a disheveled old stone hall overlooking an untidy yard. That is hardly a venue befitting the King of France's visit."

"Maybe on the exterior, but the interior speaks of a rich history of a strong, loyal people," Miss Clemens expressed in a timid voice.

Her brother cast her a frustrated look. "How would you know, Adalyn?"

"I have toured the Queen's Chamber, as it was previously known, and the ceiling has a vast, clear space unobstructed by a single column. It is an architectural wonder, if you ask me," Adalyn stated, her voice gaining more confidence. "I apologize for my enthusiasm. I am fascinated by architecture."

"You and Lord Paxton have something in common," Lady Paxton said. "Lord Paxton would rather spend time looking at architectural drawings than anything else."

Miss Clemens sat straighter in her chair as she directed her next question to Lord Paxton. "Do you have the architectural drawings for the Palace of Westminster here?"

"I do, but I am afraid it is impossible for you to see them," Lord Paxton revealed.

Pushing back her glasses, Adalyn responded, "I understand."

"When I was shopping near Westminster abbey, I noticed the House of Lords' roof going through a renovation," Josette commented.

Lord Paxton nodded. "That's right. Furthermore, the prince regent tasked my team with finding a way to minimize the cost of replacing the lead that coated the roof and replacing it with Westmorland slates."

"I take it that you were successful," Morgan remarked.

"We were," Lord Paxton answered proudly. "To finance part of the roof's renovation, we sold off the lead, all one hundred and seventy-six tons of it, which also greatly reduced the pressure on the interior beams."

"How much longer will the roof take to complete?" Mr. Perier asked before taking a sip of his drink.

"Unfortunately, when the lead was removed, it revealed a more extensive decay than anticipated in the wood," Lord Paxton explained. "It could take years for this project to be completed, assuming the funds are forthcoming from the treasury department."

Mr. Blount held his glass in his hand. "It is a shame that England spent so much money on the war against France rather than use that money to help stimulate the British economy."

Morgan caught the tightness around Lord Paxton's mouth before he pushed back his chair and rose. "There are women present, Mr. Blount. We will debate this over a glass of port."

Morgan rose and assisted Josette. Leaning closer, he whispered, "Thank you for discovering which room Mr. Blount is staying in."

"You are welcome, husband." She flashed him a smile. "Go enjoy your time with the men."

Chapter Fourteen

Following the men to a room off the dining room, Morgan sat down on a brown leather sofa and accepted a glass of port from Lord Paxton.

Once all the men were seated and had a drink in their hand, Lord Paxton sat down next to him.

"Are you enjoying yourself, Morgan?"

He took a sip of his drink. "I am."

Lord Paxton smiled approvingly. "Where do you hail from?"

"Nottingham," he lied.

"Mr. Addington, how do you feel about the King of France addressing a joint session of Parliament?" Mr. Blount inquired.

Lowering his glass until it rested on the armrest of the sofa, Morgan replied, "I believe it's a great honor that the King of France is willing to travel to England to thank both houses for the support they extended during the Napoleonic Wars."

Lord Paxton nodded his agreement. "Before he was king, Louis lived in Britain for seven years, and Prinny grew close to the Bourbons. King Louis has even been the prince regent's guest of honor for many state ceremonies."

"If I recall correctly, King Louis was elected a member of the Most Noble Order of the Garter and given a knighthood," Gaspard Mancini stated.

"That's right," Lord Paxton replied, taking a sip of his drink.

"Who paid for King Louis to live in Britain?" Geoffrey asked in defiance. "Did the prince regent? No! The people paid an annual pension to him and his family."

"France is grateful for the hospitality that was shown our king and his family during their exile," Mr. Christophe Mancini diplomatically said.

"You British are fools to support the restoration of the Bourbon rule," Mr. Clemens scoffed. "There were good reasons the Bourbons were exiled, killed, or cast aside."

"Per his promise," Mr. Perier observed, leaning forward, "King Louis has not attempted to recover lands and property taken from the royalist exiles."

"And he has continued many of Napoleon's foreign policies, including the limitation of Austrian influence," Mr. Lemaure pointed out.

Gaspard rose and walked to the drink tray. "In addition, King Louis acts under a constitutional monarchy, meaning he acts in accordance with the written French constitution, not against it."

It was Mr. Blount's turn to scoff. "When has a monarchy ever *not* tried to exert more power from the people? It's only a matter of time until he lies and cheats his way back to an absolute monarchy."

Placing his arm on the back of the settee, Christophe shook his head in disapproval. "Would you rather have had Napoleon's son, a mere infant, rule France?"

"No," Mr. Blount replied. "It's only a matter of time until Napoleon rises up and claims his country."

"*His* country? Do you actually believe that Napoleon will escape the isle of Elba?" Gaspard asked with an uplifted brow.

"I have no doubt," Mr. Blount exclaimed, holding up his glass.

Geoffrey leaned forward in his seat. "There are growing movements in and around London, and these don't include the riots and protests that continually break out amongst the people. Every day, women and children are dying on the streets in the East Side. They are being denied proper housing, food, and medical care. We must help these people. Yet, our prince regent is spending the people's money on lavish estates, mistresses, and on scandalous costume balls."

"Son, I do not disagree that these people need to be helped, but it's not that simple," Lord Paxton attempted to explain.

"It is that simple, Father!" Geoffrey shouted. "The power should belong to the people, and we should have the right to remove a monarch that has abused his authority."

Lord Paxton placed his drink on the table next to him. "Whigs and their philosophies border on treason."

Geoffrey jumped up from his seat in outrage. "You are wrong. How is supporting free trade and the abolition of slavery treason?"

"Slave trading is a felony punishable by transportation. Those who are convicted are exiled to Australia!" Lord Paxton contested hotly.

"Only in the British empire," Mr. Blount interjected. "What about the land owners in the British West Indies who own slaves?"

"Then who would labor in their fields?" Lord Paxton pressed.

"Geoffrey, you mentioned growing movements in London. What are they protesting exactly?" Gaspard asked, walking back to his seat next to his brother.

"It is not just in London, but all over England," Geoffrey shared. "An uprising is coming. A king cannot suppress a nation, continue to increase the national debt, and not expect to be held accountable."

"You are a fool, son. If there is an uprising, it will be squashed, and the perpetrators will be punished." Lord Paxton rose swiftly, disappointment in his features. "Enough talk. It is time we join the ladies and end this night on a positive note."

After Lord Paxton walked out, the other guests followed him. However, when Morgan approached the door, Geoffrey grabbed his arm. "What do you believe?"

Morgan critically eyed Mr. Blount, who stood nearby watching their interaction. He wanted to grab Geoffrey and shake some sense into him, but instead he opted to say, "I side with the people."

Geoffrey dropped his arm. "If only my father realized that Tories are holding Britain back."

"Don't worry. He will see soon enough," Mr. Blount said with a twisted smile.

Nodding briefly to each man, Morgan turned to leave the room. Mr. Blount was up to something, but what?

When the men joined the ladies in the drawing room, Morgan claimed the seat next to Josette on the settee in the back of the room. He slipped his arm around her shoulder. "Did you miss me, my love?"

Josette leaned into him. "Always," she replied with a smile.

How he wished her words were in earnest. He would give everything he had to lay claim to Josette's heart. Would he ever win it? His heart ached knowing she might never return his feelings.

Lady Paxton rose from the front of the room and announced, "For this evening, I would like to invite each lady to perform. You may play the pianoforte, sing a song, or a recite a poem." She turned her attention towards Miss Clemens. "Would you like to go first?"

Miss Clemens rose courteously from a chair next to Josette. "Thank you for this honor. I would like to perform on the pianoforte," she informed the group as she stepped to the instrument. After playing, she curtsied and returned to her seat.

Josette leaned towards her and whispered, "Well done."

"Apparently, my parents did not waste their money on my lessons," she teased, pushing up her glasses.

Mrs. Perier was next, and she recited a long, drawn-out poem, eliciting yawns from several members of the audience. Clearly, there was no way that she could be a spy unless her job was to bore people into compliance.

Before Mrs. Perier returned to her seat, Miss Lemaure rose enthusiastically and walked to the pianoforte. "I would like to sing, but I require accompaniment."

"What piece do you wish to perform?" Lady Paxton asked.

"A French opera, known as *Medee*, by Luigi Cherubini," Ernestine replied, placing her hand on the pianoforte. "Although, I doubt anyone in this room is familiar with that opera."

Turning towards Josette, Lady Paxton inquired with an inquisitive gaze, "Mrs. Addington, are you familiar with that opera?"

"Indeed, I am, my lady," Josette replied, rising from her seat.

Miss Lemaure removed her hand from the instrument with a smug smile on her lips. Once Josette was situated on the pianoforte, she acknowledged the song that Ernestine requested and started playing the melody. Once the first note was sung, Morgan noticed that Josette began playing the pianoforte louder, thankfully drowning out the horrible screeching that came from Ernestine. She was terrible! What a cruel trick of a parent to tell their child they had talent, when it was so evident that they did not.

As the last note was played, Mr. Lemaure jumped up and started clapping profusely while the other members of the audience kept their gazes downward and away from Ernestine. Smiling, she curtsied, seeming oblivious to the reactions of the other guests.

Lady Paxton rose from her seat and escorted Ernestine back to her chair. "That was… a unique experience, Miss Lemaure." Clasping her hands in front of her, she announced, "We now have the privilege of hearing from Mrs. Addington."

Josette rose from her seat at the pianoforte and addressed the group. "If it is permissible, I would like to sing more than one song from the opera *Fidelio*, by Beethoven."

Lady Paxton smiled approvingly. "Of course, it is. Sing the whole opera, if you would like."

Josette returned to the bench and began playing. When she sang her first note, Morgan glanced around the room and saw the other guests staring at her in amazement. Why was her voice so magnificent? He had heard some of the greatest sopranos perform, and yet their voices didn't hold him transfixed as Josette's did. Her voice carried pain and sorrow, but somehow, it also yielded hope.

Rising, he carefully moved the short distance to the door, being mindful not to attract attention. Once in the hall, he saw maids and footmen lined up to listen to Josette perform.

In haste, he headed up the stairs and towards the east wing. Finding the first door on the left, he opened it, surprised that it was not locked. He walked further into the room, and his eyes took in the surroundings. Except for a satchel on the bed, and a book on the side table, nothing appeared amiss.

Stepping to the bed, he searched under the pillows, but found nothing. He laid on the ground and looked under the bed, then lifted the Persian carpet off the ground to see if anything was hidden. There was nothing in this room that connected Mr. Blount to *Genet*.

He stifled a groan. Maybe *Genet* didn't come after all? His eyes scanned the room one last time, and his gazed landed on the book on the table. It seemed odd that Mr. Blount only brought a satchel, but he had packed a book. Striding towards the table, he picked up the green volume with yellow piping. Opening the book, he read the title, *The Sceptical Chymist: or Chymico-Physical Doubts & Paradoxes*, by Robert Boyle.

He started skimming through the pages and a piece of paper fell to the ground. Picking it up, he glanced at it, but didn't recognize the words and assumed it must be coded. He placed the book down, went over to the writing desk and grabbed a small sheet of paper. After using the quill to copy the note, he placed the original missive back in the book.

Morgan went to the door and peered out into the hall. After ensuring it was clear, he walked out and closed the door behind him. He decided to take the opportunity to search Christophe and Gaspard's rooms as well, but that search failed to turn up another lead.

His search had taken longer than anticipated, so he decided to wait for Josette in their bedchamber. Opening his door, he walked in but stopped when he saw Miss Lemaure sitting on the bed, her dress pulled down to expose her shoulders.

Glancing back into the hallway, he thankfully did not see anyone. He closed the door and asked in an irate tone, "Why are you in my room?"

Ernestine rose from her position on the bed. "I saw that you left the party early, and I was hoping to keep you company."

"You need to leave, now!" he ordered, placing his hand on the handle.

A pout came to her lips as she suggestively walked over to him. "I was hoping we could become better acquainted."

She stopped in front of him and reached to place her hand on his sleeve. Immediately, he stepped far out of her reach. "I am a happily married man, Miss Lemaure. Whatever you are suggesting, I am not interested."

Instead of taking the hint, she took her hands and moved her dress lower on her arms. "Are you sure I cannot tempt you?"

He kept his eyes on her face, and his tone took on a stern edge. "Dress yourself and leave this room. *Immediately.*"

Huffing, Ernestine was adjusting her dress when the door was opened and bumped up against her. "Oh, excuse me…" Josette started to say, but her voice stopped when she saw him. Her eyes held uncertainty coupled with pain. She turned to leave but stopped and spun back around. "What is going on here?" she demanded.

Morgan placed his hand on the door, opening it further. "Miss Lemaure is just leaving."

"Yes," Ernestine mumbled as she moved around Josette and out into the hall.

Josette walked further into the room, and Morgan closed the door. Expecting her to rail at him, he was shocked when she asked, "Was I convincing enough?"

"Pardon?"

"Did I play the part of a jealous wife proficiently?"

He just stared at her. "You were only *acting* upset?"

She waved her hand dismissively. "We are not truly married. You do not need to explain yourself to me."

Morgan rubbed the side of his face, unsure of how to answer. Was she not upset that he was found in a compromising position with another woman? "I thought you would be furious."

"Why would I?" she asked, her voice becoming strained. "You are *paying* me to play the role of your wife after all."

"Josie, please—"

She cut him off. "Did you discover anything in Mr. Blount's room?" He couldn't help but notice that her voice was void of all emotion.

"I did." He reached into his waistcoat, pulled out the piece of paper, and approached her. When he stopped in front of her, she took two steps back, creating more distance between them. "I found this," he said, extending it towards her. "I believe it is a coded message."

She accepted the paper and the crease between her brows appeared. "I have seen these words before," she revealed, bringing her gaze back up to his. "I found a book in Mr. Antoine Clemens's room, and I thought perhaps it was a language I was unfamiliar with. Perhaps it's a code book."

"It could be. Also, I found that note in a chemistry book."

She gave him a curious look. "What color was the book?"

Morgan took a step closer to her, and Josette sat down on the bed. "It had a green cover and gold piping," he revealed.

She pressed her lips together. "That could have been the book that I saw Adalyn holding in the library."

Untying his cravat, he asked, "Are we under the assumption that Adalyn and her brother are both working with Mr. Blount?"

"I don't believe Adalyn is associated with this uprising," Josette replied. "For all intents and purposes, Antoine and Adalyn do not appear to get along. She even left France to work as a governess for six years to avoid her brother. I can't imagine them working together, at least willingly."

"Good point," Morgan said, removing his dress jacket and draping it over the back of the settee. "We can search Antoine's room again with the coded message and see if we can decipher it."

Josette rose from the bed and smoothed out her gown. "That sounds like a plan."

"Would you like me to call for a maid to help you undress?" Morgan asked.

She shook her head. "No, thank you."

"Do you intend to sleep in your gown?" He gave her a roguish smile. "Or would you prefer my assistance?"

Ignoring his comment, she walked over towards the window, opened it and leaned out. "I plan to sleep outside tonight," she announced.

"Don't be ridiculous," he declared, taking commanding steps towards her.

In a swift motion, she removed her dagger, spun around, and held it out in front of her. "Stay back, Lord Morgan."

He stopped and placed his hands in front of him. "You are clearly upset about earlier," he started, "but nothing happened between Miss Lemaure and me. I came into the room , and she was waiting for me."

Lowering her dagger to her side, Josette's bottom lip trembled. "We are not married. You are free to do as you please." Her words were filled with anguish.

"You must believe me," he said, taking a step closer, "nothing happened."

She turned her gaze out the window, and Morgan could see the indecision flicker across her face. He could tell that she wanted to believe him, but he knew she was fighting a battle within herself.

Her eyes became guarded, and Morgan knew he had come out the loser. Placing her hand on the sill, she exited the window in expert precision.

"Wait!" Morgan shouted, crossing the room in a few strides. He reached for her hand on the sill. "Don't go," he pleaded.

Josette's stare was unrelenting. "Unhand me," she warned.

Not releasing her hand, he tried again. "At least let me be the one to sleep outside."

"You need not concern yourself with my well-being," she replied, yanking her hand back.

Before he could say another word, Morgan watched as Josette scaled down the wall proficiently. It appeared that her gown did not encumber her in the least, and she landed gracefully in the courtyard. She ran towards the cover of the trees, disappearing into the night, without so much as a backward glance.

Should he go after her? No, she would come back. After all, what woman would prefer to sleep outside when there was a nice, comfortable bed waiting for her.

Leaving the window open, he sat on a chair facing the window. She would come back.

He hoped she would come back.

Chapter Fifteen

$\mathcal{D}$awn was breaking as Josette awoke from her bed of damp leaves and rose to a sitting position. She knew she'd better not dally much longer if she wanted to sneak back into her bedchamber before the servants began their day.

Standing up, she brushed off the leaves clinging to her gown. It was time for her to face Morgan. Last night, when she'd walked in and caught Morgan with Ernestine, she felt as if all of her fears had somehow become a reality. At first, she had felt betrayed, but then she realized they didn't have an understanding between them. Morgan was free to spend time with whomever he chose.

Regardless, the more she dwelt on it, the more confident she felt that Morgan was telling the truth. She reluctantly walked back towards the estate and saw that her window remained opened. But no light came from within. Despite trusting Morgan with her life, she didn't trust him with her heart. She couldn't let her guard down. No one could hurt her again, if she refused to let anyone in.

Josette had trusted her brother, but he had kicked her out of their home, forcing her to fend for herself in Bermondsey. She had survived living on scraps of food, sleeping in the slime-coated alleyway, and hoping she could survive another day.

Morgan was a good man. He was a friend, but he could mean no more to her than that. However, she knew that was not true. He did mean a great deal to her. Curse that man, she thought. Why did he stir feelings inside of her that she had sworn to suppress? And why did his mere presence provide her with comfort and reassurance?

Stopping at the back wall, Josette looked out onto the courtyard and thought about returning to London on her own. She could just walk away from Morgan and return to her school, her girls, and her home. Or she could go inside and tell Lady Paxton the truth about her situation and request the use of their carriage.

She lifted her head up and looked at the opened window. No, she had given Morgan her word. She would help him discover the identity of *Genet*. She owed him that.

Josette climbed up the wall and entered her bedchamber. Morgan was sleeping in a chair facing the window. Except for a missing jacket, and an untied cravat, he was still dressed from the night before.

Josette knelt next to him, touching his sleeve. "Morgan," she whispered.

His eyes flew open, and a look of intense relief came over his features. "You came back."

"I told you I would."

Leaning forward, he raised his hand to her hair and pulled out a large leaf. "What the blazes were you thinking sleeping out in the cold all night?" he demanded, tossing the leaf to the floor.

"I needed time to think," she replied, rising from her position.

Morgan gave her a knowing look. "No, you needed time to convince yourself that you are better off alone."

She stared at him in disbelief. How did he know that?

Morgan rose and gently sat her down on the chair he'd just vacated. "You have leaves stuck in your hair," he informed her, as he began untangling them from her disheveled locks and tossing them onto the floor.

"Thank you," she murmured.

She heard Morgan let out a loud, deep sigh. "You scared me, Josie. I didn't know if I should go after you, or if I should give you time to be alone. But every hour that passed, I grew more and more afraid that I would never see you again."

She lifted her face to look up at him. "I didn't mean to alarm you."

"I am responsible for you. Do you not understand that?" he stated, his voice rising.

"Don't you mean your burden?" she contested, tilting her chin defiantly.

Crouching down in front of her, Morgan grabbed her chin and pulled it down. "Will you please get it through your thick, stubborn, beautiful mind that you will never be a burden to me? You challenge me every step of the way, making me a better spy and a better man because of it."

His voice grew emotional as he added, "You must believe that nothing happened between Miss Lemaure and me."

"I do believe you," she confessed. "I know you to be an honorable man."

"Then why did you run away from me?"

She glanced at the door, wishing she could flee and end this awkward conversation. "I would prefer not to say."

Morgan's eyes shone with anguish. "You still think of me as a rake. Someone who is incapable of fidelity."

She held her tongue, because a small part of her did still believe that.

"Did you know that I was engaged before?" he asked, sitting on the chair next to her.

She shook her head.

"My father was tired of my reputation and arranged a marriage for me to Lady Esther, a sweet, young daughter of an earl. He informed me that if I did not marry the girl then I would be cut off and disowned," he confessed.

"What happened?"

Morgan ran his hand through his mussed-up hair. "Prior to the marriage, I investigated my betrothed and discovered that she was in love with another gentleman. She had been devastated to learn of the betrothal contract and pleaded for her father to change his mind."

"Did he?"

"No. He put his foot down," Morgan revealed, "so Esther and I concocted a plan to both get what we wanted. While I waited at the wedding ceremony, Esther snuck off with her lover to Gretna Green, and I was able to play the part of the jilted bridegroom."

Josette reached forward and placed her hand on his sleeve. "I am sorry. Would you have married her if she hadn't been in love with another man?"

"No, I would not have," Morgan said firmly.

"Wouldn't your father have cut you off?"

He shrugged one shoulder, but she could see lingering pain in his eyes. "Possibly. No doubt my father will find another reason to threaten to cut me off in the future."

It was the words that he wasn't saying that saddened her heart. Tentatively, Josette reached over and ran her hand along his jawline, feeling the dark stubble on her fingers. "Your father's disappointment in you hurts you far more than you let on."

She could feel his jaw tense beneath her hand. "Life is too short to live without love. When I marry, I will commit myself, both body and soul, to the woman I love," he affirmed, his eyes watching her with longing.

Feeling bold, she asked in a timid voice, "And if that person is never ready?"

His face softened. "Then I would wait."

"Even if it took years?"

He encompassed her hand with his. "Even if it took years, because I happen to know that she is worth the wait."

A knock came at the door before it was slowly pushed opened. A blonde-haired maid stuck her head in and asked, "Would you like me to help you dress, Mrs. Addington?"

"Yes, please," Josette said, rising.

The maid walked further into the room. "Did you sleep in your gown, ma'am?" she asked with a confused brow.

"I was so exhausted last night that I fell onto my bed and only just awoke," she lied, earning a smile from Morgan.

Looking her up and down, the maid frowned. "This may take some time. I think it might be best if we order a bath for you first."

Josette sighed. "That would be lovely."

"May I stay and watch?" Morgan whispered in her ear.

Nudging him with her elbow, she was gratified to hear him let out a soft grunt. "A simple no would have sufficed," he teased. "This is a good time for me to break my fast." He reached up and pulled another leaf out of her hair. "Have a good bath."

Heading down the hall, Morgan was surprised to see the door to Lord Paxton's study open. He peered inside and saw Lord Paxton hunched over a peculiar looking desk in the corner. He rapped his knuckles on the door to make his presence known.

Lord Paxton lifted his head, turning towards him. "Morgan. You are up early," he said, his eyes taking in his appearance, "and apparently, you had a rough night as well."

"May I come in?"

"Yes. I could use a break," Lord Paxton replied graciously.

Morgan walked over to the oak desk, noting the tilted top, and an edge that ran along the bottom, supporting the drawings. "This is an interesting-looking desk," he commented.

"I had this table built specifically for me to create and review architectural drawings," he explained. "It can be raised, lowered, and tilted by an apparatus using a lead weight."

Noting the drawings on the desk, he asked, "Is that what kept you up all night?"

Lord Paxton turned over the papers, hiding them from his view. "It is. Whenever I start working, I lose track of time." He frowned. "It infuriates my wife."

"I can relate to that."

Lord Paxton leaned back in his chair. "Is that why you look like death?"

"That bad?" Morgan asked, wincing.

"You have dark circles under your eyes, and you are wearing the same clothes as last night, although now they are wrinkled."

Morgan brought his hand up and rubbed the back of his neck as he looked at the ceiling. "Josette and I had a misunderstanding last night."

"And you slept on the ground?"

"No, the chair," he admitted, bringing his gaze back down.

Lord Paxton grinned. "Next time, try the floor. It is far more comfortable."

"I am hoping there won't be a next time."

Laughing, Lord Paxton rose and walked to the drink tray. "Trust me, there will be a next time. Marriage is a wonderful thing, but it can also be aggravating. That's how you know the marriage is working."

"I thought marriage was supposed to be harmonious," Morgan commented.

"No," Lord Paxton said, pouring two small glasses of port. "Marriage is hard. When my dear Eleanora and I got married, we had been raised so differently. We had different expectations coming into the marriage, and we fought constantly." He handed Morgan a glass. "But we were committed to each other, and our differences made our love stronger."

"Josette and I are vastly different too," Morgan stated before taking a sip of his drink.

Lord Paxton sat down on the chair next to him. "Be patient with her. I beg of you."

"Josette told me that you were friends with her father," Morgan ventured, lowering his glass to rest on his leg.

"She told you that?" Lord Paxton lifted his brow.

"She disclosed *that*," Morgan huffed, "but she guards her past fiercely. I only recently discovered that her parents and sister died, and her brother tossed her out of their home."

Lord Paxton placed his drink onto the table. "Why would you marry a woman who hid her past from you?"

Caught off guard by the directness of the question, Morgan took a moment to take a sip of his drink. His mind replayed meeting Josette in the alley the first time and how he immediately recognized her strength of character. Not only had he been attracted to her physically, but he felt a sense of familiarity with her that he had never experienced with another.

Knowing that Lord Paxton was still waiting for his answer, he replied, "I wasn't interested in her past, I only wanted to be a part of her future."

"I promised I wouldn't reveal her parentage until after the house party, but I can tell you that everyone around Josette failed her." Lord Paxton hung his head low at that admission. "She was but a mere child dealing with the death of her parents and sister, overcome with grief, and shunned by Society."

"By Society?"

Lord Paxton sighed. "Aye. But I will not say more on this matter until Josette has spoken to you."

Morgan took a sip of his drink, knowing that he did not have the same confidence that Josette would confide in him. He glanced over at the drawing table. "Do any of your sons share your passion?"

"No. My oldest son, Albert, is managing our property in Kent, we bought my other son a commission in the Royal Navy, and Geoffrey..." His voice trailed off. "Geoffrey is struggling with his identity right now."

"What are you referring to?" Morgan asked, despite already suspecting the answer.

Lord Paxton frowned. "I raised all my children with the same values and expectations but only Geoffrey has rebelled. Ever since he left for Oxford, he keeps flipping from one radical group to the next."

"Is that because he sides with the Whigs?"

"No, not all Whigs are inherently evil," Lord Paxton replied with a smirk.

Morgan chuckled. "That's good."

Lord Paxton's expression turned to one of sadness and heartache. "My wife and I have preached morality, work ethic, and loyalty to king and country above all else. But Geoffrey spends his time in gambling halls and houses of ill repute. He's involved in all types of debauchery with his chums. It is breaking our hearts, and we don't know how to help bring him back on the right path. It makes us question what we did wrong."

Morgan shifted his gaze towards the window because he imagined his father voicing the same concerns. Hearing these words out of Lord Paxton's mouth, and the pain that was expressed, it made him realize how his father must be feeling. For the first time, he felt guilty for all the pain that he had caused his family.

A silence loomed over them before Lord Paxton stated, "Frankly, I have dire concerns over Mr. Blount and his influence over my Geoffrey. There is something odd about that man, but my son seems to idolize him."

Ensuring their conversation stayed private, Morgan rose and walked over to the door, closing it. "If I may ask, why did you allow Geoffrey to invite Mr. Blount?"

Not appearing concerned by him shutting the door, Lord Paxton explained, "Geoffrey sprung it on Eleanora, and he was quite insistent about it."

"Do you know everyone from your guest list personally?" he asked, returning to his seat.

Lord Paxton shook his head. "I only know my four investors, Mr. Perier, Mr. Christophe Mancini, Mr. Lemaure and Mr. Clemens."

"Do any of them have radical views, or have they expressed opinions that raised concerns?"

"No, they are all professionals," he said. "We care more about the profit of the mine than we do about politics."

"And their guests?" he pressed.

"I can't say that I have noticed anything that has been disconcerting," Lord Paxton responded with a questioning look. "Why are you asking these questions?"

"When we first arrived, Josette and I rode into town and saw Mr. Blount preaching to a large crowd," he shared, hoping to distract Lord Paxton from his line of questioning. "He was riling up the people about social reform and handing out pamphlets."

Lord Paxton grunted. "There is a growing movement in our town and throughout England that is demanding change. I fear that more clashes may result, ending in many more deaths."

"Geoffrey has been attending the meetings at The Gutted Fish," Morgan reported, leveling his gaze at him.

Cursing, Lord Paxton rose and moved slowly to his desk. He placed his hands on it and hung his head. "What is that boy thinking?"

Morgan rose from his seat. "Be cautious around Mr. Blount. I don't trust that man or his intentions."

"We have something in common," Lord Paxton expressed firmly.

Stepping closer to Lord Paxton, he said, "I will talk to Geoffrey. Let's hope we can convince him of the errors of his ways before he does something foolish."

Pushing away from the desk, Lord Paxton gave him a weak smile. "You better hurry and change. We are fencing this morning."

"Now that is something I can get behind," Morgan replied, heading towards the door.

Chapter Sixteen

Josette lowered her needlework as her gaze drifted towards the window. The men had gone fencing on the north lawn hours ago, and the ladies were in the drawing room engaged in various amusements.

In the far corner of the room, Mrs. Perier and Miss Lemaure sat at a desk, writing letters and chatting softly. Focusing on the two women, Josette felt confident that neither could be the famed French spy, *Genet*. Both appeared to be lacking wits in many regards. Which left only one other woman to investigate.

Turning her attention to Adalyn, she asked, "Don't you wish that women could go fencing with the men?"

"Indeed," Adalyn responded, pulling her needle through her handkerchief. "I have often thought fencing sounded more exciting than sitting around a drawing room writing letters and practicing our embroidery."

"We could go outside for a walk around the gardens," Josette suggested.

Lowering the handkerchief to her lap, Adalyn looked out the window. Then she adjusted her glasses on her nose. "The sun is too high. Perhaps we should wait until after we rest this afternoon."

"Perhaps," Josette murmured.

Adalyn laughed. "Good heavens, you are easy to tease." Placing the handkerchief on the table, she leaned forward in her seat. "Do you think Lady Paxton would object to us leaving?"

"I don't see why," Josette answered honestly. "We are just taking a stroll outside."

Tilting her head towards the other two women, Adalyn asked,

"Should we invite Mrs. Dull and Miss Tedious with us?"

Josette laughed and brought her hand up to cover her mouth. "I would prefer not to."

"I agree," Adalyn said, standing up and smoothing out her pale green gown.

Leaving her needlework on the chair, Josette rose and moved towards the door.

Mrs. Perier's head popped up. "Where are you ladies going?"

"On a walk," Adalyn replied, her steps slowing.

Miss Lemaure's eyes grew wide with disbelief. "But the sun is too high in the sky."

"Exactly," Adalyn responded with a twinkle in her eye. "Josette and I are hoping to earn a few more freckles on our noses."

Josette turned her gaze towards Miss Lemaure. "You are welcome to join us." Her tone was anything but inviting.

Miss Lemaure lowered her gaze to her lap and murmured, "I would prefer to stay inside."

"As would I," Mrs. Perier said, returning her attention back to her letter.

After they were in the hall and heading towards the rear door, Adalyn asked, "Do you want to explain what that was all about?"

"To what are you referring?" Josette tried to sound confused.

"The exchange between you and Miss Lemaure."

Glancing over her shoulder to ensure no one was near, Josette confessed, "Last night, I caught Ernestine in my room attempting to seduce my husband."

Adalyn rolled her eyes. "She did the same thing to Antoine and the Mancini brothers."

"She did?"

Nodding, Adalyn added, "My brother informed me that he caught her rifling through his trunk."

That's interesting, Josette thought. "Do you think she was stealing from him?"

"That was Antoine's first thought as well, but nothing appeared to be missing."

A footman held open the rear door as they exited the estate.

"What do you know of the Mancini brothers?" Josette asked.

Adalyn pushed the large spectacles up further on her nose. "The Mancinis are one of the richest families in France, and Christophe runs all of their businesses and investments."

"What does Gaspard do?"

Adalyn shrugged. "He's the second son. So, he has more freedom to do as he pleases. From what I understand, the Mancinis have investments all over the world and Gaspard travels to inspect them."

"How poor is your eyesight?" Josette asked, as they walked through the well-manicured gardens.

"Dreadful. That's why my spectacles are so large," Adalyn explained, taking them off her face.

Taking a good look at Adalyn without the glasses, Josette saw a beautiful woman that would be the envy of the ton. She turned and resumed their walk. "Oh, I have been meaning to ask, do you still have the book with the green cover?"

"Pardon?"

"The one I saw you holding in the library yesterday," Josette clarified.

Adalyn gave her a quizzical look before replying, "I do not. My brother asked to borrow it."

Josette frowned, appearing disappointed. "I will just have to wait until he finishes with it then."

"Why are you so interested in that book?"

"When I saw you select it from the library, I realized I hadn't read it before, and it piqued my interest," Josette confessed. "I love reading about chemistry and physics."

Adalyn smiled. "I knew I liked you."

Josette returned her smile, and they resumed their stroll through the gardens. Supplied with new information, she knew she couldn't exclude Ernestine as a possible spy, since she was searching through Antoine's trunk. However, the evidence continued to stack up against Antoine.

Poor Adalyn. What would become of her if it was discovered her brother was the French spy, *Genet?*

After a vigorous bout of fencing with Geoffrey, Morgan saluted his partner and removed his mask. "Well done," he praised.

Geoffrey let out a bark of laughter as he took off his mask. "I highly doubt that. You beat me every time."

"If you keep practicing, I have no doubt you will beat me soon." Morgan extended the mask, chest padding, and sword towards a footman.

Lord Paxton approached, handing each of them a drink. He turned to Morgan. "Your fencing skills are impressive."

"That's the difference between a Cambridge man and an Oxford man," Morgan jested.

"Come and eat," Lord Paxton invited with a chuckle. He pointed to the table set up with an assortment of food. "Your wife informed our cook of all your favorite desserts and asked for them to be served."

Morgan's steps faltered. "Did she?" When did she have the time to do that, he wondered. She had already told him about the custard, but it surprised him that Lord Paxton knew about it.

"I overheard her telling a group of maids that it was love at first sight for the two of you," Gaspard said, stepping closer to him.

Josette was good, Morgan had to admit. She was definitely winning the bet.

"Gentlemen, may I have your attention, please," Lord Paxton raised his voice and requested. As they assembled, he stood in front of the group. "Now that we are away from the ladies, I wanted to discuss some business with you. The coal mine in Champagney has been in my family for generations, but it is time that I sold my majority shares. Between the estates I manage, designing multiple buildings, and supervising the work at the palace of Westminster, I am afraid the mine has become more of an afterthought. As the four main investors in the mine, I felt it would be best to offer to sell it to one of you first."

"I will buy your shares!" Mr. Christophe Mancini shouted.

Mr. Lemaure scoffed. "I think not. Why should you have first rights?"

Lord Paxton put his hands up. "I anticipated a dispute. Might I propose that my shares be distributed evenly amongst all of you who are interested in this venture?"

"I am interested," Mr. Antoine said.

All eyes turned to Mr. Perier, and he nodded. "I think that's a fine solution."

"Excellent," Lord Paxton exclaimed, regaining their attention. "I had hoped that this would be the resolution everyone would agree to. So, I took the liberties of having my solicitors draw up the contracts. That's why I asked all of you to come. This will save months of negotiating through missives and sending contracts back and forth via post."

Lord Paxton put up his hand as the four investors inundated him with questions. "I assure you that the price of my shares will be fair, but we can adjourn after dinner tonight to discuss the exact terms."

"It appears we will be spending time with the ladies while the other men hash out the contracts," Gaspard said to him.

"Which is where I would rather be anyway," Morgan replied, grinning.

Gaspard smiled. "If I had a wife like yours, I wouldn't want to spend time away from her either."

Feeling himself tense at Gaspard's comment, Morgan decided to change topics. "Do you not own any shares of the mine?"

"I do," he confirmed, "but my brother takes care of our family's investments."

"How exactly do you spend your time, Mr. Mancini?"

"Call me Gaspard," he said. "I spend my time as I please. I dabble in politics, spend time with beautiful women, all while strategically avoiding the dreaded marital noose."

Looking at Gaspard, Morgan realized that he sounded like a blundering rogue. Yet, did his cover not revolve around him acting in a similar manner? Was this how society portrayed him? A rake that only cared about himself and seeking after pleasurable pursuits?

Geoffrey walked up to them with a plate in his hand. "You should try the lavender cheesecake. It's delicious."

"I'm afraid I don't see Mr. Blount," Gaspard commented. "Did he leave the party early?"

Geoffrey shook his head. "No. He had business in town today."

"What exactly is Mr. Blount's profession?" Gaspard pressed.

"He is an orator," Geoffrey replied before taking a bite of his dessert.

"Who pays him to speak?" Morgan inquired.

Geoffrey swallowed his bite of food, then shared, "He isn't paid by anyone. He preaches reform because he is passionate about it."

Gaspard crossed his arms over his chest. "Passion doesn't pay the rent."

"I suppose Mr. Blount lives off a portion of the donations given to him," Geoffrey responded. "He spends most of his time in London, anyway."

"Have you donated to Mr. Blount's cause?" Morgan asked, stifling the urge to roll his eyes at Geoffrey's ignorance.

"It's my cause as well. I cannot stand idly by and watch the social injustices occurring daily. Between heavy taxes and lack of food, people all over England are struggling to survive. Yet our prince regent is continuing to spend money at a reckless rate, and parliament is doing nothing to stop it, plunging us further into debt as a nation," Geoffrey fumed.

"How much have you donated to this cause?" Gaspard pressed.

"In total, about £500, but I help the cause in other ways," Geoffrey said. "For example, I have helped find additional contributors."

"Do you know what Mr. Blount intends to do with all the funds that have been collected?" Morgan asked.

Geoffrey glanced over his shoulder at his father, who was still engaged in conversation with the other men. "There are other groups across England rallying together, waiting for the right time to march to London to protest the inequality in our government."

Morgan shot him a look of disbelief. "Are you speaking of an uprising?" he asked in a hushed voice.

"No, not an uprising," Geoffrey contended. "It will be a peaceful protest to demand change."

Gaspard let out a huff. "When is the 'right time' for this 'peaceful protest' to occur?"

"Soon," Geoffrey replied. "Now if you will excuse me, I want more dessert."

Morgan and Gaspard watched as Geoffrey walked back to the table. Gaspard spoke first, echoing Morgan's exact thoughts.

"He is a fool."

"He is young and idealistic, not even twenty-one," Morgan affirmed.

Gaspard shook his head. "If he continues down this path, he won't live long enough to see his next birthday," he stated flatly.

Morgan stifled a groan. Gaspard was right. Somehow, he needed Geoffrey to realize the error of his ways. He could be passionate about social injustices, but he couldn't blindly follow the first fool that shouted louder than everyone else.

If Geoffrey continued following Mr. Blount, it could only end in two scenarios; he would be marked as a traitor or be executed.

He sighed. And he was just starting to like Geoffrey.

Chapter Seventeen

Staring at the blue papered walls in their bedchamber, Josette kept her back towards Morgan as he dressed for dinner. "Should we abduct Antoine and torture him until he confesses that he is *Genet*?"

She heard Morgan chuckle from behind her. "Typically, you gather more proof before you interrogate a suspect."

Smoothing out the skirt of her gold, square-necked gown, she replied, "We've already discovered that the green book in his possession was placed in Mr. Blount's room. He has a book in his trunk that appears to contain codes. And we've found letters from Mr. Blount under his mattress."

"I will admit, the evidence *is* stacking up against him."

"I'll take the note you discovered in Mr. Blount's room and use the book in Antoine's room to attempt to decipher it." Josette drummed her fingers on the settee's armrest. "The question is why would a rich, successful man like Antoine choose to work as a spy."

"Like me?"

"You are an honorable spy," she reminded him.

"You only consider me honorable because I am British," he said. "If I were a French spy, then you would consider me the enemy."

Her fingers stilled as she mulled over his words. "Napoleon unjustly declared war on most of Europe, killing millions in the process, and weakening many countries for years to come. It would stand to reason that his spy network would also be accountable for his treachery. Besides, if *Genet* had retired when Napoleon was exiled, perhaps bought a chalet in the mountains, then we would not be attempting to capture him. Would we?"

"I would have continued to hunt him until my last dying breath,"

Morgan replied in a steely tone. "He was responsible for my brother's death."

Hearing the pain in his voice, Josette turned in her seat to face him, immensely grateful that Morgan was mostly dressed. He looked so handsome in his black trousers, white waistcoat, and black dinner jacket, although his cravat was hanging loose around his neck.

"He was only partially to blame," she said. "*Genet* may have stolen maps that showed the locations of British troops, but he was acting under Napoleon's authority."

Morgan clenched his jaw as his gaze shifted over her shoulder. "My brother's squadron was ambushed by French soldiers because of the information supplied by *Genet*."

"Were you close to your brother?"

"He was my closest mate," he replied sadly.

"I understand your pain," she murmured.

His eyes latched onto hers, conveying his compassion. "I know you do, Josie."

Fighting the urge to do something foolish like run into his arms, Josette said, "We still haven't discovered why *Genet* wanted to come to the house party. After all, Mr. Clemens has the funds to buy a passport on his own and could have boarded any ship bound for England. Why did he come under Lord Paxton's passport?"

"If Antoine is *Genet*, then perhaps he is here only to settle business at the mine," Morgan mused as he reached up to tie his cravat.

Josette arched a brow. "Do you believe that?"

"No," Morgan stated, his hands still fidgeting with his cravat, "but a spy must stay objective."

"We still need to discover why one of the Mancini brothers and Ernestine were searching through the trunks," Josette said. "We can't rule out that *Genet* brought an accomplice with him."

"Good point. We'll stick to the plan." Morgan lowered his hands from his skewed cravat.

Josette shook her head, smiling half a smile. "Why don't you have Lord Paxton's valet dress you for dinner?"

"I can dress myself," Morgan declared.

She smirked. "Your cravat is skewed *again*." She laughed as she stepped over and stopped in front of him. Without asking permission, she took a moment to adjust it. "Much better."

Josette noticed that Morgan's arms hung loosely at his sides, but his hands were balled into fists. Had she upset him? Bringing her gaze up, she saw the he was watching her closely, admiring her, his eyes filled with an emotion she could scarcely believe. *Love.*

"Josie."

At the sound of his voice tenderly speaking her name, her heart softened, allowing her to feel again. She knew she should say something, do something to take control of the moment, to stop the aching vulnerability quickly closing the distance she'd worked so hard to put between them.

His eyes darted towards her lips as he slowly leaned his head forward. Her lips parted as she realized how badly she wanted to kiss him. His mouth hovered over hers, and his warm, intoxicating breath brushed across her face, causing her heart to hope for more. But her mind pleaded for her to stop, to reconsider these fleeting emotions. Doubt crept back in, willing her to step back.

"I can't do this," she breathed. "I'm sorry." She started backing up, her eyes taking in his heartfelt gaze.

"Josie," he said, his voice filled with concern. He took a step forward.

She put up a hand. "Please, don't come any closer." Her back pressed against the wall, and she turned towards the door. Placing her hand on the handle, she stated, "I will decipher the code, then I will meet you in the drawing room."

Morgan moved closer to her with a worried frown. "Josie…"

Opening the door, she slipped out and closed it behind her. She picked up her skirts and ran the length of the empty hall, not stopping until she turned the corner. Her back slumped against the wall as a soft cry escaped her lips. What had she done? She had let down her defenses, and she allowed Morgan to enter her heart. A heart that was supposed to be impenetrable.

After this assignment, Morgan would go on, living his life, and she would be left to pine after him the rest of her days. No, she refused. She did not need his love or his pity. She was happy living on her own, and she refused to let him take that control away from her.

That blasted man! Why did he affect her so? Josette reached up to touch her lips. She had wanted to kiss him, wanted to feel his lips on hers. No, it was only a moment of weakness, she excused herself. After all, she had accepted this job believing she was immune to Morgan's charms. Now she knew she had been lying to herself all along. She had deep, unrequited feelings for him.

Morgan may claim that he had feelings for her, but men were a fickle lot. Once he conquered her heart, he would move on to another, leaving her to mend a broken heart and read about his new love interests in the society page.

Placing her hand on her stomach, she attempted to calm her racing heart. No! She was stronger than this. She could resist Morgan's charm and his devastatingly handsome face. He was paying her for a job, and *she* was not included in the bargain.

Josette straightened from the wall with renewed resolve. She was helping to stop a French spy, and she needed to keep her wits about her. She peered around the corner to ensure the hall was empty before she walked to Mr. Antoine Clemens's room. Knocking on the door, she waited for a response, but when none was forthcoming, she opened the door and slipped inside. The drapes were pulled open, and the sun was just dipping over the hill, providing her with adequate light to search.

She started to move towards the trunk but veered her course when she noticed the green book on the small round table. As she flipped through the pages, she found nothing stuffed inside of it. When had Mr. Blount returned the book to Mr. Clemens?

Placing the book down, she knelt beside the trunk and started searching for the coded book. However, all the books were gone. She had just started reorganizing the contents of the trunk when she heard a male's voice in the hallway. Closing the lid, she started to dive under the bed, but her heart nearly stopped when she saw Mr. Gaspard Mancini already hiding there.

He grabbed her arm and tugged her close to him. As she attempted to yank back her arm, he whispered in her ear, "I do not intend to hurt you. But if you keep struggling then we will both be found out." Recognizing his logic was sound, she nodded her understanding. The explanations could wait.

The door was opened, and Antoine said, "Let me just change my jacket." A black jacket dropped to the ground, and Antoine stepped to his trunk and opened it. Pulling out a new black dinner jacket, he sighed. "Well, this is better than nothing," he murmured under his breath.

Shrugging the jacket on, Antoine left the room, closing the door behind him. Turning her expectant gaze towards Gaspard, he just offered her a roguish smile. She rolled her eyes as she wiggled her way out from under the bed.

Once she rose, Josette smoothed out her dress as a ruse to gain access to the dagger strapped to her right thigh. Keeping her hand in the slit of her dress, she waited until Gaspard rose before she demanded in a hushed voice, "What are you doing in here?"

"Not here," he replied, placing a finger to his lips.

Mr. Mancini opened the door, peering out into the hall. He indicated that she should follow him, and they both slipped out of Antoine's room. They walked the short distance to his room, and he opened the door, allowing her to enter first. Suddenly, he shoved her back against the wall and placed a knife to her throat. "Why are you so interested in Mr. Clemens?" he growled.

Carefully, she slid her hand into the left-hand slit in her gown and removed the pistol strapped to her left leg, pressing it into his hip. "I don't respond well to threats, Mr. Mancini."

A flash of respect shone in his eyes as he lessened the pressure of the knife against her throat, but he did not remove it. "Why were you searching Mr. Clemens's room?" he asked, his tone not as sharp.

"I beg the same question of you," she replied. "This is the second time I've caught you in Mr. Clemens's room."

Gaspard regarded her with narrowed eyes for a long moment before he lowered his dagger, tucking it into the waistband of his trousers. "We are getting nowhere this way." He offered her a charming one-sided smile. "I believe we should start over."

Not willing to give up her advantage, Josette moved the pistol to her right hand and stepped away from Gaspard. "I don't want to have to kill you, Mr. Mancini…"

He cut her off. "Gaspard," he said smoothly. "My friends call me Gaspard."

"I will not," she asserted. "I do not become friendly with men that I may have to kill."

His cocky smile grew wider. "You won't kill me."

"No?"

He took a step closer, his eyes watching her. "We are both after the same thing."

"What is that, exactly?" she asked, keeping the pistol aimed at his chest.

"The truth." Gaspard's eyes roamed her face and her gown approvingly. "You are a beautiful woman, Josette." His eyes came back up. "May I call you Josette?"

"You may not," she replied forcefully.

Not deterred by her rejection, he took another step closer. "Why don't we take a seat and discuss this matter rationally?"

Tired of the game he was playing, Josette cocked the pistol. "Mr. Mancini, I hope you are not foolish enough to think flirting with me will distract me so you can strip me of my pistol. Your attempt will be in vain, I assure you."

Gaspard's confident demeanor faded, and he stared at her in amazement. "I may have underestimated you."

"Let's drop this charade, shall we?" Josette asked, lowering her pistol to her side. "Time is of the essence since the others are bound to notice we are missing soon enough."

His face grew expressionless as he studied her. "Who do you work for?"

Josette maintained his gaze. "I work for no one."

"Are you a friend or foe of Napoleon?"

"I'm British. What do you think?" she asked sarcastically. "Who do *you* work for?"

Gaspard frowned, placing his hand on the hilt of his dagger. "I work for the secret service in France."

She brought her gun up again. "Are you *Genet*?"

"No, I work for France. I am loyal to King Louis," he informed her. "I am here to detain *Genet*."

"Do you know who *Genet* is?"

He shrugged. "That's what I am trying to discover. An informant told us that *Genet* was traveling to Lord Paxton's house party."

"Why would France want to arrest one of their own spies?" she asked, lowering her pistol again.

Stepping to the drink tray, Gaspard poured himself a glass of port before answering, "*Genet* was one of Napoleon's most trusted agents. Ever since Napoleon was exiled to the island of Elba, *Genet* has been acting rogue, intent on ensuring that Napoleon is returned back to the throne."

She tucked away her pistol and moved to the window. "There is much to discuss, and Morgan will need to be involved in our conversation. However, we cannot be seen together."

"What do you propose..." His voice trailed off as she opened the window and stepped out.

As she started climbing down the exterior wall, Gaspard put his head out the window and asked in an astonished voice, "Are you mad?"

She lifted her head and smiled. "Only partly."

After she dropped down onto the paved courtyard, she smoothed back her hair and waved up at Gaspard before she disappeared through the rear entrance.

Holding a drink in his hand, Morgan listened as Lord Paxton discussed the upcoming hunting season, but his eyes kept drifting towards the open door of the drawing room. Josette should have arrived by now. What was taking her so long?

When he had first arrived in the drawing room, Antoine Clemens was chatting with Christophe Mancini, but Miss Lemaure had bumped into him, causing his drink to spill onto his dinner jacket. He walked with Antoine when he went up to his room to change, mainly because he wanted to ensure that Josette was not discovered. His eyes surveyed the room as Antoine changed his jacket, and fortunately, he saw no sign of her.

Now he was waiting for Josette to make her appearance, and it was wearing on his nerves. His hand clenched his glass. Perhaps she was still upset with him for the liberties he had been taking with her.

No, he thought. Josette may be unpredictable at times, but she wouldn't let her emotions affect her work. That he was sure of.

He was about to place his glass on the table and go search for her when Josette stepped into the room. Her face was expressionless, but her eyes lit up when she saw him.

She didn't stop until she was right in front of him. She rose to her tiptoes to kiss his cheek, surprising and pleasing him immensely. However, his amusement slipped when he heard her whisper next to his ear, "We have a problem. We are not the only ones looking for *Genet.*"

He nodded to acknowledge her words. When she stepped back, he asked, "May I get you something to drink?"

"No, thank you," she replied with a smile.

Lady Paxton announced dinner, and they started to move towards the dining room. In the hall, Morgan noticed Gaspard fall in line with the back of the group. Could he be the other person searching for *Genet*? Turning his gaze towards Josette, he saw that she was watching him. She nodded slightly with a knowing look.

During dinner, the same mundane topics were discussed about hunting, fishing and the weather. After dessert was served, Lord Paxton pushed back his chair and declared, "Pardon us ladies. The men have business that we need to tend to. My wife has planned some parlor games to occupy your time this evening."

Everyone rose, and Morgan offered his arm to Josette. Raising his voice a bit, he asked, "Since I'm not needed at the meeting, would you like to take a romantic stroll around the gardens?"

She smiled sweetly up at him. "What a grand idea! I would love some fresh air."

Leading her out to the gardens, they stopped and pretended to admire the foliage and flowers as they made their way towards a cluster of large birch trees near the back of the gardens.

"Do you think anyone is still watching us?" he asked.

"I doubt it, but just in case..." Her voice trailed off as she picked up her skirts and ran for the cover of the trees, smiling flirtatiously over her shoulder at him.

Knowing this was for show, he laughed as he chased after her. He came to a stop when he found Josette leaning up against a tree with a dagger in her hand. "Do you have nefarious plans against me, wife?" he teased.

"Not tonight," she bantered back, her eyes scanning the trees. "Mr. Gaspard Mancini should be here soon."

The sound of approaching footsteps behind him had Morgan reaching for his pistol tucked into the back of his trousers. He instinctively stepped closer to Josette as he kept his pistol in his right hand.

Stepping out of the cover of the trees, Gaspard came into view but stopped a few feet away.

Josette spoke up, breaking the silence. "Mr. Mancini is an agent for France's secret service."

Morgan furrowed his brow. "Do you have proof of this?"

"No," Gaspard replied dryly. "I do not carry documentation. That would defeat the purpose of the *secret* service. Josette was not forthcoming about who *you* work for."

Why the blazes did he just call Josette by her given name? "My *wife*," he said, "was correct in keeping *our* secret to herself."

"I apologize. I meant no disrespect," Gaspard responded, his eyes darting towards Josette.

"Perhaps we can hurry along our conversation," Josette suggested.

Directing her next comment to Morgan, she revealed, "Mr. Mancini has been tasked to detain *Genet* because he has turned rogue."

Shifting her gaze back to Gaspard, she added, "We were sent to arrest *Genet* for crimes against our government."

"Am I to assume you are both agents?" Gaspard asked.

"You may," Morgan replied.

Gaspard chuckled. "The British Crown employs married agents. *Fascinating.*"

"Would you be willing to share the information that you've uncovered?" Josette asked.

All humor was stripped from Gaspard's expression as he replied, "I don't know how much to share. I'm working under the assumption that Antoine Clemens is *Genet* based upon finding an unusual book in his trunk and a stack of letters between him and Mr. Blount.

However, my instinct is telling me that he is not *Genet*."

Josette stepped closer to Gaspard, and Morgan had the sudden urge to pull her back towards him. Fortunately, he stopped before making a fool of himself.

"Who do you think it is?" she asked.

"I know it's not my brother," Gaspard said firmly. "I can vouch for him."

Morgan tucked his pistol away. "We found a coded missive in a book that sat on Mr. Blount's table."

"I was hoping that unusual book in Mr. Clemens's trunks would help us decipher the note, but when I searched his trunk before dinner, I discovered it was gone," Josette shared.

Gaspard ran a hand through his hair. "It doesn't make sense. Antoine is a respected businessman, worth millions, and stands to gain another fortune with the policies that King Louis is implementing. Why would he give up all that he had worked for to aid Napoleon?"

"Perhaps Ernestine is *Genet*," Josette suggested. "Adalyn mentioned that her brother caught Ernestine rummaging through his trunks."

"Ernestine is not clever enough to be *Genet*, and frankly neither is Mr. Lemaure," Gaspard asserted. "I don't know much about Miss Clemens, but she seems too meek to be a spy."

"Well, it couldn't be Mrs. Perier," Josette confirmed. "We were chatting earlier, and her voice faded off as she got distracted by the birds outside the window."

Gaspard smiled. "I agree. Mr. Perier fell asleep during dinner. Last time I checked, I believe spies are required to stay awake when on assignment."

Josette laughed at Gaspard, which greatly irked Morgan. Drawing both of their attentions, he shared, "From what we know about *Genet*, he is cunning and ruthless. He did not pick this house party by chance. So why is he here?"

"That's what I keep asking myself as well," Gaspard answered.

"Mr. Blount and his group of rebels?" Josette suggested, fingering the dagger in her hand.

"But why would a spy of *Genet*'s caliber care about a small uprising?" Morgan asked. "It doesn't make sense. We're missing something."

"When I searched Mr. Blount's room at The Gutted Fish, I overheard him mentioning a plan that incorporated another group of rebels in London. Supposedly, it is in retaliation for England lending their support to the traitorous Bourbons," Josette informed Gaspard.

Gaspard kicked his boot against the leaf-covered ground. "The King of France is scheduled to arrive in England in two days and is speaking to a joint session of Parliament in four days. If *Genet* was targeting Bourbon supporters, then why would he come to Torquay? Why not London?"

Morgan nodded his agreement. "Even if *Genet* is hoping to start an uprising, Torquay is nowhere near London."

"May I propose we abduct Mr. Clemens and force him to tell us what he knows?" Josette asked, tucking her dagger away.

Gaspard winced as he glanced away. "We'd better be right about Antoine. If not, we risk giving away our advantage and potentially warning *Genet*."

"Could we force Mr. Blount to talk?" Morgan suggested.

"Maybe. He may have learned *Genet*'s identity since attending the house party," Josette replied.

Gaspard shook his head. "*Genet*'s identity has always been shrouded in secrecy. No one has gotten close enough to him, or they have died trying. Which is why I doubt *Genet* would reveal himself to a simple orator."

"Both of our countries want *Genet* alive, but I plan to arrest him and send him to Newgate to be charged for his crimes," Morgan stated.

"All my country wants is for *Genet* to disappear," Gaspard confessed. "I would much rather have England handle the trial and execution."

Josette pushed off the tree and stood next to Morgan. "Then if all goes well, tomorrow we will confirm *Genet*'s identity, arrest him, and return home."

Chapter Eighteen

Morgan was lying on the floor near the fireplace replaying Josette's words in his head. Once they arrested *Genet*, and delivered him to Newgate, their assignment would be done. They would return home and go their separate ways.

He had no intention of letting Josette go that easily. He was prepared to fight for her affection, no matter how long it took. He turned his head towards the bed and enjoyed listening to Josette's heavy breathing. He needed to be more cautious about declaring his intentions. Luckily, Josette was inclined to approach him and adjust his skewed cravat. That had been an ingenious plan on his part.

Moaning came from the bed, and Morgan saw Josette starting to toss and turn. Rising, he started towards her but stopped when she seemed to calm down. Then she began whispering, tossing her head side to side.

"Please don't go…"

Morgan sighed. She was having a dream about her family again. Would those dreams always haunt her?

"Please don't leave me…. Morgan," she breathed, and this time her words were more urgent.

Did she just say his name? His heart soared at the thought that Josette might need him in her life. Perhaps one day she would even accept his courtship.

She whimpered, and a tear ran down her face. He sat on the bed and ran his fingers gently across her cheek, caressing her delicate skin. Her eyes flew open, but she did not withdraw at his touch.

"You were having another nightmare," he told her, not wanting to share the specifics.

"Oh," she replied, closing her eyes. "I'm sorry for disturbing you."

"There is no need to apologize."

Her tear-filled eyes opened. "Why are you so nice to me?"

"Because you would kill me if I wasn't," he teased.

She grinned. "You can always make me laugh."

Morgan wanted to tell her that he wished he could be the one who made her laugh every day, but instead he opted to say, "You have a beautiful laugh. It suits you."

Sadness descended upon her features as she looked up at him. "After we stop *Genet*, where will you go next?"

His hand stilled on her cheek. "I suppose I will get a new assignment."

"Will it be in London?"

"It could be anywhere."

Josette placed her hand over his on her cheek. "I will miss you."

He arched an eyebrow. "You will?" he asked, hoping she would expand on that.

With a bob of her head, her piercing eyes met his. "You are my friend," she replied with a shaky breath. "I don't have very many of those."

He took his free hand and tucked a piece of hair behind her ear. "I want to be so much more than your friend, my dear Josie." He watched her carefully, knowing he was being bold in his speech. And hadn't he just convinced himself to be more cautious about declaring his intentions?

"I know," she replied, lowering her gaze for a moment. "I care for you, but you deserve better than me." She brought her gaze up. "I am a tainted woman."

"You are not an innocent?"

Josette's mouth gaped and a dark blush came to her cheeks. "I am! I meant... my name is tainted by scandal," she stammered, closing her eyes.

"Open your eyes," he urged gently. "You have nothing to be embarrassed about."

She sat up in bed. "After my father died, I was sent to live at my Aunt Winnie's estate... and my uncle died four days after I arrived.

The news spread quickly around Mayfield about the unlucky girl that caused people to die an untimely death." She flinched. "I was dubbed 'Black Josette' in the newspapers, and my friends stopped receiving me. Whenever someone recognized me on the street, they would say hurtful things to me. My aunt blamed me for my uncle's death and sent me back to my brother."

"What did your brother do?" he asked, maintaining his hold on her hand.

"At first, he taunted me with the newspaper whenever I was mentioned and informed me of the bets that were placed at Whites about me."

Clenching his jaw, Morgan couldn't wait to discover her brother's identity. He planned a slow, excruciating death for the blackguard.

"I do not recall reading about a 'Black Josette' in the newspaper."

"Thank goodness for that," she murmured.

"What does this have to do with *us*?" he asked, his heart filled with compassion.

She lifted an eyebrow. "Why do you say *us* with such ferocity? We are opposites in so many ways."

"True," he said, "but we do have something in common."

"What?"

"We have both been featured in the society pages of the newspaper," he pointed out.

Josette rolled her eyes. "We have had vastly different experiences. For starters, high society adores you. I have read that ladies carry around portrait-miniatures of you."

"I *am* handsome," he teased, "charismatic and charming…"

"And vain, my lord." She grinned.

Leaning closer, his eyes roamed her face. "You have been treated poorly by your family, but you are a fighter. You took what life gave you, and you fought back. You rose above your trials and survived."

"Living on the streets forever altered me," she said quietly. Tears came to her eyes, and she blinked them away. "After I ran out of money, I lived in a room with six other families, and I watched their children in exchange for a chance to use the mattress for four hours a night. My whole person was ragged and filthy. I worked constantly alongside the children to sweep the streets or help make small trinkets for them to sell. Eventually, I became just another mouth to feed, and I was kicked out to make room for someone who could pay rent."

Josette exhaled a shuddering breath before continuing. "Dead animals lined the streets, and I would check to see if they were fresh enough to cook. After a time, I stopped caring if I stepped in excrement and rubbish, even with my bare feet."

Morgan had been to the East side, and he could only imagine the squalor she'd had to endure to survive. "Why didn't you attempt to find employment as a governess?"

She pressed her lips together. "That was my initial plan, but I was young and foolish. I waited too long, and my dress became too faded. I even tried to find work as a maid, but no one looked past my disheveled appearance. When Lord Camden rescued me, I was still wearing the same dress that I wore when I left my home."

His heart could not take the pain in her voice anymore, and he gathered her up close to him. "You are safe now. You will never experience that heartache again."

Settling closer to him, she said, "That's why being the headmistress is so important to me. I am giving these girls hope for a brighter future."

"I understand," he murmured.

She shifted her position, so she could look up at him. "Do you?"

"Do I what?"

"Understand why we could never be?" she asked, her eyes imploring.

He shook his head. "I disagree."

"You are the son of a marquess, a lord, and I am a scandal-ridden orphan," she explained.

He huffed in frustration. "You may see yourself in that light, but I do not. Your past does not define who you are. It molds you, shaping you into the person you are today."

She offered him a tiny smile. "I fear that you may need to borrow Adalyn's spectacles."

He shifted his position until his back rested against the wall, but he still held Josette in his arms. "I'm not going anywhere, my dear Josie. You can resist it, or you can accept the inevitable."

"No wonder every woman falls in love with you."

He tensed at the joke at his expense. "I can promise you that you are the only woman I have ever wanted to charm like this."

She leaned back and out of his arms. "You speak of fidelity, but I have read the society pages. It has been reported that women attempt to sneak into your townhouse."

He sighed. "You still doubt me?"

"I fear once we finish this assignment, your feelings for me will diminish," she expressed, nibbling on her bottom lip.

He cupped her cheeks with both hands, forcing her to look at him. "We are partners on this assignment, but I cannot continue on and pretend that I don't have deep feelings for you." His eyes grew determined. "When this is over, I intend to court you." He offered her a smile. "I intend to take you on carriage rides through Hyde Park and take you to the opera. I will buy a ridiculous number of flowers and have them delivered to your school."

He leaned closer, kissing her forehead, his lips lingering on her skin. "And I will steal a kiss. One that will take your breath away and banish all of your worries."

Her eyes were wide as she watched him lean back. Thankfully, rather than argue, she remained silent, which was good enough for him. Resting his back against the wall, he gently nudged her to lay on his chest.

"It's time for bed. Once you are asleep, I will resume my spot on the floor. I just want to hold you for a little longer."

She put her arm around his waist as she relaxed into his embrace. He placed his chin on the top of her head, enjoying the delightful aroma of rosewater that scented her hair. He never wanted to leave Josette's side again, but that wasn't possible. He was an agent of the Crown and could be assigned to any mission. For the first time, he questioned whether he wanted to continue working as a spy.

Kissing the top of Josette's forehead, he realized his priorities had shifted. But he was certain they would figure it out… together.

Josette was having the most wonderful dream. She was in Morgan's arms, and she felt so safe and warm. She heard a child giggling in the tree overhead… but then, it turned into Gaspard's voice above her.

"Ahem."

She must be hearing things. Then she heard it again.

"I could have killed both of you."

Opening her eyes, she realized her head was resting on Morgan's chest, but she didn't have time to respond.

"Why are you in our room?" Morgan grumbled.

"I am disappointed in the caliber of agents that Britain retains," Gaspard replied. He stood next to the bed, frowning down at them. "I knocked, but no one responded."

"You should have taken the hint," Morgan grunted, tightening his hold around her waist.

Ignoring Morgan's chiding remark, Gaspard continued. "Then I walked up to your bed, and I could have killed you both. You really should request additional training."

"If I had perceived you as a threat, I would have killed you before you even crossed the threshold," Morgan mumbled. He shifted the covers to reveal the pistol in his left hand pointed at Gaspard.

"Perhaps you are not as lax about your safety as I perceived you to be," Gaspard admitted, raising both hands and stepping away from the bed.

Josette lifted her head off Morgan's chest and sat up. To ensure her modesty, she brought the covers up to her chin, covering her white nightgown. "Why are you in our room, Mr. Mancini?" she asked in an annoyed tone.

"Most of the men left to fence on the lawn, leaving Lord Paxton in his study, and Antoine is reviewing his ledgers in the library," Gaspard revealed. "It would be a perfect opportunity to speak to him."

Morgan extended her his pistol. "Will you hold this for a moment, my dear?" he asked, before he rose off the bed and stretched his neck. "Give me a moment to get dressed."

Gaspard lifted his brow. "Do you always sleep in your clothes?"

Moving to the settee, Morgan put his waistcoat over his white shirt and shrugged on his jacket. "My sleeping habits are none of your concern," he responded dismissively.

Turning his gaze towards her, Gaspard smiled. "Is your husband always so pleasant in the morning?"

"I'm afraid it's your presence that is upsetting him," she responded.

"Pity," he said. "I had taken him for an early riser."

Morgan sat down and put on his Hessian boots. Then he rose and retrieved his weapon from Josette. "Thank you," he murmured, tucking his pistol into the back of his trousers.

"Would you like me to go with you?" Josette asked.

Morgan shook his head. "Sometimes interrogating a suspect can be a long, intensive process, and…" His words trailed off as he frowned.

"And messy," Gaspard finished for him.

"Messy?" she questioned.

Casting a frustrated look at Gaspard, Morgan sat down on the bed. "If Antoine does not cooperate, we have alternative methods to make him talk," he explained.

"Torture," she whispered. "How will you accomplish that during a house party?"

Morgan reached up and tucked a piece of her hair behind her ear. "Very carefully, my dear Josie."

"Can we break our fast first?" Gaspard asked unexpectedly. "I would hate to have to stop our line of questioning to eat some bread."

"No wonder France lost the war," Morgan murmured, rolling his eyes.

Josette laughed, bringing her hand up to cover her mouth.

"I can hear you, Mr. Addington," Gaspard grunted.

Morgan smirked. "I would hope so. You are only a few feet away from me."

"Off with you two," Josette said. "I need to change, then I will devise a plan to keep the ladies distracted."

Rising from the bed, Morgan offered her a warm, private smile. "Try to stay out of trouble."

"That is always easier said than done," she bantered back.

As soon as the men left the room, she threw back the sheet and jumped out of bed. She had just started dressing when a maid came in to help her finish and style her hair. After she was ready for the day, she decided to go in search of the other ladies.

She walked down the hall, but her steps slowed when she saw the door to Lord Paxton's study was open. Glancing in the room, Josette saw Lord Paxton was hunched over his drawing table in the corner. A lighted candle sat near him, providing additional light as he reviewed the architectural drawings. Josette smiled at his dedication to his work, then she quietly resumed her walk down the hall.

Approaching the top of the stairs, Josette saw Adalyn storm out of the library, distress clearly on her features.

"Adalyn," she called, drawing her attention.

A frown came to Adalyn's lips as she pressed her glasses higher on her nose. "Morning, Josette," she replied in a tone that was anything but cordial.

"What's wrong?" Josette asked in concern, stepping closer to her friend.

"You'll never guess what my brother has done!" With a heated glare directed at the library door, Adalyn huffed, "He just informed me that I will lose my monthly allowance unless I marry the man he's chosen for me."

"And what did you say?" Josette gasped.

"I told him that I refused to marry for convenience," Adalyn said, her voice shaky.

"Good for you."

"So he cut me off." She raised her hand in front of her and snapped her fingers. "Just like that."

Josette stepped closer. "What are you going to do?"

"I've already secured a position in London as a governess." Adalyn swiped at the tears that fell below her glasses. "I suppose I will leave today rather than after the house party."

"You are leaving today?" Josette asked, surprised by this unexpected news.

"It is better this way," Adalyn assured her. "I refuse to let Antoine control me."

Josette gave her a sad, understanding smile. "If the governess position doesn't work out, then please send me a missive. Perhaps I can help you."

"If you can't rely on family, who can you trust?" Adalyn scoffed.

"Do you require any funds for your journey?" Josette asked, reaching out to touch her sleeve.

"No, but I thank you for your generosity," Adalyn replied with a weak smile. "I plan to take the mail coach out of town."

"Be safe, Adalyn," Josette urged. "It has been a pleasure to get to know you these past couple of days."

An emotional Adalyn embraced her. "I feel the same," she said, stepping back.

Feeling the anger grow inside of her as she watched her friend walk away, Josette found herself striding towards the library. This is a bad idea, she thought, but she refused to stand idly by while Mr. Clemens treated his sister so poorly. How dare he treat her with no regard for her feelings!

She stormed into the library and saw Mr. Clemens sitting at a large table with books spread out in front of him. He barely spared her a glance before turning back towards his ledgers.

"How could you?" Josette accused as she stopped next to him. She slammed one of the ledgers shut. "How could you treat Adalyn so callously?"

"I beg your pardon?" Mr. Clemens looked up with a baffled expression.

"Your cruel actions forced your sister to leave her home to seek employment as a governess in another country, and now you are threatening to disown her if she does not marry!" she exclaimed. "What gives you the right…"

Mr. Clemens cut her off. "You don't even know what you are talking about, you foolish chit."

Reaching into her skirt, Josette removed her dagger and plunged it into the closed ledger. "If you call me foolish again, I cannot be responsible for my actions."

His eyes narrowed at her dagger. "Why are you threatening me, Mrs. Addington?"

"Why are you forcing your sister to marry? Because of *your* actions, Adalyn is forced to take another governess position."

"Not that it is any of your business, but I never said she had to marry," Mr. Clemens replied dismissively. "I just asked her to return home to help with the family business."

"Liar!" Josette declared. "You were threatening to take away her monthly allowance, leaving her destitute."

Mr. Clemens stared up at her with bewilderment on his face. "Who told you that?"

"I just spoke to Adalyn in the hall."

"She must be confused," Mr. Clemens stated, "because I never once threatened to end her monthly allowance."

"Then why is she leaving to accept a governess position in London?" Josette huffed.

He tossed up his hands. "I don't know! Why did she leave in the middle of the night six years ago to accept a governess position in England? When did she start wearing those ridiculous spectacles? These are questions I can't answer."

"Are you saying she had a choice?"

Mr. Clemens rose and tugged down on his waistcoat. "Adalyn is a wealthy heiress, and I cannot presume to understand why she lowered herself enough to accept a governess position, even if it was for a brigadier general."

"Adalyn was a governess for an English general?" Josette asked skeptically.

"Yes, Brigadier General Arthur Slade Ballard." His jaw clenched. "Now do you understand the disgrace it was for our family? Our cousins were fighting in the war and my own sister was consorting with the enemy."

Josette frowned. Things were not adding up. "What about the books in the bottom of your trunk?"

He eyed her suspiciously, but she did not care. She needed to discover the truth. "Those belonged to Adalyn. She asked me to hold them for her because her trunk was full."

"And the green chemistry book? The one that was found in Mr. Blount's room?" she asked forcefully.

He gave her a blank stare. "I don't know what you are talking about. What book?"

"What about the letters from Mr. Blount that were in your possession?" Josette pressed, ignoring his question.

"What the devil? Why would I write letters to that irksome man?"

"What of Miss Lemaure?" she asked, eyeing him thoughtfully.

Mr. Clemens visibly stiffened. "What about her?"

"Did you find her searching through your trunk?"

Clearing his throat, obviously embarrassed, Mr. Clemens revealed, "Miss Lemaure may have come to my room, but it wasn't to search through my trunk."

They had been duped! Adalyn was *Genet,* and she was leaving the estate today. Grabbing her dagger, Josette tucked it into its sheath as she backed away from the desk. "When my husband comes to see you, tell him I need to see him immediately. Tell him we were wrong."

"Wrong about what?" he asked, his voice filled with confusion.

"Trust me. It will save you a considerable amount of pain if you just tell him," she said, before she turned and raced out the door.

Running back towards Adalyn's room, her steps faltered when she turned the corner and saw the door to the study was closed. She could hear muffled shouting coming from within, but she couldn't make out the words. When she knocked on the door, she was met with silence.

Josette attempted to open the door, but it was locked. She crouched down with one of her hair pins and picked the lock easily. Much to her surprise, when she pushed opened the door, she saw Adalyn pointing her pistol at Lord Paxton, who was still sitting at his drawing table.

"Josette," Adalyn drawled in an annoyed tone, "would you mind closing the door?"

She stepped inside and closed the door behind her without taking her eyes off of Adalyn. A confident woman stood in front of her. Except this Adalyn's eyes appeared black and cold.

"Did you get lost again?" she asked Adalyn lightly. "If you recall, the library is further down the hall."

Adalyn jerked her pistol towards her. "Go stand by Lord Paxton," she ordered. Moving the pistol into her left hand, she took off her spectacles and tossed them onto the desk. "I hate those dreadful things."

Lord Paxton cast a worried glance at Josette as she approached, but he did not say anything.

"Now back to the matter at hand," Adalyn said, aiming her pistol at Lord Paxton. "Give me your seal."

"I think not," Lord Paxton responded.

Keeping her pistol pointed at Lord Paxton, Adalyn moved around the desk and attempted to open the drawer. It was locked.

"Where is the key?" she demanded.

Lord Paxton shrugged. "I lost it."

Adalyn let out a frustrated sigh as her left hand grabbed her glasses. Shoving the end of the frame into the edge of the drawer, she twisted and turned her hand until the drawer unlocked. "There's a reason I wear those glasses," she admitted, smirking.

Adalyn's eyes never left Lord Paxton's face as her hand sorted through the drawer. After a moment, she frowned. "Where is your seal?" she demanded again.

Lord Paxton gave her an apologetic smile. "I'm afraid I lost that as well."

"If you do not produce the seal," Adalyn warned as she turned the pistol towards Josette, "then I will kill Josette."

Rising, Lord Paxton stepped in front of her. "There is no need for anyone to get hurt."

Taking advantage of being hidden from Adalyn's prying eyes, Josette slid her hand through the folds of her skirts towards her pistol.

"Why do you want his seal?" she asked over Lord Paxton's shoulder.

Adalyn pursed her lips together. "It is none of your concern."

Pressing the pistol against her side to keep it hidden, Josette stepped out from behind Lord Paxton. "It is if you are threatening to kill me for it."

Lord Paxton shot her a warning glance and placed his hand out to corral her back behind him. She met his gaze and shook her head.

Adalyn walked around the desk and waved the pistol towards Lord Paxton.

"Give me the seal, *now*."

"I had the most informative conversation with your brother after I left you," Josette said, drawing Adalyn's attention back to her.

Adalyn glared. "Is that so?"

"I learned that you were the governess for a brigadier general," she shared. "Which potentially could have given you access to British troop locations and other state secrets."

"I have no idea what you are referring to," Adalyn snapped.

"I think you do," Josette replied, scrunching her nose. "I also discovered that you asked your brother to hold onto your code book, and you most likely planted the letters from Mr. Blount under his mattress."

Lord Paxton looked at her in surprise, and she detected a hint of admiration in his eyes.

Adalyn tensed, her hand tightening around the pistol. "You are more than you appear, Mrs. Addington," she stated, her words anything but complimentary.

"Why would you go through all this trouble for Lord Paxton's seal?" Josette questioned.

Turning the pistol to point at her, Adalyn's tone became menacing. "You have no idea who you are up against."

"Oh, but I do," Josette said slowly and deliberately. "You are *Genet*."

Adalyn glared at her with such ferocity that the hate was palpable in the room. "You just signed your own death warrant," she growled.

Lord Paxton's mouth gaped. "*You* are *Genet?*"

Attempting to lengthen their conversation, Josette tilted her head. "What I still don't understand is why you would set up your own brother to take the fall as *Genet?*"

"One never goes into an unfamiliar situation without an exit strategy." Adalyn walked over to the window and glanced out. "A few innocent remarks, well-placed items, and adopting the persona of a timid woman allows me to complete my task without arousing suspicion. Plus, it is quite entertaining for me."

Josette shook her head. "But he is still your brother."

"I care not for Antoine. He is a coward. He refused to fight for Napoleon!" Adalyn exclaimed, advancing towards her.

Josette arched a brow. "You do realize that Napoleon lost the war, don't you? He is exiled to Elba."

"I tire of your cheeky comments." Adalyn cocked the pistol at her chest. "You are in over your head. It's a shame that I have to kill you," she said in a mocking tone. "I rather liked you."

"Stop!" Lord Paxton jumped in front of her, earning a scowl from Adalyn.

Taking advantage of the distraction, Josette brought her pistol up and stepped out from behind Lord Paxton. "The game is over. You have lost."

Adalyn's eyes narrowed at the pistol, then she laughed cruelly. "Oh, my dear friend, the game has only just begun." Shifting her aim towards the single lighted candle on the drawing table, Adalyn shot the brass chamberstick, causing it to propel upwards and onto the silk curtains. In moments, the curtain burst into flames.

Immediately, Lord Paxton took off his jacket and started beating the growing flames. Adalyn bolted towards the door, and Josette fired her pistol, hitting Adalyn in the upper arm. Unfortunately, that did little to stop the French spy, and she was able to run out the door.

Josette chased after her, but the door wouldn't budge. It was locked! Dropping to her knees, she attempted to unlock it, but she couldn't turn the mechanism. She rose in frustration, knowing they needed to find another way out. And quickly.

The rear of the room was on fire as it began to devour the drawing desk, drawings, and the plaster wall moldings. Her vision was starting to become blurred by the billowing smoke, but she managed to stagger towards a window near the front of the room. She opened it and leaned out, allowing her lungs to suck in the fresh air.

Pulling her head back into the smoke-filled room, she turned her attention towards Lord Paxton, who was still vainly battling the growing flames. When she opened her mouth to call to him, she started coughing and couldn't stop. The heat from the fire was becoming unbearable, and she was becoming increasingly lightheaded.

Lord Paxton dropped his scorched jacket onto the floor. She saw him open his mouth, but she couldn't hear what he was saying over the roar of the fire. Grabbing her arm, he assisted her out the open window.

Josette's breathing became more labored as she hurried out their only means of escape. She felt weak as she attempted to focus on scaling down the brick wall, grateful that it had become almost second nature to her.

She tilted her head to confirm that Lord Paxton had followed her out the window. She saw him a few feet above her, but her sigh of relief turned into another bout of coughing. Struggling to remain conscious, she finally reached the ground, but as soon as her feet hit the lawn, everything went black.

Chapter Nineteen

Sitting alone in the breakfast room, Gaspard and Morgan sat uncomfortably across from each other. The only noise was the ticking sound coming from the floor clock.

Gaspard cleared his throat. "I have been meaning to ask if Lord Paxton is aware of your assignment?"

"He is not, and I have no intention of informing him," Morgan replied firmly.

"Understood." Gaspard took a bite of his food, and silence descended again. "Were you and Mrs. Addington both agents before you were married?"

"I recruited Josette to be an agent," he replied, skirting around the truth.

Gaspard pushed his plate to the side and leaned back in his seat. "It seems rather odd that your partner is also your wife."

Taking his last bite, Morgan placed his napkin onto the plate. "It certainly has its advantages and disadvantages."

"It must be nice though," Gaspard murmured in a quiet, reflective tone. "I don't think it would be fair of me to take a wife at the moment. I would be forced to keep secrets from her and lie to her about where I was going or who I was seeing."

"I admit, it has been nice to be able to confide in someone," Morgan confirmed.

Gaspard took a sip of tea and placed the cup back on the saucer. "You married an extraordinary woman. I hope you never take that for granted."

"I won't," Morgan promised. "Earning Josette's love has been one of the hardest missions I have ever been faced with." He stilled at that realization. He did love her. Wholeheartedly.

Sitting back in his seat, Morgan observed the fine cut of apparel that Gaspard wore. "You clearly do not lack for income. Why don't you retire from the spy business? Get married and have a brood of children running around."

"Tempting." Gaspard chuckled. "I certainly don't work as a spy because I need the money."

"Then why?"

Gaspard glanced over his shoulder before replying, "Due to my extensive social and professional contacts, I was brought in to work as a spy, using my diplomatic status as a cover. Eventually, I earned Napoleon's trust, and I became one of his courtiers."

Morgan was astonished. Gaspard had been one of Napoleon's most trusted advisers!

"I know what you are thinking," Gaspard said, breaking into his thoughts. "Napoleon and I were not friends, nor were we foes. My role within his court was simple. I spoke for the people."

"What did the people say about Napoleon?" Morgan asked curiously.

Gaspard leaned forward in his seat and placed his forearms on the table. "He was not beloved by the people. He was ruthless, vindictive, and arrogant. His regime lacked credibility and seemed to mirror the emptiness in his soul."

Morgan lifted his brow at the harsh words. "I take it that your allegiance did not lie with Napoleon."

"At first, it was. I believed in his vision, his passion, and Napoleon rewarded me handsomely for my service as his courtier. But, towards the end, he became too unpredictable, too vindictive," Gaspard confessed. "After King Louis took the throne, I transitioned into the secret service to hunt down the agents that were still loyal to Napoleon. I have captured them all across Europe, including Britain."

"How did you manage to accomplish that feat?"

Gaspard smiled smugly. "I still maintain a diplomatic passport. Britain welcomes me with open arms."

"Does your brother know what you do?" Morgan reached for his glass, bringing it up to his lips.

"Yes and no." The smile dropped from Gaspard's face. "My

brother knows I go on special assignments for the king, but he doesn't know the specifics."

Turning his gaze towards the door, Morgan asked, "Are you ready?"

Gaspard nodded and rose. "Let's hope we are right."

Pushing back his seat, Morgan stood. "If Antoine is not *Genet*, then he has a lot of explaining to do."

They headed straight for the library and saw Antoine sitting at a table, his ledgers opened in front of him. Gaspard closed the door behind them, and they approached the desk cautiously. "May we ask you some questions, Mr. Clemens?" Morgan asked.

Antoine spun in his seat, his lips pressed tightly together in a line of disapproval. "Good heavens! Not you!"

Surprised by that unexpected remark, Morgan's steps faltered. "Pardon?"

Antoine huffed as he grabbed one of his ledgers and held it up. It had a large gash in the cover. "Your wife ruined my ledger when she slammed her dagger through it."

"My wife did that? For what purpose?"

Antoine dropped the book back onto the table. "She had it in her mind that I was forcing Adalyn into an arranged marriage."

Gaspard stepped closer to Antoine. "And are you?"

"No! But for some reason Adalyn is leaving today to accept another governess position," Antoine fumed. "I have no idea what my sister is thinking."

Morgan sat on the edge of the desk next to Antoine. "Josette just walked in and threatened you?"

"Yes!" Antoine exclaimed, sitting back in his seat. "Your wife is really quite frightening, if you ask me."

"What did she want to know?" Morgan pressed.

"She kept asking about books that I was holding for Adalyn, and my relationship with Mr. Blount," Antoine shared.

"Do you have a relationship with Mr. Blount?" Gaspard asked.

"Of course not." Antoine shook his head. "Why would I even associate with that horrid man?"

"Where is my wife now?" Morgan demanded.

"I have no idea," Antoine claimed, tossing his arms up. "When she left, she wanted me to tell you that you have it all wrong and to seek her out immediately."

Morgan's eyes darted to Gaspard. "Anything else?"

"Yes, she informed me if I relayed the message it would save me from a considerable amount of pain," Antoine answered, sounding skeptical.

"Do you have any idea where Josette is?" Morgan asked, frustrated by this unexpected delay.

"I don't know," Antoine answered. "She just ran back into the hall."

"Morgan," Gaspard said, drawing his attention. "We need to find Josette."

Leaning closer to Antoine, Morgan chose his words purposefully, and his tone was devoid of all emotion. "If I find that you have lied to me, I guarantee that I will return and finish this," he threatened, gratified to see fear in Antoine's eyes.

They opened the library door and charged out into the hall, heading towards the wing where the bedchambers were. Before they turned the corner, they heard a loud commotion. A group of servants were standing next to Lord Paxton's study door, and smoke was billowing out from the cracks around the doors.

"We can't get in!" a maid cried, wringing her hands.

Instantly, all thoughts of finding Josette fled. Morgan's primary focus was on rescuing Lord Paxton. Hoping he wasn't in the study, Morgan reached for the handle, but it had been broken off.

Banging on the door, he shouted, "Lord Paxton! Are you in there?"

Between the noise of the fire, and the hushed words from the servants, he couldn't hear a reply from inside. He rammed his shoulder into the door, but it was not enough.

"Let's do it together," Gaspard suggested.

Morgan counted down, and they slammed their shoulders into the door, causing the wood to splinter as it collapsed inward. The room was filled with billowing smoke, causing him to cough violently. He couldn't see any sign of Lord Paxton, and the heat and flames in the room forced him to retreat into the hall.

The butler began shouting orders, forming a long line of servants along the hall and down the stairway. Morgan and Gaspard joined at the head of the line. Morgan glanced anxiously into the room, then to the bottom of the stairs, waiting for the buckets of water to reach them.

Finally, he saw the first of the buckets being passed hand to hand up the stairs. When he had one in his hand, he threw the water on the fire. Steam mixed with the smoke, filling the air with a moist, acrid fog. He coughed, but handed his bucket back, reaching for the next. As the minutes ticked by, they poured bucket after bucket, dousing the fire with water. With each bucket, he peered through the smoky fog, trying to see inside.

It was nearly half an hour before Morgan could even think of entering the room. The flames were slowly being snuffed out, but they still flickered up here and there.

When Morgan could finally stand the diminishing heat, he dropped his bucket and searched the room, his heart pounding as he looked for any sign of Lord Paxton. Relief flooded over him as he realized the lord wasn't there. He involuntarily took a deep breath to sigh, but the overwhelming smell of smoke forced him to back out of the room, coughing.

"Lord Paxton wasn't in there," Morgan managed to tell Gaspard between coughs.

Gaspard didn't respond. His eyes were fixed on the open window in Lord Paxton's study. Brushing past him, Gaspard headed towards the window. Putting his head out, he muttered an expletive under his breath.

"What's wrong?" Morgan asked as he followed him in and approached the window.

Gaspard spun around and placed a hand on his shoulder. "You don't want to see this. Trust me."

Shoving aside Gaspard's hand, Morgan took the few steps towards the window, looked out, and his heart dropped. Josette and Lord Paxton were lying next to each other on the grass. Neither of them were moving. He hoped they were unconscious, and not…

Without finishing that thought, he sprinted out of the study, down the stairs, then ran like a madman towards the main entry door. He didn't stop running until he reached Josette. Dropping to his knees, he cradled her in his arms and felt for a pulse. He breathed a deep sigh of relief. *She was alive!* He held her close as tears filled his eyes.

Lord Paxton stirred next to him, coughing. "Is Josette… all right?"

"She is alive," he said, not relinquishing his hold on her.

"She collapsed…" Lord Paxton coughed hard, then caught his breath and continued, "after she scaled down the wall."

Gaspard ran up to them and placed his hands on his knees, breathing hard. "Is she alive?"

"She is," Morgan confirmed.

Gaspard helped Lord Paxton rise. "Let's take them inside and call for a doctor."

Holding her close, Morgan felt a tear slip down his cheek. All he could focus on was the hope that she would wake up. She *had* to wake up! He had never needed anything in his life before, but he needed Josette.

"Morgan," Gaspard interrupted his thoughts. "Would you prefer that I carried her?"

"No," he replied firmly, kissing the top of her head. "She's mine."

Josette opened her eyes and blinked at the brightness of the room. How did she end up in her bedchamber?

She took a moment to sit up in her bed, her body protesting the unexpected movement. She pressed a hand to her forehead, unsuccessfully attempting to will the pain in her skull to subside. She tried to recall what had happened to cause such a horrible headache. Suddenly, it all came flooding back. She *had* to see Morgan. She had to tell him the truth about Adalyn.

The door opened, and a fair-haired maid walked into the room. "You're awake!" she exclaimed cheerfully.

As Josette brought her hand down, she noticed how incredibly dry and dirty it was. A glance told her the other hand hadn't fared any better. The fire had also taken its toll on her gown. Not only did it smell of smoke, but the once-pastel color was now almost black.

"How long was I unconscious?" she asked.

"About three hours, ma'am." The maid held a tray in her hands and walked it over to the table. "Mr. Addington was called away, but he instructed me to cater to your every whim. I have requested a bath to be sent up."

"Where is my husband now?" Josette asked, sliding her feet carefully over the edge of the bed.

The maid kept her back to her as she organized the tray. "In the library. He is in a meeting with Lord Paxton and Mr. Gaspard Mancini."

Rising, Josette took a few shaky steps but was gratified to feel her strength returning. She needed to speak to Morgan as quickly as possible. Time was of the essence. She didn't have the luxury of lounging in bed.

The maid shouted after her, "Mrs. Addington! You should be resting!"

Ignoring the maid, she headed towards the library, pausing briefly to run her eyes over the damaged study. She shuddered when she saw the blackened, charred walls and burned furniture. The smell of smoke was still overwhelming, making it hard to breathe, even from the doorway. *Genet* had left them for dead, but they had survived.

Once she arrived at the library door, she knocked and pushed the door open. Taking in the room, she saw that Lord Paxton stood between Gaspard and Morgan and was pointing towards a document on the table.

All their eyes turned towards her, but Josette did not have time to feel self-conscious. As she started to open her mouth, Morgan closed the distance between them. He reached out and cupped her cheeks, his eyes caressing her with a look of great tenderness, as if he'd waited forever to see her.

Seeing the compassion in his eyes, she briefly forgot her purpose for being there. Her lips parted, but she couldn't seem to formulate any words. Not when he was looking at her like that. All she could do was stand there, waiting for him to say something. *Anything.*

"You're awake," he said softly. "I was so worried. I was afraid you might never wake up."

She grinned playfully. "This is not the first time I have fallen while scaling a wall."

Ignoring her attempt at humor, Morgan lowered his head very gently until he was resting his forehead against hers. "Josie…" He took a shallow breath. Then, his tone turned accusatory. "What were you thinking?"

It took a moment for her mind to register his words. "Thinking?" she asked, leaning back. "I believe it's clear what I was thinking. I was trying to stop *Genet* from killing Lord Paxton."

"For which I am immensely grateful," Lord Paxton declared from his spot behind the desk.

Morgan's piercing gaze watched her. "You should have waited for me."

"If I had, Lord Paxton might have been shot," she contended, stepping out of his arms.

Lord Paxton came around the desk, approaching them with hesitant steps. "Again, I am grateful for Josette's interference."

Morgan frowned deeply, not bothering to acknowledge Lord Paxton's comment. "Not only did *Genet* escape, but you were almost killed."

Placing a hand on Morgan's shoulder, Lord Paxton tried again. "You are not thinking clearly, son. Your wife's actions were heroic, and you are deflecting your anger at the situation onto her."

Josette saw Morgan tense as he ran a hand through his tousled hair. Rather than wait to be accused again, she started to explain. "I saw an emotional Adalyn leaving the library. She informed me that she was leaving to accept a governess position today, causing me to seek out her brother."

"What if Antoine had been *Genet*?" Morgan huffed. "He would have killed you."

Josette's eyes narrowed. "I can protect myself, Morgan."

"Apparently not," Morgan countered.

Lord Paxton stepped closer to her, his expression softening. "Thank you. If you hadn't interfered when you did, the outcome could have been fatal for me." He embraced her firmly. As he leaned back, he whispered in her ear, "However, don't ever do anything so foolish again. But don't tell Morgan that I agree with him."

"Thank you," she replied as he offered her a kind smile.

"I told Gaspard and Morgan about what transpired with Miss Clemens in the office."

"Were you able to…"

Lord Paxton put up his hand to stop her. "I know what you are going to ask. I sent footmen to search for Miss Clemens and Mr. Blount. Sadly, they have both disappeared."

"Did they search The Gutted Fish?" she asked.

Lord Paxton nodded. "Yes, but Mr. Blount had already cleared out his room."

"What you did was really brave, Mrs. Addington," Gaspard said with admiration in his eyes.

Josette smiled at him. "My friends call me Josette."

Gaspard tipped his head towards her, acknowledging her words.

Lord Paxton regarded the group for a long moment before saying, "It is clear that you three are more than you have led us to believe." He turned his focus onto Morgan. "Dare I assume that you work for the Home Office?"

Morgan met his gaze, unflinchingly. "I serve the Crown's interests."

Turning his knowing gaze to her, Lord Paxton asked, "And do you serve…" he paused, clearing his throat, "the Crown's interest as well?"

Josette glanced at Morgan, and he gave her a nod. "I do."

Lord Paxton lifted his brow at Gaspard, waiting for his reply. In response, Gaspard bowed. "I am just here for the merriment of the house party, and not because I am attempting to track down a French spy on English soil." He smirked. "Just for the record, I am loyal to the King of France."

"Interesting," Lord Paxton muttered as he watched Gaspard closely. "I believe I underestimated you, Mr. Mancini."

"Why was Adalyn demanding your seal?" Josette asked.

Lord Paxton sighed as he walked back to the table. "That is an excellent question, and I'm afraid I may know the answer." He stepped to a shelf and pulled out a long, rolled-up paper. Returning to the table, he spread it out. "These are the architectural drawings for the House of Lords."

When Josette stepped closer to the table, Morgan grabbed a chair and positioned it next to Lord Paxton. "Why don't you take a seat?" he suggested as he placed his hand on her elbow directing her towards the chair.

Why was he fussing over her? "That's not necessary," she insisted.

"Your body needs to rest," he protested softly.

Focusing on the drawings, she replied through gritted teeth, "I appreciate your concern, but my body is perfectly content standing."

"Just sit in the chair, Josie," Morgan urged. "Please?"

Why was he being so insistent about the chair? She was perfectly capable of standing on her own. Rather than continue this ridiculous fight when they had more pressing matters at hand, she lowered herself to the chair and murmured a grudging, "Thank you."

"As I was saying," Lord Paxton continued, "I am the chief architect on the new roof and general renovations. Due to the large amount of materials we are required to store, we were granted permission to store these items in the undercroft, directly under the House of Lords."

"How large is the undercroft?" Gaspard asked.

"The undercroft, or lower story, which is level with the pavement of the street, runs the length of the building. Part of it is enclosed to contain a stove for warming the chamber above, and another portion serves as the Speaker's state dining room. But that still leaves a large open area that historically has been rented out for shops," Lord Paxton shared. "However, after the gunpowder plot of 1605, the Crown bought all the undercrofts of the Palace of Westminster and refuses to rent them out to the public."

"Forgive me, but what was the gunpowder plot?" Gaspard inquired.

"It was a failed attempt to assassinate King James I and both houses of Parliament during the opening meeting of Parliament," Josette explained. "A group of Roman Catholics rented a section of the undercroft that extended under the House of Lords and planted thirty-six barrels of gunpowder there."

"Thirty-six barrels?" Gaspard repeated in disbelief. "That's a lot of gunpowder."

Morgan nodded solemnly. "Many speculate that if the gunpowder had been detonated, the loss of life and property would have been catastrophic. The blast would have not only destroyed the upper house, but the nearby House of Commons, Old Chapel, and Westminster Hall would have also been destroyed."

"Fortunately, the conspirators were all caught, tried and executed," Lord Paxton shared. "To celebrate the plot's failure, the Crown passed the Observance of 5th November Act. Some people refer to it as Bonfire Night."

Josette rose from her chair, hoping that she had sat long enough to satisfy Morgan. "It has been dubbed Bonfire Night because the very night that the gunpowder plot was foiled, bonfires were lit to celebrate the safety of the king."

Morgan frowned at the empty chair, but rather than criticize her, he turned towards Lord Paxton. "If the Crown won't rent out the undercroft, how were you able to gain access to store construction materials there?"

"There is no other place to store the materials," Lord Paxton stated, pulling out an architectural drawing and placing it on the table. "This is the map of the entire Palace of Westminster. It was originally built as a royal residence. It covers the courts known as Old Palace Yard and New Palace Yard." He pointed towards the map. "Between the palace, townhouses, merchant shops, and businesses, there is not a single open piece of land to rent out."

Josette nodded in agreement. "The buildings are practically sitting on top of each other at the palace."

Lord Paxton placed his finger on the drawing. "We were granted access to the undercroft by way of the interior courtyard." He stopped speaking, his brow furrowed as he looked up at them. "We were granted permission on one condition."

"Which was?" Morgan asked.

Reaching into the pocket of his waistcoat, Lord Paxton removed a brass seal. "The only way past the guards is by producing a missive with my waxed seal on it. If the workers cannot produce that, they are turned away."

Gaspard frowned. "Is there no other way into the undercrofts?"

Lord Paxton shook his head. "The guards search the undercrofts daily while Parliament is in session. They are diligent about looking for any signs of tampering."

"And if your seal was stolen?" Morgan asked.

Tucking the seal back into his waistcoat, Lord Paxton said firmly, "I guard this seal with my life. If it was stolen, then my life would be forfeit."

Josette's eyes scanned the drawings. "*Genet* failed to obtain the seal. Perhaps she will return home, even though she was unsuccessful."

"No, *Genet* will not run back to France," Gaspard asserted. "She will find another way to achieve her nefarious purpose."

Morgan placed his hands down onto the table and asked Gaspard, "What do you think her purpose is?"

Gaspard ran his hand along the back of his neck. "I may have left something out previously," he started slowly. "There has been talk about *Genet* assassinating King Louis, but up until now, no one gave it any credence." He dropped his hand. "I believe Miss Clemens is planning to blow up the House of Lords when King Louis addresses the joint session of Parliament."

Lord Paxton dropped his face into his hand. "That would explain why she wanted the seal. I suspect she wanted to store explosives in the undercroft. If the gunpowder was stored with the construction materials, then no one would give it any heed."

"But we stopped her," Josette assured them. "She doesn't have access to the undercroft."

"I know of another way," Geoffrey quietly announced from the library doors.

Chapter Twenty

Everyone turned to face Geoffrey, who was looking at the floor.

"What do you mean, son?" Lord Paxton asked, his voice guarded.

"I gave Mr. Blount permission to use our apartment at the palace," Geoffrey answered, shifting nervously from one foot to the other.

Lord Paxton stared at his son, blinking slowly. "Please tell me you are joking. You gave Mr. Blount, a traitor to the Crown, access to the apartment that Prinny *allowed* our family to use during the renovation process?"

"I didn't think you would mind." Geoffrey walked further into the room, his steps hesitant. "I gave him a key and told him he could only stay when you weren't in residence."

"You gave *him* a key!" Lord Paxton roared. "Are you mad?"

Morgan could see Geoffrey was attempting to be strong, but he also saw the anguish in his eyes. He was crumbling under his father's scrutiny, and with good cause.

"Where is the apartment situated?" Morgan asked, bringing his gaze back to Lord Paxton.

"It sits in the structure attached to the south-east corner of the House of Lords, known as the Painted Chamber," Lord Paxton said with pressed lips. "Because of the many long hours I spend at the palace supervising the construction project, it became quite burdensome to travel to my townhouse in Mayfair every night. When Prinny heard of my plight, he offered the solution of using the apartment. Normally, this apartment is used to host dignitaries of other nations."

Pointing at the map, Lord Paxton highlighted the close proximity of the apartment to the upper house.

"Do you have a staff at the apartment?" Josette inquired.

"Not when I'm residing there alone," Lord Paxton revealed. "When my wife joins me, she travels with the required staff."

"How did you meet Mr. Blount?" Josette asked as she approached Geoffrey.

"We met at a pub," he shared. "He invited me to listen to him speak at a rally in Templeton Square, and we struck up a friendship."

Morgan stifled a groan at Geoffrey's naivety. It was clear that Mr. Blount had arranged for them to meet. "Had you met Miss Clemens before this house party?"

Geoffrey shook his head. "No. I hadn't."

Placing a hand on his shoulder, Josette led Geoffrey towards the sofa. "Have you met any of Mr. Blount's other friends?"

"You mean the other revolutionaries?" Geoffrey asked as he sat on the sofa.

"You have been deceived," Lord Paxton scoffed. "Mr. Blount used you to gain access to me and our apartment."

"Father, it's not like that..." Geoffrey attempted, his voice growing unsure.

Gaspard interrupted him. "Has Mr. Blount affiliated himself with the Whig party?"

"I assume so." Geoffrey looked back up at him with confusion on his face.

"You assume so," Morgan repeated, sitting on a chair opposite him, "but you don't know for sure."

"His teachings are in line with what the Whigs preach... I just assumed," Geoffrey replied, stumbling over his words.

Sitting down next to Geoffrey, Josette asked, "These groups that you mentioned; have you met any of the other leaders?"

"I have not, but I have met some of the other anti-monarchs," Geoffrey admitted. "And I know there are groups similar to ours all over England."

Leaning forward, Morgan pushed, "Is there a call to arms, or are these peaceful protests?"

"Um..." Squirming in his seat, Geoffrey looked much younger

than his twenty years of age. "Mr. Blount is encouraging an uprising…" His voice faltered as he looked at his father. "But I wasn't going to be a part of that, Father. I swear! I told them it was wrong to press their agenda with violence."

"It is more than wrong. It is treason!" Lord Paxton crossed his arms over his chest and gave his son a look of exasperation. "Do you not grasp that you are implicated in all of this?"

At his father's words, Geoffrey's face paled.

"Geoffrey," Josette began, "when was this uprising supposed to occur?"

"In a few days," Geoffrey responded, shifting his gaze towards her. "Something big is going to happen that will act as a signal for the people to rally and storm London."

"Do you know what it is?" Gaspard asked, placing his hands on the back of an arm chair.

"I don't," Geoffrey confessed. "Mr. Blount left today to be with the other protestors in London."

"Leaving you behind?" Morgan questioned.

"Violence is never the answer," Geoffrey murmured. "I told him that."

Morgan stood suddenly. "I suspect that after bombing the House of Lords, *Genet* plans to use the chaos to have an uprising, plunging Britain into further panic and disorder."

"If King Louis is assassinated," Gaspard exclaimed as he pushed his chair back, "then France will have no choice but to welcome Napoleon back as emperor! Our constitutional monarchy is too weak to survive political turmoil."

"With both houses of parliament gone, Britain would not be in a position to stop Napoleon assuming the throne," Josette said. "He would be unstoppable."

"We have to get to London to stop *Genet*!" Morgan exclaimed.

Josette jumped up. "I agree."

Morgan's heart dropped. Josette couldn't go. She was still recovering from her injuries.

"You stay here and rest," he ordered her. "You are in no condition to travel, especially at the grueling pace that Gaspard and I will be forced to endure."

Josette crossed her arms over her chest defiantly. "I am going," she huffed. "If not with you, then I will go by myself."

In two strides, he closed the distance between them and placed his hand on her arm, guiding her towards the far corner.

"You barely escaped out of Lord Paxton's study with your life. You're still recovering," he reminded her. "It would be best if you stay here and rest."

Determination laced Josette's features. "You would go without me then?"

Morgan reached up to cup her right cheek, but she turned her head, so he lowered his hand. "I need you to be safe, Josie. I can't risk worrying about your safety while attempting to focus on saving England from a massive terrorist attack."

"After everything we've been through," she began, pain filling her words, "you still think of me as a hindrance."

"No, that is not it at all," he declared. "I don't want you to be injured… or worse."

Josette took a step back, the hurt evident on her features. "I have told you before, I can protect myself."

"It's not about protecting yourself…" he hesitated, his eyes imploring hers to understand, "…I can't lose you."

"I am not yours to lose," she countered.

Morgan took a step closer to her and placed his hands gently on her shoulders. "Josie," he whispered, "please don't say such things."

"You promised I would be your partner, but you are trying to control me," Josette stated, shaking off his hands. "You have no right."

"I paid you to pose as my wife at a house party," he replied in a hushed voice, "not to stop a French spy from blowing up parliament and assassinating a French king. As far as I am concerned, your job is over."

Josette's mouth parted in surprise, and Morgan realized he may have gone too far. He closed his eyes, wishing he could take back his last words.

Lord Paxton cleared his throat from across the room. "Josette, I'm afraid I must side with your husband. He is only concerned for your safety, as am I."

Turning her gaze towards Lord Paxton, Josette replied, "You're wrong. Morgan is not my husband; he *was* my partner." With one last heated glare focused at him, she spun around and walked swiftly out of the room, slamming the library door behind her.

Morgan wanted to shout in frustration that Josette had just ruined their cover. But before he dealt with those repercussions, he needed to finish the conversation with her. He had barely taken his first step when Lord Paxton's hand gripped his shoulder from behind.

"You are not married to Josette?" His words were filled with anger as his hand clamped down harder. "You lied to me, to us?"

"It's not that simple," Morgan proclaimed, turning to face Lord Paxton.

"Get out of my home!" Lord Paxton roared, dropping his arm. "You are not welcome here."

"Wait! You need to understand," Morgan shouted, putting his hands up. "I was assigned to track down *Genet*, and I was partnered with Josette."

"You shared a bedchamber with the girl!" Taking a commanding step towards him, Lord Paxton pointed to the ground as he declared, "You will do the right thing and marry her!"

"Don't you think I want that?" he exclaimed. "I want to marry Josette, but she doesn't want me."

Lord Paxton immediately calmed a bit, looking baffled. "Why not? What woman doesn't want marriage?"

Morgan tossed his head back and looked up at the rafters. "Josette's virtue is intact. I would never disrespect her so horrendously and take advantage of her prior to our marriage," he stated, bringing his gaze down. "I love her."

"But she doesn't love you?" Lord Paxton questioned.

Morgan shrugged. "At times, I can see her softening, but she keeps her heart guarded so fiercely." He walked to an upholstered arm chair and dropped down. "I can't do my job if my focus is on Josette's safety."

A deafening silence filled the room as Lord Paxton sat on a chair next to him. "What little I saw of Josette in action, it appears she is proficient with a pistol and can take care of herself in stressful situations."

"You Englishmen are fools indeed." Gaspard chuckled dryly. "France has been employing women as spies for centuries, but Britain does not believe women have the mindset for espionage."

Geoffrey sat taller in his seat as he asked, "Mrs. Addington... er... Miss Josette is a spy?"

Morgan turned his sharp gaze towards Geoffrey. "If you ever reveal that piece of information, I will kill you."

"Mr. Addington," Lord Paxton requested with a lifted brow, "will you please stop threatening to kill my son?"

"It wasn't a threat," Morgan said deliberately, "it was a promise."

With fear in his eyes, Geoffrey nodded his understanding.

Glancing at the door, Lord Paxton stated, "As much as I would like to leave Josette in the care of my wife, I believe she will be traveling to London with us."

Morgan shook his head. "Gaspard and I will not be traveling with you in a carriage. We are going to ride hard towards London. We only have three days until the joint session of Parliament commences."

"If we ride hard, we should arrive in two days' time," Gaspard affirmed, "giving us a whole day to thwart a terrorist attack."

"Sounds reasonable," Morgan confirmed, rising from his seat.

"Will Josette be coming with us?" Gaspard asked, lifting his brow.

Morgan sighed deeply. "If we don't take her, she will just go on her own. If you will excuse me, I need to go grovel to my pretend wife."

He frowned as he left the room. Why had he fallen in love with the most cantankerous, disobedient woman in all of England?

Josette had just strapped her pistol to her right thigh when she heard a knock at the locked door. Taking a guess at who was there, she ignored the knock and walked over to the bed, reaching for her cap. She placed it on her head and surveyed the room. Her dresses lay haphazardly near the trunk, but she did not care. Her focus had been on finding her training clothes, so she could leave as quickly as possible. She was sure Morgan would be furious at the condition of the room.

No, he would be angry because she left without him. Well, it was his own fault, she thought. It was his fault for trying to control her. She was not his wife. She was free to come and go as she pleased, and he could not stop her.

Ensuring her dagger was secured against her leg, Josette took a moment to glance in the mirror, assuring herself that she had everything in place. As a present, Cosette had sewn her buff trousers, fitting her tall frame, and a white shirt that hung a little snugger than most men's shirts. Kate, the Countess of Camden, had given her leather straps to secure her pistol and dagger on her thighs during her long training sessions. It was convenient having both weapons on her person and within reach.

Josette fought back her emotions as she tucked the coral necklace into a small pocket of her trousers. She sighed. At least, she had something to remember Morgan by. She walked to the window and placed her hands on both sides. It's time to go, she thought. The knocking stopped. Finally. Hopefully, Morgan took the hint. As she started to place her foot on the sill, the door opened, and she heard a deep sigh from behind her.

"Do you intend to run away every time we fight?" Morgan asked lightly.

Keeping her back to him, Josette's eyes scanned the courtyard, and she saw her chance for freedom. All she had to do was exit the window and scale down the wall. She would be free to travel to London... alone. Her heart constricted at that word. *Alone.* Suddenly, being alone didn't seem so appealing, but she didn't see another option. She heard a soft thud as Morgan dropped down onto the velvet settee facing the window.

"Just so you know, I approve of your clothing," he remarked.

She could hear the smile on his lips. Why did just hearing his voice help soothe her? She found herself feeling less angry than she had just a few moments ago.

"How exactly do you plan to get to London on your own?" Morgan asked.

"I plan to borrow one of Lord Paxton's mounts and ride there," she informed him, not bothering to turn around.

"You do realize that horse thievery is a hanging offense?"

Josette lowered her hands from the window frame. "I left a note, explaining I would return the horse after I tracked down *Genet*. If Lord Paxton takes issue, then I will pay him for the horse."

"That is a considerable sum of money," he pointed out. "But, rather than dwell on that, where do you intend to stay when night approaches?"

"I am perfectly content sleeping under the stars," she stated. "I am aware that my attire will attract unwanted attention if I approach an inn-keeper to rent a room."

"And did you think of food?"

Drats! She had almost left her reticule behind which would have made her food options considerably limited. "I would have eaten off the land."

Morgan chuckled. "Your plan sounds flawless, my dear. Have fun."

Placing her hands back up on the window frame, Josette felt her resolve crumble. She didn't want to ride out alone. She wanted to stay with Morgan. Curse her treacherous heart! Curse Morgan! This was his doing.

"Go on," Morgan urged.

Her hands tightened around the frame. He was testing her. He didn't think she could do it. Well, she would show him!

As she placed her foot onto the sill, she felt his warm breath next to her ear. "Or we can ride out together?"

She shook her head. "There is no *we*, remember? My job is over."

"I understand that." Turning, he leaned his back against the wall, his eyes watching her. "I will escort you back to London and deliver you to the safety of your school."

"Will you go after *Genet* by yourself?"

"No. Gaspard is riding with us, and he will help me capture *Genet*," he informed her. "Besides, once we are back in London, I know a few friends who can help with this situation."

"I am one of those friends, Morgan!" she exclaimed. "I helped save *your* life at The Cloven Hoof in Gravesend. Do you not recall that?"

He frowned. "Circumstances have changed…" His voice trailed off as she turned away from him. "*We* have changed."

"You are never going to view me as your partner, are you?" Josette's shoulders slumped in resignation.

He looked confused. "We *are* partners."

"No, we never truly were," she murmured. "You see me as someone you need to protect, even after everything we have been through."

"I don't understand why you are upset."

"I don't need a protector; I can protect myself," she stated, wrapping her arms around her waist. "What I need is for you to trust me."

He straightened from the wall. "I do trust you."

"Then prove it!" she shouted. "Let me help you stop *Genet* before it is too late."

Morgan's blue eyes grew serious and worry lines shadowed the corners of his eyes. "When I saw you crumpled on the ground, I thought I'd lost you…" His voice was sober, shaking a little. "The thought of losing you is more than I can bear."

Feeling the tension drain out of her, Josette replied, "If you try to control me, then you *will* lose me." She raised her hand up and her knuckles brushed his cheek. "Allow me to be myself around you; grant me that privilege."

"Why do you have to put yourself in harm's way?" Morgan captured her hand in his. "Why can't you stay behind? Just this once. For me."

"I will never be what you are hoping I will be." Stepping back, Josette held out her arms. "You are asking me to hide while you risk your life to save England. That is *not* who I am. I want to fight alongside you, help you. Not hide behind you. Don't you understand that?"

"We are trying to stop a ruthless French spy from blowing up the House of Lords and crippling the two most powerful nations in the world!" Morgan exclaimed, clenching his jaw. He turned away from her. "It's not a matter of trusting you. I know you are capable, but I can't… I *won't*, let you go into a situation where you could be killed."

"And what of you?" she asked.

He turned back around to face her. "I accepted the risks associated with being an agent of the Crown long ago. But you," he ran his hand through his tousled hair, "you aren't an agent. You were not asked to give your life in defense of your country."

"You are my dearest friend," Josette said, placing her hand over his heart. She spoke through unshed tears, surprising herself with the intensity of that admission. "Do not attempt to shelter me from the atrocities of man, because I have experienced them firsthand." She brought her other hand to his chest. "You speak of the pain of losing me, but my heart would crumble and cease to exist if I lost you."

"Oh, Josie," Morgan breathed as he embraced her. "You won't lose me."

"I know, because wherever you go, I go," she stated matter-of-factly.

She could see indecision on his face, but then his expression changed, and Morgan looked at her thoughtfully.

"If this is what you truly wish."

"It is," she replied quickly.

Lowering his head, he kissed her forehead, his lips lingering on her skin. "I can't guarantee that Beckett will go along with this, but I am willing to try, assuming, you follow all of my orders."

She beamed up at him. "I promise."

"I am mad for agreeing to this." He grunted. "Truly, utterly mad."

"I think you are quite brilliant."

Morgan walked over to the window and looked out. "Bringing your betrothed on an assignment is generally looked down upon by the other agents."

"Your betrothed?" she repeated. "But we aren't engaged."

"We are." He smirked, looking over his shoulder. "Starting now."

Her mouth gaped. "You can't just decide we are engaged."

"I believe I just did," he said, waggling his brow. "Now, out the window. It is time to depart."

She glanced out the window and saw Gaspard standing below with three saddled horses.

"I had a feeling," Morgan playfully nudged her with his shoulder, "that you would make your appearance dressed in men's clothing. So I asked Gaspard to bring the horses to our window. That way, we could depart without anyone seeing your..." his approving eyes roamed the length of her, "attire."

"Clever spy." Not thinking, she turned her head towards him, bringing their lips only inches apart.

His eyes darted towards her lips. "Do I get rewarded for my thoughtfulness?" he asked, his voice low and soft.

"I suppose that's only fair," she heard herself saying, but her breath caught as he moved closer. As his lips brushed against hers, Josette heard a throat clearing loudly from outside.

"Correct me if I am wrong, but we *are* trying to stop a French spy, are we not?" Gaspard's teasing voice shouted up.

"I'm going to kill him." Morgan's lips brushed ever so softly against hers as he spoke.

Her lips quirked. "Don't do that on my account."

Morgan leaned back far enough for her to see the twinkle in his eye. "Let's go save England, together."

Chapter Twenty-One

Morgan's eyes scanned the darkened horizon as the relentless rain came down in sheets. Soaked to the core, he hoped to secure dry lodgings for the evening.

"I see a barn!" Josette exclaimed, pointing towards a far corner of an open meadow. She kicked her horse into a run, veering towards the large structure. Gaspard rode close behind.

Eager to be out of the rain, Morgan overtook them before they reined in their horses in front of the barn. He dismounted and grabbed the handle of the barn door, wrenching it open. It gave way with a groan and rats scurried across the floor, disappearing into the darkness of the shadows. *Rats!* He hated rats!

The overwhelming odor of manure, animals, wood, and feed were mingled together. Josette appeared immune to the smell. She didn't hesitate to escort her horse into the barn. As she walked past him, he noticed the soaked clothes clinging to her body. He took off his jacket and draped it over her shoulders.

"Thank you," she acknowledged, pulling it closer to her body.

"I have to keep my betrothed happy," he said, smirking.

Josette rolled her eyes. "We are not engaged."

Working quickly, they removed their horses' saddles and found brushes to curry their wet coats.

"I will drop some hay down the chute," Gaspard informed them as he climbed up the ladder to the haymow.

After ensuring the horses were taken care of, Josette and Morgan climbed up the ladder and found a blanket hanging from a nail on the wall. Laying it over a section of hay, they sat down and leaned back. The odor of moldy hay, dampened by raindrops, hung in the air, and

Morgan heard the sound of trickling water.

"This is surprisingly comfortable," Morgan observed, closing his eyes.

"I wouldn't get too relaxed." Josette's voice held humor. "Hay mounds are notorious for rats, snakes, and all kinds of vermin."

Morgan shot up from his seat and turned to look at the large pile of hay. Gaspard laughed as he sat down near them and leaned his back against the wood frame. "Don't tell me that you are afraid of snakes, Morgan?"

"Snakes I can handle. It's rats I hate," he confessed, shuddering.

Josette patted his sleeve comfortingly. "Do not fear. I will protect you from the big, fat rats."

"How are *you* not afraid of them?" Gaspard asked Josette.

"I look at rats differently," she informed him. "I see them as a potential food source."

Gaspard's eyebrows shot up. "You have eaten rats?"

"Rats, snakes, cats, dogs…" Josette nodded as she rattled off the list. "I learned that mice aren't worth your time to cook. They have hardly any meat on them."

Suddenly, Gaspard's shocked expression turned into a wide smile. "You are teasing me. This is an example of your British wit, isn't it?"

"Sadly, it is not," she replied, twirling a piece of hay between her fingers. "I was forced to live on the streets for a short time."

Looking for confirmation, Gaspard turned to Morgan, who gave him a sad nod. He hoped that the Frenchman would drop the matter. Taking the hint, Gaspard changed the subject.

"This was an unexpected delay."

"It is," Morgan agreed, listening to the pounding rain on the barn's roof. "I had hoped to arrive in London tonight, but that won't happen now."

Bringing his leg up, Gaspard rested his arm on it. "Tomorrow afternoon is the joint session. What if we're too late?"

"We won't be," Morgan stated firmly. "We'll head out before dawn. If we ride hard, it's only a few more hours into London."

Leaning back on the hay, Morgan placed his arm over Josette's shoulders and pulled her close. "We should rest," he encouraged.

To his delight, Josette shifted her body, so she rested her face on his shoulder. He could hear her sigh contentedly, filling his heart with joy.

Morgan looked up and saw Gaspard watching them with a wistful expression.

His heart dropped as the hay next to his head rustled. Turning, he saw a black rat scurrying off the hay and onto the floor. Before he could react, Josette sat up, removed her dagger, and flung it at the rat, killing it.

She rose from her position and walked over to the dead vermin. Removing her dagger, she grabbed the rat's tail and tossed it into the corner.

"One down," she muttered, "hundreds to go."

"Hundreds?" he asked, a touch of fear in his voice.

"Don't worry," Josette grinned, then drawled, "*I* will protect you, my lord." She leaned down and used the hay to wipe off her dagger before securing it back to her leg.

"Thank you, my fair maiden." Morgan had to admit that he was pleased that he didn't have to be the one to kill the rats.

"Are you truly a lord?" Gaspard asked, interrupting their private interlude.

"Yes," Morgan confirmed, seeing no reason to deny it.

Gaspard's next question was directed at Josette. "Are you a titled woman?"

She shook her head.

"But you were born into nobility," he pressed.

"What I am, or what I am not, is none of your concern, Mr. Mancini," Josette declared.

Morgan chuckled. "Josette does not like to answer questions about herself."

"I thought we were friends." Gaspard tsked, then he smiled. "Perhaps if I went first."

"I already know everything that I need to know about you," Josette said confidently.

"You do?" Gaspard asked in an amused tone. "Pray tell."

Josette straightened as she scrutinized the Frenchman. "You are a very handsome man…"

"Why, thank you…"

"… and you use that to your advantage. You speak several languages, based upon the collection of books I saw in your room, but you hide your intellectual prowess from those closest to you."

Gaspard put his hands out and said, "That is impressive but—"

Josette cut him off. "You had your heart broken once, and now you don't believe love is tangible, at least not for you. You hide behind a mask of your own self-making, but it doesn't alleviate the pain of disapproval you feel from your family and friends. Even though you insist you are happy, you are lonely and can't find peace."

"Anything else?" he asked curtly.

Josette's voice softened. "You don't thirst for blood, but you will kill if the situation calls for it. Which is why I trust you, despite the fact that you are a French spy."

Gaspard stared at her, his mouth parted. "How did you know that?"

"My *betrothed* is very astute in her observations of others," Morgan said, smiling proudly at Josette.

"Will you please stop referring to me as your betrothed?" Josette huffed, but there was no anger in it, nor frustration.

Gaspard dropped his leg as he asked, "How did you read me so perfectly?"

Josette smiled confidently as she explained, "The books in your trunk gave me great insight into the man you are. They were scientific in nature, and were written in Russian, German, and Croatian. You underlined passages and wrote small notes on the pages, allowing me to conclude that you do not share your insights with others. However, the most worn book in your collection was Shakespeare's Sonnets, written in Italian, and it was on the table next to the bed. Leading me to assume that you read it frequently."

"You can tell all that by my book collection?" Gaspard inquired with a furrowed brow.

"We naturally gravitate towards books that speak directly to us," Josette said. "Every book we open, every page we read, it becomes a part of who we are, and who we will become."

"And the thirst for blood?" Gaspard asked.

Her tone softened. "Even though you threatened me with your

dagger, your eyes still held a glimmer of kindness."

"You threatened my betrothed with a dagger?" Morgan growled.

"It was only fair. She threatened to shoot me," Gaspard replied jovially before his face grew serious. "I wish you were on our side, Josette. The French could use a spy like you."

With a quick side-glance at her partner, Josette's lips quirked. "I'm happy where I am."

Morgan felt his chest puff up with pride. She was happy with him. Now he just had to convince her to marry him. That was going to take considerably more time.

"We should get some sleep before dawn," he said, feeling his heart leap with joy when Josette rested her head on his chest.

Josette reined in her horse as she reached Lord and Lady Lansdowne's townhouse. She dismounted as Morgan and Gaspard caught up to her. A footman ran down the steps to collect their horses as they raced up the entry stairs.

Not bothering to knock, Josette opened the large door and walked into the marble entry hall. "Lady Lansdowne!" she called.

Eliza, dressed in an emerald green gown, rushed out of the drawing room. "What's the matter?" she demanded, her steps growing hesitant when she saw Gaspard. "And you brought a guest?"

"We need to speak to Benedict and Adrien, *immediately*!" Morgan announced.

Eliza pressed her lips together. "That's impossible. They are at the House of Lords for the joint assembly."

"What? No! That was supposed to be this afternoon!" Morgan yelled.

Eliza gave a brief shake of her head. "The prince regent is attending the assembly, and they rescheduled it for the morning..." Her voice trailed off as her alert eyes grew calculating. "What's the problem?"

"Larson, we need you!" Morgan shouted at the rafters as he stepped away from Eliza.

"Good heavens, Lord Morgan, you are acting like a raving

lunatic. I urge you to consider prying eyes," Eliza warned as she grabbed his sleeve and led him towards the drawing room. She gave him a slight shove into the room, then she stepped over to Josette, lowering her voice. "Who is your guest?"

Josette met her gaze and knew what she was asking. "He is a member of France's secret service." Eliza's eyes widened, so she rushed to continue, "He is a friend, for now."

Eliza's sharp eyes roamed over Gaspard before she nodded.

"Lady Lansdowne," Josette gestured towards him, "may I introduce Mr. Gaspard Mancini?"

"My friends call me Gaspard." He bowed and flashed her a charming smile.

Eliza arched a brow. "Then I will be sure to call you Mr. Mancini."

Josette heard boots thudding down the stairs. At the stair's landing, she could see Mr. Larson and Lord Jonathon Beckett running to meet them. Both held pistols in their hands. Once they saw Gaspard, they both skidded to a stop on the marble floor and pointed their pistols at him.

Taking a step closer to Gaspard, Josette stated, "He is a friend."

"He is French," Mr. Larson growled, holding his pistol steady.

Gaspard smirked. "I am impressed. It generally takes longer for Englishmen to catch on," he joked dryly.

Mr. Larson took a commanding step forward, but Jonathon put his left hand on his shoulder. "Josette," he darted his gaze towards her, "why did you bring this man into my sister's home?"

Morgan stepped out of the drawing room. "It was my decision."

"Easton?" Jonathon lowered his pistol and tucked it into the waistband of his trousers. "What the blazes is going on?"

"Gentlemen, and Josette, may I suggest we have this conversation in the drawing room," Eliza stated in a firm tone, her eyes scanning the entry hall.

Josette followed Eliza into the room and saw her purse her lips. She knew her mentor was not pleased with this intrusion.

Once Mr. Larson followed Gaspard in, he closed the door and stood guard, his hand resting on the butt of his pistol.

"Easton, you'd better have a good reason for bringing this

Frenchman here," Jonathon warned with a clenched jaw.

"This is Mr. Gaspard Mancini," Morgan replied. "He is a spy for France."

Immediately, Mr. Larson and Jonathon withdrew their pistols and pointed them at Gaspard again.

"This is ridiculous," Josette huffed and walked in front of Gaspard, forcing the men to immediately lower their pistols. "The lives of thousands of people are at stake, including our prince regent."

Gaspard spoke up, "And King Louis."

"Yes, and him too," Josette said with a fleeting smile.

Keeping the pistol at his side, Jonathon turned towards Morgan. "Explain, *now*."

"We tracked the French spy, *Genet*, to Lord Paxton's house party, but she got away," Morgan started.

"*She?*" Eliza asked.

"Yes," Morgan confirmed. "We now know her identity. Miss Adalyn Clemens."

"You are an imbecile for letting her get away," Jonathon pressed, his eyes narrowed.

Josette squared her shoulders, refusing to let Morgan take the blame for her failure. "It was my fault," she confessed. "I found her threatening Lord Paxton, and I intervened. I was able to shoot her in the arm before she escaped."

"Why was she threatening Lord Paxton?" Eliza asked.

Morgan placed his hands on the back of a chair and leaned in. "That's why we're here." His eyes grew dark. "We believe *Genet* intends to blow up the House of Lords while King Louis is addressing the joint assembly."

"No!" Eliza cried as she lowered herself slowly onto a chair. "Not only is the prince regent there, but so are Benedict, Adrien, and my father."

"For what purpose?" Jonathon asked. "Why would a French spy want to blow up the King of France?"

All eyes turned to Gaspard. "Not everyone is pleased with the Bourbons regaining power. *Genet* was one of Napoleon's trusted agents and apparently is still loyal to him. I don't believe I need to explain the ramifications if *Genet* is successful at eliminating your prince regent and both houses of Parliament."

Mr. Larson crossed his arms over his chest. "No, *you* don't."

Concerned by her friend's pale face, Josette stepped to the drink cart and poured a glass of water. "*Genet* was planning to use Lord Paxton's seal to access the undercroft." Extending the drink to Eliza, she continued, "Fortunately, Lord Paxton refused to give it to her."

"Why would *Genet* risk her identity to obtain a viscount's seal?" Jonathon frowned. "That doesn't make sense."

"*Genet* is planning to blow up the House of Lords the same way the Roman Catholics tried in the Gunpowder Plot of 1605," Morgan explained. "Lord Paxton is the architect responsible for the renovations on the upper house and was granted permission to store construction materials in the undercroft. However, only someone who has a sealed missive by Lord Paxton is allowed access to the cellar."

Josette sat down next to Eliza. "By retrieving Lord Paxton's seal, *Genet* would have been able to store explosives directly underneath the chamber."

"And you are certain that *Genet* plans to use gunpowder to achieve her nefarious purpose?" Jonathon asked.

"We have no tangible proof at this point," Morgan answered, shaking his head, "but that is the assumption we are making."

Mr. Larson's expression grew hard. "We don't have the luxury of you being wrong, Lord Morgan."

"If any fire started at the palace, it would be a disaster," Jonathon voiced. "Every year, prior to opening Parliament, architects issue warnings against the possibility of fire in the palace. It's always on the front page. They have mentioned the narrow, dark, and unhealthy passages, as well as insufficient accommodations, amongst other things. However, their recommendations have gone unheeded."

Taking a step further into the room, Mr. Larson said, "*Genet* was unable to obtain the seal. Thus, she does not have access to the undercroft."

"Furthermore, the Palace of Westminster is heavily guarded. There is no way she could slip through the blockade," Eliza stated in a relieved tone.

Josette winced as she reluctantly revealed, "*Genet* has access to

Lord Paxton's apartment in the palace. It's tucked next to the prince's chambers, which shares a common wall with the House of Lords."

"What!" Jonathon roared as the others in the room went silent.

"A Mr. Blount befriended Lord Paxton's son and deceived him in many ways." Morgan pushed off the back of the chair. "Besides donating to Mr. Blount's cause, he also gave him a key to come and go as he pleases."

Jonathon's eyes were furious. "Those apartments are all interconnected. If someone wanted to destroy the upper house, that would put them in the perfect position to do so."

"When does the joint assembly start?" Morgan inquired.

"In less than an hour," Eliza confirmed, jumping up from her seat. "We need a plan."

"I know you don't want to hear more from me," Gaspard said, pulling a sheet of paper out of his jacket, "but we all have a vested interest in stopping *Genet*." He walked over to the table and unfolded the large paper. "I took the liberty of recreating the architectural drawing that Lord Paxton showed us back at his estate."

"How convenient," Mr. Larson growled.

"For once, we are on the same side," Gaspard commented calmly before he pointed at the drawing. "The undercroft is accessible at the pavement level. There appear to be only three entrances. Two on the east side and one at the northwest corner."

Eliza ran her finger along the drawing and shared, "The House of Lords is connected to buildings at both its north and south end. The west end opens to the Old Palace Yard. The east face is partially connected to a structure that contains the prince's chamber. The south-east corner also holds the royal entrance."

"Exactly," Gaspard said. "In addition, there is a small, gated courtyard on the east side, and it has access to the undercroft. The prince's chamber and St. Stephen's Church keep the courtyard enclosed, but it can be accessed through the royal entrance as well." He straightened and met Jonathon's gaze. "If I had to guess, I would say that *Genet* will target one of the entrances to the undercroft by way of the courtyard."

"The undercroft is also accessible inside the House of Lords," Morgan informed the group. "There are multiple doors leading down towards the cellar."

Jonathon's eyes scanned the drawings, a frown tugging his brows together. "Where exactly is Lord Paxton's apartment?"

"Near the prince's chamber," Josette answered, pointing towards the adjacent structure that connected near the south-east corner of the upper house.

"What would stop *Genet* from blowing up the apartment?" Mr. Larson asked. "The fire would spread to the House of Lords."

Morgan's face grew solemn. "The intention is not to burn the upper house, but to assassinate King Louis, Prinny, and all of Parliament."

Gaspard nodded. "I agree. *Genet* wants to kill King Louis to usher Napoleon back in as Emperor. A fast-growing fire wouldn't guarantee anyone's death."

Josette caught a pointed look passing between Jonathon and Eliza before she saw Jonathon nod.

"Mr. Larson, will you escort Gaspard out of the room for a moment," Eliza requested.

Mr. Larson turned his sharp gaze towards Gaspard and pointed at the door, indicating he should go first. No one spoke until Gaspard had left the room and the door was closed.

Jonathon glared at Morgan, his eyes bristling with barely-controlled anger. "What were you thinking bringing a French spy into Eliza's home? Are you mad?"

"Gaspard is our ally in this," Morgan contended.

"On this assignment, yes, but *he* is the enemy!" Jonathon shouted forcefully, pointing at the door. "We cannot risk revealing Eliza's identity."

Morgan stood his ground. "What would you have me do?" he countered. "Besides, there is no way that Gaspard can discern what Eliza's role is within the agency. My focus was arriving in London before *Genet* blows up our whole Parliament, and I couldn't very well leave Gaspard on the pavement while I came in to speak to you."

"Finding fault with each other won't solve anything," Eliza chided. "We need a plan. And we need one quick."

Jonathon shook his head. "We can't formulate a plan until we know what we are up against."

"I could…" Eliza attempted.

Jonathon interrupted her. "You can't, Eliza."

"Why not?"

He stepped closer to her. "If you were caught running around the Palace of Westminster in men's clothing with a longbow in your hand, you would be disgraced, or killed. It would force you to go into hiding."

"But I could." Josette stepped closer to Eliza.

"Josie, you are not ready…" Morgan started.

Eliza dismissed his comment with a wave of her hand. "Josette is ready and is more than capable of completing this assignment." Her eyes grew determined. "She will not do it alone because I am going as well."

"Eliza…" Jonathon growled.

Taking a step towards her brother, Eliza challenged him. "I refuse to stand by and do nothing. I can, and I will, provide support with my longbow on the roof."

Jonathon ran his hand through his hair. "Fine, assuming Larson goes with you."

"That goes without saying," Eliza stated. "Since Mr. Mancini will be traveling with you, Larson and I will depart separately."

"What is the fastest way to travel to the Palace of Westminster at this time?" Morgan asked.

"Leave that to me," Josette suggested. "I know a few shortcuts."

Eliza nodded. "I need to send off two missives before Larson and I depart."

"I don't like this," Jonathon huffed. "There are too many variables."

"That's what makes this fun," Josette quipped, earning a scowl from Morgan.

Chapter Twenty-Two

Weaving through the vestiges of Westminster's maze of old alleys and lanes, Josette finally arrived at Parliament Square, which was just outside the palace gates. When Morgan, Gaspard, and Jonathon stepped out into the square, their eyes widened in amazement.

Morgan turned towards her. "How were you able to navigate the side streets so proficiently?"

"Once you are familiar with the layout, their arrangement isn't as random as you might think," Josette informed them.

Jonathon nodded his approval. "Good work, Josette."

"Thank you," she said, grateful for his praise. "Follow me."

"You can't walk into the Old Palace Yard dressed the way you are," Morgan asserted, placing a hand on her shoulder. "No one may have questioned you in the alleyways, but you will be more obvious here."

She removed the pistol strapped to her leg and tucked it into the waistband of her trousers. "Better?"

Morgan looked exasperated. "Not at all."

Josette removed her dagger, tucked it into her waistband, and pulled the cap down low on her head. "Satisfied?"

"Not even remotely," Morgan contended.

"Do you hear that?" Gaspard asked as the sound of angry voices drifted out from the palace gates.

Jonathon turned towards the noise. "It sounds like protestors."

"Sounds like there are a lot of them," Josette remarked, looking anxious. "Mr. Blount has been busy."

"Not everyone is pleased with the outcome of the war, so they believe his rhetoric," Jonathon replied. "Let's go."

They swiftly passed through the gates of the palace and headed further into Old Palace Yard. Near the House of Lords, loud, angry protestors voiced their disapproval of King Louis. A line of stone-faced, red-coated soldiers, armed with rifles, stood guard along the length of the building. Two additional soldiers stood guard on the steps of the royal entrance at the southeast corner.

Josette scanned the royal entrance, her eyes admiring the Gothic corridor and the ornate flight of stairs. "There is no way *Genet* could have secured access to the royal entrance to deliver barrels of materials."

"What about the north end where the Commons passes to the Upper House?" Morgan suggested.

"I highly doubt the workers can loiter in the Old Palace Yard," Jonathon answered with a shake of his head, "much less mingle with members of Commons. It is highly unlikely construction materials would be delivered to either of these entrances."

"I agree," Morgan said. "Let's proceed to Lord Paxton's apartment. We might be lucky enough to find Mr. Blount and *Genet*." His eyes roamed the surrounding structures. "How do you suppose we gain access?"

"We go through the Painted Chamber." Jonathon pointed at the structure adjacent to the House of Lords. "It leads up to the prince's rooms. Lord Paxton's apartment can be reached through the interconnecting passageways."

Two red-coated sentinels stood guard at the Prince's Chamber's entrance. When they approached, rather than speak, the guards narrowed their eyes and gripped their muskets tighter.

Morgan offered them a smile. "I need access to this building."

"Bugger off," one soldier ordered.

"I'm afraid I am going to have to insist," Morgan replied, his smile dropping.

The taller soldier stepped closer to him and leaned forward, the brim of his bicorne narrowly missing Morgan's face.

"If you do not leave, then we will arrest you." He spat at Morgan's shiny, black Hessian boots.

"You shouldn't have done that," Morgan stated, looking calmly down at his boot.

"Why not?" the guard sneered.

Without saying a word, Morgan grabbed the rifle from his hands and clobbered the man in the face, knocking him unconscious. The other guard scrambled to place his rifle in firing position, but he wasn't quick enough. Morgan grabbed the barrel with his left hand, shoving it upwards, while his right fist punched the man, causing him to fall to the ground.

Josette kept watch as Morgan stepped over the unconscious soldiers and opened the door. Leaning down, he placed his hands under one soldier's arms and dragged him inside. Jonathon dragged the other guard inside, as well.

"We are in," Jonathon confirmed. "Follow me."

"Lord Paxton said he was staying in the Moon Chamber," Gaspard reminded them.

Racing up the stairs, Josette followed behind the men until Jonathon stopped at a door painted dark blue. A plaque next to the door confirmed it was the Moon Chamber. He tried the handle, but it was locked. Jonathon turned and nodded once to Josette.

Without saying a word, Josette grabbed a pin out of her hair, crouched down, and quickly unlocked the door. She straightened and stepped back.

Jonathon retrieved his pistol from the waistband of his trousers and threw open the door. Keeping his pistol in his hand, he stormed into the room. Gaspard and Josette followed behind. They were met with only silence.

"We are too late," Gaspard growled. "I need to warn my king. We have to stop that assembly and get him far away from the House of Lords."

"Not yet," Morgan urged as he started searching the room. "We still don't know where the gunpowder is being stored."

Josette looked into a side room and noticed some discarded materials on the floor. She picked them up and headed back to the main room. "I found rope and wadding."

Jonathon grunted. "That's not good. Both are used in transporting barrels of gunpowder."

"That was my thought as well," she acknowledged, dropping

them to the floor.

"Before we burst into the joint assembly and interrupt your king's speech, I propose we search the undercroft," Morgan recommended.

Gaspard's hand tightened around his pistol. "Fine. But if we find anything suspicious, then we stop the assembly."

"Agreed," Morgan and Jonathon replied in unison.

As they walked out of the chamber and into the hall, Josette's eyes scanned the interior courtyard at the rear of the building. She could see the two entrances to the undercroft, but no soldiers were stationed at the doors. That's odd, she thought.

"Something's wrong," Josette declared, increasing her pace. Finding a narrow flight of stairs, she raced down and tossed open the door leading into the small interior courtyard.

Before she took her first step, Josette saw two sloppily-dressed, red-coated soldiers straighten up against the wall of St. Stephen's Chapel. Their eyes grew wide at the sight of her, but they didn't question her, nor did they approach her. Instead, they stepped back to their post and resumed guarding the doors to the undercroft.

"Did you find something?" Morgan asked as he rushed through the door with Jonathon and Gaspard on his heels.

Josette turned around and lowered her voice. "Something is suspicious about those guards."

Morgan's eyes darted towards the soldiers. "In what way?"

"Well, they are not holding rifles, their shirts are not tucked in, and their waistcoats are misbuttoned," she revealed. "Until now, I have only seen sharply-dressed soldiers."

"Perhaps those soldiers are lazy." Gaspard shrugged. "It's been my experience that most Englishmen are."

Jonathon glared at Gaspard. "You are making it nearly impossible for me *not* to want to shoot you."

Gaspard smirked. "Trust me, I feel the same way about you."

A door to St. Stephen's Chapel opened, and a man walked out into the courtyard carrying a barrel bound by rope over his shoulder. He froze when he saw them, but his eyes nervously darted towards the soldiers.

Morgan took a step towards the man. "May I ask what you are

storing in the barrels?"

"Uh… construction materials," he replied, clearing his throat.

"Interesting," Jonathon stated, placing his hand over the butt of the pistol in the waistband of his trousers. "What materials require the barrels to be bound with rope, rather than iron hoops?"

"Nails," he answered forcefully.

"Nails?" Morgan repeated. When the man nodded, he continued, "Would you mind if we take a look?"

The man's face paled.

Just then, Josette heard the cocking of pistols from the direction of the House of Lords. She turned her head and saw the soldiers approaching them, only now they had pistols in their hands.

"Sam, what's the bloody hold up?"

Josette stifled a groan as she heard a familiar voice behind the man holding the barrel.

"Hurry up. We still have twenty more barrels to unload," the voice ordered.

Sam took a step to the side as Mr. Blount walked casually into the courtyard with a barrel on his shoulder. He stopped at the sight of them.

"Mr. Addington and Mr. Mancini," he called out, his voice clipped. "Who else did you bring to their deaths?" He gently lowered the barrel to the ground.

Two more men walked out of St. Stephen's Church, both with barrels on their shoulders.

"Put the barrels down over in the corner, *gently*," Mr. Blount instructed. "We need to deal with this interruption first, and we can't risk a spark blowing up the gunpowder early."

Morgan took a step closer to Josette. "Do not fear. I will keep you safe," he whispered.

Josette rolled her eyes. "Thank you for that."

"You, boy," Mr. Blount ordered, his gaze upon her, "take off your cap."

"Leave the boy alone," Morgan demanded as he stepped in front of her. "He has nothing to do with this."

Mr. Blount pulled out his pistol and pointed it at Morgan. "Unfortunately, you made him a part of this when you followed me from Lord Paxton's estate."

"Hello, Mr. Blount." Josette removed her cap and stepped out from behind Morgan.

"Mrs. Addington?" Mr. Blount's jaw dropped. Recovering quickly, he frowned as he lewdly perused her body. "It is a pity to kill such a beautiful woman."

Josette shrugged one shoulder. "I would be more concerned about how you are going to make it out of here alive, if I were you."

"You foolish woman," Mr. Blount guffawed. "There are four of you and six of us." He stepped closer, lowering his pistol. "I find you amusing, so I will give you one chance to secure your freedom."

"I'm listening," she replied.

"Help me with this project," Mr. Blount proposed with a sadistic smile, "and then spend the night with me."

Josette felt like gagging at his offer. However, rather than immediately reject him, she smiled coyly. "Or, I could take my dagger and slash your throat," she suggested in a sultry voice.

Mr. Blount's eyes narrowed. "You would rather die alongside your husband?"

"It's better than in your bed," she countered.

Obviously annoyed, Mr. Blount looked at Morgan. "You should have taught your wife how to curb her tongue."

Morgan smiled affectionately at her. "I happen to approve of the way my wife speaks."

"We don't have time for this!" Mr. Blount shouted, waving the pistol in front of him. "We need to get the barrels in the undercroft before King Louis finishes his speech." He stopped moving his pistol, aiming it at Jonathon. "You will die first."

"Me?" Jonathon huffed. "But we haven't even been introduced!"

This is not going to end well, Josette thought. How were they going to stop six men with pistols aimed at them? She slowly slid her hand behind her, reaching for the pistol in her waistband. Regardless of what happened, she was not going to stand idly by and be shot.

Her hand was stopped by Morgan's. "I am going to cause a distraction, and I want you to run."

"I won't go without you," she replied without hesitation.

"It matters not if I live or die, but I want you to live another day," he expressed, his eyes full of tenderness.

Mr. Blount chuckled cruelly. "How sweet. Young love," he scoffed as he snapped his fingers over his head. Two of his mercenaries stepped closer, taking aim at them. "You two will die at the same time."

"Since you are going to kill us anyway, will you at least tell us what your plan is?" Jonathon asked casually. Josette was not fooled though. Although Jonathon appeared relaxed, she knew his body was alert, preparing for a fight.

"It's simple, really," Mr. Blount declared proudly. "We are going to blow up the House of Lords."

"Can you be more specific?"

Mr. Blount looked at Jonathon as though he was a simpleton. "We have twenty-seven barrels of gunpowder that we will place directly under the chamber."

"Where is Miss Clemens?" Gaspard asked, his eyes scanning the courtyard. "Is she helping to unload the barrels?"

"Do not concern yourself with Adalyn's whereabouts," Mr. Blount responded, barely sparing him a glance. He cocked his pistol, aiming at Jonathon's chest. "Enough questions."

"I agree!" Jonathon exclaimed, diving out of the way and reaching for his pistol.

An arrow struck Mr. Blount in the chest just as his pistol discharged.

Taking advantage of the distraction, Josette pulled out her pistol and shot at one of the soldiers. But before she could retrieve her dagger, the fight was over. The ruffians lay on the ground. Dead. Most of them had arrows protruding from their chests.

Morgan grabbed her and pulled her tight against him. "I am so relieved you're all right, Josie."

She smiled into his chest. His arms were becoming her new favorite place to be.

Gaspard cleared his throat. "Morgan. Josette." His voice sounded worried.

Turning her gaze towards Gaspard, she saw him kneeling next to Jonathon, who was sprawled out on the ground. Jonathon wasn't moving and blood was staining the ground under his head.

Morgan and Josette ran towards Jonathon and dropped to their knees beside him. Josette leaned forward until her cheek was hovering above Jonathon's mouth. After a moment, she sighed and straightened.

"He's breathing."

Josette slid her hand under the back of Jonathon's head. When she pulled it back, it was covered in blood.

"Do you see any other injuries?" she asked, pulling her shirt out of her trousers and ripping off a large section at the bottom.

Morgan, who had been looking for other injuries, noticed the left sleeve of Jonathon's black jacket was saturated with blood. He ripped the sleeve off the jacket and saw red blood staining the white shirt. He tore open the shirt, expecting the worst, but was relieved when he saw only a single, angry, red streak on his upper arm. "The bullet just grazed him."

"That's good," Josette said as she wrapped Jonathon's head with the makeshift bandage. "He must have suffered the head wound when he jumped out of the way."

Gaspard gazed at Josette, curiosity in his eyes. "How did you learn to do that?"

"A friend taught me," she replied, grinning. "It was part of an intense training course."

Looking at her blood-covered hands, Gaspard observed, "Most women I associate with would feel squeamish at the sight of blood."

Josette tied off the bandage and carefully lowered Jonathon's head to her lap. "You will discover that I am not like most women."

Gaspard gave her a flirtatious smile. "I am well aware of that, Josette."

A low growl came from the back of Morgan's throat as he watched Gaspard flirt with Josette. Before he could open his mouth to rebuke the French spy, Eliza knelt next to him and ran her fingers along the bandage on Jonathon's head.

"How is he?" she asked Josette.

Josette's expression grew serious. "The bullet just grazed his arm and his head wound appears superficial, despite the amount of blood you saw on the ground."

"Good," Eliza muttered, watching her brother with concern on her face. "We need to get him to a doctor."

"I agree," Josette murmured. "Do you want us to help you get him to your coach?"

"No. We need to stick to the plan," Eliza said firmly. "I shouldn't even be down here, but when I saw Jonathon…" Her words trailed off as her voice hitched with emotion.

Morgan heard footsteps echoing off the cobblestones in the courtyard and looked up to see Larson crouching down by Jonathon, his breathing labored.

"I don't have the ability to scale down walls like Eliza does." He cast her a frustrated look. "I am an old man."

"You are hardly an old man," Eliza replied, her eyes not leaving Jonathon's face. "Do you have the strength to carry Jonathon over your shoulder until we can hire a hackney?"

Mr. Larson rose and stretched his neck. "That won't be a problem, but I expect you to stay hidden."

Morgan and Gaspard rose and helped drape the unconscious Jonathon onto Larson's shoulder. Morgan watched as Larson headed back into the building, but when he turned back around, Eliza was not in the courtyard. Where had she gone?

Rather than dwell on her disappearing act, Morgan turned his gaze back towards Josette, who had walked over to the barrels of gunpowder.

With a thoughtful look, she said, "Mr. Blount mentioned they were going to put twenty-seven barrels of gunpowder in the undercroft. Earlier, he said they still had to unload twenty more. Since there are four here, I assume that three barrels have already been placed."

Morgan glanced over at the building. "That's a big assumption. Mr. Blount might have included these four in his overall tally. If that's the case, then there are seven barrels of gunpowder in the undercroft."

Gaspard spoke up, "I hate to be the bearer of bad news, but if the gunpowder goes off under the House of Lords, then it could still ignite the rest stored somewhere in that church." He looked at St. Stephen's chapel and back again. "We need to evacuate the building. Even if we ignored the additional barrels, three strategically placed barrels of gunpowder could cause mass destruction."

Running a hand over the back of his neck, Morgan knew what a momentous decision this was. To interrupt a foreign king's speech to a joint assembly of Parliament would be a grave insult, potentially placing a black mark on English history. On the other hand, if the gunpowder did ignite, the entire structure could be burned to the ground."

"What do you think?" he asked Josette, surprising himself. Normally, he relied on his own instinct, and his alone. But he was learning to appreciate Josette's unique insight, forcing him to recognize that he trusted her instinct as well.

Josette pursed her lips as she studied the building. She turned back to him, her expression determined. "I would err on the side of caution and beg for forgiveness later." She touched the top of a barrel. "We already have proof of the nefarious plot, and that *Genet* is behind this."

"All right," Morgan said with a bob of his head. "I will go down to the undercroft..."

Josette shook her head. "You are the only lord here. I would never be granted access to the upper chamber because of my gender." She looked pointedly at Gaspard. "Furthermore, our soldiers will not be so cavalier as to let a Frenchman walk into the chamber uninvited."

Morgan ran a hand through his hair. "I will go in while Gaspard and you..."

To his frustration, Josette shook her head again. "Gaspard needs to help lead his king to safety. I will go alone into the undercroft."

Morgan closed the distance between them. "No! Absolutely not. We have no idea what you would be up against down there."

"We are wasting valuable time," Josette insisted. "Trust me to complete this assignment."

As much as he wanted to argue with her, to plead with her, Morgan knew that she was right. And it killed him.

"Fine, but as soon as the House of Lords is evacuated, I will come and find you."

"Sounds reasonable," Josette said, removing her dagger from her waistband and strapping it to her leg. She reached down and retrieved an overcoat pistol from her boot and examined it for a moment. "I'm ready."

"Before you go…" He slipped his arm around her waist and pressed his lips firmly against hers. It was a kiss full of promise for a shared future together. A kiss full of hope.

He broke the kiss but remained close. "Come back to me, my dear Josie."

Josette's eyes shone with longing. Her words were filled with emotion. "And you must come back to me."

"Always," he murmured, sealing his promise with another kiss.

Morgan removed his arm from around her waist and smiled. "I hope I gave you sufficient training for this assignment."

A mischievous smile graced her lips. "What training?"

"Good luck." He turned and raced towards the House of Lords, hoping Gaspard would follow.

Gaspard caught up to him and matched his stride. "Do you have a plan?"

"No," he admitted. "Do you?"

"We'll figure it out together."

At the royal entrance, two soldiers armed with rifles blocked their path. "No one is allowed entry at this time," one of the soldiers stated, his brown hair sticking out below his bicorne.

Morgan straightened to his full height and stated in a commanding voice, "My name is Lord Morgan Easton. I am the son of the Marquess of Bath."

The other soldier, who had a scar running down his right cheek, acknowledged his words with a bob of his head. "I understand, my lord, but the King of France is addressing the assembly. We are under strict instructions not to grant entry to anyone, under any circumstance."

Morgan took a step closer, and the soldiers tightened their holds on the rifles. He could fight them both, but that would take too much time, and time was of the essence. "I work for the Home Office," he revealed, "and we have discovered that a French spy is attempting to blow up the House of Lords as we speak. We need to evacuate the building."

At first the brown-haired soldier's eyes grew wide, but then he shook his head regretfully. "I can't grant you entry. I could be fired."

Better than dead, Morgan thought. But as he opened his mouth to reason with the guard, Gaspard spoke up. "My name is Gaspard-Michel Mancini, Duc of Feltre, and I am on the King of France's counsel. I demand admittance to warn my king of an impending assassination attempt." He stepped until he was toe-to-toe with the soldier and spoke in a deep growl. "I won't be turned away."

"I understand, monsieur," the soldier said, his eyes showing fear and respect. He stepped back. "If you would allow me to escort you..."

Not bothering to wait for the soldier to finish his sentence, Gaspard started running down the passageway.

"Tell your superior to start pushing these protestors back to make room for the members of Parliament as they exit the building," Morgan instructed, before he brushed past the brown-haired soldier.

"I will see what I can do, my lord," the soldier acknowledged with a salute.

Morgan took off running down the passageway and up the stairs, catching up to Gaspard easily. As they sprinted up the final steps, he glanced over at the Frenchman. "You are a duc?"

"I am. Napoleon granted me the title," he replied, keeping his eyes straight ahead. "It's not something I am generally forthcoming with, especially with English agents."

Once they reached the two large, gilded doors, they each grabbed a handle and forcefully pushed. The doors banged against the wood, loudly echoing throughout the great chamber.

Morgan rushed into the room with Gaspard close behind him. Every head in the three long sections of the room, filled to capacity, turned towards them. In the front of the room, a large stage was erected with Prinny seated on the throne, which was an elegantly carved arm-chair, ornamented with gold and crimson velvet.

The King of France was standing at the golden podium, dressed in ceremonial robes. His voice trailed off as he watched them run up the aisle.

"We need everyone to evacuate the chamber *immediately!*"

Morgan shouted. He stopped in the middle of the chamber and watched as armed guards swarmed around the stage to protect the king and prince regent.

On the stage, Prinny rose from his throne. "What is the meaning of this outlandish interruption?"

"Your royal highness," Morgan yelled, "there are barrels of gunpowder under this chamber! They could go off at any minute, so we need everyone to evacuate. *Now!*" He didn't have time to stand on ceremony.

Loud muttering erupted in the room. Morgan even heard a few people declare that he was mad. Yet, no one moved from their seat. This was not going well.

"What are you doing, Morgan?" The familiar voice coming from the front of the room sounded aggravated.

Turning his gaze, Morgan saw his father facing him, his glare of outrage was palpable. "Father, I speak the truth. I discovered a plot to blow up this chamber."

"Who wants to blow up the House of Lords?" his father demanded.

Morgan's eyes darted towards King Louis. "A French spy known as *Genet.*"

At his words, more lords grumbled skeptically. A few of the men rose from their seats. The furious look in their eyes confirmed that they did not believe him, and they intended to throw him out.

"Are you inebriated?" his father challenged.

"No, I am not," Morgan stated with firm intensity. "Whatever you think you know of me, you must acknowledge that I have never been known to lie or prevaricate." He turned his gaze towards Prinny. "I have witnessed firsthand the barrels of gunpowder."

"What say ye, Gaspard, Duc of Feltre?" King Louis stepped from behind the podium.

"Your highness," Gaspard bowed, "this man speaks the truth. *Genet* intends to assassinate you. We must get you to safety."

King Louis gave him a swift nod. "Then so be it." He started to exit the stage as Gaspard ran up to assist him.

Morgan's eyes scanned the room, surprised that no one had followed King Louis's lead. "We are wasting time! You must leave the chamber. The gunpowder could detonate at any moment."

"I believe him!" shouted another familiar voice from the rear of the room. Adrien, the Earl of Camden, rose and stepped into the aisle. "Who is with me?"

The Duke of Remington rose next and stepped into the aisle. "I am." He scoffed at the members in the room. "You're all fools not to heed his words."

"I believe Lord Morgan is telling the truth as well," Benedict, the Marquess of Lansdowne, shouted from the front of the room. His eyes grew wide and fearful as he addressed the crowd. "I smell smoke. Everyone get out, *now!*"

His words had the intended effect because everyone rose as one. The members of Parliament started rushing towards the four exits. Morgan saw that Prinny was being escorted off the stage.

"Easton!" Adrien shouted as he fought his way through the crowd to get to him. "What the blazes is going on?"

"That's what I want to know," Benedict said, now standing next to him.

"*Genet* is planning to blow up the House of Lords. She acquired—"

"She?" Benedict interrupted.

Morgan nodded. "Yes. We were able to ascertain her true identity, a Miss Adalyn Clemens. She obtained access to an apartment near the Prince's chamber and stored twenty-seven barrels of gunpowder in St. Stephen's chapel."

The chamber's exits were still blocked with men attempting to evacuate, so Morgan continued. "We were able to stop the conspirators from relocating all the barrels of gunpowder to the undercroft. We have deduced that either three or seven barrels are under this chamber." He turned his gaze towards the floorboards. "It was decided that Josette would go down to the undercroft to investigate while I evacuated the chamber."

Adrien's frame tensed. "Josette is alone?"

"I was not happy with that decision, either." Morgan shook his head. "But Josette couldn't very well access the House of Lords. She would have been arrested had she tried to evacuate the chamber."

"Good point," Adrien grumbled. "What's the plan?"

"We believe *Genet*'s main objective is to assassinate the King of France," Morgan informed them. "Will you two ensure that King Louis and Prinny are secure and away from harm?"

Benedict nodded. "Consider it done."

"Who was standing up there with you?" Adrien asked.

Morgan turned his gaze towards the empty stage. "That was Gaspard Mancini, Duc of Feltre, a member of King Louis's counsel and," he hesitated before adding the detail, "a French spy."

"You teamed up with a French spy?" Benedict's brow rose, then he smirked. "I look forward to hearing this story later."

"Frenchmen cannot be trusted. I will be keeping a watch on this Gaspard Mancini," Adrien contended.

"See that you do," Morgan agreed. "Once the chamber is evacuated, and the members of Parliament are secured, I will go down to the undercroft and help Josette." The crowd was thinning at the right rear door, so he headed towards the exit. Suddenly, he stopped and spun back around. "One more thing. Jonathon was injured."

Benedict and Adrien both slid to a stop.

"Injured?" Benedict asked, the worry evident in his tone.

"He hit his head while we were stopping some of the conspirators, and a bullet grazed his arm," Morgan explained. "He's with Eliza and Larson now." Morgan saw the rage in both agent's eyes. He was grateful that their anger was not directed at him.

"Let's stop *Genet*," Adrien stated, "then she will pay for injuring my friend."

Benedict grabbed Adrien's sleeve and pointed towards the front of the chamber. "If there is gunpowder in St. Stephen's chapel, then we need to be sure that Prinny and King Louis are out of harm's way."

"Good point," Adrien acknowledged. "Their guards probably took the king and prince regent to the Painted Chamber, which would be in range of the blast if the gunpowder detonates. We need to evacuate them to Westminster Abbey, or at least into New Palace Yard."

Both agents took off running, and Morgan was left standing behind a group of ashen-faced men trying to get down the congested stairs.

"What is the problem?" he asked.

An older gentleman turned back to address him. "The soldiers are attempting to push back the protestors to allow us room to exit the building, but they aren't cooperating."

Morgan mumbled an expletive under his breath. This was an unexpected delay. One that he had not anticipated. How was he going to help Josette if he couldn't even exit the building?

Hold on, Josie. Just hold on.

Chapter Twenty-Three

Josette cautiously pushed open the wooden door. She knew from the architectural drawings they led into the rear part of the undercroft. She stepped through the arched doorway and kept her pistol tightly in her hand.

Straining to hear any noise or movement coming from within, she made a face and looked up. The loud protesters outside seemed to mask all other sounds. Shifting her gaze towards the opposite wall, she saw empty arched alcoves systematically lining the stone wall with darkened sconces hanging between them.

There was enough light coming from the doorway and long windows running along the top of the undercroft to see the main part of the hall. In the rear of the chamber, she saw stacked tiles and wood beams, running the length of the walls. Turning her attention towards the front of the vault, her view was hampered by piles of bricks, stones, and iron beams. This is truly a construction storage site, she thought to herself.

Treading lightly on the stone floor, Josette noticed the exposed wood beams above her. She passed by a large brick fireplace recessed deep into the wall. This must have been used as the main stove back when the upper hall was originally the queen's chamber, she thought. Stopping at the pile of construction materials, she noted that up ahead, the undercroft broke off into three arched darkened chambers. Which one should she explore first?

A clang echoed off the wall in the middle chamber. Taking a chance, she kept her back against the wall and stepped through the archway. Barrels lined the room, but they were held together by iron, which meant they were not filled with gunpowder. She heard a woman's voice up ahead.

Josette listened carefully and could barely discern the words, "Go... check... imbeciles..."

A shadowy figure headed towards her, and she ducked behind a barrel. The man, dressed in a white shirt and tan trousers, walked right past her with a scowl on his face. Rather than allow him to leave the chamber, she rose silently and hit the back of his head with the butt of her pistol. He crumpled to the ground, and she dragged him towards a darkened corner.

Careful to stay crouched, she hurried further into the chamber. Luckily, barrels were scattered throughout the room providing her with more than enough places to conceal herself. As she crept closer, she heard the familiar voice of Adalyn.

"Where are those fools?"

Josette heard a muffled answer, but Adalyn's voice rose.

"You two," she growled, "go check on what's taking Albert and the others so long. We don't have much time before we have to set the fuse."

Josette crouched against a barrel and waited until the two men passed by her. She trailed behind them until she could hit one with the butt of her pistol. As the man fell to the ground, the other ruffian turned around with a dagger in his hand, but she was ready for him. With a flick of her wrist, she tossed her own knife into his heart. He dropped to his knees before collapsing to the ground. Three down, she thought. How many conspirators are there?

She rushed back towards the front and saw Adalyn standing near four burly-looking men. Three barrels, tied with rope, sat in the middle. One look at Adalyn, and Josette knew the woman was fuming. A roar of the crowd outside caused the conspirators to look to the small window along the front wall.

"Something's happening!" Adalyn declared with a frown on her face. "We're going to light the slow match and be done with it."

Josette knew she had to stop that from happening. Three barrels of gunpowder could cause a substantial amount of damage in this ancient palace. Furthermore, if the blast managed to reach the rest of the barrels, the result could be catastrophic.

"I'm afraid I can't let that happen," Josette announced as she stepped out from her hiding place, her overcoat pistol pointed at Adalyn.

Adalyn's eyes widened at the sight of her, but they quickly narrowed. "My friend has returned," she said snidely. "How exactly are you going to stop me, Mrs. Addington?"

The four burly men stepped closer to Adalyn. They each held a dagger.

Adalyn lifted her hand to stop her henchmen. "Put your pistol away, Josette. You must know that if you shoot your pistol, the spark could ignite these barrels, killing us all."

Blazes! Adalyn was right. Reluctantly, Josette tucked her pistol in the waistband of her trousers, removed her dagger, and held it in her right hand.

Adalyn smirked. "There are five of us and only one of you. Are you prepared to fight to your death?"

Squaring her shoulders, Josette nodded. "I will, if I have to."

"My feisty friend," Adalyn chortled. "You have saved me the trouble of having to hunt you down and kill you later."

"Once again, you have overestimated your cleverness," Josette remarked, her voice calm.

Adalyn regarded her for a long moment with hatred in her eyes. "Gentlemen, kill her…" she paused, a cruel smile appearing on her face, "and ensure it is excruciatingly painful as punishment for her shooting me in the arm."

Before the men took a step towards her, a feminine voice came from the end of the chamber.

"Dear me, please say that you are not having all the fun without me."

A hooded figure approached them, her face hidden from view, but Josette recognized the woman's voice. It was Cosette. What was she doing here?

Cosette didn't stop to acknowledge her as she approached Adalyn, her long, black cape dragging on the stone floor. The guards were about to step in front of Adalyn when Cosette stopped. She removed her hood.

"Cosette?" Adalyn's face paled.

"Hello, Adalyn," Cosette said with her thick French accent.

"Miss me?"

A wide smile came to Adalyn's face as she pulled her into an embrace. "I thought you were dead. Where have you been?"

"You know me. I always find a way to survive," Cosette replied smugly, stepping back.

Adalyn's eyes roamed Cosette's face. "But… how?"

"I work at an all girl's school, teaching them embroidery. It's been awful." She looked at the barrels and frowned. "I heard about your plot, and I rushed over here to see if it was true. Please say these are not the only barrels of gunpowder. That would certainly cause an explosion, but it wouldn't blow up the building entirely."

"We are still waiting on more barrels," Adalyn explained, then continued proudly. "We have a total of twenty-seven barrels of gunpowder."

A sinister glint came to Cosette's eyes. "That's good. That will decimate the Palace of Westminster, and everyone within it."

"Who told you about the plot?" Adalyn asked with an uplifted brow.

Cosette ran her finger lazily along the top of a barrel, appearing unconcerned by Adalyn's scrutiny. "I was informed by the street urchins I employ. They report back anything suspicious that happens in and around London," she explained. "I've been biding my time, hoping someone would come looking for me."

"If I'd known that you were still alive, I would have rescued you," Adalyn responded with sympathy in her tone.

"I want to go back to France with you," Cosette asserted.

"No!" Josette pleaded, taking a step closer to her friend. "You can't leave."

With a look that held a mixture of pity and irritation, Cosette stated, "I don't answer to you anymore, Miss Josette."

Adalyn glanced between them suspiciously. "You know each other?"

Turning to face her, Cosette revealed, "This *lady* is the headmistress at the school where I work. She ensures I remain a prisoner."

Josette couldn't make sense of this Cosette. She loved teaching at the school. Didn't she? Gone was her kind-hearted friend, replaced by a confident, hardened spy. Which one was the act?

"Ah, it seems *Miss* Josette has her own fair share of secrets. How fitting," Adalyn remarked. She turned her gaze back to Cosette. "Why haven't you left England on your own?"

Cosette clasped her hands in front of her as she admitted, "I couldn't. I was granted a stay of execution, on the condition that I never left the schoolhouse. I am watched constantly, and all of my movements are scrutinized."

"How did you stop the execution?" Adalyn asked, her voice still filled with doubt.

Cosette let out a light, airy, but frightening laugh. "I seduced the judge, guard, and executioner for good measure."

"That sounds about right," Adalyn teased. "Your flirtations are legendary amongst the female agents."

"It's been awful, Addy," Cosette pouted. "I've had to live amongst these Englishmen and pretend that I don't want to kill them all." She focused on Josette, but her eyes were guarded. "I was forced to be friends with them to keep up the ruse."

"That must have been awful for you," Adalyn murmured.

"It was," Cosette declared. "The British took away my freedom, keeping me as their prisoner."

Adalyn walked over to the barrels of gunpowder and placed her hand on one of the lids. "We can't wait any longer for those idiots to bring the rest. We need to light the fuse or we will miss the opportunity to assassinate King Louis."

"Will this be enough to complete the job?" Cosette asked with concern.

Tapping the top of the barrel, Adalyn shared, "We are directly under the stage. A blast here should be enough to assassinate our king and the Prince Regent of Britain."

"Brilliant!" Cosette exclaimed. "What are we waiting for then? Let's light the fuse."

"No!" Josette shouted, stepping closer to the barrels. She stopped when Cosette pulled out a pistol from beneath her cape, aiming it at her.

"Stay where you are, Josette," Cosette demanded.

"Wait!" Adalyn exclaimed. She stepped over and placed her hand on the pistol, lowering it to Cosette's side. "Unfortunately, you can't use a gun to kill her. The spark could ignite the gunpowder. Why not just slash her throat and be done with her?"

Lowering the pistol, a cold smile came to Cosette's lips. "Or we can tie her up and let the blast kill her."

A large man advanced towards Josette with twine in his hand. She gripped her dagger and prepared for a fight. In a swift motion, Cosette stepped closer, clasped her wrist and wrenched it behind her back.

"Josette, darling, you are only embarrassing yourself. I have seen you train, and you are not capable of beating me," she purred into her ear.

Removing the dagger from her hand, Cosette shoved her towards the awaiting thug, who roughly grabbed her wrists. Josette yanked them back, and he responded by slapping her face with the back of his hand. She staggered back, unable to regain her footing. The man followed her, hitting her again on the opposite cheek. She collapsed to the ground, attempting to regain her bearings.

The man advanced again, grabbing her around the throat with one large hand, and forcing her to a standing position. His hand tightened, and she reached up to scratch at the man's face. Growling, the man tossed her against the brick wall.

From her crumpled position, Josette looked up, hoping Cosette would help her, save her, but there was no hope in her friend's cold eyes. She lowered her gaze to the floor, her heart despairing at the betrayal she felt. She had only ever viewed Cosette as a friend, but it had all been an act. A tear slipped out of Josette's eye. She had been tricked, deceived... again.

"Enough," Adalyn declared. "Tie her hands and be done with it. I don't want anyone to accidently knock over the gunpowder."

The guard crouched down and jerked her hands forward, tying them in front of her. When he had her tied securely, he shoved her back against the wall. Josette felt pain coursing throughout her body.

Cosette stepped closer to the window and looked out. "With King Louis's assassination, Napoleon will be able to leave Elba. France will welcome him back with open arms," she gloated.

"Once the explosion kills the king and regent, the people will stir. Groups of revolutionaries all over England will march into London, creating even more chaos amongst the wreckage and carnage," Adalyn stated with a clenched fist. "England may never recover."

"Does Napoleon know about this plan?"

"Who do you think planned it?" Then, Adalyn's smile dimmed. "I don't understand what's keeping the others, but I promise you, everyone who failed Napoleon today will die," she declared. "With the twenty-seven barrels of gunpowder, we should have blown the House of Lords to mere slivers and rubble. It would have taken out the whole English government."

"I did see three unconscious men further back in the undercroft," Cosette informed her.

Adalyn turned a heated glare towards Josette. "You wouldn't happen to know about that?"

"I do. I am surprised at the low caliber of thugs you've hired," Josette replied, shrugging with one shoulder, "because they didn't even anticipate a fight. It was the exact same with Mr. Blount and those other men. Not very impressive fighters, if you ask me."

Adalyn crouched down next to Josette and grabbed her hair, yanking back her head. "You stupid girl, you've ruined everything," she seethed. "If I had obtained Lord Paxton's seal, we could have stored the barrels of gunpowder in the undercroft days ago." She released her hair and stood up. "Then all we would have had to do was light the fuse."

"That would have been much too easy for you, *Genet.*" Josette rested her head against the wall.

"*Genet?*" Cosette repeated in surprise, turning her gaze towards Adalyn. "You are *Genet?*"

"I am," Adalyn confirmed, continuing to glare at Josette. "That's why Josette must die. She knows my identity."

"I am not very good at keeping secrets," Josette mused as she scrunched her nose, "so I told Morgan," she paused dramatically, "and Gaspard."

"Then, I will have to kill them, as well," Adalyn vowed forcefully.

"This is where it gets tricky," Josette replied jovially. "Morgan works for the Home Office. By now, I'm sure that he's already notified his superior officer."

Adalyn's eyes narrowed with seething hate. "I hope your death is excruciatingly painful," she declared, "and when I find your husband, you can be sure his death will be slow and agonizing, as well."

Josette yawned. "I'm sorry. I had an early morning. Can you repeat your threat?" Her face grew expressionless. "It truly did sound uncomfortable."

"Give me the tinderbox," Adalyn ordered over her shoulder. "I want the pleasure of lighting this fuse myself."

One of the men stepped forward and handed her the tinderbox. "Thank you," she murmured. "Once I light the slow match, we will have five minutes before it detonates. Still, I would run and not stop until you hear the explosion." She turned her gaze towards Cosette. "If we are separated, go to the New Palace Yard. I'll find you there."

Josette watched in horror as Adalyn walked to the front of the chamber and crouched down next to the twined fuse. A loud grunt filled the air, and she turned in time to see Cosette elbowing one of the ruffians in the face.

"Cosette?" Adalyn asked, her eyes sparking in confusion.

Using Josette's dagger, Cosette stabbed the man in the stomach, twisted it, and yanked it out. She turned to face Adalyn as the man slumped to the ground.

"I can't let you do this." She dropped the dagger and kicked it over to Josette.

Adalyn rose and glared at Cosette. "You would betray your country… your countrymen?"

While Josette took the dagger and began slicing through the twine, Cosette removed her cape, and tossed it to the side. Before the cape even had time to settle on a pile of bricks, she had retrieved a knife from within the folds of her dress.

"I would to protect my family," Cosette insisted.

A thug advanced towards Cosette, and she flung her knife, hitting him squarely in the chest. After he fell to the ground, she retrieved her dagger and turned to fight another opponent. The man threw a punch but Cosette ducked, jabbing her fist into his side. The man hunched over, and Cosette took the opportunity to slash his throat.

Adalyn roared and charged towards Cosette, hitting her in the face. Not giving Cosette an opportunity to recover from the blow, Adalyn swept her leg, knocking Cosette's feet out from under her.

Just as the twine dropped to the ground, Josette rose and aimed her dagger at Adalyn's back.

"No!" Cosette shouted from the ground as Adalyn stood over her. "She's mine."

"All right," Josette said, "I guess this last dirty ruffian is mine."

The thug smirked as he charged towards her with a fisted hand, but she easily leaned to the side, and his hand met only air. Simultaneously, she plunged her dagger into his stomach. His mouth gaped before he staggered back and landed against the wall.

Josette looked back toward Cosette and Adalyn and watched as the former allies fought a fierce battle. Their fighting techniques appeared synchronized as they landed blow after blow, but neither one appeared to get the upper hand.

They started circling around each other, each seeming to anticipate her opponent's next move. "You forget that we trained together," Adalyn snarled, her right hand holding a dagger.

"I did not forget," Cosette contended, "but I have learned some new moves since then. And apparently, you have not."

"We used to be like sisters!" Adalyn screamed. "How could you betray me like this?"

"I finally found my family." Cosette's eyes darted towards Josette's. "I know where I belong."

"Napoleon will be furious to learn of your deceit," Adalyn declared, lunging forward with her knife.

Cosette stepped to the side and grabbed Adalyn's wrist, twisting it sharply, causing her knife to fall to the floor. "Napoleon is ruthless and tyrannical. He sacrificed his soldiers like a chess master does his pawns. He looted towns, leaving nothing behind, and he's responsible for the death of more than a million men, women, and children." She twisted Adalyn's arm behind her back.

"Napoleon is a liberator of the people," Adalyn fumed, her head turning to shout at Cosette over her shoulder. "He embodies expansionism and inspires men to fight for liberty!"

"You're wrong." Cosette shook her head, holding Adalyn as she struggled. "He spewed propaganda, and we followed him blindly."

"He is revolutionary," Adalyn retorted. "Our courageous imperator."

Shoving Adalyn to the floor, Cosette stood over her. "Leave this undercroft with your life. Just walk away. I owe you that."

"Never!" Adalyn began crawling on her hands and knees towards the barrels of gunpowder. "I will not fail."

Cosette's alert eyes grew compassionate. "Save yourself, Addy. Don't make me kill you."

Adalyn stilled and turned her hurt gaze towards Cosette. "You would kill me?"

"I will if you try to light that fuse," Cosette answered sadly.

"What happened to you?" Adalyn asked, her brows furrowed. "You used to be one of Napoleon's top agents."

Walking over to her, Cosette crouched down and answered, "I never wanted to be a spy. My father forced me into that role. He forced me to seduce men." Her eyes darted to Josette. "When I was given a chance to leave that life behind, to live a normal life, I embraced it wholeheartedly. I am finally free."

Adalyn's face contorted. "You will die alongside me. Traitor!" she screamed, lunging for a pistol on the ground near her.

"Run!" Cosette shouted.

Josette didn't hesitate. They were sprinting towards the rear of the vault when the pistol discharged. A loud, devastating explosion rent the air. Cosette grabbed her arm and shoved her into the brick fireplace, covering Josette's body with her own.

Then, everything went black.

As he descended the stairs from the House of Lords, Morgan saw the commotion in the Old Palace Yard. The screaming protestors had been forced back towards the Henry VII Chapel, and a solid line of soldiers separated them from the members of Parliament.

The members of the upper house congregated near the south side of the yard, leaving the members of Commons to stand along the west wall. To his surprise, a stern-faced Lord Charles Beckett met him at the bottom of the stairs.

"Explain everything," Beckett demanded, stepping closer.

Taking the next few moments, Morgan shared what they had discovered at Lord Paxton's estate, the identity of *Genet*, and the events leading up to the evacuation of Parliament. When he'd finished, Beckett bobbed his head in approval.

"You chose wisely. I would have made the call to evacuate the chamber as well."

"Sir, with your permission, I would like to go into the undercroft to see if Josette requires any assistance," Morgan requested. He felt an urgency to be sure that Josette was alive and unharmed.

"Before you go," Beckett stepped closer, his eyes narrowed, "did you treat Miss Josette with the courtesy that she deserves?"

"I did," Morgan said, "but I realized that I am tired of playing the ruse of a married couple. I want to make it a reality."

"Did you compromise her?" Beckett asked with such intensity that a shudder coursed through Morgan's spine.

"No, I love her," he declared to England's chief spymaster. "I would never treat her with such disrespect."

To his surprise, Beckett grinned. "Excellent. Eliza knew you two would suit. I was a little more skeptical." He waved his hand. "Go ensure Miss Josette is safe."

As he spun around, he heard a loud explosion coming from the undercroft. Everyone dropped to the ground. Glass shattered, and a billowing cloud of fine dust drifted out of the broken windows of the cellar, hanging over the Old Palace Yard. Then, silence descended over the crowd.

Morgan's heart dropped. *Josette.*

"Go," Beckett urged, shoving him towards the undercroft. "I need to see if the chamber is on fire."

Morgan didn't need to be told twice. He ran towards the vault's entrance. The door had been blown off and smoke billowed out into the courtyard. Approaching the entrance cautiously, he stepped inside the arched doorway and shouted, "Josette!"

His view was hampered greatly by the dust and debris filling the room. He stepped in further, his boots crunching on the broken tiles.

"Josette, where are you?" he cried. Taking off his jacket, he held it over his mouth, allowing him to breathe a bit easier.

It was slow work walking further into the room. Mounds of bricks, tiles, and wood beams had been blown everywhere. He glanced at the brick wall and saw nails sticking out the length of it. They must have taken flight during the explosion. There was no way Josette could have survived being in a chamber with so much loose debris flying around.

"Josette!" he shouted again, knowing his efforts were in vain. "Josette, please... answer me."

He heard Benedict's voice from the doorway. "Did you find her?"

"No!" he shouted back at the two hazy figures. "I haven't."

"Perhaps it would be best if Benedict and I look for Josette." Adrien spoke from Benedict's side, his voice holding only compassion.

Tears came to Morgan's eyes as he acknowledged what Adrien and Benedict weren't saying. They didn't think Josette was alive. But she had to be! They were going to start their lives together.

Blinking back his tears, Morgan began stepping over the piles of construction materials.

"Josie! Where are you?" he called again. Then, he heard a faint clinking towards the center of the room. "Do you hear that?" he asked Benedict and Adrien.

The three men moved in the direction of the noise. It was slow work as they had to move barrels and other debris out of their way. The noise continued and grew louder as they approached the far wall. However, they were forced to stop at the large mound of bricks resting up against it.

The clinking stopped. Morgan's heart dropped. He reached for his pistol and tapped the butt against the bricks. After a moment, he stopped and waited. The clinking started again. Someone was alive behind these bricks. Please be Josette!

Immediately, they began moving bricks as they tried to gain access to whoever was behind this wall. Over and over, they picked up bricks and threw them aside. After a while, Morgan's body ached, desperate for reprieve.

Finally, they created an opening and Morgan heard a woman say, "We are in here."

"We?" Benedict asked. "Will you identify yourself?"

"I will, Lord Lansdowne," the woman said with a chuckle. "It is me, Cosette, and I have an unconscious Josette with me."

"What the blazes?" Adrien shouted as he tossed another brick aside. "What are you doing in there, Cosette?"

"Eliza sent for me. Perhaps it would be best if we had this conversation at another time."

The men worked faster, and they eventually created a hole large enough for Cosette to climb through. Instead of exiting, however, she said, "I am going to pass Josette through first. We need to get her to the doctor."

Morgan stepped towards the opening and reached in to collect Josette. As soon as she was placed into his arms, he gently pulled her back towards him, careful to keep her head from hitting the bricks. He cradled her close to his chest as he exited the building, taking a moment to breathe in the fresh air.

A large group of gentlemen had made their way to the interior courtyard and watched as he came out from the undercroft. He was covered with dust, but he did not care. Gently laying Josette on an iron bench, he began searching her body for injuries. She had a large bump on the back of her head, but no blood appeared on her person.

Morgan started to wipe the dirt off her face, but he only managed to smear it more with his own dirty fingers. He wanted to shake Josette and tell her to wake up, order her to speak to him. But what if she never did?

"Josie, dear," he spoke softly. "Please wake up. Please talk to me." He gently ran his right thumb along her cheekbone. She winced and moaned. Upon closer inspection, he saw bruising on both of her cheeks. What had Josette endured in there?

This was all his fault. He should have been the one to go into the undercroft.

Benedict clasped his shoulder. "How is Josette?"

"Alive," he answered, looking up. "Where is Cosette?"

Benedict's eyes strayed towards St. Stephen's Chapel before he answered. "Adrien is escorting her back to the school." He hesitated, before adding, "You should know that she risked death to help save Josette."

"I can't even imagine what those two must have endured inside the undercroft," Morgan replied, his eyes turning back to Josette.

Benedict crouched down next to him. "It was much more than that. It was stipulated as a condition of her release that Cosette would never leave the school grounds without Adrien escorting her. If she violated those terms, for any reason, she would be remanded back to Newgate, and her original penalty of death would be enacted."

Understanding the gravity of the situation, Morgan asked, "Did anyone see her?"

"Let's hope not," Benedict stated.

Josette turned her head to the side and groaned. Morgan placed his hand on her cheek. "Josie, wake up."

She blinked heavily before looking up at him. "Is Cosette all right?"

"She's heading back to the school right now with Lord Camden," Morgan shared.

"Good," Josette sighed. "She saved my life." Suddenly, her eyes opened wide, and she shot to a seated position. "Is the House of Lords..." Her voice trailed off as she turned to look at the structure. "It's still there."

Morgan nodded. "It is. It seems the explosion was contained in the undercroft."

"I was so worried..." She stopped speaking and tried to rise.

"Rest for a moment longer," Benedict insisted. "When you're ready, will you please explain what transpired down there?"

Josette rested her back against the bench and started, "There were only three barrels of gunpowder..." She went on to explain how she was outnumbered, the role Cosette had played in defeating *Genet*, and how the explosion occurred. "Cosette protected me from the blast, but at some point, I lost consciousness," she finished.

Morgan stared at her, anger coursing through him. He was furious at Josette for the risks she had taken. How could she have been so cavalier about her life? Challenging four thugs and a French spy? Pure recklessness!

However, in a few moments, relief began to dissipate his anger.

She *was* still alive, after all. Once he felt in control of his emotions, he spoke with a firm intensity.

"You stubborn, reckless woman…" He hesitated, bringing his hand up to cup her cheek. "What you did in the undercroft was brilliant. I am proud of you."

Josette's eyes lit up, and a smile graced her face. "I was trained by the best."

Benedict coughed and cleared his throat. "Well, I wouldn't consider Morgan the best. He is adequate, but…"

"Thank you for the vote of confidence," Morgan said, chuckling.

"Josette!" a male voice shouted, his words echoing in the interior courtyard. "Josette!"

Morgan watched as Josette's face paled. She jumped up, her eyes becoming frantic. "I have to leave," she declared, turning towards St. Stephen's Chapel.

"Why?" Morgan reached out and grabbed her arm. "Who is that man?"

Josette yanked her arm back. "Someone I would rather not see again." She ran towards the chapel's door without looking back.

A tall, slender man with brown hair charged into the courtyard and ran towards the door where Josette had just disappeared. Morgan and Benedict both rushed to intercept him. They stood in the way, preventing him from following her.

"Let me pass," the man exclaimed, charging into them.

"What is your business with Miss Josette?" Morgan demanded, shoving him back.

The man's eyes narrowed. "It's none of your concern."

"It is," Morgan insisted. "She is my betrothed."

Foolishly, the man shoved Morgan in the chest. "I think not."

Morgan lunged for the man, but Benedict stepped in between them.

"What gives you the right to speak for Josette?" Benedict questioned.

The man yanked down his waistcoat. "I am her brother, Lord Craven."

Benedict let out a low whistle as he stepped aside. In one swift motion, Morgan landed a heavy blow against the man's jaw. Lord

Craven's head was thrown back as he landed on the ground and didn't move.

Benedict frowned. "Why did you have to knock him unconscious? It would have been much easier if he had traveled on his own to your townhouse."

"It was either that or kill him," Morgan admitted, shrugging unrepentantly.

"Well, if those were the only two options," Benedict joked, glancing at the growing crowd that had witnessed their interaction. "Let's have this discussion somewhere else, shall we?" He lifted his brow. "But you get to carry Lord Craven."

Chapter Twenty-Four

$\int$he door to his townhouse opened as Morgan hurried up the few steps. His heavyset, white-haired butler, Mr. Ferguson, greeted him while tipping his head respectfully.

"My lord."

With Josette's unconscious brother slung over his shoulder, and Benedict following behind him, Morgan stepped into the entry hall and addressed his butler.

"Ferguson, I do not wish to be disturbed. Whatever sounds you may hear, please tell the staff to disregard them."

"As you wish," Mr. Ferguson replied, his expression giving nothing away. "You received two missives while you were gone, sir. One was from Lady Lansdowne informing you that her brother, Lord Jonathon, is home and recovering from his injuries."

"That's great news," he said. "And the other?"

"Lord Bath sent over a missive, but it was sealed," Mr. Ferguson revealed. "It's on your desk."

"My father sent a missive?" Morgan repeated in surprise. His father had not sent him any type of correspondence since he moved into his own townhouse.

"Aye," the butler confirmed. "It arrived only moments before you came home, my lord."

Benedict leaned closer and teased in a hushed voice, "Perhaps it addresses the spectacle you made of yourself in Parliament today."

"Thank you, Lord Lansdowne, for your candor and insight," Morgan huffed.

"Happy to oblige," Benedict responded, leaning back.

"Mr. Ferguson, please contact my solicitor. I would like to see him tonight about an urgent matter."

"Consider it done," Mr. Ferguson replied.

"Let's get this over with," Morgan sighed as he started walking towards his study.

Benedict matched his stride and glanced at him curiously. "Do you often bring unconscious men into your townhouse?"

"No. Why?"

"Because your butler didn't seem to bat an eye when you walked into the entry hall," Benedict commented.

"Frankly, Ferguson is a man of few words," Morgan shared. "He had been in my father's employ for almost twenty years when I asked him to come work for me."

"Is that why your relationship with your father is severed?"

"That's not why," Morgan responded, entering his study.

He dropped Lord Craven onto an armchair, then went around to the front of his mahogany desk. Opening the bottom drawer, he pulled out a ball of twine and placed it on top. He removed the dagger from his boot and cut off several long lengths.

Morgan took the twine and lashed Lord Craven's wrists to the chair's arms. Benedict bound his ankles to the legs and added one more around his chest, tying it to the back. After their prisoner was secure, Morgan sat on the nearby settee.

"When I was younger, my father and I were always at odds, but I deeply respected him. It wasn't until I became an agent that our relationship turned sour."

"Why was that?" Benedict sat down across from him on a white settee.

With a side glance towards Lord Craven to confirm he wasn't stirring, Morgan explained, "My father is a staunch Tory. He was mortified when he discovered I had begun spending time with known Whigs. He demanded that I stop all associations with people who were affiliated with the Whig party or even those who sympathized with their cause. That was the first time he threatened to disown me."

Benedict glanced around Morgan's spacious study with striped green paneling and large windows overlooking a nicely manicured yard.

"I take it that he did not disown you."

"He did not, but he grew distant," Morgan confessed. "He never took time to discover that my opinions have always aligned with the Tories."

"I'm glad that we share the same political views," Benedict stated, crossing one ankle over the other knee.

Morgan rose and stepped to the drink cart. "Alarmingly, there is a growing number of revolutionaries that share anti-monarchic views, especially amongst the Whig party. Beckett assigned me to infiltrate these groups and assess the danger they may present."

"What did you discover?"

"That most of these groups are filled with idealistic young men who cannot seem to follow their own inconceivable notions of unpatriotic parliamentary reform." Morgan picked up the decanter and filled two glasses with port. "They idolize Napoleon, criticize the war efforts, but go home to sleep comfortably in their parents' estates. It is quite maddening to sit in these rooms and listen to the propaganda being spewed from these ignorant minds."

Morgan picked up the two glasses and extended one to Benedict. "My reputation as a rake grew after a botched engagement, and Beckett started leaking false information to the editors at the newspapers. Being featured on the society page led to a wide array of invitations to balls, soirées, and house parties." He smiled smugly as he lifted his glass up to his mouth. "I was even the guest of honor at several social events."

Benedict took a sip of his drink and observed him for a moment. "Yet, you are not happy with your lot in life."

"I didn't realize how unhappy I was until I pretended to be Josette's husband," Morgan stated as he rested his glass on his leg. "I feel complete when I'm with her, as if I was born to love her."

"How does Josette feel about you?" Benedict asked, swirling his drink around the glass.

"I know she cares for me, but she keeps her heart locked up so blasted tight!" Morgan dropped his head against the back of the settee. "I don't know how to convince her to be with me, but I will make it my life's work."

"Didn't you call Josette your betrothed in the courtyard behind the House of Lords?" Benedict asked, amused.

"I did," Morgan admitted, smiling. "I just haven't convinced Josette yet."

"Let me offer you some advice," Benedict said earnestly as he placed his glass onto a side table. "Josette is very similar to Eliza in many ways. Both would rather fight their way through a hundred armed ruffians than become vulnerable by sharing their emotions. But unlike Eliza, when Josette was cast aside by a loved one, she was forced to live in the rookeries. I have no doubt that took an immense toll on her ability to trust."

"No doubt." Morgan took a moment to glare at Lord Craven before asking, "Did Josette share her experiences in the rookeries with you?"

"No." Benedict shook his head. "She has revealed nothing about that time in her life."

"Then how did you know she lived in the rookeries?"

"Adrien shared with us how he was able to track down Josette near Templeton Square. He reported the horrific living conditions she was enduring." Benedict raised an eyebrow knowingly. "She confided in you, didn't she?"

"She did," Morgan confirmed.

"Good." Benedict bobbed his head in approval. "It's time she learned to trust her heart."

Lord Craven moaned as he rolled his head from side to side.

Morgan placed his glass on a table and moved behind Josette's brother, slapping him in the back of the head.

"Yow!" Lord Craven exclaimed as his head shot up, and he started struggling against the bindings. "What is the meaning of this!" He glowered at Benedict. "Why am I tied to this chair? I demand to be released at once!"

Benedict leaned back in his seat and draped his arm along the back of the curved settee. "You are not in a position to make demands, Lord Craven."

"I have seen you in Parliament before. You are Lord Lansdowne," Lord Craven declared.

Benedict glanced up at Morgan. "It appears his memory is intact."

"Where is my sister?" Lord Craven asked, turning in his chair to look behind him.

Morgan grabbed an arm chair and positioned it directly in front of Lord Craven. He sat down and glared at him with such ferocity that he could see fear in Lord Craven's eyes.

"Is… this about… your supposed engagement to Josette?" Lord Craven stuttered.

Morgan shook his head. "No. I will get to that later."

Lord Craven swallowed slowly. "Then why am I here when I should be out looking for Josette?"

"We know where Josette is," Morgan assured him, removing his pistol and resting it on his leg, "but I would die before I ever let you near her again."

Lord Craven's face softened, relief evident in his features. "She is safe, then." His words were more statement than question.

"She is safe," Morgan confirmed.

To his complete and utter surprise, Lord Craven's next words threatened to disarm his hostility. "Thank you for keeping her safe. I have been so worried," he stated, his tone sounding sincere and forthright.

Morgan stared at Lord Craven. The man was good, believable even. But he knew better. "If you were so worried about your sister, then why did you throw her out of her home?"

"That was not my finest moment." Lord Craven's sigh seemed filled with regret.

"No, it was not. Or any day after that when you failed to find your sister," Morgan growled. "You discarded her like waste."

Lord Craven grimaced at his words. "I bungled that, to be sure. I was so overcome with grief, guilt, and my own selfish pride, that I drank to excess that night. After I collapsed on my bed, I didn't wake up until the following evening, but I was still suffering from my overuse of the drink. I stayed in the darkness of my room and fragments of my conversations with Josette from the night before would pop into my head. But it didn't seem real." He hesitated, before adding, "I didn't want it to be real."

Morgan shot up from his seat, shoving it backwards. "If that was the case, then why didn't you search for her?"

"I did!" Lord Craven exclaimed. "The next morning, I knocked on Josette's bedchamber door to apologize, but she was gone. I spoke to my staff, and I was able to piece together what I had said and done the night before. Immediately, I started searching for her in the rookeries and even hired the Bow Street Runners a few days later."

Benedict spoke up from the settee. "Why did you suspect she went into the rookeries?"

"One of my maids informed me that she saw Josette running in that direction the night she fled from our townhouse," Lord Craven explained. "I kept hoping she would come home." He dropped his head, staring at the floor.

"I don't buy it, Lord Craven. If you cared so much about Josette, then you wouldn't have flaunted Society's poor treatment of her in the newspaper," Morgan remarked callously.

Lord Craven brought up his gaze, the regret visible in his eyes. "I had a reputation of getting angry when I was inebriated. After my father died, I drank all hours of the day to take away the pain of his death. Before that, I never would have thought I could be so cruel as to abuse my own sister. I have not had a sip of alcohol since that night, nor have I ever stopped searching for her."

Morgan stormed towards the window and placed his hands on the sill. Blast Lord Craven! He seemed genuinely remorseful and appeared to be telling the truth, which irked him even more. This was not part of his plan.

"I believe him. Do you?" Benedict asked, coming up next to him.

Morgan dropped his head, reluctant to reveal his answer. "I do, as well."

"Should we untie him, or did you still want to kill him?" Benedict teased.

"I should probably take him to see Josette."

"That sounds like the best course of action," Lord Craven responded from his chair.

Benedict chuckled as he walked over and started untying Lord Craven's binds. "You may not think so after she's finished with you."

Morgan turned and leaned back against the window sill. "Perhaps it would be best if I went without you and gave Josette some time to warm up to the idea of meeting with you."

"Josette has never been fond of surprises," Lord Craven agreed as he rubbed his sore wrists, "but I would really love to see her."

"She might kill you," Morgan warned, "or stab you with her dagger."

"Are we still speaking of Josette?" Lord Craven looked baffled. "She has never been prone to fits of violence."

Benedict started laughing but turned it into a cough when Lord Craven turned his head towards him.

Morgan straightened and took a step closer to Lord Craven. "I will take you to see Josette, but if she refuses to see you, then you will accept that."

"I will, for now," Lord Craven replied.

"All right." He walked towards the door, opened it, and shouted into the hall, "Ferguson, prepare my carriage."

In all the excitement, Morgan forgot to read the missive from his father. He walked back to his desk and tucked the note into the pocket of his waistcoat. He would read it later. Right now, he was going to escort Lord Craven to meet with Josette. He had no doubt that she would be furious, initially.

Morgan truly hoped that she would not see it as a betrayal of her trust.

Josette kept playing her brother's voice over and over in her head as she soaked in the bath. When she'd seen Hudson at the House of Lords, her heart had stopped. He had almost caught up to her! She should have confronted him right there, in front of all those lords milling about. But she couldn't. She needed time to focus and think about her next course of action.

The next time she saw her brother, it would be on her terms, not his. He would rue the day he banished her from their townhouse and attempted to steal her inheritance.

Josette had just stepped out of the metal bath tub when her lady's maid slipped into her room.

"Did you enjoy your soak?" Abagail asked, bringing her a towel.

"I did, very much."

After drying off, they began the arduous process of dressing her.

Josette stepped into her square-necked, periwinkle afternoon gown and waited patiently as Abagail fastened the ornate buttons down the back.

"Why did you select this particular gown today, Abigail?"

"You left most of your gowns in Torquay," Abagail explained, finishing with the last button, "but this was one Miss Cosette altered, so your dagger and pistol can be accessed, if required."

"Now that I'm home, I'll send a missive to Lady Paxton requesting that my trunks be sent to the school." Josette walked over to the dressing table and picked up her dagger. After strapping it to her right leg, she sat on the chair. Her swollen cheeks had started bruising, turning black and blue.

"If you don't mind me asking, why did you leave your trunks behind?" Abagail asked as she started brushing her hair.

"Ouch," Josette murmured as the brush grazed a tender spot on her head.

Abagail's hand stilled. "Should I stop?"

"No, please continue," Josette said. "I left my trunks behind because we were in a hurry to depart."

Abagail laid the brush down. "I would like to apologize for failing to attend to you in Torquay," she said softly. "It was wrong of me to leave you alone."

"No apology needed." Josette met Abagail's gaze in the dressing table glass. "I understand why you left, and I wasn't alone. Lord Morgan, many footmen, and an entire household staff were with me at the estate."

"I hope Lord Morgan wasn't as insufferable as you first described him," Abagail remarked as she twisted Josette's hair into a chignon.

Josette smiled. "Lord Morgan and I reached an agreement of sorts."

"I am glad," Abagail replied solemnly as she placed a hair pin in place. "Did… um… he cause all these bruises, ma'am?"

Josette started to shake her head but stopped when Abagail held her head firmly to insert a pin.

"Oh no, the bruises on my cheeks are not from Lord Morgan," she rushed to say.

"And the bruising on your head, around your neck, and along the length of your back?" Abagail asked worriedly. "Did he hurt you?" Her voice was filled with so much concern that Josette's heart felt as it if would burst with gratitude for this kind young woman.

"No, Lord Morgan did not lay a hand on me," she reassured her. "These bruises are from something entirely different."

Abagail nodded, but she didn't appear convinced.

Josette turned her head when she heard a knock at the door. "Come in."

"Good. You are out of the bath," Cosette observed as she entered. She looked stunning in her dark blue, long-sleeved gown with intricate floral designs embroidered along the neckline.

Abagail placed the final pin in her hair and stepped back. "Is there anything else you require, headmistress?"

"No, thank you," Josette replied, turning so she could admire her hair in the mirror. "Your hair styles are becoming much more elaborate. I'm impressed."

Abagail curtsied. "Thank you," she gushed as she rushed out.

Cosette's eyes remained on the door for a moment. "A few kind words go a long way with that girl."

"Thank you for saving my life," Josette said as she draped her arm along the back of her chair. She hoped it sounded as heartfelt as she meant it to.

"It was nothing." Cosette smiled softly, then winced as she sat on the bed. "You would have done the same for me."

"Are you in pain?" Josette asked, eyeing her with concern.

"No more than you, I imagine." Regret came to Cosette's eyes. "I'm sorry I allowed that guard to hurt you. I was attempting to gain Adalyn's trust and—"

Josette spoke over her. "I understand why you did it." She gave her friend a tentative smile. "How did you know where I would be?"

"Eliza sent over a missive, informing me of everything that was transpiring and requesting my help. When I learned that Adalyn was *Genet*, I knew I had to help you. She always had a ruthless side to her."

"She spoke of training with you," Josette said. "Were you close?"

Cosette shifted her gaze, looking over Josette's shoulder. "We trained together, and even went on a few of the same assignments.

Adalyn was a gifted spy, but she thrived on deceit and bloodshed. She was a master of disguises, but she must have grown complacent. She never would have used her own identity before."

"She had me fooled into thinking her brother was forcing her into an unwanted marriage," Josette huffed.

"That doesn't surprise me. She can read people and exploit their vulnerabilities."

"How did you fool her then?"

Cosette laughed out loud. "Because, my dear friend, I have always been a better spy than her."

"I have to ask you something." Josette rose from her chair and walked over to the bed. "Did you mean what you said about being a prisoner here?"

"No," Cosette answered with a shake of her head. "That was a strategic lie. I am happy living here at the school and teaching these wonderful girls about embroidery."

"But what about your dream of opening a modiste shop? Do you ever long for that?"

She pressed her lips together for a moment, then replied, "That is the great thing about dreams. I always believed I wanted to own a dress shop in Paris, but my dream evolved. I found a new dream."

Josette heard the wistfulness in Cosette's tone and suspected she wasn't telling her the full truth. As she opened her mouth to prod her further, a knock came at the door.

"Come in," they answered in unison, then grinned at each other.

The housekeeper poked her head into the room. "Lord Morgan Easton is here to see you, ma'am."

"Thank you, Mrs. Dawson." Josette jumped up from her seat. "Will you show him into my study?"

"Yes, headmistress," Mrs. Dawson murmured, then closed the door behind her.

Cosette arched an eyebrow. "You seem quite interested in seeing Lord Morgan."

"Do I?" Josette asked, trying to sound innocent. "I am just curious why he came to call. That's all."

"Right," Cosette replied dryly. "You might want to work on your acting skills."

"I'd best not keep Lord Morgan waiting," Josette hedged, walking towards the door, hoping to end this line of questioning.

Remaining seated, her friend stretched her arm behind her and leaned back, observing Josette.

"Lord Morgan seemed quite frantic when he was searching for you."

"That's logical. We are partners."

"*Just* partners?"

Josette placed her hand on the door handle as the memory of his lips touching hers came to her mind. "For now," she responded with a hint of a smile.

Descending the stairs, Josette saw Morgan leaning against the wall near her study door. He was watching her intently as she approached him, and the tenderness she saw in his eyes made her heart race.

She stopped in front of him, suddenly feeling shy, and gave him a tentative smile. "Lord Morgan."

His lips quirked. "Miss Josette," he replied. Although he addressed her formally, his tone held affection, tenderness, and intimacy.

"Come. Let's talk in my study," she said as she reached to open her door.

Morgan's arm shot out and grabbed her arm. "Not yet. I would like to speak to you for a moment."

"Oh?" She lifted her brow in confusion. "Is there a reason you prefer not to speak privately?"

"Josette," he reached for her hand and intertwined their fingers, "I brought someone with me."

"May I ask who?" she asked cautiously.

Morgan glanced down at their hands. "Your brother."

"What!" she exclaimed, staring at him in disbelief. Yanking back her hand, she retreated two steps. She glanced around the entryway half-expecting her brother to step out of some dark corner, looking drunk and angry, the way he had that fateful night so long ago. When he didn't appear, she glared at Morgan, her tone accusing. "You brought Hudson here? To my home? To my school!"

Morgan took a step closer to her, but she put her hand up to stop him. "It would be in your best interest to hear what he has to say," he urged.

Josette stepped further away from the door and turned her back to him. How could Morgan betray her like this?

"I didn't betray you," Morgan said, guessing her thoughts.

She spun around. How could he read her so well? It was infuriating and flattering at the same time.

"After you ran away," he continued, taking a step closer to her, "I knocked Lord Craven unconscious and brought him back to my townhouse for questioning."

"Questioning?" she huffed. "Did you not think to consult me? Or does my opinion not matter to you?"

"Your opinion matters a great deal to me, Josie. You know that."

"Do I?" Josette countered. "I want you to take Hudson and leave my school. I will call—"

"Josette."

She froze. That voice! She knew that voice. It was the same voice that had haunted her nightmares these past two years, and now it was coming from *her* study. Her brother might look the part of the gentleman, but he was a cruel, conniving man. Reaching into the folds of her dress, she pulled out her dagger.

Morgan stepped in front of her, stopping her. "Put the dagger away," he ordered. "He means you no harm."

"You're wrong," she insisted, attempting to step around him. "Hudson deserves to pay for what he did to me."

To her brother's credit, he didn't cower at the sight of her anger. He just stared at her with a look of compassion and pity.

"Headmistress," Cosette spoke from behind her, drawing her attention. "It would be best to have this conversation in your study and away from prying ears." She stepped closer and whispered, "I will be nearby if you require assistance disposing of the body."

A small laugh escaped Josette's lips at her friend's unexpected offer, relieving some of the tension in her heart.

"Thank you, Cosette. That's what a true friend does."

"Miss Cosette..." Morgan began, obviously displeased by the joke.

Ignoring him, Cosette placed a hand on her sleeve. "That said, I believe you should trust Morgan's intentions."

Josette stared at her friend and confidante for a moment, then, with a slight nod, she brushed past the two men. She didn't stop moving until she was in front of the bay window in her study.

Hudson stepped into the room, wisely keeping his distance, but Morgan approached her. Despite her anger at him, she did need to rely on his strength and was grateful for his nearness. But of course, she could not admit that to him. Not yet.

Josette started tapping her foot as Hudson continued staring at her. He appeared genuinely awe-struck by her presence. Finally, he opened his mouth. "I can't believe I've finally found you. I have been searching for you for more than two years."

"Well, here I am," she replied sarcastically before turning her gaze towards Morgan. "Are we finished now?"

"I am sorry," Hudson started, his words shaky. "I am sorry for getting drunk, for ordering you out of our home, and I am especially sorry that I scared you so thoroughly that you felt you had to flee into the night." Tears filled his eyes. "My job was to protect you, and I failed. I cannot express the regret that I feel."

Josette was stunned, speechless. Hudson sounded genuinely remorseful, and it threatened her resolve to hate him for his past transgressions. She turned her shocked gaze to Morgan, who was watching her closely. He gave her a knowing smile.

"I thought you might want to hear what he had to say."

Hudson looked down at the dagger in her right hand. "Is that father's dagger?"

"It is," she replied, gripping the hilt tighter.

"May I see it?"

She hesitated, unsure of his intention. "It's all right, Josie," Morgan whispered next to her ear, his voice providing her with much needed reassurance.

Reluctantly, she extended the dagger, and Hudson stepped closer to accept it. He gently ran his finger over the ornate, white hilt. "I remember father always kept this dagger on his desk. I've wondered where it was."

Josette held her hand out for the dagger. "After you tossed the glass at me, I grabbed it to protect myself."

"Words can never express how truly sorry I am." Hudson closed his eyes, tears trickling down his cheeks. After a moment, he returned the dagger to her hand, took out his handkerchief, and wiped his wet face. "Nor can I comprehend what you have been forced to endure."

At the sight of his tears, Josette found her heart softening.

"I'm going to leave you two to talk privately," Morgan interjected softly. "I think it's best if you two have a chance to speak alone."

"You're leaving?" Josette asked, facing him. "You can't leave."

Nodding once at Hudson, Morgan placed his hand on her elbow, escorted her out the study door into the hall, past a smirking Cosette, and around the corner. He took her hands into his and brought them up to his lips.

"If you would like me to stay, then I will. Just say the word," he promised, his eyes roaming her face. "But I think you two need to spend time alone together, especially now that you know your brother meant you no ill will."

She bit her lower lip. "I don't think I have the strength to meet with my brother alone."

"You're wrong, Josie," he disagreed gently. "You are the strongest, bravest woman that I know."

"I'm not so brave," she admitted.

"I disagree." Morgan's eyes were beseeching, and she found herself unable to look away. "You survived living in the rookeries, and you just faced down a notorious French spy." He grinned. "I'm confident you will survive talking to your brother."

Taking a shaky breath, she gathered her courage. "When will I see you again?"

"It almost sounds as if you will miss me when I'm gone," he teased. His grin grew into a cocky smile, revealing the dimple on his left cheek that she was so fond of.

"I believe I will," she murmured, holding her breath nervously.

The smile slid from his face as his eyes reflected longing. "I will miss you, too."

He looked her in the eye as he started to lean closer. She tipped her lips to meet his, anticipating his kiss. But just when his lips hovered over hers, the door at the end of the hall opened and the sound of girl's voices filled the air.

They jumped apart, and Josette did not miss the look of regret on Morgan's face. Once the girls had turned the corner, Morgan gave her an impish grin. "I miss being married to you. We enjoyed a lot more privacy."

Josette laughed. "We were never truly married. It was just our cover."

"It was a good cover," Morgan joked as he escorted her back to the study. "I will call on you tomorrow," he hesitated, appearing anxious, "assuming that is agreeable to you."

She stopped at the study door and smiled coyly at him. "Until tomorrow, then."

"Yes, tomorrow," Morgan replied, his voice surprisingly hoarse. He turned to leave but stopped and spun back around. Stepping closer to her, he asked softly, "Um… are we… still engaged?" His eyes were vulnerable, raw, and he held his breath as he waited for her answer.

It would be so easy to say yes, but that would be selfish of her. He deserved better. "As I explained before, you can't just *decide* that we are engaged," she replied, softening her words with a smile.

His shoulders slumped, and he appeared genuinely disappointed by her answer. After a moment however, he straightened, and the familiar boyish grin reappeared.

"I don't accept that."

His words were so unexpected that Josette laughed aloud.

"I shall see you tomorrow," he declared as he bowed flamboyantly, grinned, and exited the front door, his head held high.

Placing her hand on the door jamb, Josette watched Morgan's retreating figure. The thought of marrying him made her smile.

It wouldn't be the worst idea, she mused.

Chapter Twenty-Five

Josette stepped back into her study and saw Hudson looking out the window towards the courtyard. His brown hair was the same shade as hers, but his fair skin favored their father.

Hudson turned around and pressed his lips together. "How did you become the headmistress of a school in the rookeries?"

"That is a long, difficult story." Josette clasped her hands in front of her.

"I have time," he replied.

She pointed towards the settee, indicating he should sit. Once she sat in a nearby chair, Josette started, "After I left the townhouse—"

"You mean," he interrupted. "after I ordered you out of our home."

"After I escaped into the rookeries, I held some glimmer of hope that you would find me. Sadly, as days passed, that hope faded. I sold mother's jewelry and tried to live the best I could, but eventually, all hope was gone. I came to the realization that no one wanted me, and that I was truly alone in the world."

"No... no... no," Hudson muttered, shaking his head. "I searched for you every day, hoping I would find some lead as to where you had gone. A Bow Street Runner located the merchant that you sold mother's jewelry to, and I was able to buy it all back."

"All of it?"

He nodded. "All of it. And it *all* belongs to you."

Tears filled Josette's eyes. "I was heartbroken when I had to sell her jewelry, but I saw no other way to survive."

"About a year ago, we received a tip that a girl matching your description was begging in Templeton Square. We searched everywhere, but we couldn't find you."

"That must have been when I started living with Lord and Lady Camden at their refuge for women."

"Why didn't you come home, Josie?" her brother asked.

"At the time," Josette glanced down at her hands, "I thought you hated me and would try to hurt me again. I thought it would be better to live on the street than be subject to your ridicule and mockery."

"Why didn't you seek out any of your friends?"

"When the society page started predicting whom I would kill off next, my so-called friends wouldn't receive me any longer," she admitted. "If you recall, you told me about the gentlemen's wagers at Whites."

Hudson wiped his hand over his face in disbelief. "I had no idea it had gotten so bad for you. I was insufferable to tease you so horrendously."

Josette saw the pity in his eyes, and she couldn't take it. She rose and stepped to the window. "After I lived at the refuge for a year, I was offered a position as Mrs. Martha Maddix's companion during her debut season."

"So, it *was* you at Lady Martha's ball." Hudson sighed deeply. "My eyes had scanned the room, and I caught a glimpse of you, but I blinked, and you were gone. I thought I had imagined it."

"After Lady Martha became engaged to Dr. Maddix, I was asked by Lady Lansdowne to run their family's school," she shared.

"That would explain your association with Lord Lansdowne," he said, "but when were you introduced to Lord Morgan Easton?"

"I met him for the first time in an alleyway behind Lady Martha's townhouse." She smiled, remembering that fateful, wonderful day.

"In an alleyway? Tell me you are not in earnest."

"It's true," she confessed. "We have become friends, in a roundabout way."

"Lord Morgan is under the assumption that you two are engaged."

She wrapped her arms around her waist. "He has yet to ask."

"But you would marry him if he did?" Hudson inquired, his eyes watching her closely.

"Perhaps... I don't know," she stammered. "I do care for him greatly."

"You do realize you are promised to Mr. Arthur Moore, Lord Paxton's eldest son?" Hudson pointed out.

"I think not," she huffed. "Besides, Lord Morgan and I attended Lord Paxton's house party under the ruse that we were a married couple."

"I beg your pardon?" Hudson asked, leaning forward in his seat.

Josette tilted her chin and chose her next words carefully. "You must understand that living on the streets changed me. I had to fight to stay alive, against all odds. Once I was given the chance to learn weapons training, I embraced it." Her gaze grew determined. "I cannot expand on the past few months, but I will say I have used those skills to help people."

"I believe you." Hudson looked at her knowingly. "I have an inkling of what you've been doing. I saw you dressed in men's clothing. Since you were covered in dust, I must assume you were in the undercroft."

"I was, but that's all I can reveal," she replied, lifting her chin.

His eyes grew solemn. "And the bruising on your face and neck?"

Josette placed her hand on her neck, remembering how it felt when the thug tightened his hand around her throat. She dropped her hand, deliberately banishing the thought, and answered defiantly, "I will not apologize for who I have become."

"I wouldn't ask you to," Hudson asserted. "I am proud of the woman standing here."

She stared at him for a moment, attempting to gauge his sincerity. He appeared to be in earnest. "Thank you," she murmured softly.

"There is another matter I wish to discuss with you," Hudson said, leaning back in his seat. "The matter of Craven Steelworks."

"Go on." Josette kept her face expressionless, wanting to see if her brother would be completely forthright.

"You should know that Father's will stipulated that you were entitled to half," he began, "but I have decided to give you my percentage, as well."

Josette's mouth gaped. "Pardon?"

"After father died, I spiraled out of control. I drank to excess, blamed others for my misfortune, and even forced my own sister to live on the street. I was bitter and felt that everything had been taken from me. What I failed to recognize is that you were in the same position. In fact, because of my behavior, your position was even worse than mine. I was so overcome with grief that I mistakenly blamed you for everything that had gone wrong in my life."

"When I discovered you were gone, I was devastated," he shared, "and I have not taken a sip of alcohol since that day. I spent all my time looking for you and expanding Craven Steelworks."

"Is Craven Steelworks profitable?"

"Oh, yes," he confirmed. "I set aside all the profits in an account for you, in hopes that you would return and claim it." He paused, smiling. "It has over £75,000."

Her eyes grew wide. "That's a fortune."

"That's only the beginning," he assured her. "I will continue managing Craven Steelworks," he hesitated, "with your permission, of course."

Josette sat in the chair behind her desk. "That offer is not acceptable."

Hudson tensed. "Oh?"

"I want you to keep your percentage in the company," she declared. "I am perfectly content with owning half of Craven Steelworks, assuming you continue to run it."

"No," he protested, shaking his head. "After everything I have done to you—"

"I insist," she said, speaking over him. "I have come to realize that we both grieved our family members' loss differently. I think it would be best if we started grieving together."

Tears came to his eyes. "Do you still miss them?"

"With every breath," she replied.

After a moment of silence, he rose and adjusted his waistcoat. "Are you ready to go home, Josie?"

"I *am* home," she responded, looking confused.

"The school is your home?" he asked, his brow furrowed.

"It is."

Hudson stepped closer to the desk and tapped his finger on the corner. "I am so grateful that you're alive that I won't argue with you… for now. But I will never stop trying to convince you to come back to our townhouse and regain your proper place in Society."

"I am happy here." Josette smiled, leaning back in her seat. "It gives me purpose."

"If you wish to work, then you could help run Craven Steelworks," Hudson offered slowly.

Her brow shot up. "You would allow me to work at Craven Steelworks?"

"If that's what you want." Hudson smiled indulgently. "I have no problem working beside my formidable sister."

She grinned. "No, I will leave the family business for you to run."

"Regardless, the money in the account is yours." He raised his hand when she started to protest. "I won't take no for an answer, especially since you have been gracious enough to let me stay on as part-owner of the company. Besides, I inherited the townhouse in London, our country estate near Yorkshire, and an estate in Scotland. I daresay that I will not lack for funds."

"That's good," she acknowledged.

"Now that you know you are an heiress, would you like to come home?" he attempted again.

She rose her seat. "Thank you for the kind offer, Hudson, but I will stay where I belong."

"You belong with me at home," he argued gently.

"Not anymore." Her voice was as gentle as his. She rose and moved around the desk. "I have no desire to return to my life in high Society. I prefer to stay where I am."

"I think I understand," he replied, "for now."

The sun was setting, and Hudson frowned as he looked out the window. "I arrived in Lord Morgan's carriage, and I am worried about securing a hackney in this part of town."

"I can help you secure a hackney, Lord Craven." The door opened revealing a smiling Cosette.

Hudson's eyes lit up with interest when he saw her, and a smile came to his lips. "Unfortunately, it is not safe for you to be outside the school's fences either, miss."

Cosette's laugh echoed throughout the room. "You are a delight, Lord Craven."

"Hudson, I would like you to meet one of my teachers, and a dear friend, Miss Cosette," Josette introduced.

Hudson bowed respectfully. "It is a pleasure to meet you."

"Follow me, Lord Craven," Cosette invited as she turned back towards the entry hall. "I will ensure that you arrive home safely."

Turning back towards his sister, he asked, "May I call on you tomorrow?"

"I would love that," she replied.

Hudson leaned closer. "Is Miss Cosette in earnest? Does she really intend to secure me a hackney?"

"Don't fret." Josette patted his sleeve. "She will keep you safe."

"But she is just a woman," he replied, glancing over his shoulder.

"No, she is not *just* a woman," Josette revealed. "She is the woman who saved my life."

Hudson nodded. "Then I shall trust her with mine, as well."

Josette returned to her chair, her mind whirling with what had just transpired. Her brother had been searching for her the entire time she was gone. And the money. She was an heiress!

Oh my, she thought. My life has just changed dramatically... again.

Morgan gripped the missive in his hands as the message from his father continued to repeat in his head.

"Call on me at your earliest convenience."

He had no doubt that his father wanted to chide him for his behavior today. Frankly, all he wanted to do was go back to his townhouse, eat a quick supper, take a long soak to remove the grit from his body, and fall into his bed where he could dream about Josette.

Did he dare propose tomorrow? Or perhaps he should take it slowly, possibly court her without it being official? Regardless, he needed to send his solicitor over to the school to pay her per their agreement. She might even be so grateful that she would shower him with kisses. One could only hope, he thought.

The carriage jerked to a stop and the door was wrenched open.

Morgan stepped out and stood in front of Brighton Hall, his ancestral estate. The large, four-level, brick home was set back from Mayfair and was only accessible through the guarded three-fingered gatehouse. The estate appeared even more intimidating with only a few rooms illuminated this time of night.

He sighed. Let's get this over with, he thought, as he walked up to the door.

The familiar aged face of Mr. Thorne greeted him. "Lord Morgan, what a pleasure to see you this evening."

"Thank you." Morgan smiled as he removed his gloves and handed them off to the silver-haired butler. "Is my father at home?"

Mr. Thorne nodded. "He is. He's expecting you."

"In his study?" he asked as his eyes took in the entrance hall and the twin staircases with the rich, red carpet adorning the steps. The deep walnut wall panels, carved cornices, and gold leaves embellishing them brought back such fond memories of his childhood.

"Aye," the butler confirmed. "Would you like me to announce you?"

Morgan shook his head. "That's not necessary."

"It is good to see you looking so well, my lord." Mr. Thorne smiled warmly at him.

Reaching out, Morgan placed a hand on the butler's shoulder. "I've missed seeing you, Thorne. I trust that you are well."

Mr. Thorne nodded reflectively. "I am. However, I miss having your family all under the same roof."

Morgan lowered his hand. "As do I."

He headed towards his father's study on the first floor but saw light originating from the drawing room. He had a feeling he knew who was occupying that room. He stepped through the doorway and saw his mother sitting next to a candle, embroidering a white handkerchief.

He leaned against the frame and took a moment to admire her. She was a handsome woman, with her faded brunette hair and tall, thin frame. Her face was starting to show her age, and he noticed more wrinkles than he had seen last time he'd been here, almost a year ago. Lady Bath must have sensed his presence because she lifted her head and looked in his direction. Her eyes grew wide as she rose from her seat.

"Morgan," she said reverently. "You have come home."

"I have missed you, Mother." Morgan closed the distance between them and gave her a firm embrace.

"I've missed you, too, my son." Her arms held him close as she whispered, "My heart is full seeing you again."

After a moment, he stepped back. "Thank you for writing me faithfully. Your letters meant a great deal to me."

"Oh?" She smiled at him through misty eyes, even as she teased, "I could hardly tell since I only received a note from you every few months."

"I am sorry. I have not been a very good son, have I?" he asked forlornly.

Bringing her hand up to cup his cheek, she stared at him for a long moment before speaking. "Whatever happens in your life, just know that you have a mother that loves you above all else."

"Thank you," he replied as he battled to control his own emotions. "I love you, too."

"Please say that you'll stay for dinner?" she asked, her hand still on his cheek.

Knowing that he could not disappoint his mother, Morgan nodded. "Assuming it will be acceptable to father."

"Don't worry about him," she said, withdrawing her hand. "I will go and ensure the cook prepares your favorite dessert. Is it still custard?"

Hearing the dessert reminded him of how Josette learned that fact about him and asked the cook to prepare it. "Yes, it is. Thank you."

"Come." She looped her arm through his. "Let me take you to your father. He's been expecting you for hours."

"He has?" Morgan asked, attempting to act surprised.

"Your father told me the most outlandish tale today," his mother remarked as she led him across the marbled floor. "He said that you barged into the House of Lords, interrupted the King of France's speech, and demanded everyone evacuate at once." She glanced over at him. "Did I leave anything out?"

"No." Morgan kept his gaze straight ahead. "That sounds accurate."

When they arrived at his father's study, his mother stopped and knocked on the closed door. "I am proud of you, son," she said quietly as she opened the door.

His father, the Marquess of Bath, was sitting at his large oak desk with ledgers spread out, but he did not look up from his writing when they entered.

Morgan turned his attention to admire the dominating ornate, black mantle sitting atop the fireplace. A small fire was burning in the hearth, providing sufficient light to the room. Blue-papered walls with black trim and bright red drapes highlighted the large window behind the desk.

"George, look who has arrived," his mother announced cheerfully, but Morgan did not miss the stiffness in her voice.

His father sighed as he laid the quill near the inkpot. "Would you mind if I spoke to Morgan alone, dear?"

"Of course not," Lady Bath said with a forced smile. "But Morgan *will* be joining us for dinner."

Morgan stifled his smile at his mother's firm tone. His parents' marriage may have started as a marriage of convenience, but it had turned into a love match over the years. By the time he was old enough to remember, their home had been filled with love and laughter.

Lord Bath leaned back in his seat. "Yes, dear. Morgan is always welcome to come home. Isn't that right?" he asked, looking pointedly at his son.

Morgan eyed him with suspicion. Why didn't his father speak his mind, so he'd know what game was being played?

When Morgan didn't answer, his mother murmured, "I will leave you two alone, then." She shot a warning glance at her husband. "Be kind, George."

Once his mother had left the room, closing the door behind her, Morgan walked over to the mantel. He picked up a vase and admired it before returning it to its spot. Why was he nervous? He was a spy for heaven's sake! Yet, speaking to his own father made him feel anxious.

"Would you like to take a seat, son?"

"I received your missive," Morgan commented as he sat in an armchair opposite his father with the desk between them.

"Thank you for coming so quickly," his father replied without the hint of censure Morgan expected.

"I've been rather busy," he said, meeting his father's gaze.

"I have no doubt."

Wiping a hand over his mouth, Lord Bath appeared uneasy, which was odd. Why would his father be nervous to speak to him? Clearing his throat, he began, "I wanted to apologize for my behavior today."

"Pardon?" Morgan asked, straightening in his seat. Whatever he had been expecting, it hadn't been that.

Wincing, Lord Bath rose and walked to the window, clasping his hands behind his back. He stared out of the darkened window for a long moment before he turned around to face him.

"When you barged into the House of Lords, spouting a ridiculous tale about a French spy blowing up the chamber, I immediately assumed the worst of you. I thought you were drunk and had intentionally planned to ruin the joint assembly."

Morgan stayed silent, not sure how to respond. He knew his father did not have a favorable opinion of him, but it hurt to hear it out loud.

"Then, I saw that Lord Camden, his grace, the Duke of Remington, and Lord Lansdowne were defending you adamantly." With a heavy sigh, he continued, his eyes filled with remorse. "Those are fine, stalwart men, and I saw the way they rallied around you. After I evacuated into the Old Palace Yard, I searched for you, but I could not find you anywhere. I finally saw you rush down the stairs, only moments before the explosion in the undercroft."

Morgan shifted in his seat. "I had to ensure everyone was evacuated."

"Like most of the lords, we decided to move towards the interior courtyard to separate ourselves from the protestors." Lord Bath walked back to his desk and sat on the edge. "That is when I saw you emerge from the undercroft with a boy in your arms."

"It was not a boy," Morgan admitted.

His father huffed in amusement. "I know. I could tell that when I saw you tenderly caressing her cheek. Who is she?"

Morgan pressed his lips together, debating how to answer. "She is someone very special to me."

"I see," Lord Bath said, crossing his arms over his chest. "Do you intend to marry this woman?"

"Yes," he replied firmly.

His father nodded. "I assumed as much." Silence descended between them before he asked, "May I ask how you discovered the plot to blow up the House of Lords?"

"I cannot tell you that, Father," he asserted, abruptly rising. "Is there anything else you wish to discuss?"

Lord Bath put his hands in front of him. "Don't leave. I won't ask you for specifics, but is that what you have been doing all these years?"

Returning to his seat, Morgan attempted to find the right words. "Society has a certain perception of me, but that is not who I am. You raised me better than that, but I assume that persona for a specific purpose."

"I perceived as much," his father answered slowly, "after seeing you risk your life today for England."

"Father..." Morgan frowned. "I am unable to say anything more—"

Lord Bath interrupted him. "And I respect that. I hope you will forgive a foolish, judgmental man. Over the years, I have thought the worst of you, but..." he hesitated, "I was wrong. You are a better man than I, and you have proven that to me today with your heroic actions."

Unaccustomed to such praise, Morgan shook his head. "I did no such thing—"

His father cut him off again. "Now, back to the girl. Who is she?"

A smile formed on his lips as he thought about Josette. He thought about refusing to answer, but he would eventually need to reveal her past. He might as well start now.

"Her name is Miss Josette Northcott. She is the sister of Lord

Craven."

Lord Bath rubbed his chin thoughtfully. "If I recall correctly, Lord Craven is a baron, is he not?"

"He is," Morgan confirmed.

"That could work. Lord Craven is the owner of Craven Steelworks," his father murmured. "I had hoped you would marry someone of higher social standing though."

"I do not require your approval," Morgan growled as he rose quickly. "I would marry Josette even if she spent her childhood as a chimney sweep."

To his surprise, his father's face broke into a wide smile. "You love this girl." It was a statement more than a question.

"I do," he stated firmly.

"Then you have my blessing," his father announced. Then he grinned. "Whether you want it or not."

"Thank you." Morgan tugged down on his waistcoat. "However, your opinion might change when you learn that Miss Josette was ostracized by Society a few years ago after the unfortunate deaths of three of her family members and an aged uncle."

Lord Bath straightened from the desk. "That poor girl," he stated softly. "Is there anything else you think I should know before we announce the good news to your mother?"

"Well," Morgan winced then revealed, "She lived in the rookeries for a year, after her brother abandoned her, until she made her way to Lady Camden's refuge for women. While she was there, she learned weapons training and is now the headmistress for The Beckett's School for Girls in the East Side."

Lord Bath blinked slowly as he appeared to mull over what he had just heard.

Morgan walked over to the mantel and stared at the fire. He had no doubt his father would rescind his blessing on their union. His father hated scandal, and Josette was a walking scandal.

"Miss Josette sounds like an interesting choice, son. I look forward to meeting her."

Morgan turned his head towards his father. "Do you mean that?"

"Yes. From what little I know about Miss Josette, I believe that she is brave and fearless. She was in the undercroft when the explosion occurred, which leads me to believe that she was working with you to stop this French spy."

Morgan opened his mouth to contest his conjecture, but Lord Bath put his hand up to stop him.

"I am many things," his father said, "but a fool is not one of them. I have a suspicion about what you do, about what Josette does, but I dare not say it aloud, for it is not my story to share."

"Thank you for understanding," Morgan replied.

Lord Bath put a hand on his shoulder and tenderly met his gaze. "Between my friends and yours, we will squash any scandal that may arise from your engagement to Josette. She will be embraced by our family and Society, I can promise you that."

"Thank you," Morgan stated. Surprised by the surge of emotions he felt for his father, he reached out and pulled him into a warm hug.

"When do I get to meet your fiancée?" his father asked.

Morgan chuckled. "After I get her to agree to marry me."

His father's brow shot up. "She hasn't agreed yet?"

"No," he replied. "She has been very hard to convince."

"I see." Lord Bath grinned, finding ample amusement in his words. "I have read the society pages and have seen you interact with the ladies. I thought all women were unable to resist your charms."

"I thought so, too," Morgan joked.

Placing his arm around his son's shoulder, Lord Bath led him towards the door. "Do you have a plan of action?"

"Yes, I plan to call on her tomorrow."

"And…" His father looked expectantly at him.

He shrugged. "That's it. That's all I have."

Lord Bath laughed loudly. "Perhaps we should ask your mother for advice over dinner."

"That sounds like a reasonable course of action," Morgan confirmed.

As they walked down the hall, Morgan felt a sense of astonishment wash over him. He hadn't thought a reconciliation with his father was even possible, but here he was, back in his ancestral home. What's more, his father had admitted he was proud of him!

Now, if he could convince Josette to marry him, his life would be complete.

Chapter Twenty-Six

The second level hall was silent as Josette walked towards the stairs with a pile of books in her hand. The girls were in classes, so it was the perfect opportunity to curl up next to the fireplace in her study and read.

"Headmistress. A word please," a woman with a Scottish accent said from behind her.

Josette turned to see Mrs. Somerville, the mathematics and astronomy teacher, walking towards her. "What can I do for you, Mrs. Somerville?"

Despite her thick, dark-brown hair, the guest instructor was a plain-looking woman. She had a long nose, and an oval face with an overly-pointed chin. But Mrs. Mary Somerville's eyes glistened with wisdom and intellect, making her a uniquely fascinating woman.

"I'm sorry, Miss Josette," she began, "I'm afraid this will be my last week at the school. I would dearly love to stay on, but I have scheduling conflicts."

"I understand," Josette sighed. She'd known for a while this day was coming. "We have enjoyed having you as a guest instructor for these few weeks."

A smile came to Mrs. Somerville's lips. "When Lord Morgan Easton approached me about working at your school, I had my reservations. However, I have thoroughly enjoyed my time with the girls."

"Lord Morgan?"

"Oh, dear me," Mrs. Somerville replied, her hand covering her mouth. "I was not supposed to mention that detail."

Shifting the books in her hands, Josette pressed, "I thought Lady

Lansdowne approached you?"

Mrs. Somerville shook her head. "My husband, William, and I met Lord Morgan at the Royal Society. We struck up a conversation, and he asked if I would consider guest lecturing at The Beckett School for Girls, offering me a rather large wage."

"I assume he offered more than the £10 that I have listed as your wage."

Mrs. Somerville glanced over her shoulder before confessing, "Lord Morgan paid me £100. The money has allowed me to expand my library with books related to the physical sciences."

"That's wonderful! I am grateful that you took Lord Morgan up on his offer," Josette said sincerely. "Having a woman of your great intellect as a teacher, our girls have seen firsthand that society can value women's contributions to the fields of science and mathematics."

Mrs. Somerville beamed at her. "You are doing a good service here, Miss Josette. I wish you the best of luck."

Josette tipped her head graciously. "And I look forward to learning more about your educational pursuits."

After Mrs. Somerville excused herself and returned to her classroom, Josette stood in the hall, baffled. Why would Lord Morgan take it upon himself to secure Mrs. Somerville a guest position at the school? And, more importantly, why didn't he say anything? Well, he was calling on her today. She would ask him directly.

As she descended the last stair to the main level, Mrs. Dawson walked swiftly towards her with a card in her hand.

"Headmistress, Lord Morgan Easton's solicitor, Mr. Babbage, is here to see you."

"Did Mr. Babbage state what his business was?" she asked, shifting the books in her hands to accept the card.

"Not specifically, but he did say his matter is most urgent."

Josette studied the card in her hand. Did anyone bother to read the sign out front? The one that specifically states no men are allowed in the all-girl school? Although, she had to admit she was curious why Lord Morgan sent his solicitor to see her.

"Tell him that he has five minutes."

"Yes, headmistress," Mrs. Dawson said. "Should I escort him to the drawing room?"

"No. Please bring him to my study."

As the maid swept away, Josette stepped swiftly into her study, placing the books on the edge of the desk. Taking a moment, she smoothed out her lavender gown with a rounded neckline and puffy sleeves. Her hair was piled into a side bun and tendrils framed her face. She had taken the luxury of spending extra time preparing herself, knowing that Morgan would be calling today.

Mr. Babbage knocked at the door before he entered. He was a short, pudgy man with blonde hair, stern features, and round spectacles on his nose. Holding a file in his hand, he bowed. "Miss Josette Northcott, I presume."

"Yes, you presume correctly, Mr. Babbage," she replied as she gracefully sat behind her desk and indicated that he should sit as well.

"I have come at Lord Morgan's request," Mr. Babbage stated as he accepted the offered chair directly across from her. He opened the file on his lap, removed two pieces of paper, and placed them on the desk. "He asked me to prepare a bank note in the amount of £15,000 for services rendered. The other paper provides details on how to secure your funds."

Josette looked at the bank note but did not attempt to retrieve it. Now that she had discovered she had her own money, she had no intention of taking Morgan's, job or no job.

Mr. Babbage sat on the edge of his chair and extended the file towards her. "If you could sign this contract which acknowledges the compensation, then the money rightfully belongs to you."

"I have decided not to accept the payment from Lord Morgan," Josette said.

Mr. Babbage stared at her in disbelief. "That's a lot of money for a woman in your position."

"Pardon?" she asked, hoping she misunderstood his intention.

Furrowing his brow, Mr. Babbage placed the file on his lap before taking his finger and slipping the papers closer to her. "Perhaps you don't understand how much you are turning down."

"I assure you," Josette warned, "that I am fully aware of how much £15,000 is."

Mr. Babbage leaned back and took off his spectacles. As he

wiped them with a handkerchief, he said, "Lord Morgan asked me to be discreet about this transaction, which leads me to believe this is a delicate situation." He held up his glasses and looked through the lens before placing them back on his nose. "I daresay that I doubt Lord Morgan would be more forthcoming with funds."

"I am not asking for additional funds." Josette clasped her hands in her lap. "I *am* telling you that I am not interested in taking a single shilling from Lord Morgan."

Mr. Babbage gave her a look of pity. "I understand that your pride is prohibiting payment for your..." he cleared his throat before continuing, "*services*, but I assure you that you have earned this money."

"What exactly did Lord Morgan tell you about the payment?" Josette asked, narrowing her eyes.

"Nothing, other than you are entitled to this small fortune."

"Why did Lord Morgan not come himself?"

"Lord Morgan Easton is a very busy man. He does not handle these trivial matters," the solicitor explained, picking up the file from his lap.

"Trivial?"

"If you would just sign the contract," Mr. Babbage extended the file towards her, "I will be on my way. Clearly, you lack funds, or you would not be working at this school."

"This meeting is over, Mr. Babbage." Josette rose quickly. "Please notify Lord Morgan that I will not be accepting his money."

Mr. Babbage frowned as he rose, reluctantly. "Would you like me to tell him anything else?"

"Yes, I would." She placed her hands on the desk. "Tell him that he won the wager."

"Wager, miss?"

Blinking rapidly, she attempted to stop the tears she felt forming in her eyes. "He convinced *me* that he loved me."

Without saying another word, she stepped around the desk and headed towards the drawing room for a moment alone. Why had Morgan sent his solicitor to offer her payment? Why hadn't he done that himself?

Now that the mission was over, Morgan couldn't be bothered to call on her. Instead, he sent a solicitor who'd wrongly assumed that she was his mistress. How dare he!

Sitting on an upholstered arm chair, Josette realized that it wasn't as far-fetched as she first assumed. In Society's eyes, she was a spinster, working to provide for herself. No one was aware that she was a daughter of a baron and an heiress.

Tears leaked from her eyes, but she did not bother to wipe them away. No matter what she did, she would never be good enough for Morgan. She was caught between two worlds, but neither appealed to her.

Morgan was the son of a marquess. Even if she hadn't been kicked out of her townhouse, and had maintained her place in Society, she was still not worthy of his notice. She was just a baron's daughter.

It was fortunate that Lord Morgan had sent his solicitor this morning, because if Morgan had come himself, she might have done something reckless, like accept his marriage proposal.

One thing was clear. There could be no future between Lord Morgan and herself.

Morgan finished writing his report for Beckett and was just signing his name when his butler knocked at the door. "My lord, Mr. Babbage is here to see you."

"Send him in," Morgan replied, placing the paper aside.

"My lord," Mr. Babbage entered his study with a stern look, "I visited Miss Josette, per your request, but she refused to accept your payment. Furthermore, she was quite haughty about it."

Morgan placed his hands on the desk and leaned in. "What exactly did you say to her?"

"I just told her that this was a fortune for a woman in her position—"

"Woman in her position?" Morgan growled, cutting his solicitor off. "What exactly do you mean by that?"

Mr. Babbage squirmed in his seat. "I was under the impression that she was your former mistress."

"Mistress?" Morgan repeated, his jaw clenched. "Mr. Babbage, you were speaking to my future wife."

His solicitor's eyes widened at the declaration.

"What gave you the impression that she was my mistress?" he asked, barely able to control his anger.

"You asked for the payment to be made discreetly…" The solicitor's voice trailed off when Morgan jumped up from his seat, came around his desk, and stood over him.

"How exactly did she react to your misguided efforts?"

Mr. Babbage cleared his throat. "She said she wouldn't take a shilling from you and that you won the wager."

"Wager?" Morgan repeated in confusion.

"Miss Josette said that 'you convinced her that you were in love with her', but then she left the room without providing further clarification," Mr. Babbage shared.

Morgan stepped over to his desk chair, grabbed his riding jacket, then turned to glare at Mr. Babbage. "You are fired, effective immediately. I do not employ idiots."

"Ferguson!" Morgan yelled as he donned his jacket and headed out of his study, leaving Mr. Babbage sitting with his mouth hanging open. "I need my carriage, *now.*"

"Yes, my lord," the butler answered from the far end of the hall.

After a short drive, he pulled up in front of The Beckett School for Girls. Reaching his hand out the window, he opened the door before the carriage even came to a complete stop.

"Wait here!" he ordered as he headed towards the entry door and knocked.

"May I help you?" Mrs. Dawson asked as she opened the door.

"I would like to see Miss Josette," he requested.

Mrs. Dawson frowned. "I am sorry, Lord Morgan. The headmistress specifically asked me to turn you away if you came to call."

Morgan ran his hand through his hair. "Please, Mrs. Dawson. My solicitor said some things…" He stopped, rethinking his words. "I need to apologize to Miss Josette and set things right."

"I am sorry, Lord Morgan. I truly am," Mrs. Dawson replied, "but the headmistress was insistent."

Before he could reply, she closed the door in his face. Not ready to give up, he went to the stone fence lining the school's interior courtyard and scaled the wall. His boots landed with a thud on the cobblestones on the other side. Approaching the bay window of Josette's study, he looked in and saw Josette sitting at her desk, her head laying in her arms. She appeared to be crying.

Morgan tapped on the glass, and Josette's head popped up. She turned her head towards the window as she wiped tears off her cheeks. Rising, she stepped over and opened the window.

"What are you doing here, Lord Morgan?"

Lord Morgan. She was back to using his blasted title… again. "I think it's rather obvious. I'm here to call on you," he declared as he started to climb through the window.

"I thought visiting a headmistress was too trivial." She stared defiantly at him but stepped back to allow him to enter.

He sighed. "I don't know what exactly my solicitor said, but he was not expressing my feelings at all. I fired him when he told me of your conversation."

"Oh," she murmured, but she didn't look fully convinced. "I did not like that man."

"Why didn't you accept the money? You earned it." Morgan leaned back against the wall.

"My circumstances have changed since I agreed to act as your wife."

"Have they?" he asked. "Do you require more money as payment?"

"No," she stated. "As part of my inheritance, I own half of Craven Steelworks, and my brother presented me with an account of £75,000."

Morgan's mouth gaped. "You are an heiress."

"My circumstances may have changed, but I am the same person," Josette insisted as she picked up a paper off her desk, her eyes skimming the words, before placing it down in another pile. "I intend to keep working at the school."

He nodded. "I would not expect less… at least until our first babe comes."

"You presume too much." Josette turned away from him.

In two strides, he gripped her arm, turning her to face him.

"Marry me, Josette, please."

"No," she answered, shaking her head. "The meeting with your solicitor reminded me that we are from two different worlds."

"You are the daughter of a baron. We are from the same world."

"Perhaps once, but not anymore," she replied softly. "My experiences, the life I've led, have changed all that. Now, I am tarnished, despised."

"That's not how I see it," Morgan attempted.

Josette placed her hand on his chest and looked up at him through watery eyes. "You are a good man, Morgan, the finest that I have ever known. You have helped me overcome so many obstacles, and I will be forever grateful for that." Tears streamed down her cheeks, but she made no effort to wipe them away. "You deserve someone better than me. A woman that does not have such a sordid, complicated past. You need a wife that is above reproach."

Morgan wiped her tears. "You are wrong, Josie. You are exactly the woman I need as my wife."

"And when the papers get wind of who you intend to marry?" she asked skeptically. "What if you stop receiving invitations to social gatherings? You won't be able to do your job as an agent."

"Then I will stop working as an agent," he declared. "You are more important."

"I don't believe that. You love working as a spy." She furrowed her brow so tightly that a line creased in the middle. "We had a wonderful adventure together, but it has clouded our judgement. Once we spend some time apart, you will see that I am not right for you."

He placed his hand on the back of her neck. "I don't want to spend one more moment apart. I love you," he declared.

Josette's eyes widened slightly, then she shook her head again. "You are just confused, which is why I need you to let me go. You deserve better."

"No," he replied, pulling her closer. "I refuse to."

She opened her mouth to protest, but he pressed his lips against hers, demonstrating how much she meant to him… without words. Taking advantage of her parted lips, he deepened the kiss and pulled her closer.

After a blissful moment, he leaned back to ensure that Josette knew she had the power to stop him if she so desired. Instead, when he looked at her beautiful face, he became mesmerized. Her eyes were closed, her black lashes fanning her delicate skin. A smile graced her lips. That smile was his undoing.

Morgan kissed her again, with as much control as he could muster. He kissed her lips, her cheeks, and her jaw. He wanted to show Josette how much he loved her, needed her, and wanted her in his life. She was not a passing fancy, but his future. He wouldn't let her go without a fight.

Josette returned his kisses with equal fervor, bringing her arms up his chest and around his neck. Her fingers threaded through his hair as she kept him close. There was no hesitancy in her lips, or actions, and he could feel the love she felt for him. So, why was she fighting the inevitable?

Leaning back, he lowered his forehead until it rested against hers. "You cannot kiss me like that and expect me to just walk away."

"You don't understand." Josette's hands tightened around his neck. "I will never be good enough for you, and when you recognize that, you will grow to resent me."

"You're wrong, Josie." He saw the indecision on her face, and recognized he was fighting a losing battle. He needed to regroup so he could win the war.

"This is not over," he said, stepping out of her arms.

Morgan saw the tears forming in her eyes, and he wanted to pull her back into his arms. But he was already starting to formulate a plan. A plan that would forever topple Josette's defenses.

He bowed. "I will call on you soon, Miss Josette."

With a devastatingly-reluctant parting glance, he left the study, leaving his heart behind.

Chapter Twenty-Seven

Josette did her best to keep a stern expression as she faced the two young girls in her office. "Girls, it is never appropriate to resort to violence," she explained firmly. "We talk about our feelings. We do not pull each other's hair."

Both girls stared at their boots, their expressions downcast.

"Do we understand each other?" she asked, looking from one girl to the other.

"Yes, headmistress," they mumbled in unison, nodding. One wiped away tears from her cheeks.

Josette waved her hand, dismissing them. "Back to your classes and remember to be kind to each other."

The girls rose and walked out of the room as if being led to their executioner. Josette couldn't help but smile at them.

She turned her attention to the pile of correspondence on her desk. She needed to catch up on the never-ending stack of forms, bills, and letters that had accumulated while she'd been away. Lady Lansdowne had offered to hire a steward to keep track of the ledgers, but Josette had refused. She'd wanted to be responsible for all aspects of the school. But now, she thought the idea might warrant consideration. Hiring a steward would give her more time to spend with the girls, which was her favorite part of running the school.

She noticed a corner of the newspaper peeking out from under a stack of books. She didn't know why she even bothered to keep it. There was no mention of Lord Morgan in the society page.

Josette rose and stepped to the window. It had been five days since she'd last seen Morgan. She sighed as she rested her head against the cold window pane. Five long days had passed. She missed his smile, his strength, and his teasing nature. For the first time, he had respected her wishes and left her alone. What had she done?

She straightened from the window. It was her fault he was gone, but she was relieved. At least, that's what she kept telling herself. If Morgan had truly loved her, he would have come after her. He would have fought harder to keep her. Unfortunately, she realized, the same could be said about her. But she was afraid; hopelessly, helplessly afraid of trusting her heart to another.

Josette moved back to her desk and sat down. She didn't need Morgan in her life. She was happy, and she wanted him to be happy, as well. With that decided, for the umpteenth time, she resumed reviewing the ledgers.

Cosette glided into the room wearing a green, long-sleeve gown with matching net overlay. "I just saw Lord Camden's carriage pull up. Are you ready?"

"Yes," she replied, rising. "I am curious, though, why Lady Lansdowne would request our presence at their townhouse tonight."

Cosette frowned as she glanced at her hair. "Did you stop having Abagail fix your hair?"

Unsure of the problem, Josette reached up and touched her brown hair, which was arranged in a low side bun.

Cosette stepped up and began removing the hair pins. "It seems to me that you have stopped paying special attention to your person since Lord Morgan stopped calling."

"I've just been busy," Josette defended as her friend twisted her hair into a chignon.

"I'm pleased that you are wearing your new gown," Cosette observed as she placed the last hair pin back in place. She moved in front of her, pulled out a few tendrils, then stepped back to admire the effect.

"You should be pleased, since you made this gown for me." Josette took a moment to run her hand along the white, high-waisted gown, with its square neckline and pink net overlay.

"You look exquisite in it, just as I predicted." Cosette laughed lightly, looping her arm through Josette's. "It looks divine with your coral necklace."

Stepping into the entrance hall, they saw a sharply-dressed Lord

Camden waiting with his hat in his hand. A smile grew on his face when they appeared.

"Miss Cosette and Miss Josette." He bowed. "Have you ever noticed that your names rhyme?"

They laughed together. "Yes, the girls have pointed that out on a few occasions," Josette said, still smiling.

Once they were situated in the carriage, it jerked forward and moved into the street. Josette watched the street urchins out the window as they darted between the carriages. Vendors sold items on the pavement, and little children held the products up in their hands, showing them to people passing by.

Adrien's voice broke through her musings. "How have you been, Miss Josette?"

She brought her gaze to meet his. "Well. And you?"

"As well as can be expected with a newborn in the home," he replied, smiling. "My wife is exhausted, but she insists on spending all her time with Mary Ann."

"Is that a problem?" Josette asked curiously.

"It is when I want a turn at holding my daughter," he joked.

Cosette spoke up. "Do the gentry not employ nursemaids?"

Adrien chuckled. "Kate does not have a favorable impression of nursemaids, but we do employ two, just in case she changes her mind."

The carriage turned down a street that Josette was unfamiliar with. "I thought we were going to Lord and Lady Lansdowne's?"

"We are," Adrien confirmed, "but not their main residence. We are going to Berkley Hall, Lord Lansdowne's ancestral home."

"Is it common to maintain two townhouses in London?" Cosette asked.

He shook his head. "It's not. Benedict's older brother purchased the townhouse in Portman Square before he passed away. Benedict decided to keep it, because it allows him to feel connected to his brother."

The carriage jerked to a stop in front of a four-level white estate with columns bracketing the entire front side of the home. Josette couldn't seem to tear her gaze away from the colossal manor spanning almost an entire block. A large fountain with a gold statue of a woman sat prominently near the square cobblestone entry.

"This is…" Her voice trailed off. She couldn't seem to find the right words.

Adrien chuckled as the carriage door opened. "I had the same reaction the first time I saw this place."

He stepped out and assisted them as they exited the carriage. Offering his arms, they walked up the four long steps as two footmen held open the doors for them.

As they stepped inside the vaulted entrance hall, Josette admired the white walls mixed with wood paneling, the mirrored sconces, and the beautiful, grey, stone floor.

Lady Lansdowne's voice came from the right side of the entrance hall. "You finally made it," she said with a wide, welcoming smile on her face as she approached them.

"Your gown is lovely, Lady Lansdowne," Josette complimented her hostess. Indeed, the slate gown with its square neckline and puffy sleeves accentuated her natural beauty.

"Thank you. I am grateful Miss Cosette had time to make it for me." Eliza stopped in front of them. "I've come to take you to the drawing room. Everyone else has already assembled."

"Can you define 'everyone else'?" Josette asked, having a suspicious feeling that Morgan was included in the group.

Eliza arched an eyebrow. "Would it make a difference in your decision to stay or not?"

"I guess not," Josette replied. "However, I am not exactly sure why we've been summoned tonight."

"My uncle, Lord Charles Beckett, asked me to arrange a meeting with everyone involved with this previous mission," Eliza explained as she turned back towards the drawing room. "Follow me. I must admit that the room we've chosen to assemble in is located in the west wing. It's quite an arduous journey."

Josette trailed behind as she pretended to admire the many tapestries hanging on the wall. Truthfully, she was buying more time as she prepared herself to possibly see Morgan again. Eliza and Adrien disappeared into a room, and Cosette cast a curious glance back at her before she followed behind them.

The sound of Morgan's laughter reached her ears in the hall, and her traitorous heart leaped at it. She took a deep breath. She could do this. She did the right thing. Given time, he would recognize that he was not in love with her.

But she was in love with him. *Desperately.* So much that it hurt. What had she done? She couldn't see him, not like this. Josette turned to flee back down the hall.

"Josie." Morgan's voice came from behind her.

She turned around slowly, and her breath hitched at his full-dress attire. His brown hair was brushed forward, his jaw was smooth, and his alert eyes were watching her, carefully.

"Are you coming in?" he asked, glancing at the opened door. "We are all waiting for you."

She nodded, not trusting herself to say the words.

"May I escort you inside?" Morgan asked as he extended his arm.

She shook her head. Good heavens! When had she become mute? She could battle a French spy, but she couldn't seem to muster up the words to talk to Morgan.

"You are quite talkative tonight," Morgan joked.

She smiled, relieved that he managed to break up some of her tension. "I am just admiring Berkley Hall."

"Ah," he replied. "This estate is quite grand. I would be happy to take you on a tour after the meeting."

"How are you so familiar with Berkley Hall?"

He gave her an impish grin. "I'm not, but I am a spy. I have no doubt I can navigate around an estate even as large as this one."

She laughed softly. "Your logic is sound, my lord."

"You're wearing the necklace I gave you," he noted, his eyes drawn to her neck.

She fingered the coral stones as they locked eyes. "I… uh…" she stammered. How could she tell him that this necklace meant more to her than any of her other possessions? Because *he* gave it to her. Before she could find the words, Eliza stuck her head in the hall.

"Pardon the interruption, but we are all waiting for you both to come in," she teased. "Unless you would prefer to have the meeting in the hall?"

Josette offered Eliza an apologetic look. As she turned towards the drawing room, Morgan stood aside and reached for her hand.

Tingles coursed up her arm as their fingers intertwined, but before she could even turn her eye to look at him, he dropped her hand and stepped back, refusing to meet her gaze.

As she entered the room, Josette saw Lord Charles standing next to an armchair. Adjacent to him, Lord Lansdowne was standing while Lady Lansdowne was sitting on a settee, and Lord Camden stood next to Miss Cosette on the opposite settee. Two arm chairs were unoccupied, creating an oval seating arrangement.

Josette found an empty seat and sat down, allowing all the men in the room to take a seat. Morgan claimed the chair next to her but kept his gaze firmly on Lord Charles.

Lord Charles Beckett smiled at the group. "I have just left the palace, and I have brilliant news. But first, I have a few things we need to discuss." His smile dropped. "The explosion in the undercroft caused significant damage to the lower level and blasted a hole where the stage was situated. Fortunately, the rest of the main chamber in the Upper House only suffered minor damage. Lord Paxton will be responsible for the renovation of the undercroft after parliament adjourns for the season, and his son, Geoffrey, will not be arrested for his *assistance* with this plot."

Morgan nodded his approval. "Thank you for arranging that."

Lord Charles sighed. "You only have so many favors, Easton. I hope you won't regret calling that one in."

"I won't," Morgan assured him.

Crossing one ankle over the opposite knee, Lord Charles continued. "Due to the smaller than intended explosion, the people did not rise up, and no group of revolutionaries marched to London. Luckily, it appears that this particular uprising has diminished to a mere simmer."

"That's great news!" Jonathon declared.

"Unfortunately, I do have some bad news," Lord Charles stated. "I fear that Lord Morgan's cover has been blown by his theatrical appearance in the House of Lords." He put his hand up when Morgan started to protest. "You made the right choice to evacuate the chamber. I do not fault you for that. However, it's not feasible to assume that your cover has come out unscathed, especially since you befriended Gaspard Mancini, Duc of Feltre. I am not saying you can't be an agent anymore, but it would be in a much different capacity now."

Josette turned towards him and whispered, "I'm sorry, Morgan. I know how much you loved working as an agent."

"It's for the best," Morgan assured her, his eyes lingering on her lips. "There are other things that I value more than being an agent."

Lord Charles cleared his throat, bringing their attention back to him. "Prince George would like to present Miss Josette the Most Noble Order of the Garter."

"What?" Miss Josette stared back in surprise. "Our prince regent wishes to confer upon me the Most Noble Order of the Garter?"

"He does." Lord Charles nodded. "He was very impressed by your heroics both in Torquay and down in the undercroft to thwart the explosion. So, he wants to honor your contribution." His face grew expressionless. "However, the Crown thanks you for your service, but we cannot allow you to continue as an agent either. Too many people saw you being carried from the wreckage."

"I understand," she replied. He gave her a brief smile before he shifted his gaze towards her friend.

"Now, Miss Cosette," he paused dramatically. "The prince regent was made aware of your sacrifice and dedication in helping Miss Josette, and ultimately helping to save all of England." He reached into his jacket pocket and removed a piece of paper. "This letter states that you are a friend of the Crown, your conviction has been overturned, and you are to be awarded £15,000 for your service." He smiled. "You are a free woman."

"I am free?" she asked, her expression bewildered.

"Furthermore," Lord Charles added, "Eliza has secured a building for you, so you can fulfill your dream of opening a modiste shop."

Tears came to Cosette's eyes as Eliza piped in, "Not only have we secured a building, but we have stocked your shop with the finest ribbons, material, and everything that you could possibly need."

"I don't know how to thank you!" Pulling out a handkerchief from her pocket, Cosette dabbed her eyes. "My heart is so full with this unexpected news."

Adrien spoke up. "Prinny was so impressed that you put your

life on the line, knowing if you were caught that your punishment would be death. He wanted to reward your valiant service."

"Thank you," Cosette replied with a shaky breath. "I don't believe I did anything more than what every person in this room would have done."

Josette leaned forward. "I, for one, could not be happier for you, Cosette. You saved my life that day."

"I am also pleased to note that King Louis does not harbor any ill will for the interruption during his speech," Lord Charles stated. "The king was pleased that *Genet* has been removed as a threat to the French people, and he offers his personal gratitude for a job well done."

"I believe I got overlooked," Jonathon pouted playfully. "After all, I was the only one that was injured on this mission."

"A bullet grazed you, and you hit your head when you dove out of the way. Those are hardly notable injuries," Adrien teased.

Jonathon chuckled.

Lord Lansdowne rose from his seat. "If you will all excuse us, Eliza and I need to prepare to receive our guests." He assisted his wife as she rose. "We will see everyone in the ball room."

As if on cue, everyone in the room except Josette and Morgan rose and began filing out of the room. Josette glanced back at the door. "Where is everyone going?"

Before Cosette exited, she spun around and answered, "Enjoy yourself."

Cosette closed the door behind her, and Josette turned to face Morgan. Before she could say anything, however, he said, "We need to talk."

Morgan grabbed the sides of his arm chair and repositioned it so he was directly in front of Josette. He was determined not to leave this room until he convinced her to marry him.

He watched for any signs of distress, but Josette looked at him with trust in her eyes. This bodes well, he thought.

When he had first caught sight of her earlier in the hall, wearing her new gown, he had never seen her more beautiful. He wanted to declare his love for her then and there, to beg her to take a chance on him. But sanity prevailed, and he remembered to stick to the plan.

Morgan reached for her hands and encompassed them in his.

"Josette, I know you requested more time, but has five days been enough?" he asked, hoping. "My heart has not changed, and if anything, I love and ache for you more."

An understanding smile graced her face. "Morgan—"

He cut her off, not ready for her rejection. "For the past four days, Cosette has been giving you the wrong newspaper. I wanted to prove to you that society would love and embrace you, if only given the chance."

"Pardon?" she asked in confusion.

Morgan stood and walked to the table on the far side of the room. He picked up four newspapers and brought them back. Opening to the first society newspaper, he read the headline, "*Heiress Josette Northcott Found Alive.*"

He extended the paper towards her as he reached for the second newspaper. "*Miss Josette Northcott Volunteers at The Beckett School for Girls.*" He opened the third society page and read, "*Lord Morgan Easton is Smitten by the Lovely Josette Northcott; Vows to Love No One Else.*"

Morgan opened the last society page. "This headline is my favorite," he confessed, extending it towards her.

Josette read the paper, and her eyes darted up to his. "These were all published?"

"They were," he replied, holding his breath for her reaction. "I paid the editors a small fortune to print the first article, but the response was so overwhelming that the newspaper requested more stories."

A smile came to her lips as she read, "*Lady Eliza Lansdowne to Host Lord Morgan Easton and Miss Josette Northcott's Engagement Ball. It is to be the Event of the Season.*"

"Josette," Morgan began, pushing his chair back and kneeling in front of her, "from the moment I met you in the alleyway, I knew I'd met my match. You test me, challenge me, and make me happier than I have ever thought possible." He reached for her hands, gripping them tightly. "I know you are scared, and are afraid of getting hurt, but trust that I love you more than life itself. Rest assured, that I *will* never hurt you, my dear Josie."

"I believe you," she replied, her eyes searching his.

This was going well. "Will you do me the honor of marrying me?"

Josette was silent for a moment before she lowered her gaze to their hands.

"I was wrong," she whispered. Tears came to her eyes, but she blinked them away. "I thought I was doing the right thing by sending you away. I thought I was protecting you." She brought her gaze up to meet his. "But I know now that I was only trying to protect my own heart."

Morgan held his breath as she swallowed slowly, and her hands gripped his tightly.

"The moment I met you," she finally continued, "my heart shattered, allowing it to begin healing. You picked up all the broken pieces of me and made me whole again." She let out a shaky breath. "With you, I am complete, and I don't want to flee from you anymore. I want to be by your side, always and forever."

"Does that mean you will marry me?" he asked again, willing his racing heart to slow.

"Yes, I will marry you," she replied, her eyes glistening with unshed tears.

He jumped up and helped her rise before he brought his lips to hers. After he leaned back, he gave her a cocky smile. "Didn't I warn you that eventually you would fall in love with me?"

"You did… repeatedly." She laughed. "Just so you know, I would have said yes before you even showed me the newspapers."

"You would have?" he asked, surprised.

Josette slid her hands around his neck, threading her fingers through his hair. "I have never been happier than when I was pretending to be your wife. Although you can be vexing at times, you never once gave up on me. You always came back for me." Her bottom lip trembled as she admitted, "I love you."

"I know," he replied with a boyish grin.

"How did you know?"

"I have made it my life's mission to know everything about you.

Your happiness is the most important thing to me." Morgan leaned in and kissed her, his lips lingering. "Furthermore, if you only knew how much I loved you, then you would know why I will always come back for you."

She eyed him with curiosity. "I do have a question. Why did you hire Mrs. Somerville as a guest teacher at the school?"

"I know how important the school is to you." His eyes filled with tenderness. "I thought a teacher like Mrs. Somerville would help encourage your girls to pursue their educational dreams."

Tears came to Josette's eyes as she attempted to blink them away. "I truly don't deserve you."

"You're wrong. It is *I* that does not deserve you." He brushed the tendril off her cheek before taking the opportunity to kiss her again. "You will learn, my dear Josie, that I will give you anything your heart desires. All you have to do is ask."

"How do you think your father will react to our engagement?"

"Well," he hedged as his lips started trailing kisses down the length of her neck, "I suppose we can ask him at the engagement ball."

"Your father is here?"

"Yes." Morgan brought his gaze back up to meet hers. "My whole family is here, as is your brother, Hudson, and Lord and Lady Paxton."

"I am so glad—" Her words were cut off as he kissed her deeply, lovingly.

After a moment, he felt Josette smile against his lips. He leaned back, curious. "What is so amusing?"

"You."

"Me?"

"Aren't we supposed to be attending our engagement ball?" she asked merrily.

He smirked. "Forget the ball. Let's jump in my carriage and race to Gretna Green."

"Or," she started, flashing him a mischievous smile, "we go to our engagement ball tonight, and you secure a special license tomorrow."

Morgan leaned in and kissed her on the lips before he pulled out a folded paper from his waistcoat. He extended it proudly towards her.

Josette unfolded the paper and grinned. "When did you have time to obtain a special license?"

"Five days ago," he replied, accepting the paper back from her. "I secured one right after I left your school."

"Thank you for never giving up on me," she murmured.

Placing his arms around her waist, Morgan replied, "My dear, sweet Josie, I will never give up on you. From the very beginning, I knew I wanted the whole you, not just the woman that you allowed the world to see." His voice shook with emotion. "You were worth the wait."

Josette's face lit up with happiness. "Let's go celebrate the good news with our friends and family."

"That sounds like a marvelous idea," he agreed as he stepped back and offered his arm. "But tomorrow, we wed."

"I can agree to that," she said, placing her hand on his arm.

As they walked towards the ballroom, Morgan couldn't believe that he had done the impossible. He had convinced Josette to marry him. And not just begrudgingly. She'd wholeheartedly accepted his proposal and loved him in return.

Never had he worked so hard for anything in his life. But Josette had been worth it. Together, they were going to have a grand adventure. He was sure of that.

Epilogue

Eight years later.

Josette sat on the blanket in the fields surrounding Harrold House, holding her infant son, George, while Morgan chased their six-year-old daughter, Phillipa. Morgan had purchased Harrold House as a wedding gift for her, allowing her to maintain her close relationship with Lord and Lady Paxton.

"I caught you!" Morgan laughed.

Phillipa giggled as her father picked her up by the waist and tossed her into the air.

"Chase me again, Father!" Phillipa pleaded in his arms.

"But I am an old man." Morgan smiled lovingly at her. "I need time to rest."

"You are not old," she replied, laughing, as she wiggled out of his arms.

Phillipa ran over and threw her arms around her. "Will we practice throwing daggers today?"

"I should certainly hope so," Josette said, her words light.

Phillipa put her hands to the sides of her mouth and whispered, "Father told me that he could shoot a pistol better than you." Even though her daughter was trying to tell her a secret, her sweet voice traveled further than she intended.

"Is that so?" Josette arched an eyebrow at Morgan, and he just shrugged.

Phillipa nodded profusely. "I told him that he must be teasing because I have seen you practice shooting your pistol."

"That's right," Josette replied, smiling. "I am much more proficient in weapons training than your father."

Morgan chuckled as he dropped down onto the blanket and reached for a grape from the basket. "Phillipa, would you like to know how your mother and I met?" He tossed the grape into his mouth.

Phillipa's eyes lit up, and she dropped down on the blanket in excitement.

Morgan placed his arm behind him and leaned back. "I was tasked with saving the King George IV before he became the king. He was called the prince regent then. There was a group of bad people who wanted to hurt him," he paused, dramatically, "and your mother begged to go along with me."

"She begged?" Phillipa asked, her nose scrunching.

"Profusely," Morgan confirmed. "I decided to take pity on her and brought her along. She spent her time in her room taking naps and going on walks, while I searched out the bad men and stopped them. I even went into a dark cellar and prevented an explosion."

Phillipa's mouth dropped open. "You are a hero, Father."

"I would agree with you!" he exclaimed with a boyish grin.

Josette laughed at his version of the truth. "I recall it quite differently, my love."

"Oh?" he asked, his eyes twinkling with humor. "How do you remember it?"

"We were a team," she replied, shifting George in her arms, "and *together* we stopped a group of rebels from hurting the prince regent."

Phillipa turned her curious gaze towards Josette. "Is father telling me one of his stories again, Mother?"

"He is." Josette nodded, earning a knowing smile from Phillipa.

"I should have known." Phillipa jumped up, ran towards a tree, and started climbing up the low branches.

Morgan scooted over until he was next to her and lovingly looked down at their sleeping infant. "I hope this child has much less energy than our daughter. I daresay she hardly sits still."

"Hudson said Phillipa is a miniature version of myself at that age," she confessed.

Morgan shuddered. "Oh dear. Heaven help me if she grows up to be half as adventurous as you."

Josette laughed. "Those days are long past for me. Having children has forced me to take fewer risks, because I now have too much to lose. Do you miss working as an agent?"

"No, I don't. Being married to you and having children is adventure enough for me. There is no place I would rather be than with you, surrounded by our children. That's where my heart resides." He nudged her shoulder with his. "Do you miss working at The Beckett School for Girls and occasionally working an assignment for the Crown?"

As she thought about her reply, Josette saw her daughter climbing higher in the tree, her face lit up with happiness. "All my experience in life, the heartache, the joy, the adventure, has prepared me for my greatest assignment; being a mother." She shifted in her seat to face Morgan. "I have never been so happy as I have been with you over these years."

"I can't help that you fell in love with me," Morgan said with his usual cocky smile, the one that caused the dimple in his left cheek to appear. "My charm just comes naturally." He shook his head. "It's a burden, really."

She leaned forward and kissed him. "What a burden you must have to bear."

Morgan reached out and cradled the back of her head in his hand, keeping her close. "My greatest triumph was winning your heart. For I have never known such joy and peace as I feel when I am in your arms." He glanced down at the babe between them. "Not only have you given me your heart, but you have allowed me to be a father."

"I love you," she whispered against his lips.

"I know," he joked. "But I love you far more."

"Perhaps we should make a competition out of who loves each other more?"

He lifted his brow. "I believe I won the last wager."

Before she could argue, their daughter's voice reached them. "Father, I need your help climbing down."

Morgan turned his head and shouted, "I'll be right there!" He chuckled as he turned back and kissed his wife firmly on the mouth. "Duty calls."

Josette watched as her husband ran over to help Phillipa out of the tree, and she sighed contentedly. This was her life. A wonderful life filled with laughter, teasing, and love. Nothing could have prepared her for the ever-growing love she felt for her husband and her family.

She glanced down at George and snuggled him closer. Playing the part of a married couple was a shallow comparison to what marriage was truly like. Together, they grew closer, trusting each other, loving each other, both with the same goal: ensuring each other's happiness.

For how could she not love her husband with a fierce intensity? He fought for her, and that made her want to fight for them. And she would, until her final breath.

Coming Soon

The Unfortunate Debutante

"Sometimes, the heart must forge its own path."

by

Laura Beers

About the Author

Laura Beers spent most of her childhood with a nose stuck in a book, dreaming of becoming an author. She attended Brigham Young University, eventually earning a Bachelor of Science degree in Construction Management.

Many years later, and with loving encouragement from her family, Laura decided to start writing again. Besides being a full-time homemaker to her three kids, she loves waterskiing, hiking, and drinking Dr. Pepper. Currently, Laura Beers resides in South Carolina.

CPSIA information can be obtained
at www.ICGtesting.com
Printed in the USA
BVHW042353170519
548585BV00001B/32/P